MAGIC & MAYHEM

Edited by Nicole Kimberling, Amanda Jean and Samantha Derr

GRNW Presents

MAGIC &
MAYHEM

Edited by
Nicole Kimberling
Amanda Jean
Samantha Derr

An imprint of Blind Eye Books
blindeyebooks.com

GRNW Presents: Magic and Mayhem
Edited by Nicole Kimberling, Amanda Jean and Samantha Derr
Published by:

GRNW Press

an imprint of
Blind Eye Books
1141 Grant Street
Bellingham WA 98225

blindeyebooks.com

Cover by Lou Harper

Many of these selections are fiction and as such all characters and
situations are fictitious. Any resemblance to actual people, places or
events is coincidental.

ISBN: 9781535585378

This book is dedicated to the Readers—everything is all about you!

CONTENTS

So What is Character-Type Love Match Anyway?

NICOLE KIMBERLING

The Gay Romance Northwest Meet-Up, or simply GRNW for short, is a special kind of convention. Held annually at the Seattle Library, the conference has come to be known for its focus on inclusivity and on the readers of LGBTQA romance.

Sure, plenty of authors attend; you're likely to rub elbows with longstanding favorites as well as discover new ones. And there are panels and swag and drinks at the bar across the street, but the organizers have always been careful to remember to give readers a voice too.

Lead Volunteer Tracy Timmons-Gray has devised many ingenious ways to get the audience talking—both to the panelists and amongst themselves.

By far the most entertaining reader-focused activity is Character-Type Love Match. It's a tournament-style competition. The fun starts when audience members suggest a list of characters such as "Cop" or "Sexy Mountain Recluse." Then, by applause, the audience votes for their favorites until only two characters remain: that year's dream couple.

At the GRNW 2015, "Mage and Cyborg" took the day. The previous year, it was "Soldier and Tattoo Artist."

I personally thought, "Well, that's a swell game, but it would be a hundred times sweller if we could sweet-talk a bunch of authors into realizing the reader's fantasy and write short stories depicting their versions of the year's dream couple." So that's what I set out to do. Early in the game, it became obvious that I'd need help. Samantha Derr and Amanda Jean from Less Than Three Press jumped on board, and we were off.

Now, a year later, we're proud to present eight stories featuring the 2014 and 2015's dream couples.

But that's not all that a reader will find in this volume. Over the course of the conference's three-year run, we have had some amazing keynote speakers. Their stories run the gamut from frightening to heartbreaking to inspiring to downright funny. Once we decided to do an anthology, sharing them became an absolute must.

Hearing these personal stories was a privilege, one that brought GRNW attendees together as a community of writers and readers. My hope is that you will experience the same sense of connection—the same thrill and hope—in reading them that I felt listening to them at GRNW.

Nicole Kimberling,
Bellingham, Washington
June 2016

Five Things We Learned While Running a Queer Romance Event (and the One Thing We Still Need to Do)

Tracy Timmons-Gray

I'm writing this belatedly, with Nicole Kimberling very kindly prodding me. "Write something inspiring," is the key underlying message—something that will help make sense of what has transpired in three years after one random April evening in 2013 where, over beers (natch), an idea was tossed out into the universe, and bit by bit after that, a program was launched that's sole focus was celebrating the awesomeness that is LGBTQ romance fiction.

I'm not sure which part might be the most inspiring... Obviously the beer was helpful in oiling the gears so that people went from the creative spark of, "Wouldn't it be cool to do a gay romance conference here in Seattle? There are so many writers here in the Northwest!" to the (inebriated?) action of going home that night and actually-for-real starting the process to launch a conference where writers and readers could come together to talk about the books they love.

Inspiring beers aside, we have learned a few things since we launched the first Gay Romance Northwest Meet-Up conference at the Seattle Public Library back in September 2013. Actually, we've learned a lot of things, some harder than others, but all of it, I'm deeply grateful for. We wouldn't be here, three years later and now preparing for our fourth conference, if it weren't for those lessons and the many wonderful people who have been a part of making GRNW happen year after year.

1. Ask (You Can Do It!)

Everything starts somewhere. For us, to launch a program that eventually led to three annual conferences, 20+

free public reading events, and gathering 1,000+ books for Seattle community LGBT libraries, we had a very simple start. After the inspiring beers, we went up to strangers and said, "We have this idea of holding a gay romance conference. Do you want to be a part of it?"

We emailed queer romance authors and contacted publishers and asked them that question. We set up meetings with organizations in the community and asked them that question. By far, the response we got when we asked was, "YES."

Whether it was from award-winning authors or leading publishers or prominent LGBT community organizations, the answer was, "YES."

We aren't the first queer romance conference, nor are we the biggest. (We might be the oddest.) A lot has been done in the field, from GayRomLit to the Golden Crown Society, Bent-Con to the UK Meet. There's a lot of gold in them thar hills, and when I say "gold," I mean interest and desire from readers and writers of queer romance to meet, come together, and celebrate the books they love.

The asking part can be scary, though. I get it. What if people say no? The reality is that people will say no, but there will be also those who say yes, and sometimes they'll say yes very emphatically while hugging you. That's how much they want this thing, this idea, to happen.

That desire has not dimmed, even as the field has grown with more events and public celebrations. Three years from those inspiring beers, readers and writers have more opportunities to come together, beyond our cherished online communities and tumblr feeds, to celebrate these stories where LGBTQIA characters shine so brightly.

So, the first lesson is if that idea strikes you, then go ahead. Ask. Sometimes they say no. And other times, they say yes, and things can really blow up from there to places you haven't dreamed of yet.

2. The Community is a Powerful Ally

One of our goals was to connect our purpose—celebrating the awesomeness of LGBTQ romance—with the community around us. This meant knocking on the doors of local and national LGBTQ and literary organizations and asking them if they'd like to be involved.

We were total strangers, though, volunteers working under the kind cover offered by the startup writing nonprofit Old Growth Northwest. This meant that we were often starting these relationships from scratch. For us to actually reach the community, we had to work with the community, and work with them where they are.

This meant we had to knock on a lot of doors, and bring them our question: "We're interested in doing a gay romance event. Do you want to get involved?" For many of these organizations, this was the first time they had heard of an event like this, even for LGBT organizations. A whole conference? For queer love stories? That's a thing?

One of the most important lessons was that we didn't ask for money. We knew going into these conversations that for many of these organizations, they were nonprofit, cash-strapped, and stretched thin. They don't have extra money for a sudden appearance of some crazy conference where people may talk about the ins-and-outs of sexy queer stories. What they did have, though, was connections to the greater community and credibility. We didn't have those things, and we would need them if we actually wanted to have impact when creating a public celebratory space for these books and their readers.

So we took money off the table, and asked, "Do you like this idea? If you do, come join us. We will make you a community partner."

And in five months, we gathered ten community partners, from our now long-time partner Gay City Health Project to the auspicious literary organization Lambda

Literary to the hard-working RWA chapter Rainbow Romance Writers. Having community organizations involved helped us do things like get the word out and allowed us into spaces that we didn't have access before. Their involvement also meant that there was an actual community involved, a group of people who believed that this idea should happen, and they were willing to put down their name and their support to make it happen.

For that, we are so grateful.

3. It Does Take Money

The model for our program overall is to provide accessible opportunity for readers and writers to celebrate queer genre fiction. This means focusing on regional access, which means focusing on doing things locally to the Pacific Northwest, and doing things for free and/or cheap, so to provide financial access.

That being said, our first year's costs were around $10,000, and that was to run a half-day conference at the Seattle Public Library and a two-hour book festival at a local hotel. We covered those costs through a mix of sponsorships from publishers, ad sales, and from attendee registration costs. ($25 for registration, and something like $15 for the early-bird rate that first year.)

As a heads-up, by far the most expensive thing are hotels. Hotel space costs *a lot*. That two-hour book festival was half our budget.

We wouldn't have had the freedom to bring in community partners and really involve the community at a deeper level if we weren't able to raise the money through sponsorships and ad sales. That was the seed funding that allowed everything else to happen. For that, we are deeply grateful to our sponsors these past three years, especially in the beginning when they really took a chance on a bunch of excited strangers on the internet with a crazy idea.

4. You Will Run into Rejection, Elitism, and Bigotry

Not everyone we asked wanted to come on board, which is cool and totally happens. The worst cases were when the rejection was tied to something. That something might be derision for romance fiction, or derision for LGBTQ fiction, or derision for LGBTQ romance fiction.

We ran into all those things. That was also one of the reasons why we approached many people with money "off the table" when we introduced the idea. Our main request for people during that first year and after, especially when working with the community, was simply, "We're starting a LGBTQ romance fiction conference. Do you like that this idea exists? Do you feel comfortable saying publicly that you like that this conference exists?"

For some, like our ten community partners, it was easy for them to say yes. They could, and did, support us publicly and supported that this event existed. For others, that request was too much.

In one case, I asked a large, local chapter of an organization that exists to specifically support romance writers in the US. I asked our first year if they would like to be involved, at no cost to them, and the answer was no. I asked during our second year, and then in our third year, with each time at no cost to them outside of being able to say publicly that they like that this event exists. The answer each time was no.

I'll be honest and say that I cried after the third year.

For some, they didn't want to appear with us because they were more "literary" and we were genre fiction. For others, it was the "gay thing."

This shouldn't be surprising, since at this moment, we're fighting across the country to allow trans people the simple human right to use the bathroom.

But each time I got a creepy feeling that what I was asking was too much because our very nature was too much—either we were doing something too "crass" like reading romance or too…whatever, like celebrating queer stories—it felt like a blow to the heart.

We learned that those blows are part of the process. The lesson was to accept with gratitude those that wanted these things to happen, wanted to help make things happen, and wanted to be there as things happened. They were and are the lights that make everything brighter and make everything worth it.

And who knows? Maybe someday, those that were not excited that this idea exists will start to think, "Hey, that's pretty cool that there are LGBTQIA love stories."

The HEA fan in me likes to think that's a possibility.

5. Queer Romance is a Wide Rainbow of Voices and They Should All Be Represented

In our first year, our byline was "The LGBT conference of the Pacific Northwest," but I'll be honest and say that we were short-sighted and 99% of our focus at that time was solely on M/M romance/gay romance. After the first conference, where we were sitting comfortable with the thought that things had gone so well, we received some kind but frank feedback that it would have been really nice to have more LGBTQ authors featured as speakers, and that it would have been nice if more than gay romance was part of the dialogue.

I'm ashamed to say I did all the stock answers at first about why we were so "mono-orientation," including the old favorite of "But we tried!" The reality is that we didn't have the background, connections, or knowledge beyond the dominate shade of gay romance, nor did we—and I'll switch that "we" to "me" and take full responsibility—have the curiosity to build that knowledge, and build the foundations for a richer, more complex discussion about the many layers that make up queer romance today. These many layers include romance fiction starring lesbian, bi, trans, asexual, and intersex characters, as well as characters who are genderqueer and agender.

I'm grateful for those that stuck with us from that first year to our second, especially our community partners that were representing the full queer spectrum. By only representing one kind of queer romance, we were not doing a good job of holding their (or our own) queer community banners. To celebrate the queer community, you need to recognize and celebrate *all* of it, and not just the voices that might be dominating the conversation.

Our takeaway from our first year was that we did a nice job, but not a great job, and to do that, we would need to do better. We would need to start building relationships, making connections, and prioritizing the stories and authors outside of the "G". That's the only way to actually be a LGBTQ event.

And so, for our second year, we invited more authors, we cold-emailed more people, and we built more spaces. The majority of the programming that year highlighted a wide range of stories and authors from across the spectrum of LGBTQIA and allies. In our third year, we handed over the reins to attendees and asked for panel submissions, and this helped the programming become even more diverse.

The push and challenge to build a platform that highlights the many voices within queer romance hasn't ended or gotten easier. It's ongoing work, because many of the "underrepresented" letters in the acronym—the Ts, the Bs, the As, the nonbinary stories and the genderqueer stories—still need a lot of advocacy and spotlights to be seen over the crowd. Lesbian romance as well still needs a lot of spotlights because *for some reason* our whole system seems to skew male, and books that celebrate and elevate stories about women who love women are still fighting an uphill battle for exposure and recognition.

Through this work, and thanks to the many wonderful people who are walking with us, we've learned that we can do a better job of celebrating the vibrancy and beauty of queer romance stories, and the many voices within it. They all deserve the love, just as they all deserve a Happily Ever After.

What Still Needs to be Done

Queer romance, and romance fiction in general, and publishing in general, is at a point where people are *used* to seeing one kind of story. One kind of story dominates all other narratives, but the audience—the varied, multifaceted, complex audience—reveals that there are many other stories that can and should be told, and should be allowed to be heard.

Maybe that one narrative is a story that focuses on heterosexual romance, or a story with only white main characters, or a story that only features cisgender or able-bodied characters. What we fortunately see more and more now are calls for more stories with many kinds of characters: multiracial characters, characters who are differently abled, and characters of varying religions. Readers want stories that recognize the broad spectrum of sexual orientations and gender identity.

The thing that we still need to do to is to continue to make the space to celebrate these many narratives. And to make the space to celebrate the many wonderful authors and readers who love, live, and inspire these stories. These narratives, these stories, still have so many barriers in front of them that are preventing them from being told and from being heard. From the cost argument ("Who will buy it?"), to the capacity argument ("Who will write it?"), to the supply chain argument ("We don't sell self-published books"), to the false meritocracy argument ("I earned this spot. Why should I have to step back for someone else?"), and to the invisible argument ("I don't know anyone who would read it").

The thing is, there are people who will write it, and people who will buy it, and people who will read it. Those sales numbers will never go up if we don't offer the space and opportunity for these books to be read. Beyond sales, we also have the moral imperative. It's not as sexy as the economic one, but it still exists, and we can't wish it away, nor will it go away if you drown it out with only stories that represent one kind of person. The only way to surpass it is to meet it.

Trans kids today should be able to read stories where people like them are happy. A bi woman should be able to read a story with a character like her, and know through that story that reaching a Happily Ever After doesn't mean she has to sacrifice her identity. A black gay man should be able to find a story that reaffirms, cherishes, protects, and celebrates love for a character like himself. He should be able to find many of these stories. There should be a wealth of these narratives, to meet the wealth of readers who are yearning to read them, to hold them to their chests, and to believe in a happy ending that includes someone like them.

Something like this just doesn't happen. You can't wait for time to pass and then find them magically on the shelf. It happens because people *make* it happen. They write the stories. They publish the stories. They read the stories. They ask for more. They laugh and cry over them, and embrace the community that celebrates and loves them.

To get to that point, we have to make the space. We need to encourage people to write. Ask people to publish. Point readers to the books. And share our spaces with each other. Share spots on panels, blogs, bookshelves, and recommendation lists, and by sharing our space together, we are also sharing the load, and saying to our fellow authors and readers, "You do not need to carry this on your own. I can help."

We are at the point right now where we still need to help each other within the queer romance community. There are too many groups who are still left behind, and if we don't make space to celebrate their stories, we will be doing the same thing that "mainstream" romance (otherwise known as straight romance) has often done to the queer romance community. We will be leaving them out of the conversation, out of the events, and out of the sales lists, or if we do include them, it will be a token few to represent the many— just enough to make the room look slightly more colorful, but not really enough to change the discussion or the power dynamics.

I humbly ask you to join us in this call to action—to stand up with all our fellow authors and readers and to ask and encourage the queer romance community to *expect* and to *own* our responsibility in making this space inclusive, welcoming, and celebratory for all these beautiful, wonderful stories.

I know for many of us, we haven't reached the limit yet. I include myself, as someone who identifies as asexual and is hungry—ravenous—for happy ace love stories.

We cannot have too many Happily Ever Afters. But we can certainly have not enough.

Maybe together, we can help expand our space and our community to include all these stories and all their amazing, excited, and inspiring readers.

That would be quite the Happy Ending, right?

How to Get LGBT Romance Books into Libraries

MARLENE HARRIS

My name is Marlene Harris and I'm a biblioholic. I'm addicted to reading. I read for fun and I read *a lot*. While my first loves are science fiction and fantasy, I also read just about every kind of romance, including gay romance.

But I am also a professional book-pusher. That's right, I'm a librarian. My current position is at the Seattle Public Library, but for the record, I am not writing officially on behalf of that library.

I'm here to talk about how readers can work with their libraries to get what they want to read on the shelves, both physical and "virtual".

In order to get your book into the library's collection, you have to navigate your way through the library's methods for getting material into its collection. In other words, what are the rules for navigating past the gatekeepers?

I'm going to get specific about things you can do to get books you want to read into your local library and/or books you've written into libraries. Before I do this, I want to make one very big caveat.

"All Politics is Local"

Public libraries are creatures of local politics. They are governed by locally elected or appointed boards and are funded by local tax dollars. Therefore, to paraphrase the gentleman who said the original phrase (Tip O'Neill, former Speaker of the U.S. House of Representatives), "All Libraries is local."

Ask for What You Want

If you are a reader and want more gay romance in your library, every library has a request mechanism for the library to purchase a book. For this method to work, some points to note:

You have to be a user of that library.

If your library is in a budget crunch, there may be a limit on how many books they order per month. (Also, requests may work better on January 15 than December 15, as libraries have budget cycles.)

Be kind to whoever has to handle the back-end of this process and fill the form out as completely as possible.

If you want an ebook, even if the form doesn't say you can ask for one, as long as the library has ebooks, you can still ask.

By asking for what you want, you are demonstrating that there is demand in the community. If no one asks, then the library does not know that their users will check out gay romances.

Also, because gay romances are not published by big-name publishers, they are not heavily reviewed by the review sources that libraries use. Requesting a specific title is a big up-vote that the library should buy it, even without a review.

One warning for any author that is thinking about getting their spouse and/or parent and/or child to request their book: please don't try to trick us. We're librarians and we do research.

Does the Amount of Sex in a Book Matter?

I've been asked whether the amount or graphicness of the sex matters in whether or not gay romance, or any romance, will be purchased for a library collection.

This is an "All Libraries is Local" answer. Sex hasn't mattered at the libraries I've worked at (and that just reads wrong when I write it), but I've worked for most of my career in either big cities or college towns, and they tend to skew liberal. If you live in a community where your local library doesn't carry het erotica, they're not going to buy any gay erotica either. On the other hand, if the het romances get extremely steamy, then it's reasonable to ask them to purchase equally steamy gay romances.

Getting Reviewed Matters

Besides patron requests, how do libraries decide what to buy? And how can you as an author get a library to buy your book?

The best thing is to get your book reviewed by one of the major review magazines.

The review magazines that libraries use are *Library Journal, Publisher's Weekly, Kirkus Reviews,* and *Booklist.*

If you write YA, there is also an offshoot of *Library Journal,* the *School Library Journal.*

For romance specifically, *RT Book Reviews* is relevant, and middle-sized and bigger public libraries subscribe and use it.

Library Journal also reviews e-original romances, including LGBTQ romances, in their online *Xpress Reviews* every week.

And *Kirkus Reviews* and *Publishers Weekly* will let authors buy reviews, but it's expensive. (And even if you buy a review with *Kirkus,* there is no guarantee that it will be a good review. *Kirkus* is notoriously snarky!)

As a recommendation, *Library Journal Xpress Reviews* is always looking for more ebook-only or digital first publishers to work with. (Full disclosure, I'm one of their reviewers.)

Work with Libraries

Librarians hand-sell books they love, just like local bookstores.

For authors, you can approach your library about doing an event there. Libraries do author events and have many of the same types of author-related programming that bookstores do.

If you do an author event at your local library, the library will also stock your books for circulation. No matter what they have to do to get them. If you are the event, people will be curious about your work and want to check your work out.

Also, many libraries will either allow an author to sell their books after an author event or partner with a local bookstore to sell the author's books.

You promote your library event; you promote the library. The library promotes your event; it promotes the library and you. *Everybody wins.*

Donating Books

Ask your local library if they accept donations. Many libraries are thrilled to have local authors donate copies of their books. My experience is that the smaller the library is, the more likely this method is to work.

Whatever you do, don't drop donated books through the book drop and expect them to magically appear in the collection. Also don't drop them at the circulation desk. (Yes, I've seen both things happen.)

Let's Talk About Ebooks

When a library buys a print book, it buys a book. Just like you. We own the book; we can do what we want with it. Including sell it or give it away later.

Ebooks are not like print books. Nobody owns their ebooks. It's software and it's a license. The licensor, meaning the publisher, controls the terms of the license.

The technology for handling the Digital Rights Management is a pain in the patootie for everyone. There are very few companies who deal in the niche market of managing the DRM for ebook library checkouts. The big name is Overdrive. 3M (yes, the Scotch Tape people) jumped into the game but later jumped back out again.

So for a library to get your ebook, we have to know about it, and it has to be available to us through the supplier or suppliers that the library uses for ebooks.

For most libraries, that's still Overdrive. Overdrive deals with publishers rather than with individual authors as a general rule. That being said, there are certainly publishers listed in Overdrive who are really just the publishers of a single author's work.

In Conclusion, and Real-Life Examples

LGBTQ romance belongs in libraries.

If you are a reader and want more LGBTQ romance in your library, suggest titles.

For authors, we really do need to see where you've been reviewed.

If you are an author, working with your local library can give you more exposure.

I will bring up one example. The Gay Romance Northwest Meet-Up was held at the Seattle Public Library's Central Library on September 14, 2013. In the month prior to the conference, the Seattle Public Library purchased *240 new ebook titles of LGBTQ romance*, including titles by most of the authors attending the conference.

From the library perspective, what was great to see was that almost all those titles went out in circulation immediately, and some titles developed hold lists. The immediate circulation plus hold queues exhibited demand to the library system, which means the library will purchase more titles.

This is something that libraries do. We (libraries in general) like to meet the demands of our users, and when we see that there is a demonstrated demand, we'll keep meeting it.

Your library wants to give you what you want. You are our customers, our patrons, our users. You know what's hot in the genre that you love and what's not.

Help us do better.

Slack Tide

KARELIA STETZ-WATERS

Talk in the Quarry Cove Tavern surges like the rain outside. The pool balls crack. The Keno game chimes. A gust of wind rattles the aluminum gutters, and a wave breaks against the rocks beyond the sagging wooden deck outside, sending a spray of white into the black sky.

"Hey, Butch," one of the fishermen yells to me, pointing at a scrawl on the chalkboard behind the pool table. "That you?"

How many times have I put my name on that board and won or lost? It might be my name. I can't tell from where I'm sitting by the window. I don't feel like playing pool.

"You take it," I say.

I hated these men growing up: Cody and Jared and Tyler and Brian Greenweed, who wants everyone to call him Axel, but they never will. They leave me alone now though.

A wave crests the rocks and hits the seawall, splashing onto the deck. The men cheer like they cheer for the sports teams they've never seen live. Once Brian Greenweed was driving by the Quarry Cove Tavern late at night, and he said he saw a wave crash right over the place. No one believes him.

"Hey, Greenweed," they yell. "You better get on home. Next one's gonna be the big one."

It's nights like this I think I should pack up my shop and head inland. Tattooing is good work in the summer. The tourists keep me busy with tattoos of flowers and kanji. But in the winter, I feel the moon pulling me like it pulls on the tide, and I don't know why I'm still here.

Another wave hits the seawall. I glance at Brian Greenweed, but he's left his seat at the Keno machine. Beyond the pool table, I see the back door open. Someone enters wearing the tan camo of returning soldiers, not the army green that the boys around here wear to go hunting. There's a little swell of conversation as the men in the back recognize the soldier and greet him.

No...her.

I look again. I see the cap and the top of a duffle bag bobbing over the shoulders of the newcomer. I feel my heart seize the way it does when you hit a big swell out on the open.

Cassandra. Little Cassie. My best friend Kaylin's baby sister by two years. I want to run up to her and throw my arms around her. Even the old fishermen hug the boys who come back. They know about setting out and not knowing if you'll motor back into the cove. I remember when she decided to enlist. She was only sixteen, and she started marching around Roosevelt High in her junior ROTC or baby-Marine or whatever-it-was outfit: crisp, green blouse and shiny boots. I saluted her, and I teased her about killing terrorists. Then on her first deployment, her squadron got lost beyond someplace called Al-Nukhib. I sat waiting at the computer. Waiting and waiting. Two weeks later, they found their way back by the stars.

Who even knows how to do that anymore? What outdated interest in astronavigation saved them in that last hour?

Little Cassie strides over, but she isn't little anymore. She's tall, and she wears her uniform with a lean squareness that is all business and not a bit of pep squad. Her tan cap is pulled low over her eyes. Her hair is pulled back in a ponytail, and I don't want to make jokes about killing people because it's no joke, and because her eyes tell me she knows that.

"Selena," she says.

No one's called me that for years.

Cassie was on Facebook the whole time she was gone, except for those weeks in the desert. It seems strange that someone could be in Iraq and on Facebook. I wish we'd just had letters. I think I would have written more if it hadn't been so easy to type gibberish and a thumbs up. How could I send her a picture of my breakfast or my latest sketch when every day before I logged on I wondered if she had survived the night?

"I didn't know you were coming back," I say.

She nods. "Yep."

One of the boys says, "Well, go on and kiss her." He's drunk, but it breaks the tension.

"Nothing's changed here," I say. "Same old bullshit, same old bullshitters."

I give her a hug. Her uniform is wet from the rain.

"I hitchhiked," she says, as if reading my mind. "I walked the last three miles down the hill."

"They didn't get you a car or something?"

"The army?" Her lip cocks into a little smile. "No. They don't get you a stretch limo when you get back."

I offer her a seat in my booth by the window, and I'm glad the bar is crowded and I got the awkward booth that's just one bench and half a table. I get her a beer and me another, and I slide in next to her. She's staring at me. There's concern in her eyes and something else too. I run my hand over my bare scalp. You shouldn't feel a good tattoo, not even the outlines where the needle goes deeper, but the tattoo on my head traces the seams of my skull bones, making an anatomical study of my scalp. I think you can feel those bones more now. Sometimes the women at the Walmart whisper when I walk by. *Why would someone do that?* I feel Cassie's gaze on me, and I think she might ask the same question, but she'd also wait for the answer.

"No one wants to get a tattoo from someone who's just got a bit of flash on their arm." I pat my bicep where an anchor might go or some soon-to-be-regretted name encased in a heart. I'm trying for casual.

"Who did it?" She sounds disapproving. No...proprietary.

I like that. I sip my beer.

"A guy in Reedsport."

She reaches up and runs her fingertips over my shaved head, her fingers lingering behind my ear, sending a shiver down my spine.

"You've changed," she says.

"You too," I say. She looks skeptical, and I don't know how to tell her it's all in her eyes. Her face looks the same: round cheeks, turned up nose, a glitter of freckles. "But you're still cute," I add.

It's a joke. She's more than cute, and she must realize it. If I didn't know her already, I'd probably be too intimidated to talk to her now.

Another wave hits the seawall. The men cheer, and this time they don't pick on Brian Greenweed with his tsunami alert app and his insurance business in town.

"What brings you back?" I ask.

"I didn't reenlist," she says.

"That would have been a second...are they called terms?"

She nods. "It's been four years. I know it's crazy. I should stay in, but I got sick of moving around."

"You've done so much," I say. I don't know if it's true.

"Went to exotic places, killed exotic people?" she suggests.

For a moment I'm lost. Then I remember—when she enlisted, I went to one of the bric-a-brac stores that sell crap to the tourists, and I bought a shirt that read TRAVEL TO EXOTIC PLACES. MEET INTERESTING PEOPLE...AND KILL THEM.

On the back, was the army logo fixed up just enough so the screenprinter didn't get sued. I bought it to piss her off. Little Cassie just smiled her cheer-captain smile and told me there was a lot more to the service than going to war.

"I was an asshole. I'm sorry."

"Yeah," she says slowly. It's not an accusation.

"Where are you staying?" As soon as I ask, I want to take the question back. I didn't mean to put it out there so quickly. Kaylin, Cassie's sister, moved to Newport with her husband. Cassie and Kaylin's folks picked up and went to Arizona. They got the idea and sold their house all in one month. There's really no one here for Cassie, except for everyone. You don't grow up in a town like Quarry Cove and not know everyone. But everyone doesn't count, and I want her to stay with me.

"Haven't decided," she says.

"I've still got the place above my shop." I make a mental inventory of the apartment. It's tidy enough, but if I had known she was in town, I would have...what? Bought flowers? That doesn't seem like enough. "You're always welcome to stay with me. You know that, right?"

"Still living the dream?" She pulls her cap off and smooths down her blond hair. Then she readjusts the cap.

"Still living." I shrug. "Four years in the army. What was that like?"

"Boring. Beautiful. Terrifying. We were stationed north of Baghdad for a while. Just me and twelve other guys. We had this place out in the desert." She pulls out her phone and shows me pictures. It looks like a campground that's been blown over by a sandstorm. But then she flips through the pictures some more and shows me a city of blue, onion-shaped domes and turrets rising above sandy streets.

"I've got to get out of Quarry Cove," I say, but I'm thinking about the way her knee is leaning against mine.

"You're leaving?" She sounds startled.

"Not…no. I mean, I always say I will, but I never seem to make it out. I don't know what it is. Your folks moved, though. You gonna go visit them?"

"I couldn't just fly back to Arizona," Cassie says. "To visit, sure, but when I decided I wasn't going to reenlist…I just felt like I had to come back here. You know? Just to see."

My heart beats in my throat like a motor running in drydock. After Cassie's parents left, I told myself she wouldn't come back. And even if she did…everyone gets lonely for the people who leave. We tell ourselves stories about them. They're an answer to a question we can't quite put words to. It doesn't mean they miss us.

"You see much of Kaylin?" Cassie asks.

"No." I pause. "I think she's still mad at me."

It's an invitation, a promise. *I remember.* Cassie stares across the bar, her eyes sweeping over the men and the pool table and the old mirrors with the Budweiser logo printed across them.

"Yeah," she says. And there's that smile again, just a little pinch at the corner of her mouth. "I remember she walked into your bedroom."

"I think the gay thing freaked her out."

"She knew you were gay before that. I'm her sister. *That* freaked her out."

I let my gaze settle just below Cassie's chin, at the hollow of her neck, where a braid of parachute chord stands in for jewelry.

"Should I not have…?"

What had I done to Cassie? Seduced her? Finally? I'd invited her over to watch a movie.

"*Desert of the Heart,*" Cassie says. "It took you long enough to make your move."

"I had to wait at least until you were eighteen."

"You were just shy."

"I was shy."

"You waited until the day before I left."

I'm trying to remember when I first looked at her and saw a woman, not my friend's baby sister. I know I hated her enlistment before I realized why.

In my silence, Cassie muses, "What was Kaylin doing in your apartment anyway?"

"She wanted to borrow a crab pot."

"She had a key."

"She was my best friend."

"I remember she kept yelling, 'She's my little sister.'" Cassie shakes her head. "You just looked up and said, 'Your little sister, not *my* little sister.' You were so fucking cool. You know you could've just asked me out. I would have said yes."

We're close together in the booth now, and the surface of the table is a tiny world. Beneath a quarter inch of lacquer, stamps and sand dollars remember a time when someone cared about atmosphere at the tavern. I trace the swirl of a tiny seashell.

Cassie reaches out and caresses my head again.

"What are you going to do now that you're out of the army?" I ask.

In the back, the men start up an argument. Someone calls someone a tweaker. A pool cue crashes to the floor. Brian Greenweed wheedles, "You guys, don't!" Jared tells him to "shut the fuck up." Cody and a fisherman from Sand Creek Beach push their chests forward, their hands in loose fists.

"You want to go outside?" Cassie asks.

In old pictures, you can see the Quarry Cove Tavern set back from the ocean. It was a guest house before it was a bar, and in the historical photographs, ladies in long skirts play croquet on a lawn overlooking the sea. But the sea has eaten the lawn. Now there's just the wooden deck with its bucket of cigarette butts, then the seawall, then the rocks, and then the waves.

When we're outside, Cassie yells over the sound of the ocean and the rain.

"Tide's going out."

Only a local would know. The spray still hits our faces, and the air smells of sunken ships. The sky is so dark, I can't see where the ocean ends and the sky begins.

"I missed you," I yell back.

"I missed you too."

"I'm sorry I waited so long."

The wind lashes the rain. Somewhere a transformer blows with the sound of a gunshot. I see Cassie jump, her face all frightened angles. Then the town goes dark. I open my arms and Cassie steps into my embrace. There is enough light to see that far. I don't know where that light comes from. Maybe it lives in the atmosphere, a luminescence in the salt spray. Maybe it's her.

She kisses me hard on the lips, and that kiss is not frightened

It feels like I'm the one who came home.

Another breaker hits the seawall.

The men start to file out of the bar. There's nothing to do inside. There's no point in fighting when no one can see, and Jackson behind the bar won't serve anyone if he can't ring up the purchase. No one's ever gotten a free beer at the Quarry Cove Tavern.

"Come home with me?" I ask.

Cody whistles and Jared calls out, "It's 'bout time, Cue Ball."

He hasn't called me that since I first shaved my head. Maybe Cassie makes us all remember. I don't mind.

It's ten blocks—that is to say the entire length of the town—to my shop and my apartment. We don't talk. The wind is roaring down Highway 101. Once we get inside, I light a candle in a little jar. The apartment is clean, even if it's ugly, and the window gives a view of the ocean. There's no land. We're all clinging to the edge. In the dim light I can see that Cassie is shivering, which seems odd. She looked so impenetrable in her uniform before.

"You're cold," I say.

"I missed the rain." She pulls her cap off and drops it on my table. She looks young and not young at the same time. I step forward and unbutton the first button on her shirt.

"We don't have to do anything if you don't want to," I say. "I want you to know that. If you just want a place to crash, it's okay."

"Kaylin told me you weren't seeing anyone." She lays the words out one by one, like someone carefully setting a place at the table. "She heard it from some of the guys at the port. She said she thought you'd be happy to see me."

"I am."

I undo another button on Cassie's shirt. I've never touched a military uniform before. Lots of soldiers and vets come into the shop, and I've done enough eagles and globes, stars, and anchors to know the lines by heart, but I don't touch their clothes. The fabric is rough. She's soaked through. I run my hands down the ribs of her undershirt.

"There'll still be hot water in the tank," I say. "Can I run you a bath?"

She says, "Sure," and she looks relieved. "I've been on the road all day. It takes a long time to hitchhike."

"You know that's dangerous."

"Thanks, mom," she says.

I laugh. "Next time, call me, and I'll come get you."

Next time.

I remember that night when Cassie and I strolled up to my apartment. I'd already been out of school for two years, but in a town like this, everyone knows everyone's little sister. I had lied to Kaylin and told her I was too tired to hang out. Cassie had followed me out of Mick's Fish 'n' Chips, where we all wasted our time before we turned twenty-one. Cassie's friends had suddenly disappeared.

God, I hate the smell of fry oil, she'd complained. *What are we going to do now?*

I said, I've got this old lezzie movie.

I was teasing, and I wasn't.

"I'm always looking for an excuse to get off the coast," I add.

Only not now. Tonight there is nowhere else in the world. I move the candle into the small bathroom, place a towel on the counter, and excuse myself. I get two beers out of the fridge. Cassie leaves the door to the bathroom open and the light from the candle spills into the little hallway. I knock on the wall outside before I come in.

I can see her muscles in the flickering light, her shoulders like a swimmer's, her abs like the marble of some beautiful Greek statue. Her face—that girl-next-door smile—barely fits her body. It's like someone Photoshopped Little Cassie's face onto the body of a bodybuilder.

I kneel down beside her.

"You're beautiful," I say.

I can't remember the last time I looked at a woman like this, so closely I can see the tiny gold hairs wet on her arm. My customers don't count. They come and go. They're just a canvas. The swell of Cassie's breast is worth everything I've done without. I ruffle the water with my fingertips. She leans back.

"You know what I missed over there?" she says. "All this water. When my parents said they'd moved to Arizona, I thought, why? It's so dry."

I take a cloth from the side of the tub and smooth it over her chest. She sighs quietly. I stroke it over her neck, down the length of her arm.

"You're so strong," I say.

Then I let the cloth fall into the water, cup the sliver of soap in my hand, and run it over her shoulders. I don't touch her breasts. It doesn't seem right, when she's naked and I'm still wearing my jeans and an old sweatshirt from Salty's Rentals.

"I didn't have anyone over there," she says. "I mean, the women in my platoon were great, but I didn't have a girlfriend or anything. Most of the time we were in this quonset hut in the desert. No one was ever alone. The guys jerked off in front of each other, but I couldn't do that."

The thought of her in the desert, hot and chaste and wanting...I feel my own body wake She leans forward. I massage her shoulders. They are as hard as the rocks beneath Quarry Cove.

"That feels good," she says. It sounds like a confession.

I draw my nails lightly down her back. When she turns to look at me, I kiss her. Her breath is clean. The slight roughness of her tongue as it touches mine sends a jolt of desire through me. When we stop kissing, the water has cooled. I hold my hand out to her as she steps out of the tub. She doesn't need my help. The muscles of her arms tell me she could lift the whole tub out of its housing. I wrap her in a towel and kiss her again, her body pressed to mine.

"I want to see your tattoos," she says.

I lead her to the bedroom. She dries off and slides under the covers of my bed without invitation.

"Well?" she prompts.

I take off my sweatshirt and pull my t-shirt over my head. I haven't bothered with a bra.

At first, she says nothing.

I forget sometimes. I forget how the bones of my skull are traced in black ink, like fissures in rock. I forget the blue wave cresting over my occipital bone or how the octopus sinks the ship at the base of my neck, swirling down into the roil of waves. A giant lantern fish forever gapes its maw on my side, its lure hanging low on my belly. The tourists who come into my shop for four leaf clovers hedge about whether or not they'll still love their tattoo when they're sixty. Everyone says sixty. I forget that I've made so many annotations to my skin. In my mind, my body is as pale and unlined as Cassie's.

"They're lovely." There is a question in Cassie's voice.

I lie down beside her.

"Why though?" she asks. "I mean, you look magical, but why?"

I can feel the damp warmth of her body. I want to tell her about the boys who would follow me through the halls of our high school and then follow me down to the docks where I tried to gut fish on the line. I wanted to be a commercial fisher, but I didn't trust them out there in the ocean. And they didn't trust me either.

"I had a hard time at school."

She traces the crest of a wave breaking over my breast, then rolls my nipple between her fingers. I can feel her touch throughout my whole body.

"So this is a warning," she says, trailing her fingers down to the monster on my side. She touches its lantern. "Or an invitation?"

"It's only a warning to sailors," I say.

She glides her hand down and cups the hair between my legs, one finger just touching the opening of my body, and says, "Good thing I didn't join the navy."

Then she kisses me, holding me down, her hand on my sex, her tongue in my mouth. She handles me. I thought that I would take the lead, that I would make love to her and redress all her hot, desert days. We're only two years apart, but that's something when you grow up in the same small town. Quarry Cove fixes you in time. Whoever you were when you were nine or eleven—stupid, awkward, and shy— you remain. It's a kind of immortality.

Cassie plunges her finger into me, and she is no one's little sister. The first thrust feels dry, sticky, then my body releases its moisture. She moves her fingers in and out. My hips lift to her hand. I feel how much bigger she is than me, how much stronger. She's a soldier, and I want that. The boys call me "Butch" and "Mister" and "Sir." But I am willow branches in her hands. I am spring trillium. She could break me, and she doesn't, and the woman in me loves that so much I feel like a stranger to myself.

"I feel like such a *girl*," I whisper between gasps.

She chuckles deep in her throat. "You are."

Her breath is slow, deep, and steady, but I can feel the urgency in her movements. Eventually, she rolls onto her back and pulls me onto her so our legs intertwine. She holds my hipbones.

"If you hadn't been there at the bar..." she says as I press against her, "I would have come looking for you."

I rotate my hips around and around, pressing my thigh against her sex. The ink on my legs is a delicate pattern of scales. If I hold my legs together, I am a mermaid, but I open my legs now. I try to touch her center with mine. She lets out a sharp bark like a drill sergeant's call.

"Oh, God. Go slow, go slow," she says. "I want to enjoy it."

I can barely pull myself away from her, but I do, and I touch her, moving my thumb around her clit while I push my fingers inside her.

"Is this all right?" I ask, breathless.

Her head is thrown back. I don't know this woman, and I've always known her. And I want to tell her what I've been too sensible to acknowledge even to myself. I haven't left Quarry Cove because I've been waiting for her to wash up upon this shore.

"Please," she begs. "Harder." She repeats the world like a prayer. "Harder."

When I fear that I will hurt her if I press harder, I slide down her body. I pull her clit and all the flesh around it into my mouth, moving my tongue across her, pulling on her.

I'm not sure what perfect blend of pressure and touch I've achieved, but we hang suspended in the stand of the tide, that moment when the great force of the moon pauses and waters are still. We are motionless, like tattooed lovers inked into the sheets. Then the orgasm shakes her body, the slack water gives, the tide reverses, and she sings her pleasure.

Once she has recovered, she kisses her way down my belly, past the lantern fish whose warning was never for her, and into the deep. She is gentle with me, which is what I need. She seems to know that. When I come, she wraps her arms around my hips and holds me, her cheek against my belly.

"Will you ever get out of Quarry Cove?" she asks, stroking my side.

"I don't know."

I coax her up, so that I can wrap my arms around her. She nestles her head on my breast.

"Don't leave just yet," she says, taking my hand and clasping it against her chest. "Not tonight."

I press my face to her hair. It smells of coconuts and sea rain and sex. There's no one-if-by-land, two-if-by-sea for lovers. I didn't know when she would come home or by what rain-swept road. I think now that she's here, I can close down the lighthouse. I think all we ever really know is how to navigate by the stars.

Dear Rose

ROSE CHRISTO

Dear Rose,

Hi. Remember me? I know we haven't kept in contact over the years. It's just that we've never exactly seen eye to eye. I had the chance to be a physicist. You stopped me. I almost ran away with the girl of my dreams. You stopped me again. Coexisting with you is like having teeth pulled, only there's no novocaine, and the dentist is that creepy guy from the *Rocky Horror Picture Show*.

Consider this letter a dire warning. Yes, this is the part in *A Christmas Carol* where the Ghost of Christmas Future points at Scrooge's grave, right before she rips off her ragged cloak and ballet dances across the stage.

Catherine Batcheller is so cool.

I want you to realize that you are not the only person who has to live your life. Everyone around you is living your life, too. Your cousins. Your grandparents. Even that Cliff guy who works the deli with you but doesn't utter a single word. What you do or don't do in other people's presence will affect each of them for the rest of their lives. You might never see the impression you've left, but that doesn't mean it isn't there.

And so when you tell stories, remember that they aren't just your stories. Every story you write should be with the intention of making somebody's life a little bit happier, a little bit easier to live. I don't want to meet with you again in another five years and find out you haven't helped a single person. I think I will strangle you with my bare hands.

You are lucky to come from a community that celebrates your differences. You are Two-Spirit, they told you. You are the Shapeshifter, like Ayas. Most people are not as fortunate as you are. Do you even realize that? When you thought that you were ugly, you were taught that you were beautiful. Many people have been tricked into thinking they are ugly. It's a giant, vicious conspiracy, and that it's allowed to persist is the most aggravating mystery on this planet. Show them it's a conspiracy. Show them that they're perfect as they are. Make them feel it in their bones, in their teeth, in the tips of their fingers, and the backs of their skulls until nobody—nothing—can take it away. If you can't accomplish something so small, you might as well stop writing.

Wachiya,
Rose

Charmed by Chance

ALEX POWELL

Merritt cradled his hand, trying very hard not to jostle it. One of the miniscule screws in his thumb joint teetered on the edge of falling out, and if it did, he'd never find the damn thing again. Why had he thought that Serrah would just let it go, when he knew she had a vengeful streak?

No more, he told himself. Dating mages ended here, once and for all.

Merritt had even moved to Yasadria to get away from all the drama in the guild, and here he had just happened to run into Serrah at the local Mech collegium.

They'd been civil—or so he'd thought. Merritt had realized that all the screws in his left hand were loose only after Serrah had left. It was a nasty trick, and one that he couldn't fix himself.

He'd panicked and asked one of the Mech mages the location of the nearest prosthetics shop, and now he stood in front of it.

It looked like a very small shop, but looks could be deceiving. The door into the shop was narrower than average and made of stained wood. The hinges were lovely wrought metal that snaked its way up the door. A strange contraption hung inside the single window.

For a few seconds, Merritt stood stuck outside, wondering how to open the door with one hand holding the other one together. Then, someone exited, and he slipped inside.

The long, narrow shop had wooden floors and brick walls. Surprisingly, the well-lit interior had shelving that held all sorts of models for different metal prosthetics. On sight alone, Merritt knew he couldn't afford most of it.

A mage sat down at the end looking into a metal-and-glass contraption that magnified his work. Realizing that he had a customer, the mage raised his head and smiled.

Wait. She smiled? He?

Merritt couldn't figure out the mage's gender, because while they had a completely flat and masculine chest, they also had on full make-up and Merritt could see that they were wearing a long, patchwork skirt.

Following that realization, Merritt felt a confused pull of attraction. Oh no.

Not that he was picky about gender, but he had just pledged not to get involved with another Mech mage. Just now.

"Um," said Merritt.

Luckily, the mage could see very well what had brought him in.

"Oh, dear, let me see that," they said, ushering him over into a chair.

They pushed their current project aside and pulled Merritt's hand underneath the contraption, whispering under their breath as they started fixing the mess that Serrah had made of his hand.

The name "Verity" was stitched to the front of their apron. Merritt stayed still and quiet as Verity kept up their barely audible chanting. How powerful the magic depended on the volume at which the mage spoke. While War mages or flashy Mech mages used loud magic, subtle and quiet magic functioned well for most Mech work

Merritt could feel the difference in his hand as Verity whispered. He took the opportunity to study Verity while they worked. Shades of brown, orange, and rusty red made up their patchwork quilt skirt. The loose red shirt they were wearing somewhat disguised their unfeminine chest. Their long, dark red tresses were tied back with a leather thong.

"Confused about something?" asked Verity, and it snapped Merritt out of his study.

Merritt blinked, mouth partly open, but he couldn't think of a single thing to say in response to that.

"You're staring," Verity said with a light laugh.

"Oh, um," Merritt said, floundering.

"You're not the first one to get caught up with my apparently confusing appearance," Verity said. "Don't worry, I'm not going to hold it against you."

"Sorry," blurted Merritt.

"It's okay," Verity said. "I've finished up with your hand."

"Oh," Merritt said. "How much do I owe you?"

"Nothing. It was no trouble. I'm not busy today."

Merritt glanced at the project that Verity had put aside, and they said in response to the silent glance, "It's a private project of mine that I've been working on."

"I don't mean to be so…" Merritt said, waving his hands around, forgetting what word he wanted.

"That's fine," Verity said. "There's no need to be nervous around me."

Oh no, Verity probably thought the gender issue flustered him, when really the fact that they were so very cute and interesting was what had put him so out of sorts.

"It's not that," sputtered Merritt. "Just, it's that…I…I should go now."

"All right then," Verity said with a small laugh. "Bye now. Come in again!"

Merritt left, heart still fluttering in confusion. *What* had just happened? He walked outside the shop , blinking in the summer sunlight.

His squirming stomach told him he definitely found Verity far too interesting for his own good. And he and Serrah had just split, too. He really needed to stop falling for Mech mages.

He flexed his hand and nodded his approval. His prosthetic functioned smoothly, as good as new, with no lag from where the flesh and nerves connected with his metal arm.

Merritt needed to talk to Dak immediately about this new crush before it got too out of hand. He could find Dak easily right now. Dak worked at the Golden Butterfly public house, and the rush of late afternoon hadn't started yet.

Five main thoroughfares in the shape of a pentagon made up Yasadria, and one could locate the Golden Butterfly on the northern boulevard. That was the university district, where both he and Dak were students. The streets were lined with huge iron-wrought sculptures that were meant to look like trees and lanterns with different-colored light.

The Golden Butterfly had a gold-plated sign, and the outside was painted black with golden accents. For a place named after such a delicate creature, it looked somewhat solemn.

He walked in and plopped himself down on a bar stool at the huge metal counter. He watched as Dak cleaned glasses for several minutes, content to wait and ponder his latest crush until Dak noticed him. Dak would know what to do. Dak always did.

Dak was tall, broad, and dark-skinned. His shorn head didn't have a speck of stubble on it, and Merritt couldn't remember ever seeing any. He had golden rings all over both his ears and a huge tattoo of a mechanical dragon on his shoulder and down his arm.

"What do you want, Merritt?" Dak rumbled.

"Well..."

He knew already what Dak wanted to say. Dak knew all about all of Merritt's ill-advised entanglements, and would not be impressed with Merritt's new interest.

"Oh no, you didn't," Dak said, groaning.

"What? I didn't even say anything yet!" Merritt protested.

"You didn't have to say a word," Dak said. "Who is it this time?"

"You know how Serrah is really good at deconstructing mechanisms?" Merritt asked. "She did that to my hand."

"And what does that have to do with whoever it is this time?"

"I had to get my hand fixed," Merritt explained. "And I went to a shop close to the university. They work there. The person. I'm not actually sure what gender they are, but…"

"Not another Mech mage," said Dak, running a hand over his head. "What is it with you and Mech mages?"

"They're interesting," Merritt said. "I can talk about Mech design with them."

Merritt and Dak were both studying Mech design and architecture at the university. Mech design had a separate school from the Mech mages', although many of them took a few design classes to learn some of the basics. Neither Dak nor Merritt were gifted with Mech magic, however.

And this is after your last disastrous relationship," Dak said. "You need to wait more than a few days between dates, you know."

"I haven't asked them out yet," said Merritt sulkily.

"Yet!" laughed Dak.

"That's what I came to see you about, to get your advice!" Merritt said. "And instead you're laughing at me."

"Didn't you learn your lesson with Serrah?"

"Serrah isn't a reflection on all Mech mages," said Merritt. "Anyway, Verity is really nice. They fixed me right up, no charge."

"So you say, but Serrah hasn't been the only mage you've dated with nasty results. Remember Yasmin? She threw a wrench at your head when you broke up."

"As if I could forget that," Merritt said. "I really liked Henrick. He had a nice temperament."

"Henrick dumped a cup of tea on your lap when you broke up," Dak said dryly.

"He was distraught! I can't blame him."

"You are going to get yourself in trouble one of these days," Dak said. "So, what are they like, this Verity of famed generosity?"

"They have long hair, and it's wavy, and the same color as a copper bit," said Merritt. "They're tall and slender, like a willow, and their eyes are large and dark brown. And their magic is the whispery, quiet type, which I like."

"I can't believe you have a preferred magic type," Dak said, rolling his eyes.

"Some of us have different tastes," Merritt said primly, tipping his chin up.

"Okay, but this is seriously not a great plan," Dak said. "Not that you have a plan, as far as I can tell."

"You're supposed to be helping me make one rather than naysaying everything I tell you about them."

"You just got out of a bad relationship," Dak said. "And the time before that, you did the exact same thing. And I told you then what a bad idea dating again would be. But you didn't listen. And look where it got you."

"I have a good feeling about this one," Merritt said.

"That's what you said about Serrah, too," Dak said. "Fine! But when this blows up in your face..."

"So pessimistic," Merritt said blithely. "Okay, so they work in a shop just a few streets away from the university. We can go and see them after class tomorrow and you can help me out. You're really good at reading people."

"Why does no one ever listen to me?" Dak said to the empty air above his head. "I have a bad feeling about this."

"Don't worry!" Merritt said, patting Dak's large hand. "I'll see you tomorrow! Remember, after class we go see Verity."

"As if I could forget," groaned Dak, then mumbled something that sounded like a complaint under his breath.

Merritt had no idea what made Dak so resistant to the idea. This would be a piece of cake.

❁❁❁

It rained the next day after class ended, and Dak didn't want to go. Merritt knew that any other day, the two of them would have bunkered down next to one of the many fireplaces around campus with some friends and studied together, or even taken a nap. But Merritt never went back on plans.

"You do too go back on plans," Dak grumbled. "Just not when they're yours. Remember that Zara dumped you because you cancelled your one-month-anniversary date."

"One month anniversaries aren't that important!" Merritt said, rolling his eyes.

"And that attitude is exactly why most of your dates don't make it past one month," Dak said, scoffing. "I'm telling you, Merritt, you don't have the best track record."

"You and your negativity." Merritt waved blithely. "Anyway, we're supposed to be focused on Verity."

"Right, with a name like that, they aren't the one for you," Dak said.

"Are you suggesting I'm untrue to my lovers?" gasped Merritt. "You wouldn't say that about me. There's not a fickle bone in my body."

"You're not with them long enough to be untrue," Dak said. "You never take relationships seriously, and your dates can tell."

"You know I'd only accept this kind of talk from you," Merritt said. "Enough of the chatter for now, we're here. No bad-mouthing me to my new interest."

"Fine," Dak said. "My lips are sealed."

Merritt and Dak stepped through the doorway, which someone had propped open in spite of the rain. The humid air made the interior of the shop stuffy. Merritt took his hood off, and his dark, curly hair fluffed up with the moisture. He smoothed it down, ready to start up a conversation with the mysterious but lovely Verity, when he stopped in his tracks.

"You!" hissed Serrah.

"Whoa, what are you doing here?" asked Merritt, backing up several feet.

"What do you think I'm doing? I'm a Mech mage. This is a Mech shop. You're as clueless as you always were, Merry-Quite-Contrary."

Verity appeared from the back and looked back and forth between them during their stand-off.

"What's going on?" Verity asked.

Verity wore their hair up in a cute updo, and a metal pin kept their hair away from their face. A streak of engine grease across one cheek charmed Merritt and momentarily distracted him from the argument.

"Don't worry, Verity, my ex was just leaving," Serrah snarled.

"Wait, you know them?" asked Merritt.

"Of course. Verity is my friend!" Serrah said. "We fellow Mech mages need to stick together and keep idiotic design students at arm's length!"

"Oh dear," said Dak.

"Is that all you can say?" Merritt said, voice pitching up at the end. "Of course my ex would know...know..."

Merritt scrambled for a word to describe Verity without sounding possessive or over-familiar. He couldn't think of one, but that didn't stop Serrah from catching on. She got a sharp look in her eye, and pointed at Merritt dramatically.

"You stay away from Verity! They have better things to do than be wooed by annoying idiots like you!" she yelled.

"Now, Serrah, I can take care of myself," Verity said.

"Not from him, you can't," Serrah hissed. "He'll sweep

you off your feet, then get distracted and drop you on your head."

"I didn't drop you."

"You almost dropped me," Serrah said. "He's no good, Verity, let me tell you."

"That's not fair, Serrah," Merritt said.

"Too bad!" she yelled. "Now, you should leave before I mess with your arm again!"

"You did that?" Verity asked. "I should have recognized the handiwork."

"Handiwork is not what I would have called it!" Merritt protested, but he backed away from Serrah's threatening pose.

Dak followed him out of the shop, and then they were back out in the rain again. Merritt crossed his arms and stalked off, Dak trailing behind him silently. Serrah's friendship with Verity meant bad news. He knew Serrah. She would tell all sorts of tales about him to Verity and turn them against him. Serrah excelled at trashing other people above all else. He'd had at least one good reason to cool towards her before their split.

"Now what?" Dak asked.

"We go back to the Golden Butterfly and have a drink," said Merritt morosely. "I don't see what else I can do but drink away my defeat at the hands of Serrah."

"You gave up rather quickly," Dak commented.

"Serrah is good at bad-mouthing," said Merritt. "I admit, I wasn't the best boyfriend, but Serrah will make me out to be some kind of monster. It'll never happen now."

"So you're actually giving up?" Dak asked in surprise.

"For now," Merritt said with a long sigh. "The odds are not in my favor."

The warm and welcoming air at The Golden Butterfly relaxed Merritt, and the staff there knew him well enough.

The pleasant atmosphere roused Merritt's spirits somewhat. Some of his friends from the university came in soon after, and they all sat around the fire with drinks in hand.

Tam, a fellow Mech design student with a flair for the over-dramatic, and Jemi, a Mech mage who wanted nothing to do with dating herself but who happily listened to other people's relationship woes, both leaned in. Merritt told them the story, and they listened to it supportively, like good friends.

"I guess that's the end of that," said Merritt, slumping back into his red plush armchair.

"You mustn't give up hope," Jemi said. "This Verity may not take everything Serrah says as the gospel truth."

"If you told me that someone was bad news, I would listen," Merritt said.

"No, you wouldn't," everyone chorused back at him, laughing.

Merritt sulked and drained his tankard.

The pub filled up around them as more university students finished their classes for the day and came down for a drink. Young students loved to come down to drink at The Golden Butterfly, a popular watering hole. Merritt was glad that they had gotten there early enough to snag the best seats. They got another round, and Merritt settled in to forget his woes.

Someone tapped on his shoulder, and Merritt turned, expecting yet another one of his university friends, and he stared in shocked disbelief to find himself looking at Verity.

"Verity!" he gasped.

All of his friends turned to look with great interest. Verity smiled winsomely and dipped their head. Merritt couldn't think of a single thing to say, and his mouth opened and closed several times as he tried to force something past his lips.

"Can I talk to you?" asked Verity in a quiet voice.

"Of course!" Merritt said, standing up and almost knocking his chair over. "Let's step onto the patio for a moment."

The Golden Butterfly had a covered patio, and Merritt felt too big for his body as he bumbled over to the double doors. Verity didn't appear at all frazzled. As for Merritt, he had no idea what it could possibly be that Verity would say, and his stomach clenched with nerves. He should be used to it by now; this was what happened every time a cute person entered his vicinity.

"So, um, what did you want to say to me?" Merritt asked, trying to find a place to put his hands.

"I wanted to ask you out on a date," Verity said.

"Wait, you what?" Merritt asked, flabbergasted.

"Yes, I am asking you on a date," Verity said. "I think you're cute, so I wanted to ask you out to get to know you better. Serrah can't be right about everything."

"Didn't Serrah tell you how our relationship went?" asked Merritt in spite of himself.

"Yes, but she tends to exaggerate things," Verity said. "I've known Serrah for a while, even before she joined the guild."

"I left the guild," Merritt admitted. "I started going to school again here in Yasadria to get away from the in-fighting going on."

"I left the guild, too," Verity said. "I set up a shop, even though I didn't finish my diploma. Maybe I will go back one day, but I seem to be doing fine without it."

"Yeah, it seems like it," Merritt said, impressed that Verity could start up their own shop without even having a diploma.

"So, I wanted to go to the Gear," Verity said. "I've never been there, but I wanted to go with someone. Everyone always wants to go to the Golden Butterfly."

"Oh, yes, that sounds good," Merritt said.

Merritt never made decisions, so he felt relieved that Verity already had a plan. He didn't usually care much about the where, because what mattered to him was the who.

"I'll meet you there at seven," Verity said. "Try not to be late!"

"I won't, I promise," Merritt said.

This time, Merritt wouldn't be late.

❁❁❁

The night of his date with Verity came, and Merritt, Dak, Tam, and Jemi were at Merritt's place. The gang sat on the bed watching as Merritt tore through his wardrobe. Clothes were everywhere, and Merritt buzzed with excitement. He still couldn't believe his luck.

Dak tapped the magic-and-gear-driven contraption on his wrist, and it chimed several times.

"Hurry up, Merritt, you're going to be late," Dak said.

"It'll be fine," Merritt said, waving in Dak's direction. "Don't worry about it so much."

"It's your first date, you have to start it off on the right foot," Jemi chided, but fell silent as Merritt held up a shirt against himself.

"What do you think?" Merritt said. "I want to seem interested, but not too interested, you know what I mean?"

"Not in the slightest," Dak said. "Isn't being interested why you wanted a date to begin with?"

"True," Merritt said. "Still, if I look to eager, it might drive them off."

"You being late is what will drive them off," Tam said. "Come on, Merritt, the Gear is downtown, and you only have twenty minutes."

"At least it's not raining," Merritt said. "Fine. The mesh one it is, then."

Merritt's choice, a silvery-gray shirt interwoven with threads fine metal shimmered in the light, was one of his favorites. He liked it because it complemented his dark skin nicely; flashier outfits suited him. He slid it on, and it felt like cool fingers sliding over his body. The metal against his skin felt electric.

"Are you done?" Dak asked.

"Just cologne," Merritt said, and spritzed himself. "There, done."

"Come on, hurry," Jemi said.

"You're more worried about me being late than I am," laughed Merritt.

"Go, go!" Jemi said, shooing him towards the door.

Merritt became distracted by the mirror hanging on the back of the door, and he reached up to smooth his hair to one side. He'd styled it earlier, but everything had to be perfect. One bit kept falling in his eyes.

"For the sake of us all, please go," Tam said. "You should take this umbrella in case it starts raining."

Merritt waved him off and announced, "I'm ready now. Wish me luck."

"You'll definitely need it," Dak said, shaking his head. "Fifteen minutes!"

"Okay, I'm going," Merritt said. "Bye!"

Merritt jogged down the stairs of his apartment building and rushed out into the night air. It felt heavy with moisture, and Merritt sighed as he realized that Tam had been right. The umbrella would have been a good plan. Too late now; he only had fifteen minutes to get downtown.

He set of at a brisk pace, and as he went, he tried to calculate the shortest distance to the Gear. It was right in the middle of the entertainment district, but it was also on the other side of the shadier end of town. Usually, Merritt would go around, but the time forced him to go through it. He'd just have to keep an eye out.

As he walked, he hummed, a bounce in his step. He had a date tonight, and not even the dreariness of the street could distract him from that. Maybe he shouldn't have worn this shirt. A lot of the people in the streets gave him the side eye.

He kept walking, and he rounded the corner and came face to face with a construction site. He'd heard vague rumors of the downtown getting more housing, but he didn't often go in this area. This must be it, he guessed, and it blocked the way past. Detouring would take another ten minutes.

He considered cutting through, and resigned himself to being late when it started raining. That settled it. He could stomach showing up slightly late, but late as well as soaked to the bone was unacceptable. Without another thought, he climbed over the barricade and began picking his way through the construction site.

Perhaps this route wouldn't save him time after all. The walkway made up of uneven wooden boards slowed him somewhat, and the rain made it slippery. The rain picked up, and he started jogging.

Without warning, his footing went out from under him, and he slammed to the ground. His elbows and hip already started to smart. He climbed to his feet and saw that a group of people standing around him, with hoods drawn over their faces. He hadn't noticed them before, but they must have followed him.

"I don't want any trouble," said Merritt, trying to shield his eyes from the rain.

"That's too bad," one of them said.

The group descended upon him like a pack of dogs on prey. They tore at his shirt, and Merritt struggled to push them off him, to slip away. This earned him a cuff across the forehead that set his head ringing. He kicked his leg out and hit something. Someone cursed and socked Merritt in the jaw. That hurt even more, and Merritt sagged to the ground. He couldn't see. Why couldn't he see?

Something warm dripped in his eyes, and he wiped at it ineffectually.

"He's got a Mech arm!" someone said.

Those words made Merritt freeze in horror. He kicked out again, flailing as much as he could, but to no avail. Someone sat on his chest, and he couldn't breathe. He gasped for breath, but all the struggling and yelling did no good. No one came to his aid.

Pressure on his Mech arm made him yelp, and then a sharp pain shot through his arm. A loud screeching noise erupted, and the pressure and pain increased. Merritt screamed, and the person sitting on him hit him again. The pain suddenly overwhelmed him, and his stomach dipped. He wretched as bile rose in his throat.

Mercifully, at that point, he blacked out completely.

✿✿✿

"He's over here!" a voice said.

Merritt tried to sit up, head swimming, but a shock of pain sent him back to the cold, hard ground. He shivered hard. His wet clothes were sticking to his skin. He tried to open his eyes, but the lights blinded him. Night had fallen, and people with lanterns were standing around him.

"We need to get him to the hospital," someone said.

Dak's face appeared above him, haloed by light.

"We're going to get you to the hospital," Dak said, but he sounded far away.

A warm blanket was wrapped around him, and Merritt passed out again.

The next time he woke up, white walls surrounded him. That seemed strange, and Merritt blinked. The whiteness dimmed, revealing that he laid in a hospital bed, and there was a white sheet between him and the outside world. Everything felt heavy, and Merritt couldn't sit up. Merritt laid there helplessly, an awful feeling churning in his stomach.

❁❁❁

He didn't know how long he'd been there when the curtain around him rustled. Dak's face appeared, and he looked relieved.

"He's awake!" he reported to someone on the other side of the curtain.

A moment later, a nurse bustled in, poking and prodding him.

"What happened?" Dak asked.

"Some people attacked me," Merritt said sleepily.

"Merritt, I don't mean to alarm you, but when we found you, you were hypothermic, and well...you were missing your arm," Dak said.

That was right. He remembered a lot of pain. Merritt craned his head around to look at the stump where his arm used to be. The gears inside were all bent and twisted, and wires had been cut or snapped. It looked like a mess. He leaned back and closed his eyes. His arm had been a very expensive gift from an uncle, an uncle who had since departed.

"What are you going to do?" Dak asked.

"I don't know..." Merritt said. A thought occurred to him, and he asked, "Hey, did someone tell Verity?"

"Um, no?" Dak said. "We were more concerned that you had been mugged and beat up!"

"They probably think I stood them up," Merritt groaned.

"That's not the issue here," Dak said. "You have no arm, mate."

"But Verity doesn't know that," Merritt said. "They'll think that Serrah was right, and now Serrah is going to be vindicated in what she said about me!"

He could just picture the triumph on Serrah's face when Verity told her what had happened.

"Fine, someone will go tell them what happened," Dak said, shaking his head.

"Wait, what happened to my shirt?" asked Merritt.

"It's ruined," Dak said, sighing.

"This is awful," Merritt said. "Between my arm, Verity, and the shirt, this is the shittiest thing that has ever happened to me."

Dak looked at him sympathetically. "There's a Mech doctor coming in to shut down the nerve endings in your arm so that you don't feel the pain anymore."

"I don't feel pain right now," Merritt said. "A bit like floating."

"Yeah, you're drugged up to the gills," Dak said. "Once it wears off, though, it will really suck."

"Great."

They were silent for a little while, and then Merritt said, "You know what we should do?"

"What?" asked Dak.

"We should design me a new arm," Merritt said.

"We wouldn't be able to afford any of the parts," Dak said.

"I know that," Merritt said. "But it's better than doing nothing, stuck here in hospital."

They had nothing to write on except napkins, but that didn't stop them. Once Dak seemed to realize that Merritt needed to be doing something to take his mind off everything, he dug right in to the project. It would have been fun project if the circumstances hadn't been so dire.

Eventually, Dak had to go home, but he took the designs with him, promising to transfer the designs onto draft sheets that he'd bring in the design next time he visited. It wasn't a bad start, considering that whatever pain medication the doctors had given him made Merritt high as a kite.

Several days later, Dak waited for the doctor to come and shut his nerves off. Apparently, Dr. More had been busy with another case, but today she had time for him. Then he'd be allowed to leave and not be kept on such strong medication.

As he drew on his arm design draft with a red pencil, a nurse poked her head in.

"You've got a visitor," she said.

The curtain parted, revealing Verity, who looked hesitantly around the edge. Merritt immediately perked up. He smiled, glad that Verity wanted to come visit because it meant they weren't mad about the missed date.

"Dak told me what happened," she said. "How are you?"

"As good as can be under the circumstances," said Merritt, smiling bravely.

"What are you up to?" Verity asked.

"Just trying to design myself a new arm," Merritt said. "I know I can't afford to buy any of the parts, but it makes me feel a bit less helpless about being in this situation."

He offered Verity the scroll full of design work that he and Dak had already done. He hadn't finished it yet, but it had the base work, the skeleton, as it were. Merritt would have enjoyed the process a lot more if it had simply been a project and not his real-life problem. He hadn't even started to consider what he would have to do without an arm. On his student budget, he definitely couldn't afford even a rudimentary arm.

"I could do work like this," Verity said, looking it over with a practiced eye.

"Yeah," Merritt said. "If only I had the resources to get the materials for it."

Neither of them spoke for a moment, and then Verity said, "I thought you had stood me up."

"Sorry about that," Merritt said, smiling sheepishly. "I would've made it if I could've."

"I know," Verity said. "I had been looking forward to it,

you know."

"Really?" Merritt asked. "Even after you talked to Serrah about me? I'm not exactly her favorite person."

"She said things that were a little bit harsh, yes," Verity said. "But she also told me what drew her in to start with, before she broke up with you. That sounds like the type of person that I'd like to know."

"Yeah?" Merritt asked hopefully.

"She said you were most passionate when talking about design," Verity said. "That when you were with her, you didn't talk about anything else."

"That's true," Merritt said. "I guess it kind of got annoying after a while."

"She also said that you're easily distracted and that you're often late or forget about things like dates altogether," Verity said.

Merritt sighed. "Well, I can't tell a lie. That's pretty accurate. I'm always sorry I'm late, though, so that has to count for something, right?"

"Perhaps," Verity said. "I wanted to make sure you were all right, so I left Serrah guarding the store, but I should be getting back. I'll come visit you again tomorrow."

"Leaving so soon?"

"I'll be back!" Verity said.

"Promise?"

Verity simply smiled and disappeared behind the white curtain.

Doctor More came by during the day to disconnect his nerves from his missing arm. A tingling pain that had been buzzing in the back of Merritt's mind disappeared at last. He hadn't even really noticed it until its absence. He was grateful for its relief even so.

His lack of arm drew stares once the doctors allowed him to leave the hospital. Merritt tried to hide it beneath his cloak as much as possible. He had to borrow a shirt from the hospital, because the one he'd been wearing had been destroyed in the attack. Merritt hadn't felt lower than this in a long time, since the initial accident that left him without an arm in the first place.

Dak came to the hospital to be with him upon his release and seemed sympathetic but silent. Not that any amount of words could bring his arm back. He kept trying to use it, forgetting he didn't have an appendage there anymore. It felt like a phantom limb.

"I'm going to return to class tomorrow," he told Dak.

"Are you sure?" Dak asked. "After such an ordeal, no one would hold it against you if you decided to miss class for a while."

"I need to try and forget what happened," Merritt said. "I couldn't stop thinking about it last night. I need something to do, or I'm going to keep obsessing over it."

"Okay, if you think that's best," Dak said doubtfully. "I'll come by tomorrow and we can walk to class together."

Even so, the next morning, Merritt remained uncertain. He stalled at the door, and he could almost see Dak rolling his eyes internally while outwardly appearing calm and accepting. Or maybe he had a sense of paranoia.

"I'm not sure if I'm ready," Merritt said, even though he had meticulously gone through his supplies and packed his bag the night before.

"Okay, I'll come and see you after class," Dak said.

Dak had turned away from the door and started walking away when Merritt flung himself out the door, hollering for Dak to wait. Dak stopped while Merritt caught up to him.

Class went as awful as expected. People in the lecture hall kept looking at him, some subtly, but others turning around in their seats to stare, and it kept him distracted. He wished he had enough for even a rudimentary prosthetic. A wooden one would do at this point. Beside him, Dak grumbled about all the attention. It seemed as if the spectacle he'd become had distracted more than one person.

He and Dak left quickly after class, and to his surprise, he ran straight into Verity, who was waiting for him outside the classroom.

"Verity!" he exclaimed.

"Hello, Merritt," they said, smiling lightly. "I wanted to speak with Dak for a moment, if I may. And I would also like to see your plans for the prosthetic arm that you made."

"Oh. Okay?"

Verity drew Dak away, speaking and gesturing with their arms. Merritt wondered what Verity wanted with Dak. Maybe they found Dak more attractive now that Merritt only had one arm? Dak looked over at him, and Merritt felt bad for even thinking about his friend like that. But if Verity wanted to see the plans, it couldn't be that. Surely Verity didn't have the resources to make him a new arm.

They came back over to him, and Verity said, "We have a plan, Merritt! Don't worry, I'll take care of it."

In the days after his encounter with Verity, Dak wouldn't reveal anything about what they had talked about, no matter how Merritt asked. Dak just kept saying that he'd have to ask Verity, and Merritt eventually retreated to sulk. Dak just laughed and told him he had to be patient.

He didn't see Verity very often after that for about a week, and every time he did see them, they evaded every question, no matter how sneakily Merritt tried to bring it up. Something was going on behind the scenes.

More and more, Merritt found the other students speculated about him endlessly. Their whispers chased him down hallways and up staircases. It seemed as if they knew something, more than Merritt knew about it.

Finally, just when the dam of silence strained to the breaking point, Verity came to him.

"I don't want to overwhelm you," they started, nervously twining a strand of hair around and around their fingers. "But I started something, and it's grown more than I thought possible."

"What is it?" Merritt asked. "I know something's going on. It's impossible not to notice."

"Well..." Verity said. "I started a campaign to raise money to get you a new arm."

"Oh," Merritt said, not certain what to think of that. He had never really considered himself important enough to be the centre of a campaign. "Is that why people keep talking about me?"

"Word spread faster than I imagined," Verity said, smoothing down their skirt. "It grew out of control. I even had professors come by to help with donations. Dak helped me, and some of your other friends. He laid out all the pieces we would need to start making your new arm."

"You mean the plans we made?" Merritt asked. "There's no way we could actually afford it. I just wanted something to do to fill the time I spent in hospital. I didn't take it seriously."

"It became serious," Verity said.

"Everyone? Who's everyone?" Merritt asked, feeling a bit dazed.

"Hundreds of students who have heard about your predicament. The news spread like wildfire, and when you appeared without your arm, that turned out to be the final proof they all needed to get into gear," Verity said.

"I don't know what to say."

"Say this is all okay," Verity said, and they sounded nervous.

"Okay? It's more than okay. I just can't believe that anyone would do something like this for me, especially people that don't even know me. Not to mention someone who thinks I stood them up on their date."

"We could always go on another date," Verity said, blushing a little and playing with the ends of their long hair.

"You still want to go on a date, after all this?" asked Merritt.

"Of course I do!" exclaimed Verity.

"Well, let's go then," Merritt said.

"Right now?" Verity asked.

"Right now," Merritt said firmly, and offered Verity his hand.

Verity took it, and Merritt lead them out of the university and down the northward boulevard. It had started to flower into spring, and Merritt found it a nice walk now that it had stopped raining. The trees lining the street created a verdant tunnel above their heads.

"What should we do?" Merritt asked.

"I thought you knew already!"

"Nope, not at all," Merritt said. "I like to decide as I go. It makes things interesting."

His dates usually disliked his spontaneity, because people liked to make solid plans for when and where and what. But Verity smiled and swung their joined hands as they walked.

"Do you want a flavored ice?" Merritt asked, pointing at a windowfront.

"Let's try it!"

The shaved ice refreshed him. The two of them had to share one, because Merritt only had one arm to use. Verity didn't mind holding the shaved ice between them. They walked all the way to the Golden Butterfly, and then had beer on the patio, watching as people went by, strolling down the boulevard.

"Look at that hat," Verity said, watching as a woman went by with an enormous hat covered in feathers and beads shaped like gears.

"It looks like a Mecha hat," Merritt said

He wanted to go off on a tangent about what kind of design would be needed for an actual Mecha hat, but he stopped himself. Serrah had always stopped him mid-sentence to say that she didn't want to talk about work. Merritt had gotten used to holding his tongue whenever the subject of Mech tech came up.

"I should try to design a Mech hat," said Verity.

Merritt's mouth dropped open, and he stuttered as he took up the conversation with delight. He sketched out a design on a napkin and slid it across the table to Verity. Smiling, they took a red marking pencil out of their pocket and made some additions to the design. It was just a silly project, but Verity kept the design, folding it carefully and sliding it into their bag before they left the pub.

Merritt walked Verity to their front door.

"Don't you think it would be better if I walked you to your door?" Verity asked. "After the trouble you were already in?"

They seemed legitimately worried, and not teasing, so Merritt said, "I'll be fine. Dak is up waiting for me to get back anyway."

"I had a great time," Verity said, dipping their gaze and smiling.

"We should do it again sometime," Merritt offered nervously.

"Sometime soon," Verity affirmed. "Goodnight."

Merritt didn't expect it, so when Verity stepped in front

of Merritt and went up on their tip-toes to kiss him, he still had his mouth open to say goodbye. Verity smelled of lavender, and their soft hair brushed against his skin. Merritt hardly had time to react before the kiss ended.

"Goodnight!" Verity repeated, and then they were through the doorway of their apartment and away.

As soon as he entered his apartment, he announced to Dak, "They kissed me!" and flopped down on the nearest couch in rapture.

"Good?" asked Dak.

"Magnificent," Merritt replied dreamily.

"I'm glad," Dak replied dryly. "So now what?"

"Now what? The possibilities are endless."

"If you say so," Dak said, smiling in amusement.

"I do," Merritt said. "Just you wait and see."

"Such optimism," Dak said, but left it at that.

Dak could say anything he liked; Merritt couldn't help being hopelessly optimistic any more than Dak could help being tall.

❁❁❁

Unfortunately, the next time that Merritt saw Verity, they were arguing with Serrah. Merritt had received a note from Verity telling him to meet them at the collegium garden, but when he'd arrived, Serrah had beaten him there.

Serrah stood with a wide stance and pointed at Verity. "He's not worth it," she said.

"Serrah, just because you broke up with him, it doesn't mean that you should try and sabotage my work to try to get him a new arm." Verity looked calm, but they had a red tinge to their ears which belied their exterior mood.

People should know what kind of person he is before they aid him," Serrah replied.

"Serrah, what is this about?" Merritt interrupted them.

"You stay out of this," Serrah said.

"But it's about me, from what I can tell," Merritt protested.

"What you need to do is be quiet and let other people talk for once," Serrah said.

"I never stopped you before. Not when we were dating, either."

"The amount you chatter, it's hard for anyone else to get a word in edgewise!" Serrah exclaimed, waving her arms in the air. "And you're always talking about Mech tech! That's all you ever want to talk about. It's enough to drive a person crazy."

"I like it," Merritt said, but waited for Serrah to continue. He might as well let her get everything out here and now.

"You're a flake," Serrah said. "You're always late or cancelling plans, or changing them at the last minute. You don't think about what makes life harder for anyone else."

"So he doesn't deserve to have an arm?" Verity interrupted.

"You're always pursuing a cause without getting any background information on it!" Serrah said, turning on them. "Jumping on bandwagons, pursuing causes you know nothing about."

"What has he done to deserve not having an arm?" Verity asked again.

"Haven't you been listening to me?" Serrah said. "I heard he was cutting through a bad part of town when those thugs attacked him. You think he wasn't asking for trouble? Besides, he had probably been running late, as usual. Which is why this happened to him in the first place."

"No, the robbers are the reason it happened," Verity replied, one fist clenching.

"He's irresponsible and clueless," Serrah said. "Why does he deserve another chance when he squandered the one his uncle gave him?"

"You're not really talking about his arm, are you?" Verity

asked. "This is about your relationship."

"It applies to both things," Serrah replied.

"You're being bitter and nasty. Do you really hate Merritt so much that you think he deserved to be attacked? What kind of person are you?"

"Better than Merritt," Serrah said.

"That's not what your conduct is telling me," Verity said.

"I obviously can't talk to you," Serrah said. "Just wait, you'll see what I'm talking about. He's not worth it, especially not fighting with one of your friends."

Serrah stomped off before Verity could reply.

"She's right, you know," Merritt said. "I am flaky and inconsiderate a lot of the time."

"And I jump on bandwagons and pursue causes I've just heard about," Verity said. "Serrah isn't completely wrong about everything, but she's not doing it to benefit anyone but herself. She's doing it to be cruel to people, which I can't agree with."

Merritt nodded, not sure what to say about the argument he'd just witnessed.

Verity perked up. "You know, I was excited to see you before she showed up. Guess what? We've gotten enough of the parts together to start putting your new arm together!"

"Really?" Merritt said.

"Want to see?" Verity asked, eyes bright with excitement.

"Of course," Merritt said.

Verity showed him the arm. It was just the basic skeleton, nothing fancy yet, but Merritt hadn't expected so much, especially now that he had the strange churning feeling that he didn't deserve it. He ran his finger along the main structure which would hold all the other modifications and sighed.

"She's wrong, you know. You do deserve to have a proper arm again. You don't deserve to be attacked just because of who you are."

"I know, but if I'd just left on time, then this would never have happened," Merritt said, shaking his head.

"The attackers are at fault," Verity reminded him again.

"I guess there's a silver lining," Merritt said. "Who knew that our little collegium could raise enough funds for even a rudimentary arm?"

Verity smiled. "That's true. Look at us go!"

Merritt looked at the arm again, and a grin tugged at his mouth. He'd never expected anything good to come of an attack that left him crippled again, but his faith in humanity had been restored slightly with the actions of his fellow students—and Verity.

He hadn't expected Verity to still be there, to be honest. But they had stuck with him in spite of everything. Merritt always felt good at the start of a new relationship, but this one was different somehow.

❁❁❁

"How does that feel?" asked the doctor.

"Okay," Merritt said, rotating his new arm.

"It should be feeling more than okay," the doctor said. "Let me tweak it just a bit."

Dr. Nevin specialized in metal prosthetics, and he'd inspected the arm himself before allowing Merritt to make an appointment to get it attached. The arm had gone through rigorous testing, not to mention peer reviews from the university.

Now, the day had finally come to get it attached so that the nerve endings would connect to the arm. Merritt, more of a designer than a medical student, didn't entirely know how the nerves hooked up, but it worked.

"There," Dr. Nevin said. "Test it again."

Merritt twisted it and turned around. No twinge of pain ailed him, and the arm had full mobility. It worked great— dare he say it?—even better than his last arm.

Verity looked on with a complicated anxious but proud expression on their face. A group of reporters from the local newspaper waited out in the hallway to interview the pair of them, and Verity couldn't contain their excitement. They were going to get a lot of public attention for this project.

"It's great," he said with a smile, looking at Dr. Nevin.

"Better," Dr. Nevin said. "Take it out for a test, and see how it works. I expect to see you again tomorrow for a follow-up."

"No problem," Merritt said.

"Don't be late," Verity said with a shake of their finger in his direction.

"I'll try my best," Merritt said with a winning smile.

"Then you're free to go," Dr. Nevin said.

Merritt and Verity stepped out into the hallway where they were immediately surrounded by people asking questions without pause. The two of them looked at each other, and Merritt took Verity's hand with his non-metal one. They squeezed it, and the pair of them faced the wave of questions together.

Merritt was happy in a very easy and uncomplicated way. He and Verity were still dating, and although they both had their flaws, they had agreed to face them one at a time. His new arm worked wonderfully, and Verity had been the one to ensure that he even had it.

"What do we do now?" he asked, once they had escaped the crowd of reporters.

"What else?" Verity asked with a laugh. "We find another project, we complete it, and then we do it all again."

That sounded just fine with Merritt.

A Letter to My Former Self

Dear Rick,

Remember when you used to write horror? Gruesome stuff that made people, when they met you, wonder how someone so soft-spoken and mild-mannered could come up with such awful stuff?

Yeah, you remember. Some magazine even dubbed you the Stephen King of gay horror.

Yet now, most of your writing focuses on love stories. You have Rick bright and dark. And I wonder why you changed.

I don't wonder much, to be honest. The truth is your life changed and your writing reflected that. See, for a time the one thing you wanted from life was to find love, to find a family to call your very own.

And you worked at it. God knows you did. A marriage to a woman. A series of boyfriends, three of them live-in, that never lasted more than a couple of years. All of these left you feeling unsatisfied. They all started out pretty, like a birthday cake, and then ended up like a birthday cake dropped on the floor, still traces of sweet, but with dirt, grit, disappointment, and heartache mixed in with buttercream frosting.

Yeah, you know what I'm talking about. And you know how that relates to writing horror. You understand that the heartbreak and fear of loneliness and being alone drove you to create troubled characters, people who were out of control, people who were desperate and who feared that the worst could—and sometimes did—happen.

People who were like you, and your love life that never worked out. In retrospect, it made sense that you wrote horror.

But then, about fourteen years ago, something changed. You answered an ad online and, contrary to most of those tenuous web-based connections, there was something there when you started e-mailing this one guy. He made you laugh. He got you. You talked. It was enough to make you want to meet in person after a couple of weeks.

You did. And you remember that first sighting of this guy when you went to pick him up, sitting on the steps waiting for you. He was wearing jeans and a blue pinstriped T-shirt. And with just one look, you fell in love.

It was scary. Even though things were good right from the start, you had too many scars to believe that, maybe this time, you'd be lucky. Maybe this time, he'd stay. So you resisted and clung desperately to what you told him you needed— your independence.

That lasted for all of three or four months.

You couldn't help it. It was too true. You were in love, real love this time, and it felt like more than just the heat of passion; it felt like the beating heart of family, in the truest and best sense of the word.

So you went on and nested and, unlike all the other relationships that had crashed and burned, you never once questioned your decision to be with this man. You still don't. And now you're legally married and looking forward to growing old with this person you never thought would cross the threshold into your life.

And to my younger Rick or Ricky, I would say, embrace both your dark and light, in both your writing and your life. But be thankful to fate, god, whatever force brought you to this man you call husband, soul mate, family…because he made it possible to be a romance writer.

And that really means something.

Broken Art

by Dev Bentham

Jim stared up at the sign: Broken Art Tattoos. He'd called a few days before to make the appointment.

That had been one mortifying conversation.

Now all he wanted was to turn around and head back to the ship or into a bar or anywhere to disappear. Except slipping into a bar was what had gotten him into trouble in the first place and besides, he didn't drink anymore. Thirty-eight and he was as nervous as a teenager. People who'd been sober a lot longer than he had told him that was part of it, he'd need to grow up all over again.

He straightened his shoulders. This wasn't anything to be scared about. He'd seen what the guy could do with a bad tattoo. One of Jim's shipmates had a tat of his ex-girlfriend's name in this really ornate script. The Broken Art Guy had turned it into a rose that anyone would be proud to have on their biceps. Jim took a deep breath and pushed open the door.

As he stepped into the empty front lobby, the door triggered a buzzer in another room. The walls were covered in display cabinets full of hearts, angels, devils and the usual assortment of postage stamp-sized images to adorn the human body. It smelled of scented candles, witch hazel, and floor cleaner—much better than smoke and cooking oil, which was Jim's only clear memory from the Taiwanese tat shop all those years ago. Passing out drunk and somehow ending up in a strange tattoo shop surrounded by assholes who'd just discovered he was gay hadn't been one of his better choices.

The whir of a needle gun stopped and a voice called, "Be right with you." The whirring resumed.

Jim stepped closer to peer at some of the artist's more original work. He had an appealing use of color and a roundness of line that had drawn Jim to his work when he'd seen the rose. Of course, Jim's bad tattoo wasn't exactly some girl's name. There might be more embarrassing tattoos out there, but Jim hadn't seen one. He was having a hard time imagining how his could be transformed into something halfway decent. He almost expected this guy to turn him away once he saw the actual ink, but Jim had to try. The thought of going into civilian life like this made him shudder. And this would be a hell of a lot faster and cheaper than getting the damned thing removed.

There was a murmur of voices from the other room. Then a beaded curtain clattered open and a young woman emerged. Makeup streaked her pale cheeks, but she was smiling. A man followed her out. Jim caught his breath. This was the tattoo artist? Jim's shipmate hadn't mentioned that he was gorgeous. But then, he probably wouldn't have noticed, beyond disapproving of the eyebrow piercing. The artist was a tall, thin man in black jeans and a black button down shirt, with the sleeves rolled up to the elbows, exposing a flight of crows down his right arm and the elegant twining of tree limbs down his left. His dark hair was cut short on the sides but long on top, and he had startlingly blue eyes. He was as far from military as Jim could imagine. And Jim was ready to be done with the military.

The tattoo artist smiled and thrust out his hand. "You must be the masochist who's booked the rest of my day. I'm Andy."

Jim fought his impulse to blush, fumble, or explain and shook the other man's hand, curling his fingers around crow wings. Andy's grip was warm and firm. Something about the assuredness of his hands was calming. Jim's shoulders started to relax.

Andy handed him a clipboard and waved toward the beaded curtains. "Go on back. I'll be there in a sec but you might as well fill this out while you wait."

Given the candles and beads, the tattoo room wasn't what Jim had expected. Well lit, with a drafting table on one side and on the other a big black recliner surrounded by mirrors and lights. The tattoo station itself was tidy, with a huge spectrum of colored inks in tiny bottles laid out in two straight lines. The walls were surprisingly bare, except for framed licenses and awards. Jim didn't know quite what to do with himself. He looked at the recliner, but if all went well and they settled on a design, God knew how long he'd be in that chair. He leaned against the wall and got to work on the paperwork.

Just as he'd finished, the beads rustled and Andy appeared. "Sorry about that. It's just me. Used to have a receptionist, but he quit a few weeks ago. I haven't had the heart to hire anyone new." He took the clipboard and set it aside, then perched on a chair beside the drafting table. "We're fixing some unfortunate tats on your ass, right?"

Jim nodded as the familiar wash of shame engulfed him. For years he'd tried to ignore the tattoos, drowning his embarrassment in enough Jack Daniels to make anyone forget. But in the year he'd been sober, he hadn't dared have sex with the same man twice. And always in the dark. Which was where he wanted to be right now. Every fiber of his being was screaming for him to run. But Andy wouldn't be able to fix what he couldn't see.

Jim bit down on his lower lip. "Let me show you." He turned around. Not seeing the look on Andy's face when he saw the tats would be a blessing. Jim unzipped his jeans and let them slip down. Hoping the blush didn't extend to his butt cheeks, he held up his tee shirt so that Andy could get a good long look at his mutilated ass where line drawings of a giant cock arched over the curve of each butt cheek, each cock squirting tear-shaped drops toward his asshole.

He winced at the low whistle from behind him. "There's a story in that one, I bet. They're even more graphic than I expected." He gave Jim's calf a gentle pat. "Okay, pull your pants up. I'll show you the designs I mocked up based on your description. With appropriate modification any one of them would do the job."

Exhaling his relief at the short reprieve, Jim pulled up his pants and turned back to Andy. He took a moment to let himself be distracted by the sight of Andy's strong shoulders and long back. Maybe if he focused on how attractive Andy was, there wouldn't be space for thinking about himself.

Andy had three designs spread out on the drafting table. He glanced up at Jim with a half-smile playing on his face. "Even if you decide not to do anything today, I gotta tell you that this was the most interesting design challenge I've had in a while."

Jim felt the blush creeping up his neck. It didn't matter what Andy had come up with. He was determined to get inked over as soon as possible. Anything would be better than what he had now. He looked down at the desk. His eyes widened. Real art.

Andy pointed to the first one, an arched black and white banner surrounded by geometric symbols. "This one is probably the most obvious fix and the cheapest, maybe five hours of work. Now that I've seen them, I'd add a more ornate cornice piece on the ends to disguise the penis heads and incorporate the droplets into the design. If you have a favorite quote, we can put that inside and voila, mission accomplished. "

Jim nodded. Did he have a favorite quote? One he'd want

to live with for the rest of his life? Probably not. He turned his attention to the next one, a rich bouquet of flowers that would spill down his ass cheeks.

"I don't know about this one." Andy tapped the parchment. "Your ass might be a garden of earthly delights, but maybe that's not what you're wanting to advertise anymore. Flowers are great for hiding bad tats—you saw the rose on the arm of that girl who just left? You'd need to look pretty closely to find her ex-boyfriend's face in there."

But Jim was already focused on the third design, a flame-spitting dragon. The image was mesmerizing, a confluence of swirls that reminded Jim of a stormy sea. It radiated a fearsome strength. This wasn't a creature to mess with.

"Yeah." Andy's voice was low. "That would look hot." He trailed his finger down the tail of the dragon. "You've got a great ass. I can just see the tail curling around and going down your thigh." He looked up at Jim. "But I need to warn you, this baby will take a lot of time, maybe ten hours. So it ain't cheap, could run as high as two grand."

Jim tore his eyes away from the dragon and met Andy's gaze, which turned out to be just as mesmerizing. "Can you do it in one sitting? I ship out tomorrow afternoon."

"I could do a lot, but I couldn't finish. I can give you a copy of the design so you can get someone else to do the rest." Andy held Jim's gaze. He took a deep breath and glanced at the clock. "I can definitely cover the problem today, but are you sure? That's a long time to have someone drilling away at your skin. It'll be after midnight by the time we're done."

Jim stood up straighter. He wasn't the toughest guy in his crew, but he was a Navy man, after all. He dug out his wallet, counted twenty hundred dollar bills, and dropped them on the drafting table. "Do as much as you can."

Andy looked from Jim to the money and back again. "You're crazy. But I guess I am, too." He stood, walked to the recliner, and by making a few adjustments, straightened it out into a table. "I'll go close the shop. Lay down on your belly, the more clothes you're comfortable taking off, the easier it'll be on us both." With that, he walked through the jangling bead curtain.

Jim stood for a moment with his hands on his jeans. Theoretically, he could just pull them down to his knees and expose the salient parts. But that was ridiculous, like a reverse modesty, exposing only the dirty bits. He unzipped his jeans and stepped out of them. He was pulling his shirt over his head when the beads jingled again. He stood there naked, staring at Andy, who was staring back, but not at Jim's face. A second later, Andy's gaze flicked up. He gave a little shrug and pointed to the table.

Jim lay down, adjusting his dick so it wasn't pushing into his gut. Andy sat in the chair beside him, ran a soapy cloth over his ass, and shaved him all the way from his lower back to his inner thigh.

The machine whirred to life. Andy lay a hand on Jim's lower back. "You obviously know how this goes. Do what you need to do to stay still."

"Yeah, sure." Except Jim couldn't remember anything from the night of the hideous tattoo. It was the first shore leave of his first sea tour. He had a vague memory of drunkenly hitting on a marine and getting shoved away. Embarrassment and fear had made him down more shots. Then they'd all walked down a dark alley to the tat shop. The rest was a blank, until he'd woken in his berth, fifty miles out to sea, so bruised and stiff that it wasn't until he'd tried to button his pants that he registered the burning pain on his ass cheeks.

Thank God for shower stalls. When Jim joined up, the military was deep in the throes of *Don't Ask, Don't Tell*. After that night, for Jim, getting naked was the same as coming out. Just in case someone saw his ass, he'd made up a story about two women, twins, who'd insisted on…Christ, it hadn't made sense even then. Who knew if anyone had believed him the few times he'd had to use it. Mostly he'd tried not let anyone see it and not to think about the tat or about who thought what about his ass. Imagining what they were saying behind his back always sent him on a bender. Which meant that if he had any chance of staying sober, the tattoo would have to go.

Jim took a sharp inhale as the needle hit his skin. Like a hot knife. The pain instantly wilted his dick. He breathed deeply, consciously relaxing the muscles of his ass. Ten hours suddenly sounded like a very long time. When he was eighteen, four years had seemed like forever, but at the end, he'd been offered a hefty bonus for six more years, and then again for another six, and after that it had only made sense to round out his twenty. If he could do twenty years, most of which had been spent working hard to hide who he was, he could sure as hell do ten hours of this.

"How ya doing?" Andy asked.

"Okay." He was surprised to find it was true. He was getting used to the burn, burn, swipe rhythm. Maybe it was like the Navy after all—he just got used to it.

"This is old artwork." Andy's tone was conversational. "Any reason in particular you decided to get it fixed now?"

"I should have done it years ago." Except, for some reason, it hadn't occurred to him. Probably because he'd been butt drunk every chance he could for nineteen of his twenty years. "Now I'm celebrating. I'm getting out after this next sea tour."

"Congratulations." Burn, burn, swipe. "You going to miss it?"

"No." It came out with the force of a torpedo.

Andy paused.

Jim glanced over his shoulder. "Don't get me wrong. I'm not a peacenik or anything."

"God forbid," Andy said, smiling.

Jim lay back down and Andy started up again with burn, burn, swipe. "A strong military is crucial for our nation's survival."

"If you say so."

"I sound like a recruiter, don't I?"

"A bit."

Jim rested his head in his hands. "Yeah. Well, I do think what I was doing was important. I just never really fit in."

"What were you doing? Or is that top secret?" There was a lightness in Andy's tone, and Jim wasn't sure if he was being teased.

"Fixing airplanes. I'm a mechanic."

Andy laughed.

"What? You don't think that's important?" Jim turned to peer over his shoulder at Andy.

Andy put a hand on his back. His touch was warm, even through the latex of his gloves. "Relax. I laughed because that's what they call me—the mechanic. I fix tattoos instead of airplanes, but it's the same thing, isn't it? Taking care of mistakes, tuning up aging work, mending broken things. It's good work, man. You should be proud."

"Thanks. I guess I'm touchy about it—maybe because the Navy's been a complicated place for me." Jim rested his head back on his hands. "I mean, I stayed in, didn't I?"

"And now you're leaving." Burn, burn, swipe. "What are you going to do?"

"I don't know. Find a job. Settle down. Stay in one place for once." A nice guy and a white picket fence. It wasn't such a bad dream, was it? Not that Jim expected a hot tattoo guy to understand.

Andy kept going, but the burn barely bothered Jim anymore. Getting used to it. After a while, Andy said, "Settling down. I thought that's what I was doing, but things don't always work out like we plan."

Jim had guessed Andy's age at early thirties, but the resignation in his voice sounded older than time. "Someone break your heart?"

Andy was silent for a moment. The only sound the buzz of the tattoo machine. Eventually Andy broke the silence. "I think I'm more disappointed than heartbroken, which I suppose just goes to show that it wasn't meant to be. That receptionist I told you about earlier? I really thought we had something."

"Sorry to hear that." Except how could Jim really be sorry that the hot *gay* tattoo artist was single? He tried to sound compassionate. "You want to talk about it?"

"Naw. Thanks."

This time the silence stretched out. Jim couldn't think of anything to say. Eventually he relaxed into the buzz and burn.

After a while, Andy stopped, draped a sheet over Jim, and called for a break. He left the room. Jim's right butt cheek was on fire. Holding the sheet to keep from exposing himself more than he had to, he rolled onto his left side. Andy came back carrying two tall glasses.

Jim stared at the glass Andy extended to him. Water beaded on the sides. He cleared his throat. "I, uh, I don't drink."

"Sounds dehydrating."

"I meant..."

"I know what you meant." Andy smiled. He still held out the glass. "Water."

God, he was an idiot. Like Andy needed to know all about Jim's struggles with sobriety. Fuck-all crazy tattoo AND a drunk. How would that surprise anyone? Jim propped himself on one elbow and accepted the glass as graciously as he could.

Andy set his own glass on his workstation. He rolled his head from side to side, then stretched his arms overhead. He seemed oblivious to Jim, which was good since Jim didn't think he could look away if he tried. It had been a long time since he had been anywhere he felt safe to just plain appreciate another man's physique.

Andy dropped his arms and shook out his hands. He smiled at Jim. "How about we order some pizza. I'll be done with this side by the time it gets here."

As if on cue, Jim's stomach growled.

Andy laughed. "I'll take that as a yes."

The whole conversation, negotiating what kind of pizza and who would pay, felt surprisingly natural. Like breathing. Although when Jim looked at it objectively, there was nothing natural about lying on a table draped in a sheet with his ass cheek throbbing, talking to a hipster guy with leaves and crows inked down his arms. The situation wasn't like any Jim had been in, and yet, it felt like he'd been there all his life.

Before they started up again, Andy put his foot on the side of the table. He pulled up the cuff of his pant leg. There, on the outside of his ankle, was a circle with the triangle inside—the NA symbol—and a date. "Four years in April." He dropped the cuff and brought his foot back down.

Jim stared at Andy's ankle. Maybe he had more in common with Andy than it might look like from the outside. When he rolled back onto his belly and let the sheet drop, Jim felt relaxed, really relaxed for the first time in a long time.

Even when the burn, burn, swipe started up again.

"You want to look?" Andy asked once they'd stopped.

Jim stood with the sheet wrapped around his waist, leaning his non-wounded butt cheek against the table while he wolfed down pizza.

He shook his head. He'd wait until it was all done. That way he'd never have to see the remaining piece of ugly again. He nodded toward Andy's arm. "Does that tree go all the way up?"

"Oh, you do want to look. Just not at yourself." Andy smiled as he unbuttoned his shirt. He let it drop and Jim stared. The branches on Andy's forearms were from a giant, ancient looking tree that covered his chest. A strong wind was blowing all the branches down one arm while a huge flock of crows flew out of the tree, down his other arm and onto his hand.

"Wow." It was astonishing, so beautiful that Jim had a hard time not reaching out to touch. He cleared his throat and forced his gaze back up to Andy's face. "Did you do that yourself?"

"Most of it." Andy turned around and showed Jim his back, which was covered in swooping crows. "I had to get a friend to do my back. But it's still my design."

"Gorgeous," Jim whispered.

"Thanks." For the first time since Jim had met him, Andy looked like he didn't know what to say. He scooped up his shirt and shrugged it back on. "You ready?"

Later, as Andy worked on Jim's other side, he said, "I fix a lot of tattoos for military guys, and I gotta say, this one's a first. Not the usual stuff of hiding names or cleaning up bad art. What's the story?"

So Jim told him about being young and stupid and drunk and how he'd tried to seduce the wrong guy. He told Andy how he'd been making up stories to cover it up for twenty years. As the night wore on, to the rhythm of Andy etching on his skin, Jim told the truth as he remembered it.

About the tattoo, the Navy, his whole ridiculous life. Andy murmured sympathetically at some parts and laughed with Jim at others. The conversation was more than passing the time. It was magnificent.

Everything comes to an end eventually. Andy's machine stopped buzzing, and the burn, which had been creeping down Jim's leg, stayed where it was. After hours of listening to the machine buzz, the quiet boomed in Jim's ears. Outside, the traffic sounds had died down. It had to be after two.

Andy helped Jim off the table and kept his hand under Jim's elbow until he felt steady. Jim's skin was on fire. He wouldn't be sitting down for a long time. He held the sheet in front of him and stood looking over his shoulder at the dragon in Andy's full-length mirror. For the first time in twenty years, he liked what he saw. His skin was bright red and blotchy. The dragon stared back, a magnificent creature covering Jim's lower back, his butt cheeks and down one thigh. *He's got my back.*

Jim caught Andy's gaze in the mirror. "Thank you."

Andy nodded. His eyes were focused on the dragon. "You ship out this afternoon? How long will you be gone?"

"Six months." Jim turned to face Andy. He'd have plenty of time for dragon gazing later. He wanted to take in the man.

Andy met his gaze. "Come back in when you get to town."

"You think it will take that long to heal?"

"If you keep it clean and don't scratch, you should be fine in a month." Andy licked his lips. "I spent a lot of time tonight getting to know your ass. It's a nice ass. I'd like to see it again."

Jim's heart rate jumped. "Really?"

A slow smile spread across Andy's face. "It's really sexy that I'm the only one who knows there's lust under your dragon."

Jim thought for a moment that Andy might kiss him. But instead, he ran his hands down Jim's arms. "Something to think about while you're out there sailoring. In the meantime, we need to bandage you up."

Jim let the towel drop. He took Andy's face in his hands and kissed him. Andy opened to him and Jim poured in everything—the humiliation and gratitude, twenty years of hiding and hoping. When he broke the connection they were both panting. Jim stared down into Andy's gorgeous blue eyes, knowing there was no way his poor, battered body could do what he wanted it to do right then. Andy seemed to know this because he put his hand on Jim's chest and held him away. Jim imagined that the flock of crows flew from Andy's hand and circled his heart.

He smiled. "I'll be back."

To My Future Self

E.E. Ottoman

This is not writing advice.

Not for you—my future self—and not for anyone else.

I suspect that at this point you are a very different writer from me, who writes very different things. Just as I am a very different writer from the writer I was five years ago, ten years ago, fifteen years ago. That's what happens when we get older; we change into different people, with different stories to tell. I hope that you write things that I cannot hope to write and that you look back with fondness at the stories I wrote ten years ago, five years ago—the stories I am writing now.

No, I'm not going to give you advice, but I do have some things to say.

First off, I hope you write what you love, what makes you happy, what makes you come alive. Not because that's what writers always say, that phrase that can sound so patronizing, so naïve, when you're trying to get by on two hundred dollars every quarter.

But because your life is too short not to be proud of yourself, not to come alive, and be in love with something that you have created. Not because anyone wanted you to, but because you wanted to, and you were enough.

Sometimes you just need to say "fuck it."

And do it anyway.

I hope you still do that.

Mostly, I hope you are still in love with writing, with telling stories, with the process, with the craft. With the long days measured in sentences and cups of coffee. The editing while trying to balance your laptop on your knees on a moving train. Those moments when you could be walking down a street, sitting in a coffee shop, standing on the front porch in the very early morning watching the fog roll in, and you know, completely and profoundly, that you have done something amazing.

Know that you do make things that are beautiful and powerful, and hold that knowledge in a secret place, the hollow of your chest where no one can take that away from you.

This is something that you did.

No one else made these stories.

Only you.

Only you could.

I hope you are still loud without apology and that you speak your mind. I know sometimes it can feel like everyone is sick of hearing the sound of your voice, and wouldn't you just be quiet already?

And there are the days when you're sick of your voice too and every word feels like hypocrisy and tastes like poison and self-doubt.

But this is who you are and what you believe in. I know for a fact every time you speak there are people who listen and people who care. And every time you speak, you learn to be a little stronger, a little kinder and a little more sure that you have something to say worth saying.

And while we are on that subject, I hope you are learning to take up space—not just for you, but for your words and the stories you create. You who were taught to be small, to be quiet. You who was taught that your stories and the stories of people like you did not matter, were meaningless, worthless. That there was no room for them on bookshelves, in libraries, and in bookstores. That characters who were like you would never live interesting and remarkable lives, never do heroic and unusual things, never fall in love, never be happy, never not be alone.

This was the story you were taught from birth: to be small, to be quiet, and to not bother looking for things that would not be there.

But this story, it is a lie. You know that.

And you made a promise a long time ago to the child you once were: that you will not be small, that you will not be quiet, and if someone does look? There *will* be stories there to find.

So if there isn't room for you or those stories, you are going to make room. On those bookshelves, and libraries, and bookstores. You are going to demand it, as loudly as you have learned to be.

And you are going to write.

This is who you are and what you love and how you are powerful.

I hope you are proud.

Proud of your books, especially the smutty ones, and the ones that scared you more than a little bit to write. The books that came easy and the ones where writing felt like crawling through a tunnel filled with wet sand. The books that got good reviews and the ones that didn't.

I hope that you are proud of the person and the artist that you have become.

I know I am proud of you, and I haven't even met you yet.

Caroline's Heart

AUSTIN CHANT

Chapter One
Texas, Summer of 1885

The morning tastes dusty and hot, like a pinch of pepper might have been mixed into the air. Roy is the first to observe it, rolling out of his bunk and pulling on his boots with sweat already prickling his underarms and the back of his neck.

Of the men on the ranch, he has the honor of being the earliest riser. He has an uneasy relationship with sleeping, and on warm nights—most nights—sweat gathers underneath his breast-bindings and wakes him in itching discomfort. These days, the earth doesn't seem to let go of the heat in the soil even to the next morning, so dawn comes sullen, stale, and dry. Roy leaves the rest of the ranch hands asleep and dresses in solitude.

He's grateful for this time of day. It's just about the only time he doesn't feel such a pressing need to watch his back in case someone sees him exposed. He even takes a few extra moments to breathe with his bindings off, his ribs aching as they expand, before wrapping himself up again and buttoning his shirt. Some days he feels like he has an old man's spine, squeezed and contorted out of shape to keep his body flat and hidden.

In the back of his mind, he counts his coin every time he takes a breath that hurts, and counts himself one day closer to a different life. To a job in town, a house of his own, or maybe—if he's really dreaming—his own ranch.

Some mornings taste like hope. This one tastes bitter.

❁ ❁ ❁

Cook knows to expect him early in the kitchen. She's a busy woman with greasy skin and nails blunted by scrubbing pans. She gives Roy a cup of coffee when he leans in the door.

"Thanks," Roy says. His voice comes out little better than a rasp. He has a swallow of coffee, clears his throat, and tries again. "Dry as hell today."

Cook laughs, sharp as the oil snapping in her pan. "You know you wouldn't lose your voice if you used it."

Roy shrugs. His voice does seem to get coarser with disuse, but that comes with the advantage of making him sound more like the other men. "Funny smell in the air, too."

"They're trying to smoke the Devil out," Cook says. "Keep him from moving in while that witch is visiting."

"She's here already?"

"Don't know. Might as well have been from the moment they invited her. If you ask me, once you invite a witch in, there's no asking her to leave." Cook shakes her head. "No matter how long you keep those candles burning."

Roy wouldn't much care if the ranch were infested with witches, so he shrugs and drinks his coffee until the rest of the men come in for breakfast. Freddie and John are, as usual, laughing about something; Isaac, the youngest, trails in with sleep in his eyes. There's six of them, not including Roy. They never do include Roy. Of all the kinds of men in the world, these ones he's never destined to have much in common with, and they can tell. Whatever boasting, swaggering boyhood they're all infused with is absent in him.

It used to frustrate him. He tried to stamp out the gentleness and quiet manners his upbringing had infused in him, tried to slap his chest and drink like the best of them. But it felt no more authentic than skirts and gowns. He'd grown up to be just like his father, an affable man with no patience for the company of squabbling boys.

And yet here he is, with neither the money nor the skills to keep any other company but that of the poor cowboys serving on Weber's ranch.

Halfway through the meal, there's a knock at the door and Mr. Weber comes in, knocking dust off his boots. Most everyone straightens up, except Isaac, who's still half-asleep in his beans.

"Morning, boys!" Weber says. He's an imposing man for one whose hands are soft from lack of honest work; he's big and sharp-eyed, always smiling unpleasantly. He doesn't much like it when employees talk back, so the most they offer him is a collective mumble of, "Morning, sir."

"I'm sure the word's got round, but in case there's no gossip in the kitchen this morning, I figured you ought to know about our guest."

Cook blushes and ducks out of sight.

"The witch, sir?" That's Isaac, who's never grasped the idea of keeping his mouth shut.

"The lady," Mr. Weber corrects him brusquely. "She's coming to take a look at Gracie's leg, bless the cattle births, and take some retired leathers for use in her spellcraft. Roy, you'll be in charge of collecting them for her."

Roy nods

"She'll be on her way by nightfall. Nobody need pretend to like magic for her sake, but keep out of her way and keep a civil tongue in your head. History says she won't lay any hexes on any man who doesn't annoy her." He grins around at the table. "Understood?"

"Sir," John says. "How are we supposed to know what annoys a witch?"

"Maybe you just ought to keep your mouth shut," Mr. Weber says, and a chuckle runs around the room.

"Pretend you're Roy for the day," Freddie says. "Can't annoy her if you don't say anything."

Roy smiles and doesn't say anything.

✿✿✿

Roy looks up the hill toward the house while he's putting the horses out to pasture and sees a pair of tall, smoldering candles on stakes planted outside the porch, giving off that curious, prickling smoke. It makes him sneeze and tickles at his throat.

He keeps an eye out for the witch but hasn't seen a hair of her when it comes time to retreat into the stables. There's a repair to be done—one of the mares kicked a hole in the door of her stall. It's dusty work. He barely notices the air growing warmer, more agitated. Not till a coil of soft heat, like a cat's tail, brushes the back of his neck.

Roy straightens, startled, and glances over his shoulder.

There's nothing out of the ordinary, just the saddles and tack and a bare wall. But the air pushes urgently around him, swelling with thick heat. And as he watches, a seam of light splits the wood of the wall, drawing along it in a rectangle the size of a door.

"Holy—" Roy gasps and grabs for a nearby post as the air surges, threatening to throw him to his knees.

Then the door cracks inward, and the pressure goes all at once. The heat tears out of the room, leaving behind cold, thin air that smells of flowers.

Roy sags against the post, shivering, staring into the eyes of the witch.

She looks straight at him, not in the forthright way that some people do, but like a cat watching an insect. Her eyes are black, alert, languid—her eyelashes are so thick and dark they seem to pull her eyelids down for each dispassionate blink. Roy can't quite breathe until she turns away to pull the glowing door closed behind her.

He hadn't expected a witch to look so pretty. She'd make him stumble over his tongue if he met her in the street. She's dressed like Mr. Weber's young wife, in gray and white, with a bow around the high collar of her dress and a straw bonnet

trimmed with silk. Her lips are rosy, her cheekbones striking and warm with healthy color. Her hair is dark and tame,
pulled back into a shiny braid that's coiled at the nape of
her neck, loose ringlets curling over her brow and along her
cheeks.

When she catches his eye again, he blushes. "Do you
need something, cowboy?" she asks in a cool drawl.

Roy snatches his hat from his head and presses it to his
chest. "Pardon me, ma'am. You wouldn't happen to be the
lady guest, would you?"

Her red mouth twists as if he's made a joke. "I prefer
'Cecily.'"

Roy swallows, torn between wonder at her beauty and
the sense that he ought to be afraid. "As you like, ma'am.
May I show you up to the house?"

"No, thank you. I know my way around."

Then she sweeps out of the stables, leaving him behind.

❁❁❁

Roy sees her from a distance on occasion for the rest
of that day as he's gathering up the old leathers for her ap-
praisal. Sometimes she's sitting on the porch with Gracie,
the Webers' daughter, who walks on an enchanted leg. Other times he sees Cecily walking the length of the grazing
land, accompanied by Mr. Weber, who stays at a respectful
distance.

Roy can't help feeling jealous of her. He wishes he could
open a magic door and be somewhere else. He wishes he
could afford to be seen as different and be feared for it, respected even. If he'd been born with the power, it wouldn't
matter what else he was: he could magic himself into a new
job, a new life.

He wonders if she could magic one for him.

The evening's coming on with a blessed trickle of cool
air when Roy treks out to the cattle pasture to join Weber

and the witch. Cecily is stroking the nose of a pregnant cow through the fence, and she looks up when Roy clears his throat.

"I have those leathers stacked up by the shed, Mr. Weber."

"Good. Whatever she wants, you pack up for the next run to Austin." Weber turns to Cecily, ducking his head like he's scared of meeting her eyes. "Will you join us for dinner, ma'am?"

Cecily shakes her head. "I'm afraid I must return to the city as early as possible."

Weber could stand to look a little sorrier than he does in Roy's opinion. He melts away and leaves them in each other's company.

"This way, ma'am," Roy says, and sets off for the shed. Cecily gathers up her skirt to follow, her hands clad in soft white gloves. Her boots are embroidered all over with flowering vines, low heels lifting her feet above the straw. They pass John as he's herding the pigs into their enclosure, and his eyes go very wide at the sight of the witch trailing after Roy in her elegant white clothes.

The leathers are piled in the grass beside the shed, stacks of worn saddles separated from retired gloves, boots, and belts. Cecily crouches in the grass, taking off her soft white gloves and running long, curious fingers over the embroidery of a ruined saddle. That particular saddle is in such poor shape, Roy thought it was almost insulting to show her, so he'd stacked a few others on top of it.

He's alarmed to see Cecily trying to delicately drag it out from underneath the others. "Er—ma'am! I can shift those for you. Don't trouble yourself."

Cecily turns her disinterested eyes on him, and Roy prepares himself for whatever a hex feels like. Only nothing happens. Cecily gives a little sigh and, with an air of concession, turns away. "Very well."

Roy crouches beside her to pull the old saddle out from under the others, wrinkling his nose at it. But as soon as he breathes in to ask what she wants with it, he inhales her perfume.

It's rosy, light, and faintly sweet, like honey. It's lovely.

It makes him forget how to talk until he draws away.

"Why, uh—why this saddle, ma'am? It's awfully broken down."

"Its condition doesn't matter." Cecily runs her fingers over the saddle horn, glancing in Roy's direction without quite looking at him. "I use leather in most of my work. The skin carries energy from all the life it comes in contact with. It holds the energy of the horse and of the men and women who rode in the saddle. I find that energy particularly easy to channel for my enchantments." She waves him back over. "This is a good one."

Roy hefts it and pulls it away. "So some have better energy than others?"

Cecily nods absently.

"Why is that? Better cows? Better cowboys?"

She raises her eyebrows, and the corner of her mouth turns up wryly. "Not quite. Sometimes the energy is stronger, or it takes a different shape. It depends on the life of the leather. On the experiences it shared. On what I'm using it for."

Cecily assesses the other saddles without approving of any of them and picks through a heap of belts next. Roy can't think of anything else halfway intelligent to ask, and he likes to watch her, so the time passes in cordial quiet. The fading sunlight casts pretty shadows across Cecily's face through the lace edge of her bonnet.

She inspects piles of gloves, boots, chaps, whips, and hats without taking anything. She's nearly finished when she picks up a pair of old riding boots with white stars stitched into the front shaft and pauses.

Roy startles. "Hey—those were mine!"

Cecily lifts her head sharply, and the look on her face stops him dead.

There's a sudden color in her cheeks, a flush of rage or fever, and her eyes—he's only ever seen a snake look at him like that. "I *know* they're yours," she says coldly.

Roy's skin crawls. He's struck with a sudden, disorienting idea. Certainly she's looking at him like her eyes could go straight through him—and who's to say a witch couldn't? Couldn't see past his bindings and his men's uniform and know exactly what he is.

She's feeling his energy through the leather of his old boots. And now, for the first time, she's looking him in the eye with unfathomable dislike.

Her fingers are gripping the toe of his old boot tightly. "You have a distinctive walk," she says.

Roy swallows, finds his voice. "Do I, ma'am?"

"Yes," she says.

She pulls her gloves back on and gets abruptly to her feet, tucking Roy's boots under her arm.

"Those are awful dirty, ma'am. I can carry them for you—"

"I am *perfectly* capable of carrying them, thank you."

He's never heard a thank you that felt more like a slap.

"I will expect to have that saddle delivered within the month." Cecily snaps. "These I'm taking now."

Without waiting for him to answer, she turns and draws a door in the air. It swings open to a blast of cold air, and Roy catches a brief glimpse of a dark, dusty shelves on the other side before Cecily wrenches it closed behind her.

Chapter Two
The Oregon coast, three weeks later.

The spell-frame rests beside the window in Cecily's long-abandoned attic, with Caroline's heart in the center.

Cecily brushes her fingers reflexively over the delicate metal casing of the prosthetic heart as she stands before it and feels its energy stir. The air grows warm as the spell wakes, bringing with it the scent of distant spice and flannel, cut grass and earth. The scent of a body that once lay close to her.

Caroline's heart shares its energy with the other components in the frame: the grasses and feathers and bones and beach stones suspended in the web of spell-threads, spun with jewels and marbles, glass eyes; the pieces sewn around the wooden frame itself, like the scarf Caroline would wear outdoors, the leathers.

The sight of the star from the cowboy's boots stitched into the corner of the frame still makes her throat tighten unpleasantly.

It feels undeniably strange to have met the man and to feel the energy he shared with Caroline. The recognition had gone through her as an unpleasant shock. Up until that point, he had seemed benign enough—more attractive than most of the ranch hands she had encountered in her time working for Arnold Weber, with an oddly pleasing habit of ducking his chin and looking up st her with round, owlish eyes.

Then her fingers had traced the star on his boots, and it was as if he had thrown Cecily back five years to a memory of Caroline's footsteps echoing on the front porch. To *her* boots resting by the door. To the quiet that followed.

Through no fault of his own, but damn him.

Even now, it's difficult for her to think of those boots as belonging in the frame. For the most part, her spell components are gathered from utter strangers—from the dusty memories associated with saddle leathers, disconnected from names and faces. At least she doesn't know his name.

Yet his eyes nag at her while she studies the frame,

touching each piece of it in turn. Each component evokes Caroline, but only a fractured piece. A scrap of her coat, a whisper of her hair. As Cecily touches it, energy bleeds from her fingertips into the frame, into the resonance that binds each component together, and the spell billows like silk in the wind. It whispers with a voice that went silent long ago. She closes her eyes and the leather beneath her hands becomes skin, her nose fills with the scent of their sheets, and in the distance—

In the distance she can hear the murmur of Caroline singing to herself in the kitchen, the creak of the floorboards under a pair of leather boots.

It fools her heart, and nearly fools her mind. Until she opens her eyes and finds herself gripping the white star.

Damn that cowboy. The illusion is spoiled, and she pulls her hand away with a bitter taste in her mouth. The spell in the frame is stronger now, but not enough to pull Caroline back through the veil. There are pieces still missing, energy she has yet to trace.

The threads of the spell pull at her as she turns away. They pluck at her heart and leave it shivering.

✿✿✿

She leaves the old coast house to its loneliness, taking the enchanted door back to her workshop. The shop in Austin is unusually quiet, which isn't entirely a bad thing; it means that nobody is in need of her urgent assistance. Still, enough customers stop by to keep her thoroughly distracted from the work of building new prosthetics. A few pretty young women and their interested suitors come by in search of what Cecily thinks of as souvenir magics—one wants "good luck", another wants "happiness", and both are perfectly content to receive mere charms of tooled leather that contain a warm suggestion of magic. A pair of wealthy parents bring in their daughter, for whom Cecily crafted a hand, because the girl has been complaining that it itches. Cecily gives the girl a bracelet of silk that glows with witch-light.

The day trickles on like this, interrupted every hour or two by the arrival of a new pilgrim, and Cecily is just putting the finishing touches on a seeing glass eye that should only have taken her half the morning when the bell over the door jingles again.

For a moment, her mind doesn't recognize the silhouette, the dusty clothes, the hat tugged down over his eyes. Then the man lifts his head, and with a nasty jolt, she recognizes the cowboy from the ranch.

She draws herself up, shaken. "May I help you?"

"I've just come from the ranch with that saddle, ma'am." He keeps his eyes down, no doubt intimidated by their last meeting.

She had quite forgotten about the saddle in all that she had thought about him. "I see. Well, you may leave it over there." She indicates a corner near the door, far away from herself.

He mumbles his assent and goes outside, and Cecily watches him walk away. As much as the sight of him disturbs her, she also finds him pleasant to watch. The energy, she thinks. He doesn't look anything like Caroline; he's stockier, with soft gray eyes where Caroline's were bright and hawkish, his nose and jaw both round and stubborn where Caroline had features perfectly fine. His hair is dark and awkwardly shorn, and Caroline's was neat and golden. Yet something about him charms her. It *must* be the energy.

She pretends to be busy when he walks back in, but watches him out of the corner of her eye. He sets the saddle carefully on the floor and turns toward her, apprehension written in every line of his body.

"There you are, ma'am," he says. "Will you be needing

anything else?"

He clearly wants the answer to be *no*, and she has no reason to keep him, but Cecily finds herself reluctant to dismiss him. "Possibly," she says.

The cowboy fidgets with his hat and says nothing, ducking his head and looking up at her with those large eyes. Waiting.

Looking at him makes her stomach hurt and her heart twist.

"Those boots of yours," Cecily says. "I used them to make a set of new prosthetics. You have a...particularly useful energy. An unusual energy."

He rocks back on his heels, looking alarmed. Cecily recognizes in his face the familiar fear of someone not used to magic. "Is that so, ma'am?"

"There's no need to be superstitious," Cecily says impatiently. "It's not a bad thing."

He hesitates. "It's not?"

"No. As a matter of fact, if you happened to have any more discarded leathers, or perhaps other items you had carried close to your person—"

"They'd be valuable to you?"

Cecily can see the glitter of greed in his eyes. She frowns. "Well, yes."

"What kind of valuable?"

He wants *something*, clearly. She can sense it in how quickly he latched on to the idea, like a man snatching for a lifeline. It's all the more annoying because Cecily has little use for money and keeps no more than she needs for maintenance of the shop. "Perhaps we could arrange some sort of barter," she says.

"Sure," he agrees. There's a spark in his eyes. "As a matter of fact, I could use a new job. D'you need a hand around your shop?"

"No."

"But…if you need more of my energy, surely it'd make sense for you to keep me close by—"

"*No*." The word snaps out of her like a whipcrack.

Her vehemence startles both of them. The idea of keeping him around, having to see him every day in exchange for scraps of Caroline's resonance, fills her with nausea. It would confuse her, corrupt the spell. His eyes would haunt her every time she manipulated the frame.

"I have no need of an assistant," she says quickly. "I could offer you my services in future, should you ever have need—"

"I don't need a wooden leg, ma'am," he says. "I just need an opportunity."

"Then I cannot help you."

"If you want something of mine…"

"Then I had better be prepared to pay whatever price you conjure up?" Cecily turns her back on him. "You overestimate your value. See yourself out, please."

He doesn't move. She hears his boots scrape on the floor as he shifts in place, and she grimly resigns herself to using the usual tactics necessary for removing belligerent men from her shop. The suggestion of fire and damnation is usually sufficient.

She's opening her mouth to threaten such when he speaks, startlingly soft:

"I'm sorry if I offended you, ma'am."

Cecily lets out a breath, unbalanced by his gentleness. "Not at all. But I don't believe we have any more business to discuss, and I have work to do."

"I'd accept money, too," he says hopefully. "I just haven't got as much need for it. At the rate I'm going, I'll never be able to afford to move to town—"

"That is not my problem, nor my concern." Cecily flicks her wrist backwards, sending a rush of air and listening to him gasp and stumble toward the door. "Leave, please."

"Yes, ma'am," she hears him mumble as he scrambles out.

She can almost feel the presence that slips away with him, and for a moment, it's so unbearable that she wants to turn and shout after him.

❀❀❀

After Roy's last cattle drive, he'd expected a break of some sort, exhausted after months on the range, days upon days of hard riding. But there had been work to do back at the ranch, and Weber paid well, so he'd returned without a wink of honest rest. Until now.

After the long drive to Austin, him and the rest of the men have been rewarded with a night in town.

Roy's not sure he finds it relaxing. The ranch has the advantage of being the same every day, presenting all the same dangers and the same hard work. The city's new. Bristling with strangers and customs he's barely familiar with. Like *witches*, for example.

The saloon where Roy and the other men are staying is cramped downstairs, tables bursting and chairs crushed together with barely space to walk between them once the evening trade picks up and the gambling gets hot at the faro tables in the back. An old man in a dusty suit bangs merrily on the piano, filling up any gap in conversation with cheerful noise. Not that there are many gaps to fill when John and Freddie are yammering.

"Roy," John says with inebriated certainty. "You know what your problem is?"

"No, John," Roy says. "Why don't you go and tell me."

Freddie guffaws and pats Roy on the shoulder. "He knows, John. He knows he's too short for a woman to love him."

Roy grins tolerantly. It's not as if there isn't a grain of truth in it. Certainly he's too short for a woman like Cecily, he thinks.

John, briefly distracted by his need to laugh at Freddie, swivels back toward Roy. "You know what your problem is?"

"No, John."

"Well, I'll tell you. Man like Freddie has many faults, but he knows what to do when he's in the city, not stuck up on the ranch with only maids and horses for company." Roy groans, already sure of where this is going. "Meanwhile you, you come to the city, you never spend any time with women. Bet it's been so long you don't remember what a woman's like."

"Is that true?" Freddie asks, giving Roy a considering look.

"I think I could identify one," Roy says. "I'm almost sure I saw a barmaid earlier."

John punches him in the arm. "That's the first step. Remember the rest?"

"Listen." Roy leans back from the table. "I'd never be one to judge what you gentlemen do. But I'm focused on my work, that's all."

Freddie and John exchange a look. "You got urges, though, don't you?" John asks.

"'Course I do," Roy says patiently, because the alternative would be to admit that he spends too much time exhausted and afraid to want much of anything from other people. "Just no need to satisfy them."

"Dangerous way to live," John says. "Spend too long without a woman, you could turn queer."

Roy stiffens, feeling a cold plunge of fear. He tries to force himself to be angry instead, like a man should be. One of these men, anyway. "I don't think I'm in any kind of danger of that, John," he snaps. "Do you?"

John opens his mouth. Then there's a commotion from the gambling tables, a chorus of outraged voices and one distinctive, familiar voice of triumph. Roy twists around in his seat to see Isaac standing up from one of the faro games, yelping with excitement. He shoves his way through the crowd back to Roy's table. "I'm buying the next round, boys!" he shouts, dumping a heap of dollars on the table, drunk enough not to notice the tension in the air.

"Look at you," Freddie says. "Didn't cheat, did you?"

"I'd never do such a thing," Isaac says, with a huge grin. "I've got a lucky streak a mile wide. Can't seem to lose."

Roy ignores his boasting, more concerned with the men he's just noticed following Isaac from the faro table.

Five of them, all roughly dressed. The ringleader, who's a clever-looking man in a nicer suit than the rest, taps Isaac on the shoulder with his cigar. "Need a word with you, son."

Isaac chuckles. "If it's about your money," he says, "you *can't* have it back."

Roy snatches at Isaac's sleeve. "Hey." None of the others will flinch from a fight, but he doesn't like the look of these men. "What do you gentlemen want?"

The ringleader smiles dangerously. "I want him to give back what he cheated—and promise to be a good boy at my table from now on."

Isaac gasps and swings around. "I'm no cheat!" he yells. "I don't owe you a cent!"

"That's right," John growls, grabbing the handful of cash Isaac left on their table and stuffing it into his pocket. "You crawl back to your table, now, or me and the boys'll—"

"John!" Roy supposes he ought to be glad the subject of his sex life is apparently forgotten, but instead, his eyes are fixed on the guns dangling from the belts of the four big men standing behind the ringleader. "Let's calm down, now." He stands, looks the ringleader in his nasty eyes, and smiles firmly. "We're not here for trouble, and I'm sure he didn't cheat you. Look at the man. He can hardly stand up—I wouldn't expect him to pull a fast one on an intelligent bunch of gentlemen like you."

"Didn't say he did a good job of it," the ringleader says, his grin sharp. "Otherwise he wouldn't have had to run back to his friends like a coward."

Isaac reels. "I am *not* a coward, you son of a bitch." And then he punches the ringleader in the jaw.

To Isaac's credit, he hits hard for a drunk man. The ringleader falls on his ass with an undignified yelp. Isaac whoops in triumph and spins around, grinning at Roy.

One of the men behind Isaac pulls a revolver from its holster and takes aim at his back.

Roy's heart freezes in his chest. But before the man can pull the trigger, his eyes catch sight of something across the room, and Roy becomes conscious of an eerie silence spreading across the drunken crowd.

He turns and sees the witch standing in the doorway.

She's radiant in the glum light of the bar, tall and striking and wrapped in a white lace shawl that stirs gently in a breeze from the doorway. Her dark eyes make a quick study of the crowd, and then they land on Roy.

She stares at him, and everyone else in the room stares at her.

Then she walks forward, and there's a general scramble by the bar's patrons to get out of her way. Men scattering left and right, chairs being overturned and dragged away. No one seems to want to touch her. "What the hell is *she* doing here?" That's the ringleader, having regained his feet and his wits.

"Miss Witch?" Isaac asks, high and startled.

Cecily ignores both of them. She walks around the table and stands before Roy. "I've reconsidered," she says coolly.

"Witch!" the ringleader spits. "You're not wanted in here."

Cecily doesn't even look at him. "My business is with him, not with you."

"What do you mean, reconsidered?" Roy asks softly.

Cecily raises her eyebrows and opens her mouth to reply, but the next thing Roy knows, he's been shoved aside, the ringleader pushing between them and waving a pistol in Cecily's face. "We don't want any of your tricks," he spits. "You get out and stay gone—"

"Get away from her!" Roy snaps, lunging forward and seizing the man by his gun arm, twisting it away from Cecily. One of the ringleader's bodyguards grabs him from behind, trying to pull him off, and Roy swings an arm loose to elbow him in the jaw. But as he does so, the ringleader tears free of his grip and spins around, fury in his weasel eyes, gun in hand.

Roy catches a glimpse of Cecily over the man's shoulder. She looks startled, annoyed.

Then the gun goes off.

Chapter Three

Cecily stares at her cowboy, at the blood spilling down the back of his hand as he clutches his chest.

The bar erupts with noise, but Cecily's world narrows to the sight of his knees buckling, his body crumbling to the floor. The cowboy's drunken friends are bellowing, throwing themselves upon his attackers with angry fists, leaving him to fall forgotten.

She lunges forward before his head meets the ground, catching him in her arms. His eyes are glassy and wide, his mouth open in shock.

Cecily grips his jaw in one hand, feeling the uncertain bite of his pulse at her fingers, its rhythm unsteady, like an engine sputtering. She feels the energy in him leaking out of the wound in his chest and spilling with each breath. But what she can feel, she can control. Drawing the power of the air inside her, she reaches for the life inside him and takes mastery of it. She forces his breath and heartbeat to stop; she silences his body and preserves it. She feels the effort of it in her fingers, like dragging a heavy weight. A bottle shatters somewhere above her, and glass rains down the back of her neck. Cecily barely flinches.

She draws a deep, steadying breath before she plunges her hand into Roy's chest. She reaches past skin and tissue as if it were water, following the path of the bullet, and finds his ribs splintered and his heart mangled.

Cecily jerks her hand out of his chest with a shudder and sees him draw a frantic breath as her control slips for a moment. She channels power back into his body to hold him steady, to keep him slipping any closer to death.

But to what purpose? He needs a new heart, now. It would take her hours to forge one, even if she were not sustaining his life with her own energy.

She needs something quickly. Or otherwise it will be just like Caroline, just like—

Just like Caroline.

"Roy!" One of the drunkards screams, and Cecily snaps back to reality as he tries to pull her cowboy out of her arms. "Christ Jesus, he's cold—"

Cecily bats him aside with a snap of energy that sends him reeling into a nearby table. She looks back at her cowboy's blank, staring eyes.

Roy.

All at once, Cecily knows what she can do to save him. And it horrifies her.

She lifts him with an effort, grateful for his slightness. She carries him through the crowd, paying no mind to the strangers she throws aside as she passes. She slings a spell onto the door and wrenches it open to her own attic.

When she slams it shut behind her, the noise stops and she is alone with Roy and the frame.

Cecily's mouth feels dry as sandpaper, her chest squeezing with fear and her stomach twisting. She leaves Roy on the floor and approaches the spellframe. Caroline's heart rests in the center, surrounded by the tangle of bright threads. The white star of Roy's boot.

If he lives... his resonance will be enough to rebuild the spell.

It must be. It will *have* to be.

When Cecily reaches through to grasp the heart, she feels the resonance stir with playful familiarity. Cecily feels so sick she can hardly stand. Everything was built from the heart. Without it...

She looks over her shoulder at Roy, his body frozen on the verge of death.

A stranger. A stranger's life for Caroline's heart.

His eyes would haunt her forever.

The heart resists being pulled free, bound as it is to the other items in the frame, but she doesn't have time to kindly disentangle it. She wrenches it out and feels the spell rip painfully.

Almost without noticing, she begins to cry. Even as she falls back to her knees at the cowboy's side, there are tears running down her face. She wipes them away bitterly and takes hold of herself, steadying her hands.

Taking Caroline's delicate heart in both her hands, she places it inside his chest. The heart warms to him as she weaves a binding spell around it, carefully joining it to the sinew and muscle of his chest.

It hardly needs invitation to begin beating.

❁❁❁

At first Roy thinks he's home, sitting by his mother's knee at the piano and listening to the steady tick-tock of the metronome. Any moment now, she'll tell him to sing, and he'll have to tolerate the voice that leaves his throat—the high voice that his mother calls sweet and that his father always smiles to hear, the voice trained to curl softly over each note.

He'll focus on the words and try to forget what he sounds like.

Instead, he wakes up.

The ceiling above him is dark, glossy wood. His chest aches like everything inward of his ribs is bruised, and his heart is the metronome in his ears, beating in his throat with a steely *tick, tick, tick.*

He's lying in a wide, white bed. He rolls his head to the side slowly and sees the witch sitting in a chair beside him.

Her eyes are closed, her arms splayed over the sides of the chair and head tipped back. Her dark hair is loose of the strict braids that bound it before, wild strands hanging around her face in tired curls. Her face is gray.

Roy tries to sit up, and that's when he realizes he's wearing someone else's shirt. There's a bandage wrapped around his chest, but it's loose, soft, not like his bindings. She *undressed* him.

His heart begins to pound with bafflement and terror. And then it doesn't seem to know how to stop itself.

From uneasy beating to panicked thumping, it escalates to a tinny drumming and a pressure in his chest that seems to bang around in his ribs. Dizziness sweeps over him, sudden numbness in his fingers. When he tries to breathe, it comes in frantic little snatches of air, shorter each time, and when he tries to yell, it comes out as a frightened sob.

Cecily's eyes snap open and she springs from her chair.

Her hand comes down on Roy's chest.

"*Breathe,*" Cecily orders. Silky strands of her dark hair hang around his face like unspooled thread, and Roy stares up at her, gasping senselessly. Warmth spreads from her palm, a soothing and steady heat that seems to wrap around his anxious heart and quiet it. "*Slower.* Breathe."

He sucks in one deep breath, and then another. One for each slow circle that Cecily rubs over his heart, a rhythm he can follow. She slides an arm under his back and pulls him into her arms, and Roy shudders with the blessed comfort of it, despite the way his skin crawls at her unfamiliar touch.

As the fear recedes, it leaves him more exhausted than before, and he wants nothing more than to turn and bury his face in the darkness of her robe. Cecily lifts him slightly, propping him against a pair of pillows, keeping her hand on his chest and petting softly. It's been a long time since anyone touched him like that, and Roy shivers again, less pleasantly.

"Ma'am?" he manages. His voice is raw. "I'm all right now."

"You certainly are, for having nearly killed yourself a second time," Cecily snaps. She lifts her hand, and Roy can breathe again.

"My... my heart's okay."

"Your heart was destroyed. I gave you a new one."

Roy gapes at her. "Just like that?"

"No, *not just like that.*" No matter how she's cradling him, her eyes are still cold and distant. "Be gentle with it. It's actually quite old."

"*Old?*" Roy yelps, his heart giving an uneasy little jump.

Cecily frowns, brushing her fingertips over his chest, and his heartbeat steadies once again. "Parts of it are old. It will serve you well. But you must stay calm and let it settle."

Let it *settle?*

Roy takes another deep breath. He's in a witch's house, and she's taken his clothes off. Seen him. "I am calm," he says, his pulse loud and steely in his ears. "Who else saw?"

"Saw?"

"Me. My—" He gestures shakily at himself.

Cecily's eyebrows arch and she averts her eyes. "No one saw. I brought you here before I treated the wound."

Roy rubs weakly at the front of his shirt, feeling the outline of a bandage through it. He swallows and breathes past the butterflies in his stomach, not meeting her eyes.

"Now," Cecily says, "*stop* overtaxing that heart."

"Yes. Thank you, ma'am."

"I will consider it thanks enough if you do everything in your power to heal quickly so that you may leave my home." Cecily pulls her hair back and looks away. She looks unwound since the last time he saw her. And though he never would've imagined that saving someone's life would be easy work, he still feels an irrational pang for having put her to such a struggle.

"I never even introduced myself," he mumbles. "I'm Roy. Roy Jones."

He offers an unsteady handshake. Cecily's fingers are cool when she touches his hand. "Mr. Jones." The curtains are drawn over her eyes. "You were very lucky today. I would suggest you do the best you can with your second chance at living."

"I intend to, ma'am."

"Good." She withdraws from him, sinking back into her chair. "Such chances are rare."

Chapter Four

Cecily has not, in all her years, had a house guest. She has never had the inclination, nor any particular guests clamoring to visit a witch's house. Still, she concedes that Roy should probably be fed, and so conjures food from a kitchen she likes in Austin. He must also be watched to be sure his heart doesn't fail or start beating its way out of his chest again, at least for a few days. As soon as she is done feeling responsible for his survival, she decides, she will send him away.

In the meantime, she sleeps in the chair beside his bed and develops an unpleasant twinge in her neck.

Roy, for his part, refuses to rest easy. She finds him in the kitchen the next morning, holding himself upright against the counter with shaky hands.

"Get back in bed," Cecily says curtly.

Ignoring the order, he jerks his head toward the window, through which a dusty bit of sunlight is shining. "We're not in Texas."

She senses a wary edge in his voice, a demand for answers. As if she makes a habit of kidnapping men after she replaces their mangled organs. "No. I live in Oregon."

"Could I go back to Austin if I wanted?"

"Yes, in about thirty seconds. Think—you woke up here perhaps an hour after you were shot. You don't think I had time to throw your body in a wagon and take it across the country, do you?"

Roy frowns. "How's it work, then?"

"The same way I transported myself to your ranch last month, except this connection is more permanent. There's a door in the back of the house that leads directly to my workshop in Austin."

Roy's eyes light up with intrigue at that. Cecily gathers quickly that, in addition to being fearful of magic, he's fascinated by it. That evening, when she spins an orb of witchlight to read by, he cradles it curiously in his hands.

"It tickles a bit." The light catches in his eyes, warming them. "What is it?"

"Just a bit of air taught to glow."

Roy shoots her a curious smile. "It sounds so nice, the way you put it."

"I take it you aren't used to hearing witchcraft described in nice terms."

"Well, no." He looks a little embarrassed. "People have a lot of ideas..."

"Which ideas would those be? That I commune with the Devil every morning before tea or that I am, prosthetic by prosthetic, secretly turning the townsfolk into my helpless thralls. Or perhaps that my mother conceived me out of an unholy union with some wild beast." Roy blushes. "Or perhaps you've heard all of those."

"Not that last one," Roy mumbles.

"There's a certain breed of young man who, when drunk, turns up on my doorstep with his friends in the hopes of having a witch hunt, and he usually has something interesting to say about the circumstances of my birth."

Roy stiffens. "They do that? Haven't hurt you, have they?"

Cecily snorts at the idea and at the look of concern on Roy's face. "I suppose if they were ever particularly bold they might try," she says. "But they generally change their minds if I threaten to hex them."

"I thought that gambler at the bar was going to shoot you."

The tension in his words is...touching. "I wouldn't have let him," she says lightly. "You were the one in danger."

"I know that. Still makes me sick." Roy hunches over, gathering the orb of witchlight close to his chin and staring into it.

"I hate those men," he adds, with startling bitterness. "Near every day for the last eight years I've wondered how I could have so much in common with them and yet so little. Wanted to get away and—I don't know. Set my own ranch up somewhere I could just be alone."

The tug of isolation and longing in his voice is familiar; it pulls at a string in Cecily's chest that hasn't been plucked for a long time. She tries to think of something to say, an example of her own life that might give him hope, but instead she feels a swell of loneliness.

She's surrounded by people, and yet their lives glance off of hers every time they meet, never forming a connection. Not that she would invite one. There's only one person she wants back at her side, and that person is dead.

"You're older than you look," she says.

Roy winces. "Usually get taken for eighteen, maybe. I'm twenty-five this August. Left home when I was seventeen."

"That's a long time."

"Yeah. Took me a long time to get work since I started later than most cowboys. By the time I realized I hated it, I was five years deep, no savings to speak of. I've been putting away what I can ever since, but it's slow going." He rubs his chin. "Suppose I'll be getting back to it once I'm well enough. Don't think I could stand to go back to work for Weber's ranch, though."

"Where will you go?"

"Don't know." Roy glances at her with a sudden, sweet smile, like he's grown tired of bitterness. "Unless you want to hire me after all."

Cecily laughs, and it startles her. It's been quite a while since someone made her laugh. "I'm afraid not. But...I will need other items of yours for a spell I'm weaving, and I'll find some way to compensate you."

"You don't need to pay me," Roy says. "I owe you my life."

❁❁❁

The next few days form a pattern. Roy wakes early, alerted by the strange new ticking of his heart, and gets up quietly so as not to wake Cecily. He brews tea in the kitchen and peers outside at the garden and the tall green trees beyond the gate, the dry golden grass blowing in the wind. Oregon, Cecily said. But without him having felt the travel, it's hard to believe.

He occupies himself by poking around in the kitchen. He used to love helping his mother cook, proving how grown-up he was by carrying the eggs without cracking them. Cecily keeps a sparse pantry, mostly preserved food with little in the way of fresh ingredients. She must be busy with her witchcraft and have no time for cooking. There's a sack of beans in one cupboard, but it's desiccated.

When he asks her about it, Cecily simply lifts one shoulder in a careless shrug and says, "There's a spell on the house to preserve the timbers, but I suppose that preservation doesn't extend to beans. I'll get rid of them."

But she leaves them there.

Dust seems to have trouble settling on any surface in the house. Roy comes to suspect that the cleanliness of everything comes not from Cecily's efforts but from witchcraft and disuse. Beyond the bedroom, which she claims is her own, she doesn't really seem to occupy the house. She floats around in the kitchen like she barely recognizes it before retreating once Roy agrees to come back to bed. She summons food with a twist of her fingers instead of cooking.

When Cecily goes back to town to deliver the prosthetic hand she's been working on, Roy hauls himself up and goes exploring.

The garden is in much the same shape as the desiccated beans, overgrown with weeds and the occasional remains of useful plants. Roy circles around the whole house, finding an abundance of abandoned equipment—most of it rusted to pieces—and copious spider webs. A few enterprising scrub trees are crawling in through the back fence.

He returns to the front yard and surveys the house, the pristine wooden face and its tired windows. Now that he's looking, there appears to be an attic of some sort, but he hasn't seen a way up. In stark contrast to the rest of the house, there are flowering vines growing down from the attic window, and beneath them, the timbers look black and rotting.

He nearly jumps out of his skin at the sound of a voice. "Pardon me, sir?"

Roy whirls around and sees a young woman standing outside the front gate. "Who are you?"

"I'm Mary. I live in town." Her eyes are wide. She has a funny, soft accent. "Are you the witch's man?"

"I'm her guest," Roy says, although it feels presumptuous to say. "What town?"

"Rockaway. Just down the road, sir. Did the witch come back?"

"Did she go away?"

"No one's seen her for years. Not since I was ten."

Roy approaches the fence, and Mary doesn't shrink back, though she stares at him with unbearable curiosity. So she isn't afraid of him by association with Cecily. "She's been living somewhere else, I think."

"Well, we never forgot her," Mary says with a firm smile. She crouches down in front of the gate and Roy leans over to see her surrounded by a tremendous bed of flowers, all colors, growing at the gate and all along the outside of the fence. "We kept bringing flowers for her garden. We couldn't get inside the gate, so we grew them outside."

"That's sweet of you," Roy says. He wonders if Cecily has even seen them.

"When I saw you, I had to come right over. Is the witch home?"

"Not right now."

"Well, does she need anything? That man she used to have wanted eggs and milk every week, plus meat from the butcher."

Roy blinks. "Er—yes," he says. "How far is town?"

❁❁❁

Though he still feels weak, he has a few dollars in his pocket, so Roy walks the half mile into town. Mary supports him by the elbow and introduces him to everyone they pass. Roy notices several strangers, especially the elderly, propped up on artificial limbs much like the ones he's seen Cecily stitching together.

From what he gathers, Cecily hasn't been seen around the town for five years, and she was always reclusive; it was her man Carl who people knew personally. But they all hold the witch in high esteem, and so Roy finds himself returning to the house with an overflowing basket of food, including meat and cheese and fresh bread, and a sturdy cane to help him walk. Mary insists on accompanying him back to the gate so she can share the load.

Cecily is still gone when he shoulders his way through the front door, so he sets himself to cooking. It's been a decade since he had a good kitchen at his disposal and good food to cook with, but he hasn't forgotten how, and a witch's kitchen seems to operate in much the same way as any other. He makes skillet potatoes, roasts onions and carrots, and is frying a pair of gorgeous steaks when Cecily breezes in.

"What on earth is that smell?"

"Dinner," Roy says. The startled look on Cecily's face is worth every step he took in carrying the supplies back from the village.

"Where did all this come from?"

"Rockaway. Where else? Everyone seems to miss you."

Cecily looks off-balance. "Do they really? I would've thought they'd have forgotten about me by now."

"They grew you a flowerbed outside the fence," Roy says, gesturing towards the window with a wooden spoon.

"Well. That's kind." Cecily smiles uncertainly and makes her way over to the stove in a sideways sort of movement, like a stray cat approaching an offer of scraps. She leans over the pan to inspect the steaks, and Roy knows hunger gleaming in a person's eyes when he sees it.

"Should you be walking or cooking in your condition?" she asks.

"I'm fine."

Cecily sighs. "Very well. But keep in mind that your heart is just getting used to being in your body and you might give it time before you start straining it."

"Me and this heart are getting along," Roy retorts. "And it's telling me that I'm *fine*."

Cecily makes a scornful noise, but a smile dashes across her mouth before she turns away. She goes and sits at the table, arranging herself in one of the wooden chairs as if it were a throne. It gives Roy a warm stir how she's letting him wait on her; he has no idea how he can ever repay her, but he was afraid she wouldn't even let him start by making dinner.

"Did you know your garden's overgrown?" he asks.

"Is it? I suppose no one's been out there in a while."

"Five years?"

Cecily frowns at him. "Did they tell you that in Rocka-way?"

"Over and over. They said there were children born after you left who'd love to be introduced to a real live witch someday."

"Children do love magic."

Roy takes the steaks from the pan and scoops potatoes, onions, and carrots onto the plates, adding a large hunk of buttered bread to each. He serves both plates onto the table and then more or less crumples into the chair opposite Ceci-ly, exhausted but proud of himself.

"This is quite a feast," Cecily says.

"I'm happy to do it, ma'am. I'm a good worker. Better than this when I'm healthy."

"You're so tenacious," she murmurs.

"Just trying to find employment."

"So I gather. It's funny."

Funnier to Roy is the fact that he's sitting at a witch's dinner table and feeling the most comfortable he has in years, talking more than he's talked to anyone since he ran away from home.

Cecily cuts into her steak and chews delicately on a slice. Her eyes close for a moment.

"This is wonderful."

Roy glows and digs in. "Down in Rockaway they kept talking about some man who used to be your assistant or something. Carl?"

Cecily sets down her fork with a sharp click. Roy glances up from the next bite he'd been contemplating and stops.

"Sorry," he says. "Forget I asked."

Cecily's jaw is tight, and she seems to have to work for a moment before she can speak. "I suppose it's natural for them to talk about her."

"Her?"

Cecily shoots him a cold look, and Roy leans back in his chair. "You may as well know," Cecily says, "that her name was Caroline, not Carl. This was her house. She presented herself as a man for the purpose of owning property and avoiding any unwanted men poking their noses into her business. The townsfolk never knew her any other way."

Roy's stomach does a flip for an entirely different, but equally unpleasant, reason. "So that's why you weren't surprised by me."

Cecily frowns. "Well—"

"That's not—" He doesn't mean to interrupt her, but stumbles guiltily on through his sentence when she stops and watches him. "That's not how I am. It's no disguise for me. And I can't tell you how or why, but I consider myself a man."

"Yes," Cecily says. "That's what I thought." And before Roy has the chance to stop reeling, she goes on: "I imagine Caroline would have had a harder time understanding than I do. I once had to explain to her that what for her was a disguise was, for me, the truest way I could present myself."

Roy takes a moment to digest that, staring at his plate while the cogs turn in his head. Then he looks up at her, at the perfect comprehension on her face.

"Do you mean to say the two of us are the same?"

"Yes."

"I didn't know."

Cecily raises her eyebrows. "Obviously." She lifts her fork again, skirting it around the edges of her plate. "I had a very queer childhood; the two things I understood earliest about myself were that I was a girl and that I was a witch. Both, you understand, were incomprehensible to other people." Cecily lets out a little sigh. "Caroline was the only person I ever cared to explain all that to."

"Well, you don't have to explain it to me," Roy says. He smiles. "Except maybe the witch part. If you ever feel like it."

Cecily shakes her head, a faint answering smile on her lips. "Maybe we can speak of it tomorrow," she says. "Assuming that you take it upon yourself to cook again."

"It's a deal, ma'am."

When they've both finished, Roy leans over the table to take Cecily's plate and stacks it on his. "Strawberries for dessert," he says, and is so distracted by Cecily's laugh that he doesn't notice the weakness in his knees until he tries to stand up. And falls over.

Or nearly does. The dishes slip out of his hand, but they never hit the ground because Cecily flicks her fingers out and the plates are suddenly suspended in the air on threads of magic.

"Easy, cowboy," she drawls.

Roy finds himself supported by an invisible presence under his elbows, holding him upright as his knees wobble. He stares at the plates floating in front of him.

"It's a wonder you ever stand up if you could just make everything fly like that."

"What a *good* use of magic that would be."

"I'm just saying it would be a temptation, if I were you."

Cecily rises and matter-of-factly plucks the plates out of the air, setting them safely on the table before she catches Roy by the waist, wrapping an arm around his back and taking one of his hands. Whatever magic is keeping him from falling vanishes, and he sags against her, supported entirely by her arms.

"It *is* a temptation," she says lightly, and she's only looking at him.

Chapter Five

Fragments of the resurrection spell float through the air around the frame, like cobwebs torn by a careless hand.

Cecily stands before the frame, sifting her fingers inconsolably through the broken threads. For a night and a day she had been unable to face the damage to the spell, buried herself in thoughts of her work, of keeping Roy stable. She had braced herself to find the spellframe dead, all its energy dispersed. What remains is almost worse. The spell is hollow, gaping open around its absent heart, the broken threads of power refusing to join across the space where Caroline's heart should be.

The resonance remains, bound into the threads, into other objects in the frame. But when Cecily strokes the leather sewn around the frame, feeds power into it, the energy that surges at her touch is changed. No longer does the presence in the room stir with the scent of spice and morning sunlight, the whisper of cloth. Instead it rises in a flurry of broken threads that snatch at the air, keening and sour. It is hungry, starving and incomplete.

Cecily pours magic into the frame, threads of light she tries to spin across the absence of the heart, but each thread breaks and melts into that lonely void. When she has exhausted herself, the frame remains alive but shattered, filled with directionless energy that stirs the room but does nothing, conjures nothing.

She sits for a while, staring at it, clasping her hands together until her fingers go numb.

She has no idea how to fix it. The spell was always experimental, theoretically impossible, but it had been *working*. Despite every spellbook's insistence that the dead were forever beyond the veil, Cecily had found ways to channel power into her memories of Caroline that seemed to call her back, albeit piece by piece. One day, her soul would have slipped through and stood in the room with Cecily, spoken to her through the frame.

But now…

Staring at the place where Caroline's heart should be, Cecily has a sudden, savage urge to tear it out of Roy's chest.

But when she imagines him without it—without the life that fills his wide grey eyes and cautious smiles and stubborn jaw—she feels as lost as she does staring at the broken spell.

Then a glitter catches her eye from the base of the frame. There are grains of clear crystal salt suspended in the spell like dew in a spider's web. Salt and fine flecks of black pepper.

Cecily hasn't kept anything in her kitchen for years, having no use for it. But unbidden the memory of Roy's cooking rises in her mind, the crunch of salt on her teeth and the mild bite of pepper on her tongue.

She straightens up with a strange mix of hope and apprehension. If Roy took something from the frame, perhaps he is also the key to putting it back together.

His energy. His sweetness.

If he stirs something in her that she has not felt for years, perhaps he can do the same for her spell.

❁❁❁

Cecily doesn't have an abundance of experience with horses. In general, animals regard her with vague distrust, sensing more of her magic than humans do. Accordingly, she avoids animals with the capacity to hurt her if they ever decided to kick.

With a cowboy in the house, she might have known it was only a matter of time before she had to grow used to them. As soon as Roy realizes how near they are to the oceanside, he insists that they should borrow a cart and horse from the village and drive out to the shore one day.

He is almost certainly recovered enough to return to his other life. This should be the moment when Cecily scoffs at his appealing eyes and casts him from her house.

Instead, they go to the coast.

She has to admit, the wind pulling past them as they drive through dry gold fields and evergreen trees is a delightful sensation. The pine-scented breeze is determined to drag her hair from its braid.

Roy ties up the horse when they reach the shore and immediately gets to work building a circle of rocks in which to house a bonfire. He's brought a heavy pot and a kettle to cook with, and more food than Cecily thinks they can eat.

Cecily stands and looks out at the ocean stretching away before her. There are few things in the world that make her feel small, but the expanse of the water and sky is one, the thick clouds rolling over the horizon.

"Could you find a good log for sitting on?" Roy calls.

"I've never encountered a comfortable log," Cecily retorts, but she walks up the beach, the sand tugging at her heels, and soon locates a suitable log, which she persuades to slide back to the fireside with her.

"Perfect," Roy says, with a grin. "I've wanted to sit and watch the sunset on this beach ever since I heard about it. Mary said it's the best view in the world."

Looking at him, Cecily can't quite bring herself to agree.

He gets the fire blazing and then smoldering gently, and then starts to cook, grilling bread with garlic and tomatoes for a snack and barbecuing a chicken over the flames. He slices and skewers vegetables from the village, roasting them until they soften and char. The air fills with the smells of wood smoke, chicken fat, the vegetables cooking earthy and sweet.

Cecily perches on the log, impatient not so much for their lunch as she is for Roy to join her. She is beginning to find his attention woefully gratifying.

He pops the cork out of a bottle of wine and pours it into a pair of glasses.

"Do you think you're supposed to drink wine on the beach?" he asks.

"I don't think anyone could argue with the idea if they saw us now."

"No." Roy presses slightly against her side and tips his head back to meet her eyes, grinning from under the brim of his hat. "They sure couldn't."

Cecily has put up with quite a bit from him in the last week, but by far his most unbearable trait is the way he makes eyes at her, usually from a distance. Tempting, but remote.

And now here he is, inches away, and she finds she has absolutely nothing to do but kiss him.

Roy goes quite still as soon as her mouth presses to his, and then cautiously leans forward, the tip of his nose brushing hers as he catches her lower lip between his.

"Wanted to do that since I first saw you," he says softly.

"Yes, I noticed."

Cecily plants another kiss at the corner of his mouth, savoring the way he turns hungrily toward her, his lips parting.

Instead of indulging his desire to kiss her, she presses her mouth to his jaw, peppering kisses down to his neck.

His eyes are especially owlish when she draws back.

"If you keep doing that," he murmurs, "I'll never even get to see the sun set."

"Is that a challenge?"

"It's a surrender, ma'am."

Cecily snorts. "I'm starting to think you mean something far less polite when you call me *ma'am*."

His blush is answer enough.

Cecily isn't quite sure of what she's doing—only of what she wants; despite the vague guilt that she is kissing him while the spell hangs broken in her attic, waiting to be restored, the feeling of *wanting* someone again is so delightful, so unexpected, that she finds it impossible to resist.

They finish the wine and the feast and wait for sunset, and Cecily can't help leaning over every few moments to remind herself of how his skin tastes. He shivers every time she noses at his neck, presses her mouth to the precious heartbeat in his throat. The evening is cold, but it doesn't occur to Cecily to spin a spell for warmth when Roy is right there, ready to heat her fingers with the skin just beneath his shirt. When her cheeks and nose grow cold, she presses them into the crook of his neck.

He retaliates by sliding shy fingers under her skirts, warming his hands on her bare, soft legs.

The horizon turns orange and pink and gold and spills down into the water, draining itself into the sea until the sky turns black and bright with stars. And by then they're back in the cart, driving slowly home in the gathering dark with a host of bobbing witchlights to illuminate the horse's way.

❀❀❀

Cecily pulls Roy's hat from his head the moment they step through the front door, tossing it to the floor and pulling him into a far more thorough kiss.

Roy sways, wrapping his arms around her waist and letting her command the kiss, eager but yielding. Cecily cradles his face in her hands, intolerably charmed by the way he rises on his toes to follow her movements, holding each kiss for a moment longer than she would, like he finds it hard to draw away. God knows she does. But even more than this, she wants to be closer to him, to hear more of the gentle hitching moans that catch in his throat when she paws at the buttons on his vest.

"Come to bed with me," she whispers.

Roy gasps against her mouth. "Yes, ma'am."

She takes his hand and leads him back to the bedroom, to the white sheets that have felt empty for years. She pitches him onto the bed, and he claws off his coat and vest, fumbling with his shirt. Cecily leans back to undo the collar of her dress and his eyes follow her, curious and craving.

"Can I ask you to do something for me?" Roy says, his voice hushed in the near-dark.

"Yes?"

"Can you tell me you'll always see me for who I am?"

Cecily pauses in the midst of taking her hair down. "Of course." She lets her hands fall to his hips, tracing their outline in the dark. "You see me for who I am."

"I surely do. The most beautiful woman in the world."

Cecily tuts, pressing her fingers up beneath his shirt and undoing the lowest button.

"I mean it."

"I know you do." It would be hard to doubt the sincerity in his eyes.

"Can I tell you something else?" he asks, breathing shaky as she opens his shirt.

"I don't know why you feel the need to ask permission."

"Just don't want to spoil the mood with all my talking."

Cecily gives him a look. "I don't mind talking. I'm not going to bed with a sack of flour."

He blushes and smiles bravely at her. "Well, I wouldn't know. I wouldn't know what spoils the mood, I mean."

It dawns on her what he means. "You've never been with anyone."

"No. There was no chance." When she's silent, momentarily stunned by the revelation that she is to be his first, and responsible for making sure he enjoys it, Roy looks nervous and goes on: "Mind you, I thought about it. I know some of the boys I worked with years ago would sleep in each other's tents. And I wouldn't have minded joining them, except..."

Except for the fear, Cecily thinks. "Well," she murmurs, "I think you'll find it isn't really so difficult." She brushes her fingertips over the closings of his trousers. "May I show you?"

"*God*, yes."

Cecily tangles his legs up around her shoulders, his thighs thick and strong from squeezing the saddle. She leans in and he's breathing hard even before she takes him into her mouth. She licks him over till he's whining through his teeth, gripping fistfuls of the sheets and rolling his head back. Then she stops to hear him gasp for the loss of it. It's been a long time since Cecily felt so merciless, or so pleased. She leans up to press kisses all over his belly, sliding her fingers between his legs instead, drawing with her fingertips wide and teasing circles around his tender flesh. He trembles under her mouth, his own mouth gone slack, throat working with each helpless noise he makes.

"Oh, *Cecily*—"

Cecily smiles against his stomach. "Would you like me to let you finish, darling?"

Roy gives a wild, breathless laugh. "Yes, ma'am."

Cecily shoulders his thighs apart and pins them open under her hands, sinking her mouth down on him again and persisting, this time, until he bucks and cries out and comes for her. She runs her palms over his legs, chasing the shivers that run through them.

"Oh, Lord." Roy reaches for her and she goes to him, curling into the crook of his arm and walking her fingers down his chest. Roy beams at her, wide-eyed, sweat curling the hair that hangs over his brow, and Cecily doesn't think she can bear how sweet he is.

"You called me darling," he says.

"I didn't think you'd mind."

"I don't." He wraps a hand around the back of her neck and kisses her warmly, and Cecily lets herself fall into it. "But can I call you the same?"

"I suppose," she drawls, and he grins against her mouth.

Though he apologizes preemptively for his lack of experience, Cecily finds only more that she enjoys about him when he reciprocates the attention. He kisses all over her thighs with worshipful care, touching her with gentle and eager hands, and—damn him—brings a flush to her face and sets her heart pounding as it hasn't in years. And then he goes down on her. If his shoulders are shaking and his mouth a little clumsy, well, it doesn't really make a difference; what matters is that it's him, and that he is marvelously enthusiastic about pleasing her, and that by the time she comes, Cecily is utterly senseless.

Roy climbs into bed, looking quite satisfied with himself, and Cecily grabs him, kisses him, and rolls him over so that she can rest her head on his chest. Roy's hands find her hair, stroking it out and coiling it around his fingers as the two of them breathe.

"Darling," he murmurs.

As the clamor of Cecily's heart recedes, she becomes aware of the sound of his heartbeat where it knocks against her ear—the familiar steely click, the rhythm as patient as a ticking clock.

Guilt coils with satisfaction in a heavy tide that washes over her until she falls asleep.

Chapter Six

Roy has odd dreams that night, where he's replanting the garden outside Cecily's house, vividly aware of the sweat trickling down his back as he digs up weeds and leaves new seeds to grow in the tilled earth. The garden is flourishing, crops and flowers growing almost as quickly as he can plant them, sprouts bursting from the rich brown dirt and unfurling as he watches. Kids from Rockaway are scrambling along the outside of the fence, calling out to the witch's boy.

Roy straightens up from a bed of roses and sees Cecily smiling at him from the front porch, and he smiles back, so in love with her he can hardly speak.

He blushes scarlet when she wakes him, concerned over his twisting around in his sleep.

Cecily spends the morning working on a pair of prosthetic feet while Roy cooks breakfast and brews a couple mugs of tea. She seems content, peace in her eyes that he's never seen before.

She smiles when he sets her tea in front of her, thanks him in a murmur. But when she takes a sip, she frowns.

"Something wrong?" Roy asks.

"No," she says. "Strong, with lemon and sugar."

"Just how you like it," Roy agrees. Then he freezes. "How'd I know that?"

He could've guessed that Cecily would like her tea strong, but it hadn't been a guess. More like a certainty.

Cecily hesitates, and he can see she's unsettled too. "It may be the house," she says vaguely. "Memories can be… animated by magic."

Roy chews on that, and his dream from the night before, while he watches her work.

"I hope you didn't overexert yourself last night," Cecily says. Roy blushes, speechless, and Cecily glances languidly at him. "I was thinking we might…discuss things further. About your stay here. Perhaps over dinner."

"Yes, ma'am."

Cecily shoots him a heavy-lidded look and rises from her chair, bundling the prosthetic feet into her basket. "In that case, I will see you tonight, Mr. Jones."

She slips out, back to the workshop. Roy runs his hands down his legs, flushed with joy.

❀❀❀

He's energized, restless. *Hopeful* like he hasn't been in years. He wanders out into the garden, intending to take stock of which plants used to be growing there and whether any of them can be saved.

He bends over a row of soil where he remembers flowers growing in his dream. And there he feels a *tug*.

Without meaning to, he straightens up and looks toward the attic.

Strange how he's never seen stairs leading to it.

He goes inside, feeling odd, like he's still dreaming. He means to make another cup of tea, but instead he finds himself searching. He wanders down a hallway he'd previously only glanced down and finds a ladder set into the wall. It leads up to a door in the ceiling.

He looks at it dubiously. Even after their night together, he doesn't like the idea of sticking his nose into a part of the house he's never been invited to.

But then—

It's like his whole body is plucked like a string, a shiver and a *pull* that runs through him.

Before he knows what he's doing, he's stepped forward and put a foot on the bottom rung. Whatever the feeling is, it keeps prickling in his chest, not so much dangerous as inviting.

Roy hesitates again as he reaches up for a handhold, but it feels like a futile effort; the way he's being strummed is hard to ignore, hard to even think through. He pulls himself up, hand over hand. At the top of the ladder, he braces his shoulder against the trapdoor and pushes it open.

He emerges into the low attic he'd seen from outside. It's even more barren than the rest of the house, except for what looks like a large, thin picture frame resting against the far wall. For a moment, he thinks it's a mirror because there's a glassy, swimming quality to the air inside the frame. There are things hanging inside it, suspended on threads of magic—feathers and stones and baubles, swaying stiffly with the movement of the air like flies caught in a spider web. There's a hole blown through the center of the web, a place where the threads are loose and drifting in the absence of something. As he approaches, he realizes that the frame itself is stitched mostly of leather and cloth, bare wood showing through in a few places.

Near the top left corner, at chest height, he recognizes a familiar embroidered white star. He reaches out and brushes his thumb over the embroidery.

Fire lances up his arm.

Roy yelps, paralyzed like a man struck still by lightning as a burning energy seethes through his bones, up into his shoulder and spilling into his chest, ragged and seeking and hungry for—

His heart gives a painful lurch in his chest. Roy wrenches himself away, falling and scrambling backwards across the floor, but the broken threads in the cobweb frame are surging up, billowing in the air, glass-bright.

They descend on him faster than he can move. They seize at his chest, driving like hot knives between his ribs and grasping for his heart, tearing at it like they mean to rip it right out of him.

Roy screams.

"Cecily! *Cecily!*"

Chapter Seven

Cecily feels the shiver that runs through the spell-frame like a sudden chill, gripping her with cold delight in the middle of a hot street in Austin.

In all the five years since Cecily began weaving that spell, she has never felt anything like it—a *stirring*.

She spins around and hikes up her skirts, racing down the street toward the workshop. There's no reason why the frame should wake, certainly not now that she has left it without a heart, without a focusing energy. Unless, somehow, something else is giving it power.

A ghost? Or someone else, whose energy is the same?

She throws the door of her workshop closed behind her and whirls to face it, drawing on the energy of the frame—which is surging, *bursting*—to anchor her spell.

When she yanks the door back open, it opens onto the attic.

It opens to Roy screaming her name.

He's on the floor in front of the frame, thrashing in the midst of so much feral magic she can hardly see him. The broken threads of the spell have wrapped around him in a mass of clutching limbs, and she can feel the anchor of their focus, the single point, the heart stolen from the frame and placed in his chest.

"*Roy!*"

"Cecily!" Roy howls, clawing at the floor and trying to drag himself toward her. Cecily lunges into the midst of the surging energy, and it feels like plunging underwater. The spell is cold and thick in the air and lashes at her skin, throwing her to her knees.

She crawls to Roy and seizes hold of him, pulling him into her arms. She throws out her hand and carves signs into the air, severing spells to break the threads and release him.

She feels Roy slump suddenly as he's freed.

"Christ Almighty," he gasps in a voice wild with fear. "Cecily, what in Hell was —"

She doesn't hear any more. Because the next time she breathes in, she tastes cinnamon. She hears the breath of a sigh, a remembered sound that had once brushed against her ear. Lifting her eyes, she sees a shadow taking shape before the frame. A body stretching itself free of the spell, broken threads bound to its arms and legs, blurring at its edges like a reflection on rippling water. Its outline nearly breaks before snapping back into the shape of limbs and torso, shoulders and head. In the face, there are eyes almost too dark to make out, there and gone again as the shadow trembles.

But in a fleeting moment, Cecily meets the shadow's eyes and knows them. And as it takes a step forward, she recognizes a dozen things at once, all flickering into view for a second: golden hair, shirt buttons gleaming, sarcastic mouth, fine nose, freckled cheeks, fingernails with the sheen of pearl.

Appearing, then vanishing, as if this were a glimpse of Caroline at the bottom of a deep, dark, river, her face caught only by a shivering beam of sunlight that glanced momentarily through the water.

"Darling?" Cecily whispers.

The shadow stretches a trembling hand toward her, and Cecily reaches back, ignoring Roy's startled protest. The shadow moves slowly closer, pulling itself further outside the frame with obvious effort.

"Caroline," Cecily manages, her throat dry. "Is that you?"

The shadow whispers, *Yes, my love.*

A drop of sorrow lands in Cecily's chest and spreads like an ink stain, gutting her before her mind even recognizes what's wrong.

She knows those words, far too well. She has heard them ringing in her memory for years, the same exact tone, the same inflection. It is Caroline's voice, but old and stale. Like wind blowing through a canyon that just happens to sound like singing.

It isn't real.

Still, she cannot lower her hand. The shadow reaches out to her, and she expects its fingers to pass right through her palm.

Instead, it seizes her.

Her whole body lights up as if a spark was struck inside her lungs, all the air in her body—all the power—suddenly burning, being dragged out of her through the connection to the shadow. It is drawing from her, draining her. Cecily shrieks with alarm as she tries to pull her hand from its grip and finds her arm lifeless. She feels its attention turning from her, the power in her veins surging away to fuel it as the shadow turns toward Roy.

Toward the heart. The heart, which is its sole desire.

"Cecily!" Roy screams, seeing her caught by the shadow. He lunges to his feet and starts to leap forward, ready to throw himself into the spell. Cecily summons what power remains in her body and calls a gust of wind that knocks him back across the floor.

"Run!" Tears of effort streak down her face as she struggles to resist the draining of her power, fully aware that it will not stop until it has taken her life. "It will kill you for the heart! Run, now—to Austin, and keep running—"

But Roy picks himself up and sprints not for the ladder, but for the frame. He dives past Cecily and the shadow, seizes the frame in both hands, and swings it against the sharp edge of the window frame.

The frame folds in half, timber splintered and bent, and the spell comes free of its moorings. But the energy that has bound the components in the frame together for years, the energy Cecily poured into it, still twists through the broken frame. It sucks the shadow back into itself, releasing Cecily, and rises in a hungry cloud above Roy, wild and warped, now nothing but a ravenous thing in search of a heart.

Cecily throws out her hands as it descends upon Roy and makes fire.

The spell lets out a terrible wailing, smoke pouring from leather and bones as they shrivel, fire consuming every inch of the frame. *Caroline.* Cecily feels the smoke and the terrible heat in her own lungs and wonders if she's going to burn too. She feels the moment when the spell gives in to the flames, its energy bursting and dispersing, the threads flailing like the limbs of a tortured marionette.

It feels like a blade lodged in her chest.

The frame blackens and crumbles and collapses into dust, the threads breaking and going limp, and Cecily sobs and sobs and sobs.

❀❀❀

It takes Roy a long time to get Cecily down from the attic. For a while he sits beside her while she weeps into his chest, while he wraps his shaking arms around her and strokes her hair. When her tears run dry, she stays in his arms, silent and clutching the back of his shirt.

The ashes of the frame drift through the air around them, stirred by leftover heat and an energy that Roy can feel, an aimless power with no more purpose than dying embers. The attic reeks of charred leather and bone.

Caroline. He knows little of magic, but enough to know that whatever came from the frame was not Cecily's lover.

At least not anymore.

Roy wants to get her away from the wreckage.

He coaxes her downstairs slowly. She moves like a ghost, not speaking, her eyes elsewhere. He takes her to her bed, and she folds herself under the blankets, quietly curling over away from him.

He pauses there, trying to find a word to say to comfort her, but before he can open his mouth, she whispers, "Please go."

He sees himself out.

He sits out on the sofa and watches the sun go down. Yesterday he would have been bold enough to ask her to watch it with him.

Eventually he finds a blanket in the cupboard and lies down on the couch, but sleep evades him for hours, and when he does finally fall unconscious, he dreams about fire.

❀❀❀

When he wakes up the next morning, the smell of foul smoke from the attic has spread to the rest of the house.

Roy hauls himself up, rubbing at his heart through his chest, grateful for its steady ticking. He throws open the windows and props the door open, letting in fresh air.

He makes breakfast, though he can't bring himself to eat more than a nibble of bread. He makes tea, strong, with lemon. He piles it all on a tray.

Then he goes to check on Cecily.

His heart jumps into his throat when he sees her already conscious, albeit contemplating the ceiling. Her eyes flick towards him when he comes in, and Roy ducks his head, wishing he had a hat to hide his eyes. He walks forward, slides the tray onto her bedside table.

Cecily's voice is rusty. "What's this?"

"Breakfast."

She gives a little nod. "Thank you."

She makes no move to touch it.

"You should eat something," Roy says, staring at the floor. He has a terrible feeling that she won't be able to forgive him for causing the loss of whatever was inside the frame.

And if she doesn't, at least he wants to leave her looking better than she does now. She looks half-dead, and the thought of her wasting away alone hurts more than the idea of her telling him to leave.

"I'll eat later," she says, distantly.

"Now."

Cecily gives him a startled glare. "What?"

"You've got to be hungry. You've been sleeping the better part of a day." He bumps his hip against the tray gently. "I'll leave if you have something to eat."

Cecily frowns, but she slowly levers herself into a sitting position. Roy slides the tray into her lap, and watches as she picks up a fork, wincing with each shift.

"Cecily? Are you hurt?"

She lets out a breath. "I am very, very tired. And nearly had the life torn out of me." She glances sidelong at him, her lips pressed tight together. "Oh, sit down. I can't tell you to leave, even if I should. For your sake."

Roy sinks onto the edge of the bed, watching her.

"Was that thing trying to hurt us?" he asks.

"No. But it *would* have killed you."

"What was it?"

"A spell. My own." She looks desolate, in her quiet, bitter way.

"I'm sorry," Roy mumbles. "It was important, wasn't it?"

"Not as important as I thought it was." She wraps her hands around the mug of tea, and when tears roll down her face, she doesn't try to wipe them away.

"That heart in your chest belonged to Caroline," she says. Roy glances down involuntarily. "It was the only part of her they brought back to me. She was visiting her family, trying to reconcile with them. Some part of the spell gave; her heart stopped." Cecily sucks in a sharp breath. "I wasn't with her when she died. Her family buried her. They didn't want the heart to go into the grave with her. They thought it was ungodly, like the way she loved me. So they buried her body and they brought the heart to me." Her mouth twists.

"I repaired her heart. And then I built that spell around it, thinking I could bring her back. And of course every treatise and spellbook I could find said it was impossible, but I couldn't believe that." Roy reaches over to grip one of her hands as she talks; her fingers tremble, then lace tightly with his. "The frame was made of things that called to mind her memory. I knew something would resonate with the heart if it stirred me to remember something particular about her. And with each piece, it grew stronger and easier to remember."

She squeezes his hand, tight enough to hurt. "But that's just it. The more I built it on the back of my memories, the stronger my memories were. Until they felt real. Until they were standing in the room with me. Until I could almost have made something that looked and smelled and sounded like her. I was never bringing her back. I was trying to recreate her. I was making a thing that would never have been *my* Caroline. I knew it at the moment I stepped into the attic. The spirit in it wasn't her. It was *me*. And it wanted your heart because I taught it to."

Roy rubs his fingers over the back of her hand and tries to swallow around the lump in his throat. "I'm so sorry, darling."

"You could have died, Roy." She almost looks at him then, her eyes damp and weary. "I nearly killed you."

"Cecily, I wouldn't be here anyway without you. Or without her." What ache there is in his chest is for her. "And

I'll stay here and help you for as long as it takes to get you back on your feet."

"It might be some time. I've never been so tired."

"Either way, I'll stay. So long as you want me to."

Her jaw tenses, and fresh tears gather in her eyes before she dashes them away. "I do want you to stay," Cecily says.

Roy lets out a breath of pure relief and presses a kiss to the back of her hand.

"In that case," he says, "you won't mind me giving you a little advice."

"Oh…won't I?"

"You won't. It's my ma's advice. Eat your breakfast. Nothing in the world can't be helped by breakfast."

Cecily makes a strangled noise that might be a laugh.

"Come on, now. Drink your tea."

"I said you could *stay*," she says, faintly smiling. "I didn't say you could give me orders."

"Just friendly advice," Roy says.

Cecily wipes her eyes on her sleeve, picking up her fork. "I wish it didn't smell like smoke down here," she murmurs.

"I'm airing it out. But all the ash upstairs ought to go."

"I'll take care of it once I can stand."

Roy frowns. "What do you think I'm here for? I'll take care of it. And when you're feeling a little better, I'll get you out on the porch so you can smell the fresh air—and all those flowers they've planted for you."

Cecily glances at him, startled, and then her eyes soften. "Yes."

Sad Queer Characters and the Revolution of Joy

AUSTIN CHANT

I want to talk about *Brokeback Mountain*—but more on that in a minute.

When I was growing up, there was no "reading queer literature" as far as I knew. Every so often I would come across a story with a minor gay character in it, or—more commonly—a cartoonish villain who read as a caricature of a queer person. Gender nonconformity and queer desire were shorthand for deviancy and corruption. This feeling of queerness being freaky and wrong and tragic even permeated many ostensibly LGBT-friendly stories I read as a young person.

I *loved* all those sad queer characters, because even early on I could recognize that I had something in common with them. But I'd be lying if those characters didn't make me believe some terrible things about myself. Picture a child feeling like he has more in common with campy Disney villains than Disney heroes. That's what happens when the only examples of fictional queer people are evil, tragic, dead, played for laughs, or simply treated as unworthy of having their stories told. It doesn't lead you to expect that you, a little queer kid, are a good person. And what kind of a future can you expect to have when people like you are vanquished by the heroes at the end of the story? When happy endings are for other people?

Which brings me to *Brokeback Mountain*. I love *Brokeback Mountain*, but I wish it were a romance novel. Or at least I wish there had existed, in 2005, a popular romance equivalent. Because when I first watched the adaptation, I was still young enough that it was dazzling to see any film where two guys kissed, let alone one that depicted such an intense, passionate, romantic love between a same-gender couple. But as I watched the film, I grew afraid.

I wanted so much for it to *not* be a tragedy, but I knew it was going to be. Because that was what queer stories were to me: stories of deviance being punished, stories of unrequited love, homophobic abuse, transphobic violence, death, tragedy, death. And I didn't want another story like that. I didn't want something about the evils of the human condition. I didn't want the murder of queer people used to prove a point about the cruelty of the world, to jerk a few tears out of the audience.

I wanted a love story. Specifically, I wanted a story that told me that I could be loved. I didn't want to watch these people suffer and die like I *always* watched the people I identified with suffer and die.

So—imagine with me—what if *Brokeback Mountain were* a romance novel? We know what would happen, right? Jack and Ennis would have their meet-cute on the mountaintop, and certainly there'd be some raunchy sex scenes, some gut-wrenching twists and turns and moments where it all seemed bleak and hopeless. But in the end, we'd see two people fall in the kind of love that lasts a lifetime, and we'd see that love triumph and find a way. We, as romance readers, would know from the start that this was a story destined to end happily. We would know with certainty that Jack and Ennis would get what they deserve: joy, forever.

I'm not saying that stories like these always end happily in real life. We know that they don't. But stories of enduring love and happiness, stories of safety and joy and recovery, are so valuable. So true. So important. And so real. Quite honestly, they are undervalued—and to me, growing up, they would have been life-changing. I didn't read queer romance as a young man, when I was questioning both gender and sexuality, but I wish I had. I wish I had picked up the kinds of books I read today.

Because when I read a queer romance novel, I know I won't be martyred at the end. I won't be left alone and heartbroken, a victim of this awful world. Instead, I'll be loved.

And that's actually pretty revolutionary. Telling different kinds of stories about queer people is revolutionary, and romance narratives are *very* different. Romance narratives promise the opposite of tragedy, and let us reclaim ourselves from stories about deviance and shame. Romance says: we deserve to be loved; we deserve to have our stories uplifted. We deserve a world where our partners respect and care for us, where we get the help we need, where we succeed in loving each other the best we can. Where we are beautiful, sexy, and desirable, and *safe*.

Here's another example. Do you know how often, since I came out as a trans man, I've had people tell me that *Boys Don't Cry* is a must-watch? In case you're unaware, *Boys Don't Cry* is a film about a trans man being murdered. What if, instead (or at least in addition), people valued and recommended stories where trans men are respected, loved, protected, and adored by their partners? Give me *Burnt Toast B&B* by Heidi Belleau and Rachel Haimowitz or *A Boy Called Cin* by Cecil Wilde or *A Matter of Disagreement* by E. E. Ottoman—all romance novels released in the past few years that have made me feel touched, blessed, and loved. These stories make me feel as though the authors see my *potential*—for love, for success, and for joy. These stories are fantasies for those of us who desperately need to dream.

If I've reached any personal conclusion, it's that we must keep reading, writing, and sharing queer romance. We must keep telling these stories. And we must keep loving and valuing each other as best we can—with our words, with our actions, and maybe most of all with books.

Romance for the Rest of Us

JESSICA BLAT

I was a voracious reader when I was growing up. I still am. However, I didn't read much romance—at most a few novels. You see, my sister went through a period where she thought she'd pursue romance writing so I read a few that she had on hand. In truth, the shirtless heroes and fainting damsels on the covers did not capture my interest much. What I inferred from that small sample as the standard formula of "Boy meets girl, girl hates boy generally for pretty good reasons, boy seduces girl, girl somehow redeems boy, end of story" seemed uninteresting at best and offensive at worst. I didn't see myself in these characters. I didn't realize there were other options in the genre. At that time—and I'm actually going to date myself here because I think the timeline is relevant—around the turn of the century, which seems ancient when you phrase it like that but actually wasn't that long ago, there really wasn't that much queer romance that I could easily have found as a kid in the suburbs.

Fast forward a few years. I was out, I was in college, and I went to the Seattle Gay and Lesbian Film Festival. They were screening a free viewing of *Tipping the Velvet*—were any of you there? Cinerama was full to capacity, mostly with lesbians. The show starts, gets to a climactic moment where our protagonist realizes she has been betrayed by her lover, and the credits roll. Almost 600 people myself included, gasp in shock. We need to know how it's going to turn out! You can't roll credits! The story has to have a happy ending; we understand that in our hearts. Turns out it was a miniseries and they did go on to play all the parts. As you might have guessed since I'm talking about this at an LGBTQ romance event, Nan, our protagonist, gets the girl. Happy ending. 600 lesbians and friends leave Cinerama elated.

That night there was also Q&A with Sarah Waters, the author of the novel they'd adapted for the screen. I don't remember most of what she said though I do remember thinking, *My god, someone is writing books like this. And they're getting turned into TV on the BBC.*

It certainly wasn't the first queer book I'd read (I did go read it after watching the movie), but it was one of the first where the protagonist didn't die or have some other tragic ending even if things were a bit dicey in the middle. And that's really the magic of romance, after all, right? The key genre definition: it must have a happily ever after, or at least a happy for now, which is what makes it so powerful.

Watching the explosion in the last few years of LGBTQ romance has, to me, been watching the growing acceptance that we can have happy ending too. As the genre (and our society) has matured in recent years, we're also seeing that those happy endings don't necessarily have to be in spite of being LGBTQ. In other words, we're not quite there yet, but I'm looking forward to gayness as a source of underlying conflict driving the will-they-won't-they—either due to internalized fears or external homophobia—being entirely relegated to historical romance.

And I'm thrilled for the kids of today and tomorrow that, thanks in part to many of the people in this room, they'll be able to find so many more kinds of romance than I did as a youth in the suburbs: romance not precisely confined to exactly one shirtless guy and exactly one fainting damsel.

Thank you.

Sun, Moon, and Stars

E.J. Russell

Chapter One

Just. Bloody. Marvelous.

Ever since he'd gotten assigned to the northern circuit, the bridge to Corvel-on-Byrne had been a pain in Zal's arse. He'd had to slap a new reinforcement spell on its rickety span every time he passed through on his rounds. Sun magic never lasted long over water, but that wasn't the problem today.

A boulder the size of his cottage now stood where the bridge used to be, sending the river off-course to eat away at its banks. One more blasted thing for him to deal with before he could finally leave off traveling and return home for his annual respite. He'd be lucky if he made it halfway there before the winter storms roared in from beyond the mountains.

Why anybody would choose to live this far north was beyond him.

He sighed, shrugged his pack off his back, shed his cloak and coat, and prepared to rebuild the bridge. Even if the present emergency hadn't called him to Corvel-on-Byrne, the river-locked village at the base of Star Mountain, he could hardly leave its citizens without a way to escape their homes all winter.

Zal planted his staff with its captive Sun Stone into the earth on the river bank. Grasped the handle and called on the Sun, its size, its strength, its irresistible pull, to convince the boulder to rise from its landing spot. The glow of the Stone bathed the river bank, a sunrise contained in the amber rock the size of his two fists.

He clenched his teeth, muscles straining. Although Sun and Stone delivered the power, the mage had to control it. And that boulder was heavy, unwilling to leave its new home in the river bed. As it rose in the air, Zal saw why: the base of it was easily three times the size of the top, the part that had shown over the water. He was lifting something the size of the House of Mages.

He gave one last mental shove, levitating the boulder until it was safely away from the river, and let it drop. He'd intended to move it beyond the fields, rough with stubble from the harvest and already rimed with frost, but without stronger sunlight to power his stone, he couldn't manage it.

I'll come back early in spring, when the Sun is on the ascendant. Move it before first planting. It meant he'd have to cut his respite short, but there wasn't much to do about that now. He needed to conserve enough power to remake the bridge.

Luckily, that took less time, since the villagers kept a goodly supply of replacement slats and coils of rope on the far bank. Zal used up the whole lot, but at least the bridge was back, and the villagers could spend their fierce, interminable winter replenishing the stock.

Zal walked across the bridge and through the outlying fields, passing a few of the citizens about their end-of-season tasks.

The streets of the village were busy enough. Here and there among the brown-skinned earth-born, he caught a glimpse of darker skin like his own. Unusual for a sun-born to venture this far north. None of his people appreciated the cold.

He strode down the muddy main street, past citizens bustling about their business as if the mountain hadn't exploded over their heads not a fortnight ago. As he approached the town hall, the village reeves hurried out to meet him. The man, Barkon, outpaced Netta, the women's representative, as he always did. Zal was surprised the men of the town didn't elect a different reeve, one who wasn't so nervous.

"Magister, thank the Earth you've come." Barkon panted to a stop in front of Zal, wringing his hands. "We have a...a situation."

"I'm aware of that, Elder. That's why I'm here." Zal gestured to the top of Star Mountain—or rather, to where the top of Star Mountain had been until something had blown it away.

"Yes, yes. But this is a *real* emergency."

"What Barkon means," Netta drawled, dusting her hands on her breeks, "is that this affects him personally. So it must be more important."

Barkon scowled at her. "That's not the point. If the mountain decides to fall on us, how can we stop it? It will fall or not, no matter what we do. But this other problem is right here, in our village, in our *hall*."

Zal glanced between them. Barkon avoided looking at Zal's face, as the sight of the eye-patch apparently made him even more nervous. He always focused his attention on Zal's collar-bone. Netta at least met Zal's single-bored gaze but didn't offer any clarification.

"Suppose you tell me of this situation, then."

Barkon swallowed audibly, his throat working behind his collar of office. "After the...the event on the mountain, the next day, we found a...a person. On the river bank."

Zal's attention sharpened. "Someone was caught by the river when that boulder came down? Were they injured? Sun and stars, man, where are they? You stand here, whining in the street when—"

"Peace, Magister." Netta showed her palms. "No one in the village was hurt. This person is a stranger. We suspect he came from the mountain."

Zal blinked. "A star-born? Here?"

Netta's brows drew together. "Not a star-born, no, although who can tell? Nobody's ever seen one that I can remember."

"Then what? Earth-born, sun-born?"

She shook her head, grim satisfaction in the set of her mouth. "Moon-born."

"Impossible." Zal's hand tightened on his staff. "The moon-born are gone. Dead these twenty years and more."

"Nevertheless…" She shrugged. "We found a person, not sun-born and not earth-born, naked on the river bank."

"Naked? In this weather?"

"Well, mostly naked. I wouldn't call what he was wearing appropriate for a dash to the privy, let alone a swim in the river."

"Where is he then? I should examine him. Treat him for exposure—"

Barkon licked his lips and jerked his head toward the hall. "She's in the cellar. In the gaol."

Zal frowned. "'She'? Netta said 'he.'"

"Yes, well, there's the issue. We have a bit of a disagreement on that point."

"How long," Zal tighted his hand on his staff to keep from throttling Barkon, "has the *person* been in gaol?"

"Since…ah…since we found her." Barkon pulled at his collar. "The day after the explosion."

Zal's sun-driven rage began to build, a burn in his belly. "You've kept him—"

"It's not a him," Barkon insisted.

"Then you've kept her—"

"It's not a her," Netta said.

Zal clenched his teeth. "You've kept the person locked up underneath the town hall for a bloody fortnight? I ought to report you all for hospitality infringement."

"You don't understand, Magister. She—"

"I told you, Barkon, he's a man."

"Elders. Please. Obviously the person in your custody is two-natured." The reeves looked blank. "You've heard of the two-natured, surely?"

"Hearing is one thing, Magister," Netta said. "But seeing? We've never—"

"Apparently you have now. But let us leave the issues of sex and gender out of this discussion. It's irrelevant to your treatment of a stranger."

"Not just a stranger, Magister." Barkon tugged on his collar again. "A mage. An unregistered one. Has to be. No other way to account for the spell."

"The spell, you say? What spell?"

"Anyone who goes in there, anyone at all, gets overcome with a…well…a *need*, if you get my meaning. An urge."

"Earth and sky, Barkon, when did you turn into a stripling?" Netta crossed her arms and glared at Zal. "Whoever goes in that cell turns into a bitch in heat."

Barkon bridled. "I never—"

"You did. Your pants were around your ankles, man, your pecker in your hand. If it weren't for the bars between you, you'd have—"

"Enough." Zal thrust his staff between them before Barkon's head exploded like Star Mountain. "Regardless of the details, it sounds as if the hospitality laws aren't the only thing being violated here. Barkon, did you seriously expose yourself to a captive stranger? Did you bother to ask their leave? Give them a proper choice?"

Barkon's throat worked. "I—it was the spell, Magister. You know I would never…No one in the village would ever do such a thing."

"Much as I hate to agree with Barkon, he's right. The same thing happens to everyone. Once they're within ten feet of him—"

"Her," Barkon grumbled.

"—they're suddenly desperate to swive. Do you know how difficult it's been to keep all the apprentices out of there? We need you to take him away to prison in the capitol."

Prison if they were lucky. Zal shuddered. An unregistered mage, using sexual coercion spells? That was enough to get anyone beheaded, drawn, and quartered, in whatever order the Congress was in the mood for on judgment day.

"Right, then. Let's waste no more time." He waited, but neither Barkon nor Netta moved, both of them gazing at the muddy street. "Well? Which one of you is the gaoler?"

"The thing is, Magister..." Barkon swallowed noisily again. "We don't like to go in there because of, well—"

"He's afraid he'll have another uncontrollable *urge*. Although to be fair"— she patted her coronet of braids—"so am I."

"Very well. The key?" Zal held out his hand, and Barkon handed it over.

"Could you take him his meal?" Netta held out a burlap bag and a water skin.

"You haven't even fed them?" Zal's rage rose higher, power bleeding from his Sun Stone until his braids lifted and swirled around his torso.

"Of course we do."

"He doesn't eat much. Less lately. I think he's sickening for something."

"Did you bother to pass them a healing stone?"

This time Netta wouldn't meet his gaze. "We're...ah... running low. With several confinements coming this winter—"

Zal snatched the bag and water skin. "I expected better of you, of the whole village."

"Don't judge us until you meet her, Magister. But if I were you, I'd don your fiercest protection charms. There's not a man, woman, or child in this village—"

"Child? The adults are afraid of uncontrollable urges, and you send *children* in—"

Netta held up her hands in a placating gesture. "Stay, Magister. The children don't have the same reaction. Yes, they're drawn to him, but as if he were a kindly uncle with a bag of sweeties."

"That's what I'm worried about," Zal muttered.

He left Barkon and Netta staring one another down and stormed up the steps into the hall.

Just Zal's luck to run into another rogue mage. He'd been the one to bring in Loriah at the Congress's orders. He'd resisted. They'd grown up together, trained together, taken their oaths together. Regardless, he'd had to deliver her to the Congress of Mages and Seigneurs personally—but not before she'd half-blinded him.

Her execution was the first thing he'd seen one-eyed. It had not been pleasant. They'd ripped her Stone away—almost worse than death for a Sun mage, although her death hadn't been pleasant either. The Congressional tribunal hadn't been in a merciful mood that day.

Zal descended the stairs from the hall proper to the cellar that housed the gaol. The rough stone walls breathed damp and chill, antithetical to Zal's sun-born blood.

The chair at the bottom of the stairs, where he'd expect to find a guard, was empty.

"Cowards," Zal muttered and stomped down the short hallway to where two tiny cells were cut out of the bedrock. The one on the right was empty. He had to turn his head to compensate for his missing left eye. The cell on the left …

"Sun, moon, and stars," he breathed.

The person in the cell stood under the narrow slit of a horizontal window. They wore a ragged brown robe, an obvious cast-off from the charity box. The fabric had fallen away from their arms as they stretched them up toward the window, fingers straining for the sliver of light that was all that made it past the screen of dirt and weeds.

Even in the near-dark of the cell, Zal could tell those arms were as pale as new milk.

Shite. The reeves were right.

Moon-born.

Zal's gut tightened. *I'm not qualified for this.* This was the first encounter with a moon-born mage since the Lunaria virus had swept through the population, killing every last moon-born on the continent, regardless of what anyone could do. This was a job for the Congress, not a half-blind Sun mage patrolling the arse-end of beyond.

Zal had no idea what Moon magic was like. When the plague hit, he'd been a boy, catching snatches of his parents' whispered conversation of a star-born conspiracy from his pallet under the eaves. Even afterward, no one would discuss it, as if they feared mentioning it would call down the same fate on their heads.

Sun mages specialized in healing, in counseling, in dispensing justice outside the capitol. Earth-born held no magic potential whatsoever, content with farming and government. What had the moon-born done? What magic had they wielded? At this point, they were as mysterious and unknowable as the star-born.

Zal cursed the boulder again for draining most of his reserves. If he was to face down a rogue Moon mage, he needed every trick at his disposal, every scrap of power. He'd learned, however, that what he couldn't counter with magic, he could often handle with physical intimidation. He was tall—one of the tallest of the sun-born, and they were all taller than the earth-born—broad across the chest from chopping his own firewood, lean from constantly walking the length and breadth of his circuit for ten months of every fourteen. Plus, the eye-patch made everyone uncomfortable.

"You."

The Moon mage flinched but didn't turn. Zal noticed their hair hung lank and matted, only reaching the base of their neck. Cleanliness was one thing—*the reeves could have at least allowed them a bath*—but the length was another story. Only criminals had their hair shorn. Zal's own dozens of narrow braids hung past his hips. Barkon kept his gathered in a loose-woven snood, not as tidy as Netta's plaited crown.

Had the villagers cut the mage's hair because of the alleged spell? If so, they had more to answer for than simple hospitality infringement. Only the Congress or a mage on the circuit, as the Congress's official proxy, could order a shearing, and then only after clear proof of guilt.

He steeled himself against an unwelcome surge of pity. "You have serious charges laid against you. What do you have to say?"

The Moon mage lowered their arms. Their shoulders rose and fell once, and thin fingers clutched their ragged robe as if they were gathering power for a strike.

Zal braced for attack. He'd never felt sexual desire in his life, but what if Moon magic was stronger than his will? If he were overcome by the spell—if he broke the vows he made when he took up his Sun Stone—he'd lose more than his reputation.

He'd lose his life.

Chapter Two

The man looming outside the cell was enormous. He was taller than any of the Infomancers or Lab assistants and easily twice Torian's breadth, even accounting for the bulk of his sheepskin vest and heavy, fur-lined cloak. The shivers that had chased across Torian's skin since the moment they'd stepped out of the Lab—woefully underdressed for the climate, despite the meteorological data at their disposal—increased exponentially at the promise of the warmth inherent in those garments.

They recognized the man as what the Infomancers called the J-4 strain. The planetary subjects called it sunborn. Dark skin, dark eyes. Black hair braided close to his scalp, dozens of finger-narrow plaits falling to below his waist. Square jaw—smooth, of course. The originators had engineered all subjects to be beardless.

He held a wooden staff. *Oak-equivalent, heartwood, twenty-seven point three cycles old*, according to the cybertronic sensors threaded along Torian's veins. The huge chunk of amber chrysocite contained in the cradle at the top of the staff identified him as a solar energy manipulator.

A mage. Higher in status than anyone else in this primitive habitation. None of them had been any use at all. Perhaps this man would be able to help. To get Torian away from the Laboratory and its chaos before the Infomancers noticed Torian was gone and mounted a recovery operation.

This helplessness was intolerable. If Torian had been allowed even an hour to charge their power grid in the sun, this prison would have been laughably inadequate. But Torian had lost consciousness after fighting free of the icy river. They had awoken after full dark, a captive in this dreadful hole. With no artificial lights to provide even a glimmer of power, Torian was close to emergency shut-down.

If Torian didn't act quickly, they would have insufficient power to drive their body enhancement modules and convince the mage that they could fulfill his needs. Contingent, of course, on release from this cage.

They studied the mage, who glared balefully out of his single eye, but could get no sexual preference read at all. He registered as null on their sensor array. *Why can't I read this one? Is it because he is a mage?* Or perhaps it was nothing more sinister than Torian's lamentable lack of reserves.

Very well, then. As the Infomancers told the Lab assistants, nothing can be verified without experimentation. Frame your question. Test your hypothesis. Reframe the question. Test again.

Torian could apply their methods here, although as always, they shrank from the subterfuge of the enhancement modules. Male, female, balanced—all three were intrinsic to their nature without the need of additional programming. But the Infomancers had installed the modules anyway, claiming it was for Torian's benefit, so they wouldn't slip and adopt an unsuitable aspect.

Very well. In the absence of better data, they would begin with the default. *If male, then female.*

"Well?" The mage's voice was deep, as befit the barrel chest.

Torian activated the female module. The changes were subtle. Attitude, posture, presentation. They looked up from under their lashes as they'd learned to do when servicing the Infomancers who preferred the female in manner. They could manufacture few of the supporting pheromones any longer, not without a recharge, but they'd found that most males seeking a female didn't require much in the way of enticement.

Not so with the mage. He glared at them, but seemed angry as opposed to aroused.

"What are you playing at?"

Not the default, then. They reversed the polarity to male, standing straighter, shoulders back, meeting the mage's eye without any overt subservience. The Infomancers who sought male sexual partners typically preferred stronger, less pliant behavior. It gave them something to subdue and added to their illusion of superiority.

Since the mage looked strong enough to break Torian in two should he choose, the need to pretend physical inferiority was clearly moot. Torian felt a small frisson of fear before they damped down their feedback circuits. No Infomancers had ever damaged them beyond the odd bruise or two. They were too valuable a resource. This man, though, had no such restriction.

Nevertheless, if the mage was a means of escape from the Infomancers, Torian was ready to take the chance.

They raised their chin and smiled, forcing the last of the pheromone enhancement from their depleted backup stores.

It did no good. The mage still glared.

"I see why the reeves couldn't agree on your nature. What are you?"

Torian lowered their gaze. "I can be whatever you like."

"Then I want you to be yourself. Or do you know who that is, since you seem determined to play turnabout?"

"I...I suppose I am both." Torian deactivated the module and reverted to their balanced state. "Or neither. It depends on circumstance."

"Like who you're trying to seduce into getting your way?"

The heat of a blush, the one involuntary response the Infomancers hadn't been able to program away, started at the base of Torian's throat and rose all the way to their forehead. They were mortified at being caught out but grateful for the heat.

The mage blinked. With a single eye, it looked almost like a wink, although the way the rest of his face went slack, Torian didn't mistake it for a response to their sexual overtures.

"I apologize. But you have me at a disadvantage, you realize. If you...if I...oh." Torian's knees buckled and they reached out, but missed the wall entirely.

Reserves depleted. Shut-down commencing in three... two...one.

Chapter Three

The Moon mage crumpled like a broken doll, landing gracelessly in the cell's scuffed straw.

"Shite." Zal had been so startled by their impossible presence, mesmerized by the way color rose across their skin like sunrise after a night of rain, that he'd forgotten his duty, forgotten the water skin and food still clutched in his hand.

Clearly the Moon mage—fool that Zal was, he hadn't bothered to ask for a *name* yet—was on the edge of starvation. Their face was thin to the point of gaunt, cheekbones sharply prominent, dark circles under eyes the color of storm clouds.

Ah, bugger it. Whatever Moon magic had affected the villagers had had no effect on Zal. They seemed dazed and nearly unconscious in the noisome straw. Not much of a threat.

Zal unlocked the cell and walked in, propping his staff in the corner and calling forth a low glow from the Sun Stone, just enough to see better in this miserable hole. He lifted the Moon mage, settling the dark head in the crook of his arm. He pulled the cork from the water skin with his teeth and set it to their parched lips.

"Here. Take a sip. Not too fast."

Zal needn't have made the warning. They ignored the water, focusing instead on the staff.

"Oh." They reached out a trembling hand, and for an instant, the light from the Stone seemed to flow through their long, thin fingers like honey. "Chrysocite. It emits solar power. I'd forgotten."

What in the name of the Sun were they on about now? "Listen, you—what's your name, anyway?"

"I'm called Torian."

"Torian, then. Zal here. Take a drink before I have to force it down you. You're dehydrated. I can tell."

Something else was going on with Torian too. Their life energies felt peculiar, jerking along in uneven bursts rather than flowing smoothly. After they took a few sips of water and turned away to stare avidly at the Sun Stone, Zal set the water skin on the floor. He placed two fingers on the pulse-point in Torian's wrist.

Shite! He snatched his hand away, fingers tingling. He tried the other pulse point, at the angle of the jaw, and got the same tiny jolt, oddly the same sensation as when he touched his Sun Stone directly—not that he was fool enough to do that, not unless he was dead certain it was fully depleted.

Did Moon mages carry magic in their very skin? Could Torian hold other secrets, pose other threats? They might seem no more dangerous than a half-drowned kitten right now, but wasn't helplessness the best way to lull an enemy? That ploy had certainly worked for Loriah.

Zal sighed. *So much for getting home before the storms.* He'd take Torian to the capitol, as the reeves wanted, to let the Congress of Mages and Seigneurs sort it out. That was their job, after all. His job was to deliver Torian to the tribunal for judgment.

Sun willing, he'd survive this go-round with a rogue mage without losing any more body parts.

"Can you stand?"

Torian hesitated, turning away from the staff with obvious reluctance. "I think so."

"Good. We've got a journey ahead of us. You've got to face the Congressional tribunal, explain your magic, justify using it against citizens."

"I have no magic."

"Bollocks to that. You cast your seduction spell on everyone who came near."

"But not on you."

"No. Not on me." Though not for lack of trying.

Torian nodded. "Will you be the one to take me to this tribunal?"

"Nobody else seems up to the job."

"Then I will go."

"You don't have a choice. I'm sorry about that."

They blinked luminous gray eyes, eyes all the larger because their face was so gaunt. "I see."

Zal stood and helped Torian to their feet. At least they didn't seem to be playing gender guessing games with Zal anymore.

As Zal helped Torian negotiate the stairs, he noticed they were barefoot. "Haven't you any shoes at all? Clogs? Boots? Slippers, even?"

"No. I left in rather a hurry."

"Even so, who forgets shoes?"

Torian glanced up at Zal and lifted one dark eyebrow. "Someone who's never worn them?"

"Never? Who never wears shoes? Especially in winter?"

"It wasn't an issue. The Lab is climate-controlled." Fear flickered across their face. "Or was."

"That so? Well, it's an issue now. Welcome to the edge of winter in the north."

They stepped out the hall door into the street. The instant they cleared the roof of the hall, Torian gasped and scrabbled at the neck of their robe as if they were about to strip it off.

Zal grasped their wrists, bracing himself against the zing of nearly familiar power. "Oi. None of that. You're already in a world of trouble for that kind of thing." Zal squinted at Torian's soft white hands. Was that a glint of gold under the skin?

"But..." They peered up at the pale winter sun, such longing in their face that Zal nearly relented. "Very well." They shrugged their ragged cloak back over their shoulders, but surreptitiously kept their hands out, palms up, as if to cup the watery light.

Zal released their wrists and ran a hand over his head. "Ah, bugger it. You can't make this trip barefoot and in rags."

Torian didn't respond, simply stood shivering in the muddy street, their face turned up to the wan sun, their eyes closed, and an expression as if their last, best dream had come true.

Zal spotted Barkon hovering in the lee of the blacksmith shop, Netta at his side. A gang of the village youths, boys and girls old enough for apprenticing, lurked behind the livery stable, watching Torian's every move. Zal glared at them until they dropped their gazes. *Hmmmm. Up to no good, that lot.* He gestured to the reeves, but they wouldn't come closer than a dozen yards away.

"You're taking her, then, Magister?"

Zal glanced down at Torian, who hadn't reacted to Barkon's use of pronoun. Maybe it didn't matter to them. Or maybe, as they'd said, they became whoever the other person wanted. Barkon wanted female, so Torian was *she*.

Not Zal's problem.

"I'm taking them, but not like this. They need a proper kit. Leggings, shirt, tunic, vest, cloak, boots, pack. A hat."

"But...but...we...the village stores...we can't afford—"

"Don't push me, Barkon. I've a mind to report you for hospitality violations on food, water, *and* shelter. Not to mention you deprived a citizen of choice. You know what that means."

Barkon clutched his snood. "No. Not shearing. I didn't—" He turned to Netta. "It was her, too."

Netta cast a disgusted glance at Barkon. "Give over, Magister. What were we to do? Seemed like a rogue mage to us." She peered at him from shrewd dark eyes. "Clearly you don't know what to do with 'em either."

"I know enough to feed them and keep them from dying from exposure. For that, they need clothing, and that's your duty under law."

"Much as I hate to agree with Barkon, you've caught us at a disadvantage. A lot of the citizens are decamping, heading south for the winter, in case Star Mountain decides to spew on us again. We've not got much to spare."

Zal sighed. He had no time or heart for bargaining. He swung his pack off his back. "How much?"

"We could do with some extra healing stones. As I said, we're running low and it never hurts to have spares."

"And prosperity stones," Barkon blurted. "For protection. From the mountain."

Zal dug in his pack, pulling out two of the leather scraps he kept for dispensing supplies. He wrapped up four healing stones and handed them to Netta. He glanced at Barkon, who fairly danced in place at the notion of four prosperity stones. *Not likely.* Zal wrapped a single prosperity stone and handed it over—to Netta.

"That do?"

"In a pinch." She pointed to the gang by the stable. "You, there. Farren. Morvan. I've a task for you." Two of the older apprentices slouched over, cutting a wide berth around Zal.

While she gave them low-voiced orders, Zal turned to Torian. "We'll get you sorted with some essentials. I worry about your feet, though. No boots Netta can scare up are likely to fit you. You'll likely be rubbed raw by the time we make camp every night. I can treat you then, fix them up for the next day, but during the day?" Zal shrugged. "I'm afraid it'll be brutal."

Torian lowered their chin, turning their face from sun contemplation, but Zal didn't miss the half-fearful glance at the mountain. "Will we be going away from here?"

"Aye."

"Then I'll make do."

❀❀❀

Zal didn't force the pace the first afternoon—or at least didn't think he did. But Torian was a good foot shorter than he was, still recovering from near-starvation, and unused to hard tramping, if indeed they'd ever done any at all.

The way they lifted their feet, as if the boots Netta had found were leaden weights, made their claim of having never worn shoes believable.

By the time Zal found a reasonably protected campsite in a fall of rocks that shielded them from the vicious wind, Torian was limping visibly. But they'd never complained. Not once.

Zal shed his pack and his cloak and pointed to a fallen tree. "Sit there. I'll gather wood for a fire, then see to your feet."

Torian sank down on the log. "Thank you. Can I be of assistance?"

"I don't know. Can you? Ever made a fire?"

"Of course." They struggled to their feet. "Where's the accelerant?"

"Don't know what that is, but pretty sure we don't have any. Just sit. I'll handle it." Zal unstrapped his ax from the pack and turned toward the woods.

"Wait. Are you…that is, you trust me here alone?"

"Not a matter of trust. I don't think you could move another step, not if the whole of Corvel-on-Byrne was after you with fire and pitchforks."

By the time Zal got back with a double armful of wood, Torian had removed their boots and the three pairs of socks Netta had come up with to try to make the things fit better.

Their pale, narrow feet were rubbed raw at heels, ankles, and toes. Guilt curdled in Zal's belly. After he'd given the reeves shite about cruel and unusual, he'd done the same by forcing this march.

He dropped down in front of Torian and took one foot in his hand. This time, the ping against his skin was stronger, running up his arm in a not-unpleasant way. He ignored it—*no harm so far*—and turned the poor foot this way and that, his healer's skills assessing damage, considering treatment.

Torian sucked in a breath. Zal glanced up to see them clenching their eyes shut, teeth sunk into their full lower lip.

"I'm sorry. Did I hurt you?"

"No. It's just…one of my regulars had a…a thing for my feet."

"Your regulars. What regulars?"

Torian opened their eyes, shadowed and wary now. Zal cursed the accusatory tone of his voice. "I…one of my jobs at the Lab was sex aid."

"Sex aid? You were a sex worker? Like in a Comfort House?"

"Yes. I suppose you could say that. If the Infomancers or Lab assistants required release, it was my duty to provide it."

"Your duty? Not your choice?"

"It was my job. I was compensated, like any other Lab assistant."

"Could you have gotten a different job if you'd wanted?"

"I wasn't qualified for anything else."

"So you didn't have a choice." Zal's fingers tightened on Torian's foot, and they flinched. "Shite. I'm sorry. Look, we need to talk more about this. But for now, I need to treat these wounds."

Torian nodded, hunching deeper into their oversized jerkin and dusty second-hand cloak.

Zal considered the medicines he had in his pack. Rudimentary for the most part. Magic was a marvelous thing, but sometimes it was just as good to treat a cut with a little protective salve, keep it clean, and give it time. But this wasn't one of those occasions. Not if he expected Torian to walk tomorrow.

He'd have to use his staff, despite the fact it was still depleted from moving that thrice-blasted boulder, followed by a half-day's march under heavy cloud-cover.

He handed Torian a crumbling meatroll from his pack. "Here. Eat this,while I get things ready."

"I don't really—"

"Eat it. You're nothing but bones, and you need your strength."

Torian's eyes widened at the fierceness in Zal's tone. "I'm sorry."

"Don't be. I'm not mad at *you*." But he was completely out of charity with the citizens of Corvel-on-Byrne and the Infomancers, whoever they were, in this Lab, whatever *that* was.

They'd been following the river all day, so Zal stumped down to the bank and filled both of the water skins and the cook pot, considering his options. While it was the duty of the circuit mages to serve the citizens in their jurisdictions, it was the duty of *all* mages to advance learning and to share that knowledge for the betterment of all.

Who else had had the opportunity in the last two decades to speak with a moon-born? To understand their magic? Zal had no illusions. Once he turned Torian over to the tribunal, there was little chance he'd see them again, let alone have this chance for uninterrupted conversation.

The sin of all mages was insatiable curiosity. Curiosity and, in Zal's case, a very inconvenient compassion.

When Congress had sent him to arrest Loriah, Zal had almost let her go, believing her tale of misunderstanding and persecution. Then she'd gone for his eyes, the look on her face as feral as any mad dog.

This time, he'd keep his guard well up.

Zal stalked back up the trail to the campsite and set the pot on a flat rock next to the fire to warm the water. Planting the staff so it would stand at his back, he took his place in front of Torian, his medicine kit next to him, a length of rough toweling across his lap.

Before he picked up Torian's foot again, though, he remembered to ask. "May I?"

Torian nodded, still hunched and clearly miserable.

Zal lifted one foot and wiped the raw flesh gently with lambs-wool soaked in a mild cleanser. "You know, don't you, that what you did in the village was wrong?"

"You mean trying to convince them to let me go?"

Zal stilled, the sponge resting on Torian's instep. "Is that what you were doing?"

"Of course. I needed to get away." They looked back toward the village, where the topless mountain loomed over the trees. "I still do."

"Doesn't matter, you know. Using magic that interferes with free will is illegal. Our whole society is based on the right of every citizen to choose. When you bespelled them—"

"I'm not a mage. I can't bespell anyone."

"You cast the same spell at me. Twice. It didn't work, but that doesn't make it any less unlawful."

Zal set Torian's foot on the toweling and tested the water in the pot. Warm enough. He tossed in a handful of soothing herbs to reduce the discomfort of the healing process. Rogue mage or no, Torian had had precious little pleasantness lately. "This may sting for a moment." He eased Torian's feet into the warm water, holding their ankles firmly when their feet twitched. "If you're to be able to walk tomorrow, I'll have to speed the healing with a spell."

"Isn't that illegal?" A faint note of irony laced Torian's voice. "Aren't you bespelling me?"

"Technically, I'm bespelling the water. You have the choice to remove your feet if you wish." Zal lifted his hands, nodding at the pot. "Up to you. You're the one who has to walk on them tomorrow, and we'll be on the trail for a full day rather than just a half."

"Very well."

Sulky, now, are we? Zal hid a grin. *Perhaps you're not so different from anyone else.* "Right, then." Zal focused his attention on his task, reaching for the link to the Sun.

"I'm not certain I understand the nuances, but—" Torian sucked in a breath when the Sun Stone began to glow. "Oh. Yes." The word was spoken like a prayer.

Zal circled the tip of his finger over the water, and it began to swirl, turning from clear to opaque white to gold. He murmured the healing words under his breath.

"That is…I've never…please don't stop."

Sun, moon, and stars—Torian sounded as if they were deep in the throes of lovemaking, not in the midst of medical treatment in the wilderness. If this was another attempt to ignite Zal's non-existent sex drive…

Zal glanced up, and the words of reproach died on his lips. His finger stilled, and the water stopped swirling and lost its glow, but the light didn't fade. Because the glow was *inside* Torian, illuminating them, a pattern of gold weaving under pale skin like a web of fire.

They blinked, disappointment clouding their gaze. "Oh. You've stopped."

"What *are* you? Is this what a Moon mage does? Suck up the light of the sun?"

"I'm not a mage. I told you."

Zal backed off, knocking his staff to the ground and dousing his Sun Stone. "That's for the tribunal to decide. But I warn you, I'll have to give testimony about what I've seen you do."

"I understand." The last of the gold lattice faded. They looked unhappy—who wouldn't, when faced with legal action?—but less malnourished.

Zal pretended he believed it was the meatroll, but he wasn't fooling himself. Torian had absorbed the magic from the Sun Stone, taken it in like they were *feeding* on it.

Think about it, man. Isn't that what the moon is? It had no light of its own, only reflected light stolen—or at the very least, borrowed—from the sun. Is that what the moon mages were? Parasites? Leeches who could drain the power from a Sun Stone, from a sun mage, whether the sun mage chose to allow it or not?

Perhaps it was a good thing there weren't any more of them—and perhaps this was why.

Zal tossed the second bedroll at Torian's now-healed feet. "Here. Get some sleep. We march out at first light."

He'd get Torian to the capitol, turn them over. Then they were someone else's problem and Zal could go home and forget all about them.

Chapter Four

The next few days were torture for Torian, almost making them wish to be back in the Lab. Zal had given them a quartz-laced pebble and told them to keep it in a pocket so their feet wouldn't get quite so raw during the journey.

Although Torian's feet managed better, their legs and back were not so fortunate. Apparently the pebble's healing properties were quite localized. Torian stored that piece of data for later consideration—automatically framing a report to the Infomancers, recommending further study.

No. That life is well over.

They repeated that litany as they marched, but every night, their gaze was drawn to the broken top of the mountain and the ruins of the Lab, still faintly glowing in the dark. The glow never altered, neither fading nor flaring, giving no clue whether anyone still remained inside.

After four long days on the trail, Torian had at last begun to believe pursuit unlikely, that the Infomancers had all either perished in the attack or fled off-planet as they'd been scrambling to do when Torian escaped. What was one cyborg compared to all their lives, after all—a cyborg manufactured from one of their own failed experiments?

To keep their mind off their discomfort, and to bury the fear of pursuit, Torian began to log information about the journey, simply because they wanted to and no one was there to forbid it.

The trees, as an example, in their endless variety and aspect. Somehow, the information in the data banks didn't do justice to the way the deciduous specimens bent in the wind, their bare branches creaking, dry leaves crunching underfoot. Or the soughing of the evergreens, their pungent smell, the prick of their needles as the travelers pushed through a close-grown stand.

Just as well Torian was accustomed to the company of their own observations and thoughts because Zal hadn't spoken to them again since the first night. Or only orders, such as "Sit here," and "Eat this," or warnings such as "Mind the ledge."

Energy reserves were another problem. If Torian could simply lie bared to the sun's rays, allowing the solar network on their back and shoulders to absorb the energy, recharge completely, they'd be able to manage the discomfort themselves with the body enhancement modules. It wasn't only good for complementing secondary sex characteristics. It amplified Torian's recovery subroutines. It could ease sore muscles, even subtly augment their muscle mass so they weren't so pathetically weak compared to the strapping mage, who apparently never tired, never hurt, and never slowed down.

That afternoon, Zal announced camp in his bass growl while the sun was still above the horizon but below the persistent cloud cover. After he stomped off to gather wood, Torian quickly stripped off cloak, jerkin, and shirt, baring back and shoulders, with their embedded solar grid, to the light.

Torian sighed with relief as power thrummed along their circuits, even though their skin pebbled in the cold. While soaking up the last of the sun's rays, they scanned the edge of the clearing, their awakening systems allowing access to data on edible flora. Perhaps, if they were to prove their good will and ability to assist in the journey, become something other than a burden and a duty, Zal would relent and *talk* to them again.

After sunset, while Zal still crashed about in the woods, Torian scouted the immediate undergrowth and along the river bank, collecting wild onions, a handful of desiccated berries, the leaves of a kale-equivalent. By the time Zal returned, a bundle of wood under one arm, a string of fish dangling from his other hand, Torian had a fairly respectable selection spread out on a rock.

Zal stopped, letting the wood drop from his arms. "What's that?"

"A salad. I thought our diet might benefit from some fresher items."

"Salad, you say? Looks like a mess of weeds to me."

Torian tilted their head. "Technically, they *are* weeds. That doesn't mean they're not edible. Don't you eat greens?"

"Of course. But not on the trail. And not in winter."

"Do you object to them?"

Zal scowled as he squatted to build the fire. "No."

"I'm afraid we'll have to eat them plain. I have nothing to dress them with."

Zal snapped his fingers and a flame leaped onto the kindling. "I might have something that'll do." He heaved a sigh and glanced up, the flames dancing in the depths of his eye. "Thank you."

In the end, they had the greens and a fish stew flavored with the onions and wild thyme. Torian didn't normally concern themselves with organic food—their cybertronic energy could sustain them, provided they remained sufficiently charged and hydrated—but there was something satisfying about sharing a meal with Zal, a meal they had prepared together.

Zal apparently felt the same way because he began to talk again, to Torian's intense relief. The Infomancers had spoken *at* Torian rather than *with* them, but Torian found they missed the communication, however utilitarian.

"Are you really moon-born?"

"Yes. Or so they tell me."

"'They'? You mean these Infomancers you talk about?"

"That's right."

"What under the Sun is an Infomancer anyway?"

Torian gazed into the fire, the warmth of the flames comforting even if the firelight couldn't add to their energy reserves. "It is…a joke, I suppose. You've called them star-born, and in a way, that's more literal than calling you sun-born or me moon-born. Those terms originated as references to your genetic make-up, expressed in skin and hair color, body characteristics and aptitudes. But they—the In-fomancers—are literally from the stars."

Torian leaned back and stared into the dark sky until his eyesight recalibrated. He pointed to the lower-most star in the constellation the subjects called the Galleon. "That star right there, as a matter of fact."

"Get away with you. They're not even from here?"

Torian turned his gaze to Zal. "Neither are you, you know."

Zal frowned and tossed a twig into the fire. "I was born outside the capitol, in the same cottage where my mother was born, and her father, and his father. Of course I'm from here."

"Not originally. All the life on this planet was seeded by people from the third planet orbiting that star. The Lab on the mountain was constructed so the originators could monitor their experiment."

"I mislike that notion," Zal growled.

"Nevertheless, it's true. They set the basics of your society in place and let it spin. But the latest researchers to staff the Lab have taken more onto themselves than was intend-ed by the originators. They're starting to interfere."

"Interfere how?"

"The Lunaria plague, the one that wiped out the C-27 strain—"

"You mean the moon-born massacre."

Torian inclined their head. "Yes. That was a mistake. An experiment gone wrong. They'd intended to seed a new ability into the population, instantiate a C-28 strain. But in-stead, it turned lethal."

Zal stabbed the air with his forefinger. "You see? This is why it's illegal to practice magic on someone who doesn't choose the path."

"It wasn't magic. It was science."

"I don't care what you call it. It was wrong."

"I can't disagree."

"So how'd you escape? And how'd they get their hands on you?"

"They rescued me as a baby, but I would have died too, so they..." Torian gestured, a sweep of their hand indicating their body, "...Improved me. Replaced the dying parts with synthetic ones. Over the years, they've made other modifications."

"Tell you all this as a bedtime story, did they? Rocking you to sleep with the tale to keep you grateful?"

Torian snorted at the notion of the Infomancers deigning to provide any justification for their actions. "Hardly. One of the modifications they made was in my data storage. Within the storage cells in my spinal column, I hold the entire data bank for the Lab, including the files on my origin and subsequent schematics. Theoretically, I can access the data, provided I'm given the correct search parameters."

But now, Torian held more, from their escape, from their journey. Direct experience was a heady thing. Empowering. *All because I chose to leave.*

"So you know what they know?"

"I contain it. My data access protocols aren't very efficient. My brain is one of the only fully organic parts of my original body that remains."

"Did you choose this?"

"I was an infant. I had no concept of choice."

"What about later? All these modifications of theirs?"

Torian shrugged. "By then, it was habit."

"I don't like it."

"Zal, I owed them. If they hadn't taken me out of the village after they unleashed the virus, I would have died too."

"If they hadn't unleashed the bloody virus, you'd have been in no danger in the first place. They murdered a whole race, Torian. There's no excuse, no way they can atone."

Torian picked at the edge of his travel-stained cloak, unable to meet Zal's furious gaze. "So you think they should have let me die?"

"Shite, no." Zal's big hand was suddenly there, covering Torian's fingers, stilling their fidgeting. "You deserve to live, but you shouldn't have to thank them for it. And they shouldn't have expected you to keep paying for it forever."

The warmth of Zal's hand sent an entirely anomalous data set coursing through Torian's secondary processors. His touch didn't come with the expectation of sexual release—Torian wasn't entirely sure that was a good thing. Zal was a very impressive specimen, and kind. They wouldn't have minded if he wanted the one thing Torian was certain they were proficient at.

Could that be respect they detected? Simple affection, perhaps? They'd never had either from anyone at the Lab. Little wonder their sensor array was going haywire.

Zal took his hand away, and Torian was immediately colder than ever.

"I don't think much of your Infomancers. *Infomancers.* What a stupid-arsed name. You said it was a joke?"

Torian nodded. "There's a quotation from an ancient author from their home world. He wrote speculative fiction. He said, 'Any technology, when sufficiently advanced, is indistinguishable from magic'. So the researchers like to joke that the subjects—"

"You mean us. The citizens of this world."

"Yes. They call you subjects. They joke that if any of you, being primitive and believers in a system of magic, were to witness any of their technology, you'd consider them magicians. But they wield the magic of advanced information. So, Infomancers."

"Arrogant arseholes," Zal muttered.

Torian found his attitude unexpectedly comforting. "That was their downfall."

Zal gazed into the dark, toward where the moon hung low over the mountains. "They've fallen then? The star-born? Is that what the explosion was about?"

"Yes. Word reached their supervisors of the nature of their experiments. The supervisors...disapproved. And reacted strongly. With ionic weapons."

"Serves them right."

Torian ducked their head and peered at Zal from under their lashes. "Do you think I deserve punishment too? For what I did in the village?"

"I'm not so sure now. You say you're not a mage. I begin to believe you." He leaned forward, resting his elbows on his knees. "What's likely to happen to your Infomancers?"

"I think—I hope—that they're gone. Dead, fled, or taken into custody. Their trip back to face justice will be far longer than ours. Although," Torian lifted one foot in its heavy boot, "much easier on the feet."

Zal's mouth dropped open for an instant, and then he laughed. A great, rolling, basso profundo laugh that echoed through the trees. *I could listen to that laugh to the end of days and not get enough.* The Infomancers had never laughed for joy. Torian had forgotten that such a thing existed.

"Do you sing, Zal?"

Zal's eyebrows popped up. "Now and again, if nobody's around to complain of the noise. Why?"

"Your voice is pleasant. So is your face and your...your body."

Zal shifted on his tree-stump chair. "Thanks, but best not get into that. Get us both into trouble."

"You weren't affected by the body enhancement program, nor the pheromones. I realize you haven't seen me at my best, but why weren't you affected?"

Zal shrugged. "You say you know all about this world."

"Only what the Infomancers knew. I'm beginning to think they missed more than they realized."

"Did they know that Sun mages are celibate?"

Torian blinked. "I—no, I don't believe so. Is that a recent requirement?"

"Only three centuries or so." Zal's tone was dry.

"So you resisted because of your magic."

"I resisted because I don't feel desire. Not that way."

"So when you take up your vocation, your desires are stripped from you?"

"No. I've never felt them. Used to wonder what all the other lads were on about, strutting around after their manhood trials, telling lies about their conquests. I never saw the point."

"Never?"

"Not once." He shrugged. "Never felt like I was missing much, if you want the truth. Of course, if you pass the magical aptitude tests and qualify to take up a Sun Stone, you have to take the vow of celibacy or have your potential stripped from you. Pretty effective way to weed out the folks who aren't serious."

"But you are."

"Aye. Easiest vow I ever took. Not like I was giving up anything. Although I do miss my sister and her family. Once you take to the road as a circuit mage, your time belongs to the land, not yourself. I haven't had the chance to go back to see them but once every three or four years."

"That must be lonely."

Zal squinted up at the stars. "There are compensations, but not many think they're worth it. Every year, fewer candidates present themselves for training. Fewer of the qualified who are willing to make the sacrifice."

"Why did you do it?"

"The work's important, and somebody's got to do it. I'm qualified. I'm competent. Why not me? Everyone in society is expected to give back somehow. This is my way."

Give back. If Torian wanted to fit into this world, they had to find a way to contribute. But how? The only thing they'd ever provided was sexual release to people too consumed with their own importance to find another compatible partner. While Torian was well aware that this world placed no shame on honest sex workers, the notion of returning to that occupation had little appeal.

"Zal."

Zal had been staring into the fire, but he met Torian's gaze over the flames. "Hmmm?"

"I don't—that is, if I pass whatever tests your tribunal sets me, what will happen then? I don't have any outstanding skills. The tools I know how to use aren't available here. How can I give back?" *How can I find a place to belong?*

Zal grinned. "That's an easy one. You know everything. Things no sun-born or earth-born has ever dreamed of. Things only the star-born know. So tell us."

Could it be that simple? "That's it? Just...talk?"

"Or write it down." He lifted one brow. "You can write, can't you?"

"Of course. But—"

"Try it on. Tell me something from the old world, the one where you say we came from."

"What?"

"I don't know. Anything. A joke."

"A joke." There had been few reasons to laugh at the Lab, but the archives held everything. Torian sent a query through the appropriate channels, although the resulting data was dubious. "Knock knock."

Zal stared at him. "That's it?"

"No. It's a challenge-response sequence. You say, 'who's there'?"

"Who's there?"

"No, wait until I start again. Knock knock."

"Who's there?"

"May."

Zal scowled. "That's not very funny."

"You have to say 'May who'?"

"Why didn't you say so? Do I have any other lines?"

"No. That's all. Knock knock."

"Who's there?"

"Justin."

"May who?"

"No, you see, I changed the challenge, so you need to change your response."

"But you said I had to say 'May who'. Now it's different?" Zal threw a pebble into the fire. "Your Infomancers have a piss-poor sense of humor. Let's leave off the jokes."

"All right. I've told you something of the old world. It's your turn to tell me something of this one."

"I don't think that joke counts. It wasn't funny, or even finished."

"That was your choice." Torian allowed a hint of slyness to creep into their voice and was rewarded with Zal's flashing smile.

"Point taken. What do you want to know?"

"I've never seen this world from anything other than a monitor, or lived anywhere other than the Lab. What is your home like?"

"My home? It's not much. Just a cottage. Couple of rooms below. Loft above for sleeping."

"Does it have indoor plumbing?"

"What's that?"

"Never mind. Please go on."

"The cottage isn't all that grand, but it sits on a cliff overlooking the Inland Sea. When the sun rises in midwinter, it skates a red path across the water, right into my window. That's a beautiful sight, let me tell you."

"It sounds lovely."

"Of course, the canton where I live is south and west, so winters aren't so vicious there. Truthfully, I enjoy winters. I don't have to travel. Can sit at home by the fire with my books. Or walk on the shore when the wind is from the west and brings the scent of other lands."

"Yes. Scents. I hadn't imagined what they would be like. Although not all are pleasant. The cell in the gaol." Torian wrinkled their nose. "I hope never to smell that again."

"Lab of yours doesn't have privies, then? Don't your Infomancers shite and piss?"

"They do. But that's what indoor plumbing is for. I'll show you when we—" Torian stopped. They wouldn't be showing Zal anything. The point of this journey was to turn Torian over to some other group, who would judge them and categorize them and compartmentalize them just as the Infomancers had done. None of those unknowns would have a liquid dark eye, a voice to rattle bones, or a touch to soothe.

I am a prisoner still. I cannot forget. I cannot mistake Zal's moral center for liking or even for grudging tolerance.

Zal seemed to remember too. He picked up the long stick he'd used to roast a bit of fish and poked the fire, sending a shower of sparks leaping up to die in the dark.

"Your turn again. This time make it something that makes a bit of sense."

Something that made sense? Nothing made sense anymore. Certainly not the Infomancers' absolute certainty that they owned the subjects—the people—on this planet to do with as they pleased.

Torian had never thought about the rightness of the workings at the Lab. It was how things were. Form a question. Conduct experiments. Draw conclusions. Repeat. Inside that sterile world, Torian had been the anomaly—both subject and co-worker. Had they truly been a co-worker, though?

They'd been part of experiments and research, but primarily as the subject, not the scientist. They'd never refused an enhancement proposal or turned down a sexual release assignment. Would it have been allowed?

Choice. The only true choice they'd ever made was to run.

The Infomancers considered themselves benevolent, their research here intended to improve the lives of others—but the others on their home world. Not these people here on this planet, whom they treated like a live-action simulation. Expendable. But these people weren't simulacra. Zal was real. His concern for his world, for his duty, for *right*, was far more benevolent than the Infomancers had ever dreamed of being.

Assuming they dreamed at all.

From the music data banks, Torian lifted a song that had always fascinated them, both from the concept of natural consequences and because the tune was so haunting.

"This ae nighte, this ae nighte,
Every nighte and all,
Fire and fleet and candle-lighte,
And Christ receive thy soul.
When thou from hence away art past
Every nighte and all,
To Whinny-muir thou com'st at last
And Christ receive thy soul.
If ever thou gavest hosen and shoon,
Every nighte and all,
Sit thee down and put them on;
And Christ receive thy soul.
If hosen and shoon thou ne'er gav'st nane
Every nighte and all,
The whinnes shall prick thee to the bare bane.
And Christ receive thy soul."

WhileTorian sang the ancient tune about the rewards of

charity and the penalties for its lack, Zal's gaze never wavered from their face. When their last note died away, he heaved a deep sigh. "Sun, moon, and stars, Torian. That tune runs right down the spine and shivers there, doesn't it?"

Torian nodded. "That's exactly how I've always felt."

"One thing, though. Who's this Christ?"

Torian shrugged, unwilling to go into the details. "I think they may be a bit like me. Three-natured. They seem to be in a lot of songs, although many of the songs are depressing. I fear they didn't come to a very pleasant end."

"Ah, well." Zal stood up. "You get some rest." He picked up his pack and swung it onto his shoulder.

"You're leaving?" Anxiety bubbled up in Torian's chest, and none of their disaster recovery programming could tamp it down. True, Zal disappeared each evening to tromp around in the woods, but he'd never been so far away Torian couldn't hear him. He'd never taken his pack before.

"Not for long. Got a bit of scouting to do. Maybe trap something for our meal tomorrow. You've plenty of wood here, so keep the fire stoked." Zal tapped his staff on the ground. A subtle wave of energy flowed outward, ruffling Torian's hair and stirring the branches of the trees surrounding their campsite. "That'll keep the wildlife at bay. I'll be back in an hour or two."

"An hour or two." Torian huddled next to the fire. Surely they could manage that long. They'd spent hours alone at the Lab. But the Lab had walls. The Infomancers and Lab assistants hadn't been friendly, but they'd been predictable. Here, with the vast, unknown dark pressing at their back, Torian became aware of how dependent they'd become on Zal in such a short time.

Unacceptable. Zal wasn't a constant. He would turn Torian over to the tribunal and move on. Best to learn some self-sufficiency now, while they still had the opportunity. Best to consider options as well, because if it looked as if the tribunal would treat them no better than the Infomancers, Torian intended to be ready to run.

Chapter Five

Zal batted branches out of his way as he stomped off through the woods. He couldn't deny he was running away like a coward, but he also couldn't deny he was beginning to doubt his own convictions. His training and his knowledge of the laws screamed that Torian was a rogue mage—a practitioner of unknown power who used illegal spells of coercion, depriving citizens of proper choice.

But with everything Torian had told him about their life in that Sun-forsaken Lab, about the star-born Infomancers, about the origins of this world, *his* world, Zal's doubts grew.

Why did this world not have a story of its beginnings? Wasn't it human nature to wonder, to find answers, even if the answers were pure guesswork and total shite? Had the star-born, these originators, somehow *prevented* them from even asking the questions? With what they'd done to poor Torian—Zal had seen the mess of metal glinting on their back and shoulders when they'd thought he was off gathering wood—who knew what the arrogant arseholes were capable of?

Zal began to doubt everything he'd ever learned. For instance, whether he should turn Torian over to the tribunal at all. Would they take the time to hear what Torian had to say?

Shite, that song, all about reaping what you sow. It had squeezed Zal's heart enough to make it weep. If someone were to sit in judgment on him, on the Congress of Mages and Seigneurs, on all the sun-born and earth-born inhabitants of the world, would they be found lacking?

Zal needed clarity, and for that, he needed to cast the divination stones, see the paths before him. Make his own bloody choice.

He broke out of the tree cover onto a plateau that over-looked the river. The gibbous moon rode high over the mountains and the tattered remains of the earlier clouds didn't obscure the stars. He drove his staff into the earth amid the frost-killed grass and sat, cross-legged, the staff at his back. He pulled out the worn square of leather with its four lines—peace, prosperity, principles, partnership—and spread it on the ground in front of him.

Had this come from the Infomancers too? Had they im-posed rules on the world so deeply and subtly that no citizen had ever suspected they all danced to someone else's tune?

Can't think like that. Didn't matter anyway. His spells worked. His connection to the Sun was real, palpable, *useful.* So to blazes with the Infomancers. *I refuse to let them choose my path for me.*

Zal pulled the pouch on its leather thong from under his shirt and shook the divination stones into his palm. Still warm from his skin, they shone in the combined light from his Sun Stone and the moon.

"You've always spoken true for me. I have faith you'll do so now. What must I do with the moon-born?"

He closed his eye and selected the opal by touch, its sur-face smooth and cooler than the others. "Moon for peace." He tossed it toward the divination mat, heard the soft *spat* as it landed.

Next, the agate, its roughness familiar, unmistakable. "Earth for prosperity." He cast it after the opal.

The flake of Sun Stone thrummed against his fingers. "Sun for principles." He flicked it after the others.

"Stars—" Shite, he didn't want to cast the handful of quartz chips. It seemed too much like giving in to the star-born and all their plots. But the stars didn't belong to the

Infomancers. The stars were there for all, in the sky every night. So. "Stars for partnership."

He flung the handful of quartz chips in the direction of the mat and took a moment to breathe, praying to the Sun that the answer would be obvious because Zal had never felt so uncertain in his life. Learning to live with a single eye had been less disorienting than having the foundation of his beliefs upended.

He opened his eye.

The sun and moon stones were aligned, touching in a tentative kiss, directly on the partnership line. The star stones were off the grid entirely, and the earth stone lay between principles and prosperity.

"Bloody wonderful. How am I to make sense out of that?" The stones had a worse sense of humor than the fragging Infomancers.

✿✿✿

After Zal left, Torian moved closer to the fire, settling on the same tree-stump Zal had used. The flames should have warmed them, but they didn't.

I have no notion how to make my way in this world. They'd nearly died twice over—once by underestimating the power of the river and once in the dark of the village gaol.

They stared into the heart of the fire, where the flames danced orange and blue, and tried to formulate the query that would return the information they'd need to survive in the wilderness on their own, should the outcome of the tribunal be less than optimal.

For that matter, perhaps they should search for ways to escape prison. Or methods of self-defense. If they could—

"You're wearing my cloak."

Torian's head jerked up at the unfamiliar voice, and they blinked, trying to recalibrate their vision to see into the dark at the edge of the clearing.

A male, just shy of full maturity, stepped into the light. Torian recognized him as one of the crowd in the street the day Zal had rescued them from captivity.

"I...I beg your pardon?"

"My cloak." He jerked his chin at Torian's feet and his thumb at the male standing at his right shoulder. "And Morvan's boots."

"My jerkin, Farren," said a third, whose face Torian had seen more than once peering through the cell's miserable excuse for a window. "Don't forget that."

Two more joined the first three while Torian was still formulating a response.

Torian's gaze pinged from one to the next before returning to Farren, the obvious leader. "But Zal paid."

Farren sneered. "Oh, aye. He paid the *reeves*. Din't pay *us*, did he? Din't give us *no* prosperity stones, nor anything to trade with in place of our kit." He took a step closer, the fire casting distorted shadows on his face. "You could pay, though."

Five of them and no sign of Zal. *Now would be a good time to locate those self-defense files.* Torian shrugged out of the cloak and removed the jerkin with trembling fingers. They held both out, the wind raising gooseflesh along the edges of their power grid. "Here. You can have them back."

The third male started forward, but Farren held him back. "Leave off, Avram. Go keep watch for Magister."

"But Farren—"

"Go." Avram slunk off, and Farren turned back to Torian. "Why'd we want 'em after they've been *used*? Not worth as much as before, eh? But Comfort House folk pay in trade, same as anyone else. They just got different goods to offer. I was there with Barkon, first time he talked to you in gaol. I saw. You're just like those as work in the Comfort House."

Torian let the clothing drop in the dirt at their feet, dangerously close to the fire. "That was different. I didn't have a choice."

"Maybe. But out here, looks like nobody's depriving you of choice except Magister."

"He's taking me to the capitol."

"Aye. Know what happened to the last rogue mage he took to the capitol?"

Torian shook their head. "No," they whispered.

Farren grinned, the firelight turning his teeth red, and drew a finger across his throat. "Cut off her head, they did."

Morvan nudged Farren with an elbow. "Don't forget the…" He pointed to his middle. "You know."

"Right. Slit open her belly and filled it with hot coals. Right after they tied her up to four horses and whipped 'em up. Ripped her arms and legs right out of their sockets. Left her there in the square, screaming, for a good two days, I hear, with them other mages keeping her from death. *Then* they cut off her head. Not from mercy, but 'cos they was sick of the noise."

Torian hugged themselves, hands clamped under their arms, willing the tremors to stop chasing across their skin, the danger alarms to stop pinging in their survival circuits. "He wouldn't. He's not like that."

"They're all like that, those mages. Say they're holding up the laws, but who made the laws, eh?" Farren sidled closer. "You don't have to go with him."

Torian shook their head. "I must. Zal's duty—"

"We'd hide you 'til he leaves. Take you back to the village. Then you could work in *our* Comfort House." Farren licked his lips. "'Cos we don't got nothing like you there now. Pale as snow, you are. You like that everywhere?"

"I—"

"Farren," Morvan murmured. "What about choice?

Shouldn't we...you know...ask?"

"Oh, aye. Let's see about that, eh?" Farren took another step forward. "All you got to do is say no. Well?"

Torian tried. But when they opened their mouth to refuse, their throat closed up, and nothing emerged. *What?* They traced their decision pathways and tried again but... there. A block in their programming, diverting them back to the *Yes* decision node, no matter how they tried to activate *No*.

But worse, Farren's obvious desire activated the body enhancement module, the one that Torian had always believed under their own control. *No no no.* They could think it but not say it. They felt themselves pulling in, rounding their shoulders, dropping their gaze to peer up through their tangled hair in the submissive female aspect. *I don't want this. I don't choose this.* Had the Infomancers coerced them after all, and Torian had never even known it?

"There, see?" Farren asked. "Maybe we should make sure." He began to unbutton the front of his breeks.

Morvan tugged on Farren's cloak. "We should go. Before Magister comes back."

"He's casting the divination stones. When's he ever figured their meaning in less than an hour? We've got time. Time to be sure." Farren stared avidly at Torian. "Go on. Say no."

Torian's thoughts flew in a dozen different directions, searching for a way around the block, a way to control their own programming. Suddenly, they flashed on Zal, raising a sardonic brow. *"Technically, I'm bespelling the water."*

Could Torian use their own traitorous circuits to bypass the *Yes* command? To bypass it, or at least side-step it sufficiently to send Farren and his gang away?

Torian didn't know if they'd succeed, but they were determined to try. So they let Farren approach, desperately formulating the question that would turn the situation to their own advantage.

Chapter Six

After staring at his casting for a good half-hour, Zal gathered the stones again. Tradition dictated that nobody got a second chance with divination, not with the same question. Once the stones had fallen, you had to interpret the results and choose a path.

Bugger that. He gathered the stones into his palm again, but before he could begin the ritual, he heard a shout from the direction of the camp. Not just one shout, a chorus of raucous hoots and catcalls.

Torian.

He'd protected the camp against wild animals, but he hadn't thought to ward it against people. Yet people were Torian's greatest threat.

Zal threw down the stones. He leaped to his feet and grabbed his staff, leaving his pack where it lay. He crashed through the trees, his downhill momentum carrying him into the camp clearing.

A handful of earth-born young men gathered near the fire. All of them looked to be in the unfortunate stage between the manhood trials at fourteen and citizenship initiation at nineteen. Zal recognized the biggest one—Farren, was that his name?—the apprentice from Corvel-on-Byrne, who'd run Netta's errands, fetching Torian's kit.

Farren faced Torian across the fire, and his hands, rot him, fumbled at his trouser buttons.

And Torian—Torian had shed their cloak and jerkin, nothing but the thin linen shirt covering their moon-pale skin. Their head was bowed, tilted slightly to look up at the villager from beneath the sweep of their lashes. Everything about

Torian said *promise* and their attitude had a predictable effect on the young men. All of them sported cock-stands under their trousers—a few, like Farren, had already taken them out.

The effect on Zal was not the same. Anger rose up from belly to chest to the top of his head, his braids whipping around his torso as if he stood in the center of a cyclone.

"Stand down!" he bellowed.

Most of the men flinched, the ones with their peckers out hurrying to shove them out of sight. Farren, though, hadn't budged, seemingly mesmerized. Torian didn't so much as glance at Zal. They kept their attention on Farren.

Spellbound. That's what Farren was, and if that wasn't magic, Zal was blind in both eyes, not one.

He swept his staff in a circle over his head, the Sun Stone glowing brighter than the fire's embers. The men cried out, stumbling back outside the circle of Zal's rage.

"You." He thrust the end of his staff toward Farren. "I said stand down. You—"

"Zal! Your left!"

At Torian's cry, Zal whirled to his blind side to face a reedy youth hefting a rock the size of his head. "Oh, no boyo. When you threaten a Sun mage, you need a much bigger weapon." One wave of Zal's staff sent the rock spinning away, the boy stumbling after.

Farren hadn't moved, although Torian had dropped their seductive pose when they warned Zal of the attack. He took two strides across the clearing and lifted the young idiot by the scruff of his neck, giving him a shake before shoving him to join the rest of the lads.

"Do you know what you've done, the lot of you? You know what it means to violate of a citizen's right to choose."

Farren rubbed the back of his neck. "But she chose. We asked. She din't say no."

"You mean *he* didn't," another boy muttered.

"Enough," Zal roared. "Did they say yes?"

Four of the boys shared uneasy glances, but Farren jutted his chin. "Din't say no. That's what counts."

"There are five of you idiots. You've all cleared your manhood trials. Farren, you look to be on the brink of initiation. You should all be well aware that *not refusing* isn't the same as *choosing.*"

"Seems like you're not offering a choice either, Magister, hauling her off to the capitol. Did *you* ever ask?" Farren crossed his arms. "Go on. Ask."

Guilt twisted in Zal's gut. It wouldn't matter what Torian said. The two of them had to make the trip, whether either one of them wanted to or not. He faced Torian, whose gaze was riveted to the ground by their feet. Zal could see the shudders racking their thin shoulders. Shite, they must be frozen. Zal picked up the cloak and draped it over their shoulders. "Torian. Tell me the truth. Do you want to go with me?"

Torian took a deep breath and raised their chin, although they kept their eyes downcast. "Yes."

Farren's mouth dropped open. "But...but I asked. I asked if she wanted to come with us. I asked if she wanted to say no."

Torian finally lifted his gaze, glaring at Farren with more anger than Zal had ever seen in them before. "You asked the wrong fucking question."

Zal blinked at the venom in Torian's tone. "Right, then." He turned to Farren and the other boys. "The way I see it, you lot have to answer for violating the reeves' decree to send Torian away from your village. For interfering with a mage's duty. For *attacking* a mage." He glared at the boy who'd nearly brained him with the rock. "For failing to see the difference between *no* and *no answer.* All basic lessons you've had ample time to learn. But since none of them seemed to stick, here's something to remind you."

Zal gestured with his staff and in an instant, with the overwhelming stench of singed hair, each boy's braids were burned up to his ears. They shouted, slapping at the smoldering ends.

"You tell your village elders what you've done to earn a shearing. When next I make my rounds, I'll have a talk with them to make sure you've come clean and that you've learned to be decent citizens." He shook his staff at them. "Go."

They went, although not without a baleful glance or two over their shoulders.

Zal turned back to Torian, who had shed the cloak in order to pull their jerkin over their head. They wouldn't meet Zal's gaze, and no wonder.

"Torian, it's not your job anymore to service anyone who asks."

They stopped fumbling with the jerkin's laces. "Is that what you think I was doing?"

Zal dropped his gaze, leaning on his staff. "Didn't look like they were giving you much choice. And that's on me. I shouldn't have left you alone."

"You think I would submit to them? On *purpose*?"

"Aye, well, that's how it worked with those Infomancers, didn't it? Back in Corvel-on-Byrne, too, or nearly."

Torian's eyes flashed in the firelight. "Be fair. In the Lab, it was my *job*. And what options did I have when I was shut up in that awful cell, behind bars, in the *dark*?"

"That's how all rogue mages justify themselves when they're cornered. That they didn't have a choice."

Torian's mouth turned down. "Maybe if they'd been allowed more time, they'd have found one."

"Now *you* be fair. If I'd given the last rogue I faced more time, she'd have taken both my eyes."

"Do you know why?"

Zal leaned on his staff, seeking the strength of his Sun Stone because Torian's attitude was completely unlike them. Was this the first sign of rogue instability? The notion sent his heart tumbling to his knees. "Wasn't a lot of time for asking questions."

"Maybe you should have made time. Because from where I stand, Zal, you're the one who failed to *ask*."

Chapter Seven

Torian yanked their cloak off the ground and flung it across their shoulders. They wanted to rip, to tear, to throw things. Was this what it was like to be angry? They'd never felt like this before, as if some primal beast were hatching in their chest, trying to claw its way out.

It was glorious.

Glorious yet also frightening and disorienting, and those feelings were far too familiar from their flight from the Lab.

But the look on Zal's face, the revulsion, the disappointment. Torian had been foolish to imagine for one nanosecond that Zal believed they had no sinister magical agenda, and that they had no desire to repeat any part of their life in the Lab. If Zal—who had spent time with Torian, talked to them, *knew* them in a way no one ever had—could think the worst, what of the other mages? If Zal no longer believed in them, could the hideous fate Farren described be waiting for Torian at the capitol?

Why was that thought so much less distressing than the loss of Zal's good opinion? Why did Torian crave the humor that lurked in his eye? Or the integrity that seemed to shine from him like the light of the chrysocite on his staff? But how could Torian expect anyone, no matter how decent at their core, to accept them for all that they were?

Different. Three-natured. *Moon-born. Cyborg.*

Torian's eyes burned in an unfamiliar way. They rubbed them, sniffing, and huddled next to the fire.

"Torian."

"Yes?"

"What should I have asked?"

An odd tightness gripped Torian's chest, making it difficult to speak. "It doesn't matter."

"Yes, it does. Tell me."

Torian met Zal's gaze across the dying flames. They read nothing but concern in his face now, and for some reason, that constricted their chest even further. *A malfunction? Must run a diagnostic later.* They shook their head.

Zal tossed his staff aside and hunkered down so he was at eye-level with Torian. "Please? I promise I'll listen. No judgments."

"You…" Torian pressed the heels of their hands against their eyes for a moment and took a breath before meeting Zal's perplexed gaze again. "You should have asked what was wrong."

Zal blinked, his eyebrows lifting. "I could see what was wrong. A pack of idiots forcing themselves on you."

"Not what was wrong with *them*. What was wrong with *me*." Torian clutched the edges of their cloak. "You were right."

"I was?" Zal frowned. "You mean you were coercing them?"

Torian shook their head wildly. "No. Of course not. But I couldn't say *no*. No matter how hard I tried. The Infomancers put a limiter in my program. Every time I tried to say no, it rerouted me to *yes*."

Zal pinched the bridge of his nose. "Ah, shite."

"And the way Farren phrased the question. He said, 'Say no'. And I couldn't. Not only that, but the enhancement module activated too."

"Did you know about this?"

"No. I never even suspected. All along, I had no choice. I still don't."

"Of course you do. You're not a slave to those Infomancers anymore."

"But aren't I just as captive to you and your laws? I don't know anything about your people, Zal. I've only met you and those villagers. How do I know whether the rest of the populace will be like you or like them or perhaps worse than the Infomancers? Farren told me what happened to the last mage you delivered. Will that..." They swallowed against the image of the broken, screaming mage. "Will that happen to me?"

"I can't—" Zal ran one big hand across his face. "Look. I like to think everyone wants to do the right thing. That deep down, we all believe in the precepts of our society, the basic rights laid out in our charter and the laws in place to ensure those rights. That we'd never punish someone unless their guilt was beyond question. But what can I say? People are idiots."

Torian was surprised into a laugh. "The Infomancers would agree about all of you. Not themselves so much."

"Aye, well, from what you've told me, they've got no room to judge. Those young fools from the village just now? By this age, they ought to know better. Respect a citizen's rights. Perhaps they'll think twice before they go haring off on another half-arsed quest, but I'm sorry their lesson came your expense. I should have protected you."

Torian shrugged. "You didn't know they'd follow."

"I saw them eyeing your in the village. I should have known they'd never be able to resist. You are unique in more ways than I can count."

Zal's words washed through Torian, leaving their chest hollow, as if their human heart had been replaced by the pulse of a cybertronic relay. *I'm alone. The only one of my kind. Even if the moon-born still existed, after all the modifications, there could be no other like me.*

Perhaps the tribunal would find it more convenient to eliminate the anomaly.

Torian hunched forward, burying their head in their arms as shudders racked their body. A small part of their processing cycles registered the new experience.

So this is crying.

All things considered, Torian preferred gaol.

❀❀❀

"Torian?" Shite. Zal had put his big, clumsy foot in it now. He strode around the fire and kneeled next to the huddled form, hesitant to touch them without permission. There'd been far too much of that in Torian's life already.

"I may not have a lot of say in what happens at the tribunal, but I'll do my best. Explain what your life has been like. Bear witness for you, if you'd rather not say."

"Will you wave your staff at them?" Torian's voice was muffled by their arms. "Singe off their hair like you did with those boys?"

"Hardly. They'd have my Stone if I came over insubordinate to the Congress. But even though I don't have the status I once had, they'll still listen to me."

Torian peeked up from the folds of their cloak. "Why did you lose your status?"

Zal pointed to his eye patch. "Some don't believe a one-eyed mage can see the paths clearly enough to do his duty. Others think any mage who'd be careless enough to lose his own eye won't be able to take care of the people in his charge. To be a mage, you must command the respect of the citizens. If they think you can't master your own bloody element, they won't trust you to master their problems."

"If people think you can't manage, they've never seen you in action."

Zal chuckled. "You've not had any basis for comparison. I patrol the hinterlands. The mages who serve around the capitol and down in the delta, where it's more temperate and populated? They're far more impressive than I am."

"I don't see how they could be."

Warmth infused Zal's chest at the muttered praise. He wasn't even sure Torian realized it had been a compliment. "Wait until you meet them. You'll see."

Torian hunched over again. "Is it terrible that I don't want to meet them? If I had a choice—"

"Everybody has a choice."

"Then my choice would be to stay out here with you. At least I understand what you want. I mean, you don't want *me*, not the way I'm used to."

"Does that bother you?"

"It's...different. All of the people at the Lab, they all wanted something from me. A preference as to what aspect I should display when it was their time for release. If I don't even have that to offer, why would you want to keep me around?"

"You really don't see yourself, do you?" Zal shifted off his knees and sat next to Torian. "Let me tell you, we've got a saying. The way to kill a mage is to put a man-eating beast in a cage, cover it with a curtain, and put up a sign that says 'Don't go inside'! We'd all go. Every one of us, every time. Being a mage isn't just working with the power of the Sun. It's learning. Chasing down knowledge. Bending it to new uses. Now you—you're like a whole maze full of doors, all marked 'Don't look'! No mage alive could resist talking with you, learning all you have to tell."

"There's a lot of it. You'd get tired."

Zal nudged Torian with his shoulder. "If I did, you could sing to me again, and I'd forget all about being tired."

A smile trembled on Torian's lips. "You like my singing?"

"Can't imagine anyone not liking it. It's brilliant."

"But would other mages feel that way? They wouldn't see me as some kind of artifact to keep locked up, would they?"

Zal frowned, considering what he knew of the mages elected to positions of authority in Congress. Surely some among their number remembered the nature of the moon-born. But what if they treated Torian's science as magic—and forbidden—as the Infomancers had mockingly declared?

If Torian's presence, their stories, made Zal question his convictions, would it do the same to the other mages? Would they see Torian as a resource, a way to learn about the star-born, about their own beginnings? Or as a danger that threatened the foundation of their society?

Zal wanted to believe the mages would do the right thing. But he'd said it himself—people were idiots, and mages, no matter how much power or responsibility, were still people. "I—"

"Are they all like you? Desireless?"

Zal blinked. "I have desires. Just not fleshly ones. Other mages? They've got 'em." Zal shrugged. "They might be tempted, but they can't act or they risk the loss of their Sun Stone and possibly their head."

"Oh. I hadn't realized. It's a good thing you find me repulsive, then. I wouldn't want you to risk your head."

Zal held his hand over Torian's knee. "May I?" When Torian nodded, he rested his hand there, the lightest of touches. "I may not have sexual desires, but I appreciate beauty. Believe me when I tell you that you're the first thing in a long time that makes me regret not having two eyes."

"Oh." Torian ducked their head, and that slow flush rose along their neck and to the tips of their ears. *Adorable.* "I— thank you."

"Do you really like it out here in the wilderness? Far cry from your mountaintop citadel, isn't it?"

"Yes. But it's so much more...real. Immediate. Alive. I'm not sorry for escaping. But..."

"But?"

Torian raised his chin, his smile tremulous. "I had no idea it would be *so* cold."

Zal laughed. "Aye. The north'll freeze the bollocks off you if you don't wear your woolies. Here."

Zal stood and shook out his bedroll, added Torian's on top of it, doubling up the blankets.

Torian watched him with wide eyes. "What are you doing?"

"One way to keep warm is to share blankets. Twice the wool. Twice the body heat."

"But...but you don't want me."

"This isn't about sex. It's about comfort. We could both use that, I'm thinking. Because I've got no idea how to interpret the divination I just—shite! My pack! Here, you crawl in. I've got to go rescue my things from up the hill. Unless—are you afraid the lads'll be back?"

Torian clambered between the blankets. "After what you did to them? Not likely. Go on."

Zal raced up the hillside, not willing to leave Torian alone for any longer than necessary. When he got to the spot where he left his pack, he discovered that the stones he'd discarded when he'd heard the shouts lay on the mat in exactly the same formation as his first throw.

And what that meant, the Sun only knew.

Chapter Eight

For the first time since leaving the Lab, Torian awoke warm. Zal's big body, spooned behind them, radiated heat like his Sun Stone. This was a new feeling for Torian altogether. They'd never slept with a partner before. The transactions at the Lab had been restricted to the prescribed hour during regular work shifts. Torian's nights had always been their own.

But this, the comfort of another body—moreover, the body of someone who would never ask for more than Torian was willing to give—made them want to snuggle in and never rise.

Another thing that close proximity under a double layer of blankets brought to pungent attention, though, was that the two of them had been on the trail for nearly a week, with only minimal opportunities for washing. Not that Zal's earthy male scent was unpleasant, precisely. It was definitely different from the Lab inhabitants, who all smelled of antiseptic cleansers and formaldehyde.

Torian wasn't certain if their own scent would be pleasing to Zal, however, and they desperately wanted to please Zal. Not *that* way, not now that they knew the cost, but enough to be a desirable trail companion.

Torian eased out from beneath the blankets, loathe to leave Zal's heat. For once, the big mage had slept beyond the first pinkening of the sky. Perhaps he was glad to have someone to generate extra warmth as well. *I'm good for that, at least.*

Torian took the cooking pot and the toweling and made their shivering way to the river bank. They filled the pot with water and set it on the bank, then stripped, gritting their teeth as gooseflesh rose over every square centimeter of their body. It would be worse once they dumped the frigid water over their head, but they had no choice.

Or do I?

Zal had expelled solar power stored in his chrysocite to ward off the local fauna and to burn off the village boys' braids. What was Torian but a living solar storage unit? Perhaps they could discharge energy as well as absorb and consume it.

They hunkered down next to the pot and thrust in their hands. *Cold!* Concentrating despite shivering so hard it was a wonder their cybertronic connections didn't shake loose, Torian traced the neural pathways to the power cells at their core. If they reversed the input *here* and redirected the output *there...Ah.*

The water warmed around their hands, heating until it was almost uncomfortable. Torian grinned, dipped a corner of the toweling into the water, and scrubbed away the grime of their days on the trail and trapped in the cell.

True, it wasn't the same as the perfectly regulated temperatures of the Lab showers. In a way, though, it was better because they'd done it themselves—altered their programming for a new purpose to suit their new life.

What else might they be able to do if they questioned a few of their assumptions? *Frame your question. Test your hypothesis. Reframe the question. Test again.*

By the time they were clean and clear of soap, they had compiled a mental list of their most pressing questions, chief among them how to say *no.*

Torian rubbed themselves with the rough toweling, skin turning an unbecoming shade of pink from the cold and the friction. They wrinkled their nose at the stained and travel-worn clothing. What would it be like to put on freshly laundered clothes again?

They pulled on the shirt, and as their head emerged from the neckband, they caught the white stroke of a com-trail, like a tether linking the ruins of the Lab to the sky.

Torian froze with one arm through a sleeve. Were the Infomancers still inhabiting the Lab? Had there been other launches that they hadn't witnessed? Was that an evacuation pod en route to a ship in orbit?

Torian scanned the sky, activating their infrared sensors. *There.* The signature of a cloaked shuttle, coming this way on a landing trajectory. A shuttle that could track Lab-manufactured implants with pinpoint precision.

Torian hurried into the rest of their clothes and stumbled up the trail to camp, their bootlaces still untied. Zal was just strapping the bedding to his pack. He looked up with a grin, but his smile faded when he took in Torian's state.

"What is it? What's wrong?"

"I think...I think the Infomancers may still be here. There's been a glow in the Lab ruins every night, but I thought it was just the residual energy from the breach in the walls. I thought it would fade eventually. There's a ship on its way."

"A ship. You mean a boat on the river?"

Torian shook their head impatiently. "No. An airship."

Zal's eye widened. "A ship that flies through the air? Now that I'd like to see."

"No. No, you wouldn't. Because the ship comes with at least one Infomancer. And I think they want me back."

Chapter Nine

Zal grabbed his staff and stood up. "Why? Just for the sex? They can bloody well get that from someone else. You've paid them back and more."

"Not just that. The data stores. The archives. They're here." Torian thumped their chest with a flat palm. "All of it, stored inside my cybertronics. I hadn't thought. I hadn't considered. But if the attackers destroyed the Lab computers, I'm the only backup they've got left."

"No fear. I won't let them take you. Unless..." Zal studied Torian, who looked flustered, frightened, and half-frozen. "Unless you *want* to go with them. I know this world isn't what you're used to."

Torian grabbed his arm. "I don't want to go. I want to stay here. With you."

"Now, we talked about that, my friend. That choice won't be mine to make."

"But shouldn't it be mine? You're always saying your society is founded on free will, on the right of every citizen to make their own choices. I choose here. I choose you. Unless...*oh, fuck.*" They carded trembling fingers through still-damp hair. "You don't want sex. I keep forgetting. There's nothing I can offer you in exchange for keeping me with you."

"Oi. You've got way more to offer, believe me. But just so we're clear, if you want sex, I can't give it to you. So if that's what you need—"

"No. I've had enough to last me quite a while, trust me."

"Aye. I do."

"You...trust me?" Torian's eyes widened. "I don't think anyone ever has before."

Zal brushed Torian's cheek with the backs of his fingers. "What did I tell you? People are idiots."

"Torian." A gravelly voice spoke from the forest behind them and Torian flinched.

Zal whirled, his staff held across his body, shielding Torian from the threat. "Who goes there? What do you want?"

The man who stepped out of the trees was shorter than Zal but taller than Torian and soft around the middle like Barkon. He wasn't moon-born pale or earth-born mid-brown or sun-born dark. He was somewhere between earth and moon, with near-black almond-shaped eyes, a broad nose, and an expression of total irritation.

So this is a star-born. Zal wasn't impressed.

The man didn't pay any attention to Zal. "Torian. We're evacuating, and this stunt of yours has put us seriously behind schedule."

Torian stepped out from behind Zal. "Then leave, Edric. But I'm staying here."

Edric's thin eyebrows shot up, astonishment joining the irritation on his face, as if his breakfast egg had grabbed his fork and stabbed him in the belly. "Don't be ridiculous. The facility is compromised. The recidivist faction...well, they don't intend to allow us to rebuild. It's time to regroup."

"I told you. I choose to remain."

"Have your circuits been damaged? I said we have no time. We have to activate the destruct sequence before we go, and the mother ship won't wait for us."

"Destruct sequence?" Zal's gaze bounced between Edric and Torian. "What's that? Is something in danger?"

Torian's fists clenched at their sides, their attention fixed on Edric. "You intend to go through with it, then? Destroying the whole planet, the civilization that *you* started, murdering all these people, just to cover your tracks?"

"Clearly you need a complete system diagnostic. I'll start it as soon as we've docked in orbit." Edric looked Torian up and down, his glance cold, dispassionate. "I hope the backups haven't been corrupted."

Zal had had enough of Edric's attitude. "Let me see if I understand you. You don't want Torian from affection or loyalty. You want them for what they know? As if they're nothing more than a book to open and discard at your whim?"

"It doesn't *know* anything. It's a repository and a sexual surrogate. Nothing more."

Zal took a step forward, hands tightening on his staff. "They're not an it. And they're far more than a fragging book. You don't deserve them."

"If it weren't for me, it wouldn't exist, so I own it, legally and wholly, and I intend to take it with me." Edric beckoned to Torian. "We've a task to accomplish. If you continue to behave irrationally, I'll have to wipe your memory. As if I didn't have enough to do."

Zal turned to Torian and grasped their wrist, the little zing that always accompanied contact with their skin sizzling along his veins. "Don't go with him. You can't want this. They *exploited* you."

Torian's gaze cut to Edric. "He's right, Zal. This is all I am. All I've ever been, but for this time with you. It's better this way."

"It's not. It's not better for you. And it's not better for me."

"Enough." Edric held a strange object in his hand, pointing it at Zal as if it were a mage's staff.

"What in the name of the Sun is that?"

"It's a blaster." Torian's murmur was strained. "Don't move."

"Come now, Torian. Or do I silence this fool for good?"

"Please, you needn't do that. I'm coming." Torian clutched Zal's arm. "Don't follow."

Zal's heart gave a painful lurch. "Torian—"

"You said you trusted me," they murmured. "Trust me now."

Chapter Ten

This had to work. But in case it didn't, Torian allowed themselves an indulgence. They stretched up and kissed Zal's cheek. "Thank you."

Zal blinked rapidly, a sheen in his dark eye. "Ah, shite. Don't go." His voice, laced with pleading, resonated painfully with the implants in Torian's chest. "You said you were done with them. That you wanted to stay here. With me."

Edric laughed, a thin, arrogant sound. "What foolishness. Torian is a logical construct. We've made it that way. Why would it want to stay here and be destroyed when it could return to comfort, convenience, and usefulness?"

"Usefulness? Making them think all they are is a machine for you to tinker with or a hole to stick your pecker in? I bet you've never even heard them sing."

"Sing? Ridiculous." Edric shuffled his feet, clearly on edge. "No more delays. Start data retrieval for the detonation protocol codes on the way to the site. Thanks to your antics, our launch window is too narrow as it is, so if you don't move your mechanical ass—" Edric gestured at Zal with the blaster.

"I'm coming." Torian walked toward Edric, keeping their body in direct line with the blaster. Torian was in no danger. As long as they held the backup files, Edric wouldn't fire for fear of scrambling the data. But Zal—no, Torian would not allow harm to come to him.

They'd nearly reached Edric when Zal strode forward, dodging in front of Torian to face down Edric.

"Don't do this. We—my people—we're not some trifling annoyance, like a swarm of insects for you to swat. We have homes, families, a *society*."

"Really? How long do you think your society would go on without our support?" Edric waved the blaster at Zal and Torian flinched. "That chrysocite, for instance. *We* gave it to you. Turned those worthless rocks into massive solar cells to study how a society policed with magic would work. You've got fewer than half the original number now, and lose more every year. What will you do when your magic doesn't work anymore?"

"I reckon we'd learn to cope."

Edric snorted. "You couldn't. You're too dependent on it. We're doing you a favor by making the end short. Maybe not painless, but at least quick. A brief flare and you're done, rather than a long, drawn-out descent into chaos and starvation."

"You've no right—"

"I've had enough of you." Edric adjusted the setting on his blaster. "The rest of the planet can wait for the destruct sequence. But you? I'm ending you here."

Edric pointed the blaster square at Zal's chest.

Torian didn't pause, didn't think, didn't hesitate. *They acted*, grabbing Edric's bare wrist with both hands and wrenching it downward. *I did it with the water, for my own convenience. This time, it's for the planet. This time, it's for Zal.*

Edric struggled, but Torian's infrastructure was reinforced with materials of the Infomancers' own making, and no matter how degenerate their morals, they knew their cybertronics. "What—let go. Torian, what are you doing?"

They bared their teeth. "Choosing."

Torian pushed the entire charge in their reserve banks through the conduits in their cybertronic network, out the sensors in their fingertips, directly into Edric. This time, they encountered no hidden code loops. No safety bypasses. The Infomancers had never coded for this scenario. Obviously, they'd never imagined one of their own constructs would rebel.

Their mistake.

Edric juddered and twitched, his eyes rolling back in his head. Torian sensed his heart stuttering, but still they discharged. More, more, *more*.

Reserves depleted. Shut-down commencing in three... two...

With a jerk of their chin, Torian disabled the safety protocols and *pushed*. All of it. Every last joule. Whatever it took to keep Zal safe.

As Edric collapsed, jerking, on the ground, Torian followed until the very last spark of energy flowed out of them and into Edric's corpse.

Chapter Eleven

"Torian! Sun, please, no. Torian!" Zal dropped to the ground next to where Torian lay beside the lifeless star-born.

He ripped Torian's shirt apart and pressed a hand to their chest. No little zing of awareness, not even a ghost of a flutter of heartbeat. The gold lattice under Torian's skin was gray and dull, exactly like Zal's Sun Stone when its charge was depleted.

Wait just a second. Depleted charge? Hadn't Zal noted the similarities between Torian and his Stone? Hadn't he seen that network of metal on their back, exposed to the sun the way Zal recharged his staff? They needed food for their— what did they call them?—cybertronics, and those were solar powered, just like Zal's staff.

Zal's bloody half-charged staff. But with the sun still hidden behind the mountain, it was all he had.

"Please let it be enough."

He stripped Torian to the waist, their slender body already cooling on his lap. He turned them gently, exposing that astonishing metal latticework on their back.

Zal grasped his staff and willed the Stone to life, the sudden flare so bright he had to squint. The light bathed Torian's back. Zal felt the heat on his own wrist where it supported Torian—hot, as if the sun had drawn too close to the earth. Would it burn that pale skin? Did the lattice have a limit on what it could absorb at one time?

Zal eased back on the Stone's output and knelt there, in the imprisoned light of the sun, and prayed for all he was worth that it would be enough.

Too soon, the light began to fade, although the gold beneath Torian's skin had barely begun to glimmer.

"More, blast you." Zal exerted his will, further than he'd ever tried before, forcing every last bit of energy out of the

Stone until, with a crack as loud as the death of Star Mountain, the Stone shattered, cleaving his staff in two.

Yet Torian didn't move.

I can't fail now. Not with this. Torian had sacrificed their life for Zal. How humbling, that the person he'd been half-convinced meant nothing but chaos for the world had been the one to preserve it.

Zal cradled Torian against his chest, dry sobs shaking his shoulders, his hair, a curtain around his face, lying in limp black ropes across Torian's skin.

"Zal?"

Zal caught his breath at the thready whisper. He eased Torian away from his chest and nearly broke down anew when those luminous gray eyes blinked at him, a smile curving the full lips.

Zal hugged them tight again, murmuring into their hair. "Sun, moon, and stars, Torian, don't you ever do something like that again."

Torian coughed. "No promises, but I'll try to keep the near-death experiences to a minimum." They struggled to sit up. Zal assisted but kept an arm firmly around their shoulders. "Oh. Your staff. What happened?"

Zal shrugged, his arm tightening. "Seemed like a reasonable trade-off. Got you back, didn't I?" He sighed. "Although I'll have to learn a new trade. Can't be a Sun mage without a Stone, and according to your Infomancer, there won't be more of those."

"Well, actually, he lied."

Zal peered down at Torian. "He did?"

"Or maybe his information was imperfect."

Zal snorted. "And he called himself an Infomancer. Know what? Let's move away from him. I don't like him any better dead than I did alive." He helped Torian to their feet and drew them away from Edric's corpse.

"The thing is, the originators didn't *make* the Sun Stones. They found them. Here. On this planet."

"You know this because of those data archives of yours?"

Torian nodded. "That's right. They mined the chrysocite in the catacombs under Star Mountain. They never bothered to go back after they'd set the experiment in motion, but there's more there."

"Get away with you. You mean we could mine more Stones, make more mages?"

"Technically, yes, but it won't be easy. That's one of the reasons the Infomancers didn't bother to get more."

"Right. We were the only ones being inconvenienced. Arseholes." Torian bit their lip and their gaze slid to where Edric's feet were still visible in the underbrush. "Shite. I'll wager you've never hurt anyone before, let alone killed someone. I don't blame you for being upset."

"I should be, I know, but I can't regret it. When I weighed his life against your whole world, the choice was easy."

Yet Torian's expression didn't lighten, and Zal's belly clenched. *There's something else. Something I missed. Something they're not telling me.* "What?"

"The thing is…"

Zal dropped his arm from Torian's shoulders. "I know. You only said that about wanting to stay with me because of Edric."

"What? No. I meant it. But there's the whole tribunal to get through and—"

"Bugger the tribunal. I'm not turning you in. You're not a mage, rogue or otherwise."

Torian's smile nearly blinded Zal's remaining eye. "Really? Oh." Their smile dimmed. "Won't you get in trouble, though?"

"Their own rules will trip them up there. I'll have to tell them about losing my Stone, but since I'm not a mage anymore, I'm not under their jurisdiction. As for your abilities…" Zal glanced at Edric. "Best we keep some of those to ourselves, eh?"

Torian nudged the ruins of Zal's staff with the toe of one boot. "You didn't lose your ability, though. You still have the…mage potential, right?"

"Aye. But I can't harness it without the Stone."

Torian shook their head impatiently. "You manipulate solar energy. That's a given. The chrysocite is a convenient, easily transportable storage cell, but any compatible power source would work equally well."

"Is that so? Where in the blazes do I get one of those compatible thingummies?"

"Well, there's me, of course."

Torian grasped Zal's wrist and discharged enough energy to raise his braids in a dance around his shoulders.

Zal yanked his wrist away. "Don't. Not if it means you—" His throat closed at the memory of Torian lying lifeless across his lap.

Torian patted his chest. "You won't drain me, not like I drained myself. With Edric, I had to be sure. I didn't want him to destroy the planet." They grinned. "It seemed a reasonable trade-off."

"Not from where I sat."

"Does that mean you like having me around?"

Zal thought of his incomprehensible divination spread—sun and moon together on the partnership path; stars no longer in play; earth suspended between peace and prosperity. *It was a true casting after all.* He understood the meaning now—and thanked the Sun for the explosion that took him to Corvel-on-Byrne. This was his destiny—working with Torian for the good of the world, the Infomancers be damned.

"I'm bloody sure I can't do without you now."

"Exactly. You need someone to guard your left side. And I need…" Torian shrugged and pulled their oversized cloak closer around his shoulders.

"What do you need, love?"

Torian ducked their head, as if they'd suddenly come over shy. "I need someone who thinks I'm beautiful *without* the body modification protocols. Regardless of the aspect I'm wearing."

"Aye, well, you're always beautiful to me. Have been since I first saw you, filthy and half-starved in that odious gaol. But don't imagine you can't choose to leave my sorry arse behind if you want. The Sun knows I'm no prize. Got only one eye. An uncertain temper. Won't swive. A bad bargain all around."

Torian lifted onto their toes and kissed Zal's cheek again. "There are other reasons to be with someone. Companionship. Support. Caring. We could travel together. I'd like to see your home."

Zal pictured Torian on the beach below his cottage, soft dark hair blowing in the breeze as the sun rose across the sea. *Aye, I'd give a lot to see that sight.* "The life of a circuit mage is a rough one, my dear. Are you ready for that?"

"Eventually. But first, there's something else we have to do." Torian glanced at Edric again.

"If you want, we can bury him."

"Not that. I mean, we probably should. But, Zal, I'm not sure if the other Infomancers will come back. If the mother ship intended to make its launch window, this group will have gone, but they could return. Or some other faction could show up to finish what the first ones started."

"So?"

"So that destruction device is still in place, under the mountain with ancillary charges set in the catacombs reaching all the way to the southern sea. We have to disable it."

Zal frowned. "Do you know how to do that?"

Torian tapped the side of their head. "I know everything, remember?"

"Then I guess we've a long journey ahead of us." Zal stared at the broken mountain. "Shite. The northern cantons in winter. The Sun-forsaken *mountain* in winter. This'll be a right picnic." He grinned at Torian. "In that case, we'd best find the nearest town and do some shopping. We've got to find you better boots."

Torian chuckled.

"All right, I'll bite." Zal shouldered his pack. "What's so amusing?"

"This reminds me of something from the archives. A film."

"Film? What's that?"

Torian looked blank. "It's a…if you think of a—"

"Never mind. I'll take it as given. A film, then."

"At the end of a very famous one, after one character has killed a very bad person, his companion, against all expectation, protects him. In return, he says, 'I think this is the beginning of a beautiful friendship.'"

Zal tweaked a lock of Torian's hair. "You know, my own Moon, I couldn't have said better myself."

Dear Len,

RADCLYFFE

Radclyffe here—your writer self, the one you never thought could ever be real. No one told you when you were growing up that girls could be all the things boys could be—like cops and firefighters and mailmen and doctors. No one for sure ever mentioned being a writer—if you were a boy *or* a girl. That was something people a lot different than you became. So you looked around and tried to see where you might fit, but you couldn't find yourself anywhere in the kids and families and grown-ups you saw. You looked ahead and couldn't see yourself, only what you *couldn't* be.

Then you read that book, remember? *Doctor Kate*, it was called. You were ten, maybe, and you knew that was it. You wanted to be a doctor and do something that mattered, just like Kate. It all started with a book. So many books, but for so long, none about girls like you.

Remember the play you wrote about the astronaut? You made the leader a girl, because why not? Why couldn't that happen? You were eleven. You wrote lots of stories about girls who did the things you wished you could do after that. But you never once thought of writing as anything other than a place to put your secret wishes and dreams.

Then for a long time you were too busy to think about much except becoming a doctor, until I (Radclyffe here) popped up again a couple decades later and wrote some stories about women like the one you had become. Women who loved women and were happy about it. Lesbians who lived full and satisfying and noble lives. For a while, you and I shared space pretty well: you worked days, I worked nights.

And then something extraordinary happened. *We* found a place to share our stories with other people—pretty soon, lots of people. And you discovered that writing matters, too, and not just for you. What we write and what we read and what we share has power. The power to teach, the power to learn, the power to create community. The power to say: "We have the right to love and live as we choose—come celebrate with us."

So, I am glad you finally figured out that the thing you never thought you could be has turned out to be what makes you whole. You, me, and a book. Just like at the beginning.

See you soon, Len. We have another book to write and so many more to read.

Rad

The Hollow History of Professor Perfectus

GINN HALE

The Great Stage Magician, Professor Perfectus, rolled his black satin top hat over one white-gloved hand and into the other. His expression remained placid beneath his velvet half-mask. Out in the exhibition hall, hundreds of men and women leaned forward in their seats, following his every motion intently.

He passed the hat over the supine body of the very pretty Miss May Flowers (actually called Geula Mandelbaum, but audiences expected a certain simplicity of name and function when it came to the assistants of stage magicians). Slowly she began to rise off the table. Her beaded red dress draped from her legs. A comb fell from her hair, freeing one long, lustrous gold curl. She floated upward with the slow grace of a column of incense until she lay stretched out a full foot above Professor Perfectus's slim, gray-haired figure. He passed his top hat under Geula, brushing the loose curl of her hair as he did so.

And I—a dark girl standing in the shadows, where no one watched—I drew in a deep breath, taking all the strength I could from the currents of the air that filled the large hall. I concentrated and made a motion, as if to shoo a fly aside.

At once, three white doves escaped from Professor Perfectus's top hat, winging around his suspended assistant. Gasps, cries, and applause burst from the audience and grew wilder when a mob of scarlet butterflies burst from the breast of Geula's dress. They followed the doves up into the darkness above the stage curtain and disappeared as a rain of red and white cut paper fluttered down.

Someone in the audience screamed. Concerned voices rose from amidst the applause and cheers.

I stepped forward into the flare of limelight, dressed as plainly as a governess. My hair had been pulled back into a severe bun, and a useless pair of gold spectacles perched on the bridge of my nose.

Glinting, golden things like the spectacles captured the audience's attention on a darkened stage, erasing the awareness of more subtle details.

"Good people, please do not be alarmed," I spoke slowly and calmly, suppressing the cadence of my natural accent. "Let me again assure you that none of the feats you have witnessed on this stage were the results of actual magic. The professor is not a mage or even a theurgist. What you have seen here were displays of the most ingenious slight of hand and misdirection, crafted and practiced to perfection, by a great master. My dear uncle, Professor Perfectus."

I waved my hand in the professor's direction, and he executed a deep bow and then flipped his hat back atop his head. Then he dropped his white-gloved hands into the pockets of his dark coat. Sweat beaded the back of my neck and dampened the high collar of my gray dress. Encores like this one always exhausted me, but it was very nearly over.

"I cannot give away all of my uncle's secrets," I went on in a stage whisper as I drew closer to where Geula hung in the air. "But certainly a few of you must suspect that Miss Flowers is suspended by several very strong wires."

On cue, Geula reached up and wrapped her gloved hands around the black wires. She pulled herself up into a sitting position as if she were balanced in the seat of a swing. I knelt, retrieved her glittering, gold comb, and handed it to her.

"Why, thank you so much, Abril. I must look a fright." She drew all eyes as she made a small show of fixing her blond hair and then straightening the hem of her red dress before it exposed more than her dainty yellow shoes.

And while the two of us blocked the view, Professor Perfectus stepped backwards into his black cabinet, hidden in the dark velvet folds of the back curtain. He pulled the doors closed behind him and locked the clasp from inside. With immense relief, I let his lace-cut steel body slump lifelessly back onto the supports in the cabinet. At last, I allowed my consciousness to slip from the automaton.

I took Geula's hand and helped her hop down from the wires. Then she and I stepped apart to reveal the seemingly empty stage behind us.

A roar of happy applause went up through the crowd. Young men who had become regulars at the fair tossed flowers onto the stage while a few brave women threw hand-made sachets embroidered with hearts and scented with lavender.

Strange to think how much they loved to be fooled momentarily into believing that they'd witnessed genuine magic, which they'd all but outlawed across the eastern states and most of the western territories. Yet six days a week, huge crowds paid to cheer at slight of hand and misdirection. They relished the smoke hiding all the wires and mirrors because it allowed them to conjure the presence of something amazing and dangerous. Here in the dark, they longed for mysteries and magic. But out on public streets, with carriages careening past and newsboys shouting sordid tales of scandals and murders, the last thing these decent folk wanted was to discover a free mage lurking in their midst.

That hadn't always been so.

But in 1858, during the Arrow War, mages had torn open a vast and unnatural chasm, flooding out most the southern states and dividing the east and west of America with a the Inland Sea. And up in the Rocky Mountains, behind the roaring saltwater, had come ancient creatures. Theurgists and naturalists called them dinosaurs, but most folks knew them as monsters. Twelve years after that, just as the waters had calmed and cattlemen had learned to rope and drive herds of burly leptoceratops, another battle between mages had unleashed the Great Conflagration. Eastern towns all across the salt marshes and as far north as Chicago had caught light. In Peshtigo, more than a thousand people had burned to death.

Twenty-two years on, people still hadn't forgotten the terror of those merciless flames. Hell, I'd been three then, but even I still woke shaking from dreams of my parents screaming as a blazing cyclone of brilliant embers engulfed them.

So I understood what all these good, natural folks feared. I even understood why they wanted free mages like me rounded up and placed under the godly thumbs of theurgists. They felt terrified and powerless. They wanted magic if it came with assurances, federal offices, and communion wafers. They wanted mages in the world—transmitting messages across the oceans and powering turbines—so long as they had us on leashes and electric collars

But I knew the man who'd created those damn collars, and he gave me worse nightmares than my parents' deaths did.

I'd also come to understand how corrupt theurgists could be. The papers were full of news of how the US Office of Theurgy and Magicum had ordered the 7th Cavalry to suppress Lakota free mages and their Spirit Dances. That hadn't been upholding the law; it had been a massacre. I'd rather have lived all my life as a wanted outlaw than to have lent my small power to the men responsible.

Geula and I agreed on that much. She didn't share my suspicion of all theurigists as much as she dreaded the attention of the men who hunted bounties. Audience expectation wasn't the only reason she'd abandoned her real name when she'd fled Boston ten years ago.

We weren't either of us angels—though Geula could look the part with a pair of dainty white wings strapped to her dress and a brassy halo pinned to her curls—but we didn't hurt anybody. Not with our stage performances, and not when we kissed and delighted each other in the privacy of our little room back stage.

I clasped her gloved hand, feeling the warmth and strength of her grip in my own. We bowed, applause and cheers rolling over us as the new electric floor lights bathed us in a yellow glow. Geula caught a sachet and smiled beautifully. I drew in another deep breath, taking power from the tiny whirlwinds that rose between clapping hands and in gusts of hot exhalations. Doors opened and fresh breezes blew in from the lobby. My skin almost tingled with pleasure.

Air. I ached to feel fresh air the way a landed fish desired water.

Geula glanced sidelong at me, and I caught the worry in her eyes. I forced a smile. We bowed again, and the applause very slowly died down. There were always folk who believed that if they clapped hard and long enough Professor Perfectus would reappear, though he never did.

"You worried me for a moment there," Geula whispered. "Better now, though?"

"Much," I assured her. Performing six days a week at the New United America Exhibition in Chicago wore me down, but if I could hold out a year, I'd have earned enough money for Geula and I to buy our own place out west where no one knew us.

We straightened, and I followed her gaze out into the audience. The usual bunch of young men winked and ogled her. A number of older gentlemen stared at the stage with expressions of distant longing. Then I surveyed the upper-crust we'd pulled into the box-seats. I raised my hand, pretending to straighten my spectacles and hiding my scowl.

Three women, wearing silk, lace, and dazzling strings of pearls, gazed down at me from their gilded box. I recognized them, of course. The three 'Jewels of Chicago Society', papers called them. (Though the same newsmen deemed Fatima Djemille's graceful dancing 'obscene', so their taste clearly didn't align with mine.)

Tall, long-faced Jane Adams and her mousy little companion, Ellen Starr, weren't either of them much past thirty but already famous for their philanthropy and Christian charity work. Beside them, the elegant, silver-haired widow Mrs. Bertha Porter looked like a bird of paradise perched alongside two pigeons. She controlled a vast fortune of properties and was rumored to know more about financing bars and brothels than any society lady ought to. She looked like the kind of woman who laughed a great deal at everyone else.

But what truly set the three of them apart from most women in the country and made them a trinity were their statuses as Official Theurgists. With a word, any of the three of them could order me captured, jailed, and collared.

My stomach clenched like a snail dropped in a snow bank.

"You see who is up in the box seats?" I asked quietly.

Geula didn't appear the least bit surprised. She simply nodded.

"I told you I found us patrons, didn't I?" Geula whispered.

It took a moment for that to sink in. She'd invited them here. How much had she told them?

"Abril, you can't keep working like this. It's wearing you down to your bones." Geula cast me one of her soft, sweet looks. "You're making yourself sick, darling. I know you want to make more money, but—"

"You don't know anything," I responded in a less than pleasant sort of hiss. I jerked my hand from hers.

Fortunately, the stage curtain came down before anyone in our audience could see Geula's dismayed expression or witness my dash for the back door.

✿✿✿

Geula found me across the man-made lagoons, up on the observation deck that overlooked the resplendent Hall of Natural History. I stared down at the long swath formed by thousands of people, dressed in their best hats and coats, as they poured between the huge plaster statues of proud and savage beasts. Lions, plesiosaurs, elk, and elephants posed on massive pedestals, while pigeons and small brown pterosaurs flitted overhead.

Cold winds rushed up from Lake Michigan and surged over me. I drank in the force of them, calming the air around me and at the same time regaining some of my strength.

How I loved the wind—I didn't even care if it stank of fish or coal smoke. I felt as if the gusts alone could sustain me. Though in truth, not even the most powerful of wind mages could live on air alone. And contrary to popular opinion, none of us actually controlled the wind. We drew our power from it, just as earth mages needed the ground beneath them to cast spells and sea mages required water to maintain their power.

Theurgists, on the other hand, built spells as complex as engines and powered them with alchemic stone—the same way an engineer might shovel coal into his boiler. (Though not so long ago theurgists had wired mages into their spells, using us like batteries and leaving us as drained husks.)

I'd learned that much history from my uncle—not the masked automaton that I'd dolled up to pass for him on stages and in hotels, but the gentle old man who'd died to keep me and his invention from falling into the hands of theurgists or the monsters who served for them.

I glared into the distance.

Studded with electric lights, Mr. Ferris's Great Wheel rose so high into the twilight sky that it appeared to harvest shining stars as it slowly descended. Beyond that, veils of coal smoke spread a haze over the dark streets of Chicago, making the city seem as a far shore, vastly distant from the miles of verdant fairgrounds claimed by the New United America Exhibition.

"So you gonna say anything or just stare off sulking?" Geula leaned against the cast-iron railing of the overlook. She'd brought her willow lunch basket and wore a long black coat over her beaded red dress. Several ivory-capped hatpins secured her wide black hat to her hair. One stray curl hung against the graceful line of her neck.

"I'm not sulking," I replied—though my tone wasn't so convincing, not even to my own ears. "I'm thinking."

"About?"

"Things," I replied. I adored every inch of Geula—absolutely loved her laughter and easy conversation too—but for the first time, I faced how little I truly knew of her. Three months wasn't a long time together, not even if it had been a giddy, glorious three months. I'd kept back much of my own history, not wanting her to think poorly of me. Now I wondered how much she might not have told me.

"Things…" Geula hefted her small lunch basket and drew out a sandwich. She took a bite and chewed with a contemplative expression. "Could be better, could be worse."

She offered the sandwich to me, and I accepted it. We were making decent money at the exhibition, but not so much that we could often indulge beyond sausages and mustard on a rye roll. With only one railway bridging the Inland Sea, tickets didn't come easily or cheap. Though now I had to wonder how foolish that fantasy might be if I couldn't even trust Geula not to bring theurgists to my doorstep.

I took a couple more bites and then returned the sandwich to Geula. She finished it off. We both watched as a young couple strolled past us, trailing a matronly chaperone. Geula's fingers twitched, but she didn't pinch anything from them.

"I packed up your props and the professor's cabinet," Geula informed me quietly. "It's all locked up in the dressing rooms."

"Thank you." I felt slightly guilty about having left her with all that heavy work, but on the other hand, what had she expected me to do at the sight of three theurgists? Two days back, when she'd mentioned finding patrons, I'd imagined the usual bored, bearded old men who enjoyed throwing their money around in front of young women. I certainly hadn't pictured myself facing down the Chicago Jewels.

"What did you tell them?" I asked. "About me."

"Nothing except that I thought you were smart and quick. Obviously I didn't know the half of it, seeing how fast you rabbited off." Geula shrugged. For a few moments, she stared out at the vast crowds passing below us and filling the air with their conversations and laughter.

"Did you really think I'd turn you over for a reward?" Geula asked me.

"I…" I had feared as much, but I felt ashamed of myself now, with Geula giving me that disappointed look. We hadn't been together long, but I *did* know her. I'd seen her stand up to hecklers and bullies, and I'd stood beside her when she'd block the path of a patrolman bent on beating down a beggar. Geula stuck to her principles. She wouldn't sell out a friend, not even for a hundred-dollar mage bounty, I truly believed that.

"I didn't really think. I just ran," I admitted.

"Those Jersey theurgists put some real fear in you, didn't they?" Geula asked.

This time I shrugged. It hadn't been the theurgists themselves who'd ingrained this terror into me; they hadn't needed to bother. The mere threat of them had been enough to keep my family constantly moving—abandoning homes and jobs in the dead of night; changing our names and always keeping our bags packed. I'd been brought up afraid.

And when my uncle had finally found something like a stable home for his wife and me, it had been in the isolated grounds of Menlo Park, in New Jersey. There, Mr. Edison had provided housing and employment, all the while hammering in all the horror we would suffer if we forced him to report us to the Office of Theurgy and Magicum.

"They will lock you in a prison laboratory. Feed you gruel and then dissect you like a rat," he'd often informed me with a smile. "That would be a shame."

The shocks and burns I'd endured while he had tested his electric collars had been accompanied by reminders that official theurgists could and would do far worse to me, my uncle, and my dear crippled auntie.

"I guess I should have given you more warning about the three of them coming to the show." Geula's words brought me back from my troubled memories. "I worried that knowing sooner would make performing all the harder for you."

Likely I wouldn't have set foot on stage at all. I didn't feel like admitting as much.

"So what were the Jewels after you for anyway?" I asked.

"Well, it was Mrs. Palmer who I'd worked for before," Geula replied, but then she cut herself off as a group of men in musty fur coats strolled past us, loudly proclaiming their wonder and excitement over the Machine Maid in the Technology Hall. Apparently the new automaton might well 'unburden men from the hysterics imposed by the fairer sex'.

Geula scowled at the men and I just smirked.

They weren't such catches that any of the fairer sex was likely to impose anything on them but a steep entry fee.

"Four years back"—Geula returned to her story, leaning close to me—"Mrs. Palmer's favorite cook went missing. I tracked the woman down and managed to barter her back from Roger Plant—"

"I don't know who that is," I admitted. Most of the five months I'd been in Chicago, I'd worked here at the Exposition. I'd rarely even wandered far from the theater complexes. The one exhibit I'd convinced myself to pay the ticket price to enter had been the Wonders of the Western Territories. There they'd had towers of fruit from California, heaps of Nevada borax, and live specimens of beautiful, feathered dinosaurs from Colorado farms. (Their plumes adorned a great many expensive hats worn by society ladies, I'd learned.) What I knew of the city beyond the Exhibition grounds came largely from the papers and gossip. I'd heard nothing of a Roger Plant.

"Nice for you, then," Geula replied. She made a face like she was recollecting having a tooth pulled. "He runs a place called Under the Willow in the Levee. His beer isn't worth the nickel he charges, but he pulls certain men in with the girls he keeps in his backrooms. Not all of them are there willingly. It took a little doing with my pistol, but I managed to convince him that the cook wasn't worth the trouble he'd bring down on his own head if he kept her."

I stared at Geula. I'd known she'd traveled in tough company and had been more than an actress before I'd met her in the theater, but I hadn't quite imagined this.

"So they want you to find someone again?" I asked.

"They're offering seven hundred dollars," Geula said quietly. I stared at her. That was more than I could've hoped to earn in two, maybe even three, years. I didn't doubt the Jewels could afford as much, but I did wonder who they could value so highly... Or who they feared crossing so badly.

All around us, small electric lights lit up, like ornate constellations thrown across the exhibition buildings. Four of them on the far wall formed a shining crown behind Geula's head.

"This time Miss Adams has a girl missing from her charity house." Geula's expression went a little distant and hard. "Liz Gorky is the girl's name. She's nineteen, dark-haired and doe-eyed. She took work at a hotel called World's Fair but hasn't returned for a week now."

"Seven days isn't so long, particularly not for a grown woman who's found work. Maybe she's had enough of living under the thumb of a bunch a nosey temperance women."

"I thought that too. But it turns out she left her infant daughter in Miss Starr's care," Geula went on. "And according to both Miss Adams and Miss Starr, Liz doted on her daughter and fretted over leaving her for even one afternoon. Neither of them believe she simply abandoned her child."

I didn't see what Geula or I could really do about the situation, but at the same time, I wasn't entirely unmoved. I'd lost my parents quite young and still wondered what they might have thought of me if they had the opportunity to know me. I couldn't keep from feeling sympathy for the child.

"Have they gone to the police?" Plenty of missing folk turned up in their morgues. If she wasn't there, then the Jewels likely had the pull to get a city-wide search started. That was more than Geula or I could do for them.

"Miss Starr went to them right away, but they weren't much help. They questioned Liz Gorky's employer, a man named Herman Mudgett. He insisted that Liz had met a salesman and run off with him, which was good enough for the crushers, apparently. But then three days ago Miss Adams saw Liz Gorky, here—"

"So, she ran off but not very far?" I asked.

"She wasn't attending the exhibition," Geula whispered. "She was an exhibit."

"What?"

"I'm going to see her for myself," Geula said. She started to turn away but then glanced back at me over her shoulder. "You coming?"

✿✿✿

Inside the lofty Technology Hall, a promenade wider than most city streets looped through hundreds of exhibits. The air hummed with thrilled voices, engine sounds, and the bright calls of the various men presenting the inventions on display. Here and there mechanical devices stood cordoned off behind curtains and velvet ropes; some were staged like studies, kitchens, or even gardens (complete with flowerbeds and trellises of ivy). Other innovations, like the huge, silver alchemic train engine, served as structures in and of themselves.

Throngs of men and women dressed in their best clothes—hats, bonnets, gloves, and a treasury of jewelry, watch fobs, buckles, and cufflinks—crowded around magnificent displays of gleaming brass and whirring clockwork. Children, dolled up in suits and gowns, capered between wonders, exclaiming over steam-powered miniature trains and then gaping as toy-sized alchemical airships whizzed overhead.

Towering above everything else, two huge silver columns of electric coils rose up from a stepped platform like gleaming monuments. I paused as a bolt of violet light arced up from the polished silver orb topping one of the columns. All around me, the air suddenly raced with charges. Tongues of lightning crackled through each breath I drew and seemed to set my blood bubbling like champagne. The hairs all across my body stood on end like they always did when I felt a storm coming.

Geula cast me a side-long glance and then followed my stare up to the violet bolt as it reached the second tower. "I read something about Mr. Tesla's coils making coal and alchemic stone obsolete," she commented. "But I don't recall exactly how."

"Me either, but I feel like I might start spitting lightning and thunder if I come any closer to them."

We skirted around the two columns, passing a lovely-smelling exhibit, where attendants in white aprons worked an ornate machine that stamped out exquisite bars of chocolate. Geula and I both accepted the samples offered. (If we hadn't been on something of a mission, I would have circled around for a second bar).

At last we came to the various displays of clockwork automatons and alchemic prosthetics. The wandering narrow alleys created by the numerous exhibit stalls stood largely empty compared to the crowded isles surrounding the displays of engines, guns sewing machines, and chocolates. Most of the other sightseers wandering the narrow avenue appeared to be war veterans and medical men; several even carried their surgical bags with them.

I knew that many people found the sight of artificial limbs disturbing, even those crafted from oak and hickory and inlaid with copper and gold spells, like these resting on satin pillows in glass cases all around us. But I gazed at the displays with a feeling of nostalgia and comfort. The sight of ivory fingers carved with lacey spell patterns brought memories of my aunt and uncle back to me in a rush. The subtle scent of machine oil and rose perfume seemed to float around me as I recollected carrying my uncle's creations from his cluttered workshop to my aunt's parlor. She took a little time to fit on new legs, but I always waited for the moment when she reached out and took my hand and slowly danced around the room with me.

My uncle always etched a heart into each of his designs for her.

Now I found myself looking through these disembodied limbs for that telltale trace. I stopped myself just as I extended a finger towards a delicate, outstretched hand. Of course the heart wasn't there. Both my uncle and aunt were dead. The only remains of them rested in a black cabinet back in my backstage dressing room. The one thing I was likely to do if I touched one of these finely tuned prosthetics was to jolt a spell to life and give myself away as a mage. I carefully tucked my hands into the pockets of my coat.

Beside me, Geula craned her neck to take in the banners and signs hanging in the distance.

"It's the Mechanical Maid we're after," Geula informed me. Then she drew a small square of paper from her pocket and studied it. A pale, round-faced young woman with her hair in ringlets and startlingly large, dark eyes stared up from the photograph.

"Is that Liz?" I asked. It struck me as odd that a girl so poor that she was living in a charity house could afford to have her photograph taken, much less look so imperious when she did.

Geula frowned at the image but then nodded. An instant later, she slipped the picture back into her coat. We walked deeper into the exhibits, encountering more and more complete automatons amongst the prosthetic limbs, false teeth, and glass eyes.

Clockwork birds sang from atop tiny metal perches, and delicately glazed butterflies fluttered tin wings. At the entry of one large stall, two automatons balanced atop pedestals like sentries. One stood about two feet tall and a child's pinafore covered the joints of its abdomen and groin; in place of the normal porcelain mask, its clockwork inner workings lay exposed around the two wide glass eyes. The automaton standing opposite it resembled an organ grinder's monkey, complete with grimacing white canine teeth. A key, carved from pearly alchemic stone, hung from a string around its neck, awaiting a human hand to slide it into the hole over the creature's machine heart and bring it to life.

"Can I assist you, miss?" A neat man, sporting a mustache so waxed that it looked like a pastille of black licorice, stepped out from between the two automatons. He looked to Geula, though I'd been the one lingering to study the exposed gearworks. (I myself had just finished replacing the lustrous alchemic stone, which powered the spells etched Professor Perfuctus's armature.) Between my dark complexion and quiet manner, it was common for people to mistake me for Geula's lady's maid. They were often shocked almost speechless if they discovered that I employed her as an assistant.

"No. We're simply looking," Geula informed the fellow. He frowned, then stepped forward to partly block our way.

"Many of the devices further along this aisle aren't all that suitable for the delicate sensibilities of women." He spoke in the hushed tone of an undertaker cautioning against opening a casket. "But across the hall there's an entertaining demonstration of a mechanical loom that produces the prettiest dress fabrics. And back the way you came is a charming music box shaped like a white kitten. I'd imagine that would be more suitable, wouldn't you?"

"I certainly have no idea of what you might imagine, sir. Suitable or otherwise," Geula replied, and she stepped past him. I laughed and followed her.

It soon became obvious why he'd been so anxious to keep us from strolling any further along this avenue. The designs of the automatons we passed steadily turned from entertainment or medical purposes to warfare. Blades and clubs replaced limbs, while the dark barrels of heavy guns loomed up at head-level. Few of these automatons resembled human beings, much less songbirds or butterflies. Most looked more like gigantic crabs, scorpions, and spiders but assembled entirely from armories.

And I did find it disturbing to see several of the things painted not only in military colors but with police seals emblazoned across them and badges soldered to their housings.

"As if the crushers aren't nasty enough already with their billy clubs and pistols," Geula muttered.

I considered the automaton, remembering the comments my uncle had so often made about such creations when they came up at the labs in Menlo Park.

"No city could afford to actually maintain a force of those things. Maybe they'd order one, but it would cost too much to risk on actual raids. I bet it's really meant to stand guard and simply appear threatening," I assured her. "All those joints are incredibly expensive to build and repair. And the amount of alchemic stone needed to power a platoon of them would cost far more than it would to hire an army of men."

"But there are some things—truly evil things—living folks flat out won't do," Geula replied. "Whereas an automaton couldn't care, could it? Whoever's registered on its collar as the owner could make it do anything."

"True, but that doesn't mean it would succeed," I replied. "Between the gold wires and the alchemical stone used for their cores, I suspect that even if an army of these spiders were let loose they wouldn't last too long. Seeing that seam there between the inner workings and the top where the alchemic stone is housed, I suspect that it wouldn't take more than a few minutes to sever the couplings. Once they're shut down, then, easy as you please, anyone can rip them up and even resell their parts."

Geula pulled her gaze from a looming automaton with a head like a spider's and half a dozen sabre-tipped legs. She looked to me. I wasn't sure what she read from my expression, but it brought a grin to her face.

"You really are a genius, aren't you?" Geula whispered to me. "And I bet you could stop this monster dead with your bare hands."

Briefly, I considered the hulking, insect-like machine. All the ambient power in the air seemed to crackle around me. Right now, with a touch of my hand, I could burn through the automaton's wires and cogs. Another time or somewhere else, it might be a different matter. But I loved it when Geula looked at me like this, and I wanted her to think the best of me being a mage. So, I simply smiled and nodded.

As we turned around a bend, we suddenly bumped up against a dense crowd of men. The vast majority appeared cued up to shoulder their ways into the blue-velvet tent displaying a red banner that proclaimed the many advantages of the New Mechanical Maid.

Devoted! Obedient & Adoring!
Woman, as She was Always Intended!
Built to Serve Every Need!

A voluptuous line drawing of a parlor maid with little wheels attached to her heels and a doll-like face hung beneath the banner.

"Two cents says this is nothing but a couple working girls rubbed down with silver powder and wearing copper-wire pasties on their tits," Geula whispered against my ear. "Bet they're selling the world's oldest trade as new technology."

"Maybe…" Something in the air disturbed me, and it wasn't just the dust of too much face powder. A definite and terribly familiar vibration pulsed from behind the curtains. I couldn't get a clear view of the big fellows at the front through the crush of men surrounding us, but something about their bulky figures made me extremely uneasy.

"It might be more simple than expected to get Liz out of this," Geula went on as we crept forward with the line of men. "Whoever's putting up this front won't want to risk a public scene exposing their real business."

"I don't know. I think there might be more going on—"

All at once, the crowd of men surrounding us rushed and jostled forward, pushing Geula and I ahead into the dim interior of the tent. The warm air inside felt torpid and smelled of sweat and stale cigar smoke. The mob flooded around a raised brass-colored platform and carried Geula and I near enough that I could make out the lines of the dark curtains behind the platform. Two rows of electric lights lit up its floor. It was a portable stage, I realized, complete with a hidden space in back and a generator humming below the platform.

A stocky man in his late forties, wearing a dapper brown tweed suit, parted the curtains and stepped into the light. A thunderclap of applause went up from the men all around me, and I caught my breath in horror. My pulse seemed to race so fast that it sent tremors through my hands.

Next to me, Geula appeared perplexed as she took the man in.

"Is that—"

"Edison." I forced his name out.

Looking back, I realized with growing panic that there would be no way through the throng of men behind us. The only way to escape would be to wait until the end of the demonstration and then file out past the platform and through the back flap of the tent, where two of Edison's big toughs stood guard. I recognized the stocky red-bearded man as the brute Edison had often sent after me when I'd refused to present myself at the laboratory.

After nearly nine years of hiding, I'd strolled directly back into Edison's grip.

At that thought, I felt the blood drain from my face and a sick vertigo washed over me.

He's in the light and I'm in the dark, I told myself. *He won't see me. He's too arrogant to care who's in the crowd. He won't notice me from the rest.*

I did my level best to believe that I could be right. I could get out of this place. Then, to my surprise and absolute relief, Geula caught my hand in hers and squeezed my fingers. I gripped her hand in return—just as I did on stage—sharing the assurance that we were there for one another.

"Are you all right?" she whispered.

"I…." But I didn't dare say anything surrounded by so many other people.

Geula glanced between me and the platform, and that quick look of knowing came over her. I hadn't told her anything about the years I'd spent as a prisoner at Menlo Park, but she seemed to understand that it was Edison that terrified me. At the very least, I supposed that she understood what danger a man like Edison, who worked directly for Federal Theurgists, posed to a free mage like me.

"As soon as we can, we'll slip out of here, like shadows. I promise," Geula assured me. "As long as we stay calm and don't draw any attention, we'll be fine."

I nodded and squeezed her hand again.

Up on the platform, Mr. Edison basked in admiration and applause, spreading his arms wide as if his mere existence was a marvel worthy of this entire Exhibition. His hair had turned grayer than I remembered, and his paunch had become too prominent for mere tailors to disguise, but his bland face bore hardly a single worry line.

After a few more moments, he motioned for silence. The crowd quieted.

"Good evening, gentlemen," Edison called out warmly. "It's a pleasure to see so many of you gathered here and looking so excited! As you should be, let me assure you! I am not overstating the matter when I swear that this, my latest innovation, by far surpasses any before it. Yes, previously I collared magic and brought light as bright as the stars into your homes. But now, I have improved upon God Almighty's loveliest and most flawed creation. Woman!"

He turned back to the curtain behind him and pulled the fabric aside to expose an automaton that almost perfectly duplicated the appearance of a young dark-haired woman. She wore a strangely dazed smile, and the light shining up from below cast unusual shadows across her face. Even so, it was obvious that the woman on the platform was the same one in the photograph Geula had shown me. Liz Gorky.

At a motion of Edison's hand, she stepped forward and twirled around. The thin white shift she wore turned nearly transparent as she spun through the blazing electric lights.

Metallic ribs and an automaton's shell—an armature— encased most of her body like a second skin. Only her head, breasts, and groin remained exposed, naked flesh. The tight bun holding up her long hair provided a clear view of the narrow silver collar locked tight around her throat like a choker.

Appreciative gasps and a number of hoots sounded from the men surrounding us, though a few of them appeared aghast. One portly middle-aged gentleman standing to my right looked stricken. Even in the gloom of the tent, I picked out the furious red flush rising in his pale face. His horror only increased when he glanced sidelong and caught sight of me and Geula.

"You may wish to avert your eyes, ladies," he mumbled, and to my surprise, he bowed his head to stare at his polished shoes. Clearly he'd expected something wholly more mechanical.

"Yes, lest we discover what's under our own clothes," Geula whispered to me. Then she returned her attention to the stage. "If that's make up, it's the best I've ever seen. The joints of her fingers really do look like an automaton's. And not merely any automaton's hand, either…"

I edged a step forward to study Edison's Mechanical Maid.

Geula was correct; it wasn't any automaton's armature holding Liz Gorky up on that stage. The long, graceful fingers were my uncle's design, though the wrists and ankles hadn't been crafted with the same exquisite care and looked stiff, almost chunky. Nor had the armature been fitted perfectly to the woman's body. The silver planes caging her thighs dug into her full buttocks, leaving red welts.

I didn't dare push my way closer to the platform for a better view, but I guessed that Edison had cobbled together two or more of my uncle's early blueprints. Though the inclusion of Edison's own collar and the dazed look in the woman's face assured me that this creation was far from what my uncle had intended.

The automaton's armature wasn't serving to give a disabled woman back her freedom of motion, or to empower her with even greater strength and speed that she could have hoped for from a body of flesh and blood. Edison had gutted all my uncle's ideals and crafted the remnants into a shining steel prison.

Up on the platform, Edison grinned and leaned theatrically towards the Mechanical Maid.

"Why don't you give the fine fellows of our audience a bow?" As Edison spoke, I felt a crackle in the air around the Mechanical Maid's throat. I remembered the same feeling from when Edison had tested his collars on me. The Mechanical Maid twitched once, her expression remaining wide-eyed and smiling, and then she bowed low and rose back upright.

Applause and a few murmurs arose from the crowd. The portly man looked up from his shoes and then scowled to see that the demonstration had not ended.

"A few skeptics among you might think that I've hired an actress to present to you on stage, but I assure you that this is the genuine result of my patented Mechanical Maid Automatonic Armature! At one time, this woman was a loose creature who ran wild, bringing no end of shame to her good husband. You needn't take my word. Listen to what her husband, Dr. Mudgett, has to say."

A slender man sporting a thick mustache and oily dark hair stepped from behind the curtain to join Edison. Hadn't Mudgett been the name of the proprietor of the hotel that Liz Gorky had disappeared from? Geula and I exchanged a glance, but neither of us said a word. Not in this crowd.

"Mr. Edison has indeed created a miracle here," Dr. Mudgett stated. "Before he consented to treat my wife with his amazing automatonic armature, I'm ashamed to say that Liz was a disrespectful creature, prone to hysteria and wanton disobedience. She could neither keep a fit house nor control herself. She spoke back to me endlessly, spent my money furiously, and wept when she could not have her every wish. I know in these modern times she wasn't unlike many of your wives, daughters, mothers, or sisters."

Mudgett took a moment to look out at the men gathered around him with a sincere and serious expression. And a number of them called out their agreement and grievances.

Few women knew their places, these days. They took work, rode bicycles, demanded votes, and all at a man's expense. Apparently, even the colored women were getting above themselves.

Geula rolled her eyes, and I fought the urge to send a shock through the crowd. Though there wasn't much that would have given me away more quickly.

Mudgett nodded.

"Now, we mustn't hate them for their frailty and failings. As a medical man, I can tell you that such women do themselves as much harm as they do their families." He spoke soothingly, almost as if he didn't realize that he'd been the one to stir up the audience's ire. "I have seen any number of women suffering from nervous disorders, neurasthenia, and even sterility, all because they have foolishly attempted to live as men, instead of joyfully living in obedience to men."

"Women like that aren't natural!" a spotty young man across the room shouted.

"No. Nor are they Christian, despite what they may call themselves and their organizations," Mudgett agreed while Edison looked on like a well-pleased ringmaster. "Sadly, until now the only way to deal with women like my own dear wife was either to confine them in madhouses or school them through brute force. But no longer! Mr. Edison has solved the problem without causing the slightest suffering or hardship for the weaker sex. Isn't that true, darling?"

Liz Gorky nodded.

"Gentlemen, thanks to Mr. Edison, I could not wish for a more pliable or dutiful spouse." The doctor smiled and reached out and pulled Liz Gorky close to him. Her expression didn't change in the slightest as she leaned into his arms.

"Doesn't the good book command that a wife should be her husband's in everything?" Mudgett asked her. I felt the air around her collar sizzle and knew from experience that fire seared through her mind, punishing her impulse to resist. But she betrayed no sign of the pain.

Liz—or the Mechanical Maid imprisoning her— nodded again and wrapped her arm around Mudgett, who grinned.

"Now that my Lizzie knows the pleasure of rightful submission and deference, we're both happy. And it's all thanks to Mr. Edison's Mechanical Maid Automatonic Armature!"

This time, the applause sounded like thunder. Even the man next to me gave a hearty cheer. I felt so repulsed that I had to fight down my bile.

"Well, that's mighty kind of you. And thank you, Doctor, for trusting me with the transformation of your wife," Edison said once the clapping quieted. "And thank you for allowing these gentlemen to share her story."

Again, the tent filled with applause. Neither Geula nor I even pretended to clap along.

Dr. Mudgett tipped his hat to the crowd and then escorted Liz back behind the curtain.

Edison remained up on the platform, beaming through the gloom at the crowd.

"It has been my pleasure to see all the good done by all my innovations, but none more than this one," Edison announced. "Now, if any of you gentlemen feel that my Mechanical Maid Automatonic Armature could help you to shepherd a woman in your care back to her proper place, I would advise you to leave your cards with my associates. Mr. Kern or Mr. Hays are there at the back of the tent. We are taking advance orders. I look forward to working with many of you to improve your lives."

A shaft of light speared into the tent as the flaps in the back drew open. Hays's red beard appeared almost unnaturally bright in the sudden glow. Across from him, Kern straightened his bowler, which looked absurdly small in comparison to his hulking body and giant melon of a head.

They'd both worked for Edison at Menlo; as well as I remembered them, I prayed that I hadn't made an equal impression upon either of them. The fact that I'd nearly burned down one of the laboratories made that seem unlikely, but I bowed my head and forced myself to step forward as the crowd filed out of the tent.

Twice I found myself edging forward, and both times Geula touched my hand.

"Running will only draw their attention and every one else's," she said softly.

I dropped my head again. Shoving my hands into my coat pockets, I shuffled behind Geula. The men ahead of us slowed our exit to a snail's pace, as many stopped to take or leave cards with Edison's burly associates. We edged forward, stopped, edged forward again.

Then Geula and I stepped through the tent flaps. The air outside the tent felt fresh and clean. I pulled in a deep breath and started ahead towards a display of towering automatons built to conjure up the thrill and terror of the great dinosaurs of the west. A toothy tyrannosaur gaped down, while a huge white pterosaur hung on a chain from the ceiling. Nearer to me stood several massive horned creatures, the plates on their sides lay open, exposing the huge cogs and springs that would lend the thing the illusion of life with a mere spark of power.

"There's more going on here than just one girl being carried off by a pimp," Geula muttered. She turned her gaze to me. "And what was the matter with you in there? Was it something to do with —"

"You! Stop, right there!" Hays shouted from behind us. I knew his voice better than I did his flushed face or red beard. I tensed but managed not to turn back. Next to me, Geula scowled but then quickened her step slightly. Men around us turned, confused as to who Hays addressed.

"Thief!" Hays roared.

We marched deeper into the displays.

"Come back here, you dirty little thief!"

Several startled shouts warned me that Hays followed us, shoving his way into the crowd. I wanted to run, but knew that would bring the security men down on me all the sooner. No one was easier to pick out from a milling herd than a single woman sprinting away.

"Ashni Naugai! I know that's you!"

Hearing my real name for the first time in nearly a decade, I couldn't keep from looking back. Hardly fifteen feet from me, with only twenty or so men blocking his way, Hays leered at me. He shoved two dapper older men aside.

Far across the vast hall, purple bolts arced up and the air surged with a wild charge. I drew it in and then reached out and lightly brushed my hand over the massive horned dinosaur. The automaton sprang to life instantly, rearing up and tossing its big head like a bull let loose in a china shop. Grown men screamed and shouted in alarm. When the dinosaur charged a few steps towards Edison's tent, people all around ran. It didn't matter that the automaton was already winding down. In the panic, Geula and I were merely two tiny figures among a mob that fled from the displays and out of the hall.

❀❀❀

"Ashni Naugai?" Geula demanded of me as we made our way up the stairs leading into the Women's Hall. Plaster goddesses, muses, and amazons contemplated us from pediments lining either side of the stone steps.

"Yes, Miss *May Flowers*?" I responded. That only made Geula glower at me all the more.

"I told you that wasn't my real name." Geula stopped to look around us. Deep shadows spread between the electric lamps that lined the wide walkways of the exposition. Twenty yards from us, repairmen in green uniforms mounted ladders to change the lamp bulbs that had already burned out. Around them, small groups of people wandered together, taking in the wonder of a world illuminated against the night.

I scanned the shadowy figures as they moved in and out of pools of electric light. Neither Hays nor any of Edison's other men appeared to have followed us this far. Geula and I had certainly led them on a long enough chase, crossing back and forth across the lagoons and even ducking into the terminal building as if we meant to catch a train out to Chicago or beyond. As much as I'd wanted to race directly back to the theater, I was glad we hadn't taken the chance of leading Edison straight to my uncle's automaton.

"The first week we were… together," Geula said quietly. "I told you my name."

"And I told you I was a mage, but that didn't stop you from getting us involved with theurgists," I whispered back. The moment I spoke, I knew that wasn't the real reason for my anger and agitation. It was Edison, not Geula, who'd rattled me, and it hadn't been her fault that I'd gone to his tent. I'd walked right in of my own volition.

A cold wind rolled off the lake. Geula shuddered and pulled her coat closer around her. I spread my fingers, drinking the strength from the flurry and shielding Geula from its icy bite.

"I didn't let them know anything about you, I swear." Geula frowned. "How could I, when it turns out I don't actually know anything myself?"

"You know enough to get me collared," I replied, but I couldn't summon any real anger at her.

"Yeah." She snorted. "But you didn't bother to tell me enough so that I didn't drag you straight into some trouble you're obviously running from."

I hadn't imagined the matter from that perspective. She was right, of course. How could we protect each other's secrets if we hid them from one another?

"I didn't think it would matter, not once we'd moved west together." I glanced up at the serene goddess posturing a few feet from me. A bat darted past, chasing moths that had been drawn out by all these brilliant lights.

"So?" Geula prompted me.

"Tell me about Boston first." It wasn't that I didn't trust her, but I'd never shared my history, and I didn't really know how to get the words out—or if I could.

"All right." Geula shrugged. "Judge Lowell discovered my younger brother in bed with his wife. A day later, she was murdered and my brother was charged. The judge had my brother hanged. I shot the judge."

I stared at her for a stunned moment. She made it all sound so... straightforward, as if she were describing the inevitable outcome of a mathematic equation. Perhaps, for her, she was.

"So, what about you?" Geula asked.

"It's not simple..."

"Not much is." Geula stepped up next to me and put her arm around my shoulder. "Just start at the beginning."

"I suppose it starts with my parents and uncle." I relaxed against Geula. "They came to Chicago after the floods. There were a lot of jobs then for wind mages repairing and replacing telegraph lines. They were happy, I think. My uncle met my aunt here and trained under her father as an automaton builder. Then the fire came through." I had to pause a moment to steady myself against the guilt that welled up behind that one sentence. My parents had burned to death, and my aunt had risked her life to rescue me from the inferno of their house. She'd lost her left leg and most of her right hand protecting me. "We lost my mom and dad. Abril, my auntie, she was very badly burned. After that, the Mage Law passed and my uncle took my aunt and me into hiding. We left Chicago and moved from place to place until my uncle finally found work at Menlo Park—"

"In Mr. Edison's laboratories?" Geula asked like she was guessing the answer to a riddle.

"Yes. At first it seemed like an answer to all our prayers. Uncle Neelmani set to work improving the designs for automatons, I assisted him and cleaned up the machine labs, and Auntie Abril read to Mr. Edison's wife, Mary. We lived on the grounds and were well paid." I could still remember how delighted we'd all been. Uncle Neelmani had insisted on toasting Mr. Edison at every meal. He'd been certain that with Edison's resources he'd at last be able to build an automatonic armature that would allow Auntie Abril to dance and draw as she had loved to do before the fire.

How naïve he'd been—how foolishly kind and utterly devoted. I missed him so much that it hurt to remember him and know he was gone forever. I frowned up at the dark sky overhead until my urge to cry passed.

Geula quickly pressed a kiss to my cheek. Her lips felt hot against my skin, and a hint of chocolate lingered on her breath. She knew exactly how to reassure me without saying a word.

"Nothing like goodness inspired Mr. Edison to take us in," I went on. "He wanted me so that he'd have an unregistered mage to test his mage-collars on without having to report his failings—"

"The scar on your neck?" Geula asked in horror. "Edison did that to you?"

I nodded.

"He wanted worse for his wife," I told her. "The reason he allowed my uncle to work on an armature wasn't to develop a device to improve the lives of the injured and crippled. He wanted my uncle to build a shell that would let him lock his wife up and keep her from indulging in laudanum."

"An addict, was she?" Geula asked.

"And a mean one at that. She called my auntie every filthy name she could think of and hurled plates at her if she was denied her doses."

At the time, I'd despised her for treating my aunt so badly. I'd sometimes wished Edison could have locked her up. But remembering the dull deadness of Liz Gorky's gaze, I realized now what a terribly cruel act it was to so completely deny any person control of themselves—whether or not they made poor choices. Those decisions were theirs to make and defined who they were.

"So what happened?" Geula asked.

I didn't want to go on. In some childish way, it felt like I was letting them die all over again by saying any more. But I wanted to be honest with Geula. I did owe her that.

"Auntie Abril fell ill. Her lungs had never recovered from the fire, and she was very susceptible to ague. She passed away on the thirtieth of September, only hours before uncle Neelmani convinced Edison to allow him to use the armature he'd perfected to help support her breathing—"

"It could do that?" Geula asked.

"Uncle Neelmani thought so, but he couldn't get to us in time to try it. Aunt Abril died two hours before he arrived with the armature and its cabinet." I stopped for a moment, fighting back the memories of my auntie lying in her bed like a sunken, waxy doll. I didn't want to think of her that way; it wasn't who she'd been. I wanted to remember her dancing and laughing at both her missteps and mine. But the cold image of her corpse hung in my mind.

"Without her in the house to hide the laudanum away, Mary Edison had free access. She died twelve days later of overindulgence," I said. "Mr. Edison took it very badly. He blamed our family, and in a rage, he had his assistant Hays collar me so that he could test how long a mage could survive if the collar malfunctioned and didn't stop burning. I was only saved because a newspaper man dropped by the laboratory unexpectedly to interview Edison. My uncle found me a few hours later and realized that we had to escape immediately. He packed up his armature, and we managed to get to the train station before Edison and his men closed in. I was already aboard with all our luggage… and I guess my uncle realized that if he fled he could draw Edison and his men away from me and his invention…" My voice failed me then.

Geula didn't ask me to go on. I drew in a deep breath and concentrated on the rushing, pleasant feeling of excitement in the air. Perfumes of machine oil and coal fires twisted around night-blooming jasmine. Faint vibrations rolled up from a music hall, and somewhere on a balcony above us, a woman hummed to herself and applied a spritz of lavender perfume.

I exhaled slowly, feeling that I was placing this vibrant living world out between me and the painful memories that lay dead in the past.

"I think he must have circled back and tried to burn all of his blueprints," I said at last. "It was a month later that I read about his death and the fire at Edison's automaton laboratory. I was on my own from then on."

"How old were you?" Geula asked.

"Sixteen," I replied. "Old enough to know that a woman couldn't travel alone without trouble. But if I accompanied a frail old relative in a wheeled chair, folks were far more likely to let us alone. So I stuffed a mannequin into my uncle's automaton armature and dressed it up with a wig. I explained away his mask as part of his eccentric flair, him being a being a stage magician."

"And abracadabra! Here you are with Professor Perfectus, yeah?" Geula smiled wryly.

"Well, nine years on," I pointed out. "But yes. That's my story."

"So you aren't Mexican, at all?" Geula appeared slightly chagrined. "And to think I've been trying to learn Spanish all this last month."

I laughed at that. (I'd been trying to pick the language up myself.)

"My parents and uncle came over from England, but my grandfather was an Indian sailor and a wind mage." After everything else, this seemed like such a small confession. "I used my aunt's name because I had some of her papers mixed in with my uncle's luggage. Her birthdate wasn't too hard to alter. And I knew the Edison had never known her maiden name."

"Clever," Geula said, but then her expression turned troubled. "But the armature that they trapped Liz Gorky inside? That was your uncle's design?"

"Based on it," I admitted, though the idea of how terribly my uncle's intentions had been misused still repulsed me. "But it's nothing like his actual work. If you put on the Professor Perfectus armature, it couldn't restrain you like that thing Edison created. My uncle built spells into it to ensure that it responded to the desire of the wearer. It would fit and move like a second skin, not trap you in a cage."

"A second skin of steel," Geula added.

"My uncle can't be blamed for what Edison did with his design."

"No." Geula sighed and craned her head up at the statue looming over us. "How hard do you think it will be to break Liz out of that thing?"

For an instant, the question surprised me. But of course Geula hadn't immediately discarded rescuing Liz Gorky and turned her mind to putting as much distance between herself and Edison as possible. She wasn't like me—she fought instead of running away.

"I don't know. Professor Perfectus releases with a touch. But I'd bet that Edison is using a lock like the one that closes his mage-collars." I scratched absently at the high collar of my dress. "Those have to be released by the registered owner."

Geula's scowled.

"No way around that?" she asked.

"I…" I didn't want to be dragged back into Edison's proximity. I wanted to pack up and leave with Geula tonight. And yet the thought of Liz Gorky gnawed at me. "I managed to open a few collars by draining their power so that the registration spell failed… It isn't easy, but if there was enough time, I might be able to do it."

Geula smiled at me and then nodded thoughtfully.

"Hopefully, you won't have to." Geula clasped my hand in hers and started up the steps. "We're not alone in this, remember?"

This time, as much as I wanted to, I didn't run. We strolled up the stairs side by side.

❀❀❀

An hour later, upon the second story of the Women's Hall, seated under a glass dome and surrounded by the perfume of hundreds of costly greenhouse orchids, I wondered if perhaps I'd made the wrong choice. Or maybe Geula had. We certainly didn't seem to be making much headway on Liz Gorky's account.

The Jewels were gracious hostesses, and the table Geula and I sat at all but overflowed with delicacies and indulgences. Peaches, figs, and bright gold oranges (all from California) were piled high on silver trays. Gilded chocolates, in the shapes of songbirds, studded an exotic coconut cake, and we'd already eaten our fill of lobster, potato gratin, and sweet peas.

Flutes of bubbling champagne percolated in front of us.

Across the table from Geula and I, Bertha Palmer sipped her champagne and watched the two of us with the hard, keen look of a landlady intent upon evicting undesirable tenants as discreetly as possible. To her right, mousy Miss Starr poked at her serving of cake with a gold fork but didn't actually take a bite. During the entire time that Geula had described what we'd witnessed in the Mechanical Maid display, she'd not spoken a word, nor had she appeared much surprised. To Mrs. Palmer's left, Jane Adams hunched in her chair, looking too long and angular for its dainty proportions. She'd refused both cake and champagne in favor of a strong black coffee. She worried the column of pearls wound around her throat and then seemed to catch herself and curl her large hands around her coffee cup.

Of all three Jewels, Miss Adams alone had reacted with dismay to the revelation that Mudgett had claimed Liz Gorky as his wife. Outrage had shown clearly in her face and she'd looked to Miss Starr immediately. Then, as now, Miss Starr kept her demure head down, revealing nothing and offering nothing.

"Now, I know that all you asked me to do was track down Liz Gorky..." Geula took a bite of cake and then went on. "But there have to have been other women Edison and Mudgett have done this to. The Exhibition has been going for months, and Liz Gorky could only have been part of their Mechanical Maid display for a week at most. So who did they have on display before this, and what's become of her?"

Mrs. Palmer turned her champagne glass in her hand. The other two were silent as well.

"If Mudgett is running a hotel, he likely has access to a number of women," I spoke up for Geula's sake. "Not merely his staff but guests too. The Exhibition has been drawing thousands and thousands of people from both halves of the country. Some are bound to go missing…"

"Damn it," Miss Adams muttered. She cast a brief glower in Mrs. Palmer's direction. "Didn't I say there was more to this—"

"Let us not jump to foolhardy conclusions. It isn't impossible that Liz did marry Dr. Mudgett previous to her coming to you at Hull House." Mrs. Palmer spoke very deliberately and coolly. "He could be the father of her child, for all we know."

At this, Miss Starr's head came up fast. For the first time all evening, I saw clearly how furious she was. A flush colored her cheeks, and though she glowered, her light eyes seemed to glint with unshed tears. The moment she met my gaze, she bowed her head again and crushed a piece of her cake between the gold tines of her fork.

Miss Adam's hand jumped to the pearls and gripped them as if attempting to rip them from her neck.

I remembered the photograph of Liz Gorky that Geula had shown me. This close to Miss Starr, I recognized more than a passing resemblance. Liz Gorky was too old to be her daughter, but could have been a younger sister, a cousin, or even a niece.

"Liz was not married," Miss Adams said firmly. "She told us that her family disowned her for engaging in relations while still unwed."

"So she says, but there is only her word for any of that," Mrs. Palmer replied. She favored each of us in turn with a hard, direct glance. "If we were to act directly—publically—against a man of Mr. Edison's reputation and reach, we would certainly need more cause than the word of an admitted adulteress."

I didn't recall anyone saying anything about Liz Gorky being involved with a married man, but neither Miss Adams nor Miss Starr objected. And if that was the case, it made even more sense that Mrs. Palmer feared that legal charges against Edison on Liz's behalf wouldn't hold up.

But at the same time, Geula's point about Mudgett and Edison going through other women troubled me deeply. Even if Edison's cobbled-together copy of my uncle's armature did function perfectly—and I very much doubted that it did— how long could a person survive having her will so completely suppressed and violated? How much time did Liz Gorky still have before she went utterly mad or died? She'd hardly been missing a week, but already she'd struck me as a dull, dying thing. How many more would there be after her?

"We must do something," Miss Starr murmured.

"Is there any way of finding out where they're keeping Liz Gorky?" Geula asked. "We might be able to steal her away from them if we knew that much."

Unwillingly, I thought of the cabinet where I stored Professor Perfectus.

"We could have them followed, but it will take time and would involve bringing even more people into the matter," Mrs. Palmer replied. She glanced to me. "Since it seems that the two of you were noticed by Mr. Edison's associate. He thought he recognized you in particular, didn't he, Miss Nieves?"

Geula and I exchanged a quick glance. Neither of us had mentioned that.

"No," I replied. "He mistook me for another woman, but after witnessing that Mechanical Maid, I wasn't inclined to remain in his company long enough for him to realize his error."

"I see." Mrs. Palmer's level gaze reminded me suddenly of the unwavering stare of a snake. "Well, it would seem that after that incident, Mr. Edison took it into his head that this other woman was here at the exhibition. He appears to be quite interested in an automaton in her possession. If we could somehow locate that, then we might have a chance at trading it for Liz's release."

"He actually said that?" Geula asked.

"He has his agents searching the exhibition grounds," Mrs. Palmer replied.

I had to suppress the desire to leap up and rush back to the theater. I had no doubt that Hays would recognize the cabinet if he found his way into the theater's dressing rooms.

"Of course, I've made certain that, for propriety's sake, Edison's men were not allowed to intrude into the private rooms or dressing rooms of any women. I informed him that I would oversee any such search beginning tomorrow morning."

"Oh for Heaven's sake," Miss Adams cried out, and she looked to me. "If you have the damn thing, then say as much. We'll pay whatever you ask. Just let us get Lizzie back."

"Yes!" Miss Starr cast me a pleading look. "Whatever you want, it's yours."

I didn't miss Mrs. Palmer's annoyed expression or Geula's pleased smile as she looked between Miss Adams and Miss Starr. I said nothing, but Geula leaned forward on her elbows like a card sharp preparing to reveal a winning hand.

"Two thousand dollars and two tickets for California," Geula said.

Mrs. Palmer made a face like she'd bitten her tongue, but Miss Starr and Miss Adams agreed to the price. I glowered at Geula. She couldn't actually believe that I would ever hand my uncle's armature over to a man like Edison. He'd made a monstrosity of the imitations he'd built. I didn't want to find out what horror he'd create if he got hold of all the subtle innovation and spells that made up the real armature.

"You do realize that this won't stop Edison and Mudgett from replacing Liz with another woman," I said. "Or doesn't that matter?"

Miss Starr shot me a look of raw fury.

"I don't know how things are done where you come from, Miss Nieve, but here in America, we look after our own!" She jabbed her gold fork at me. "Lizzie is one of us, and we are going to do whatever it takes to get her back safe and sound to her daughter!"

Instinctively, I drew in a deep breath and felt the air around me grow cool as I drained the power from it. Geula must have felt the change because she straightened and cast me a worried look. As much as I wanted to slap a stinging charge across Miss Starr's face, I resisted. And not merely because I'd be a fool to reveal myself in front of three theurgists, but because it occurred to me that Geula wasn't being quite straight with them. She might promise a simple exchange of the armature for Liz Gorky, but there had to more in her mind than that. She'd been as appalled as I had at Edison's Mechanical Maid.

"Where I come from," I began, "all people are created equal and every life has value regardless of how poor or unprivileged their family and friends are. So obviously, Miss Starr, my America is a different one from yours."

To my surprise, Miss Starr's entire face seemed to quiver. She gave a sob and then leapt from her chair and rushed off to the balcony.

"Ellen!" Miss Adams called after her. She began to rise from her seat with an awkwardness that I remembered my aunt suffering when her prosthesis didn't sit quite right.

"No, Jane." Mrs. Palmer said. She stood swiftly and easily. "She's overtired, that's all. Let me talk to her. In the meantime, I'd very much appreciate if you'd finish the rest of this up." Mrs. Palmer indicated Geula and I with an offhanded gesture, and then she strode after Miss Starr (who I could still hear sobbing out in the dark).

Miss Adams sighed heavily and took a slug of her coffee like it was whiskey.

"You bring Liz here, and I'll have your money and railway passes waiting for you. Are we agreed?" She looked to Geula briefly but then turned her full attention to me. "I'll send word to Edison that we're willing to make the exchange. It can't happen here, but would the theater serve?"

"No." The still air inside the auditoriums would stifle me. Edison wasn't likely to agree to meet out in the open air, not knowing me as he did. But the vast space of the Technology Hall would seem familiar to him—like territory he owned. At the same time, it offered me air charged with currents and the cover of countless displays for Geula. Edison and his men couldn't control them all. "I'd rather we make the exchange in the Technology Hall."

"Tonight?" Miss Adams asked.

I nodded. Best not to give Edison much time to muster more of his resources. He was a smart man but not particularly quick, so striking now would serve us doubly well.

"What time do you think?" I asked Geula.

"Two hours from now," she replied after considering for a moment. Then she looked to Miss Adams. "But give us a good hour before you contact Edison. I'd like to already be in the building and prepared before he even catches wind of what's going on."

Miss Adams nodded and took a more refined sip of her coffee. She frowned and added a sugar cube. As she stirred her coffee with a gold spoon, she said, "Despite what Ellen said and what Mrs. Palmer might have indicated, we do want Edison stopped here and now."

"I guessed as much." Geula nodded.

"But you don't want it traced back to any of you, correct?" I asked.

Miss Adams paused and seemed to study me. I didn't bother bowing my head or lowering my gaze.

"We have to protect the movement, above all else," Miss Adams replied. "Women's national suffrage depends upon men viewing us as virtuous, kind, and non-threatening. Rightly or not, Mrs. Palmer, Ellen and I have come to symbolize those traits within the suffrage movement. We can't be publically linked to… to whatever it is that may become of Mr. Edison or his Mechanical Maid project. You understand that, don't you?"

I did. We couldn't have men suddenly realizing how little difference there really was between a demure society miss and a calculating murderess. I just didn't like which side of the divide that relegated women like Geula and I to.

"Yes, I understand."

Miss Adams sipped her coffee and seemed pleased with the effect of the sugar cube. Then rather dismissively, she added, "It would seem that you have two hours to prepare. I wish you the best of luck."

"We don't need luck," Geula replied. "But make sure you have the money and railway tickets. Because we *will* be coming for them tonight." Then Geula raised her glass, and I took up mine as well. We tapped the crystal together and drained our small portions of champagne.

❁❁❁

In the abandoned quiet of the Technology Hall, I picked out the hum of the distant coal-powered generators. During open hours, they provided electricity to many of the displays, but now with the exhibitors and crowds gone, they simply lit the long rows of spotlights flickering overhead. Shadows fluttered and danced across the drop cloths and curtains that covered most of the displays.

Mr. Tesla's towers stood silent and the sleek, silver train engine crouched on its track as if the short length of velvet rope in front of it had frozen it in place. Bats winged between the steel rafters far above us while a nervous chatter of clock-work cogs clicked and tapped away from behind countless displays.

I drummed my fingers against the cabinet that normally housed Professor Perfectus. It resounded with a hollow knock, and I stopped. Only a mannequin hung on the supports inside. But I felt certain that the sight of the glossy cabinet would draw Edison's attention. With luck, it would delay him from studying our surroundings too closely.

I resisted the urge to glance back to the looming statue of Hephaestus and reassure myself that Geula hid in the shadow of the lame god's hammer. I didn't need to look to feel certain that she held her pistol close to her chest, ensuring that the overhead lights didn't glint off its long barrel. She wasn't the one likely to grow nervous or make a mistake.

I took in another slow deep breath. The space overhead seemed to whirl with the tiny cyclones of my warm, rising breath. I wasn't one to pray, but briefly I thought of my uncle assuring me that wind mages like me were special to Aditi, goddess of the sky.

She who unbinds and grants freedom, she who protects all who are unique—she is surely your guardian, my dear. Never fear.

I'd always wondered at him describing me as unique. Now it occurred to me that maybe he'd known about me and accepted me, even before I had. It was a strange time for such a thought, and yet the idea calmed me some.

I studied the oversized double doors at the front of the hall. The flickering bulbs made them appear to shift. A mere trick of the light. When the doors did open, I'd feel fresh air pouring in between them. That was one of the reasons Geula and I had picked this spot. It also offered us a quick escape if things went badly.

As my thoughts drifted, the lights overhead flared. I concentrated, focusing on pulling the energy from them, and they dimmed again. I wanted Edison in the dark in every sense.

Suddenly, clockwork timepieces throughout the hall rang, gonged, and shrieked. I started and the lights flashed out of my control. Then I realized all the uproar simply heralded the arrival of midnight. I clamped down on the electric lights, drinking in as much of the power flowing to them as I could manage. Tiny tongues of light sparked in my hair, and my skin felt as if it was humming.

Then, as the last mechanical clock chimed its twelfth note, both doors in front of me swung open. Edison, dressed in a formal black swallow-tail coat, strode in with Liz Gorky gripping his arm. Her hair hung in ringlets, and the white gown she wore disguised most of the armature holding her, except the silver collar around her throat and steely plates that encased her arms. She stared off past my head. But Edison glowered at me directly.

Cold gusts whipped through the air, and lamplights from the walks outside shone like distant constellations. Then Mr. Kern and Mr. Hays stepped in behind Edison, and the doors fell closed after them. I wondered if he hadn't been able to call Mudgett to him on short notice, or if he hadn't wanted to inform the other man that he might barter away his "wife".

"Miss Naugai," Edison called out. He smiled at me like a monkey baring its teeth. "I received your message, and I'm here in all good faith."

I didn't have to see clearly through the flickering light to recognize that Mr. Hays carried a pistol. Mr. Kern appeared to feel that a blackjack would be enough to deal with me. It had been when I was twelve, so why not now as well?

Though from their almost bored expressions, I guessed they weren't either of them expecting much by way of a fight.

"Take the collar off Liz Gorky, and you can have what you're after." I laid my hand on the cabinet.

All of them but Liz looked intently at the cabinet. For just an instant, I imagined that Edison might comply—it would have been so easy if he did. But Geula had been right. A man who double-dealt, stole, and lied as much as Edison wouldn't be easily fooled. But at least I had their attention focused on the cabinet.

That bought Geula a moment more to take her aim.

"I tell you what," Edison said. "I'll send Miss Liz here over to fetch that cabinet, and once she's done, she can be all yours."

The air around Liz Gorky's collar crackled wildly. She shoved her hands into the folds of her dress.

We hadn't planned on it being Liz that Edison sent across the distance to retrieve the cabinet, but I could hardly object. I had to hope Geula could still manage a clean shot. If not, then we'd have to improvise.

"All right, send her over," I called.

Liz Gorky lurched forward, still clutching her dress. Earlier, she'd twirled quite gracefully, but then her collar hadn't been searing the air with electricity as it overpowered her will. As much as she must have hated putting her arms around Mudgett this afternoon, there was something in this walk towards me that she loathed much more. Something that she fought against with all her will. She'd nearly reached the halfway point that Geula and I had agreed upon, when I noticed something dark buried in the folds of her dress.

I wanted to call out, but for Geula's sake I couldn't. Everything depended upon me releasing the brilliant flare of lights to blind Edison and his men and keep them from seeing Geula when she broke from her cover.

Liz stepped over the marker and started to raise her hand. At the same moment, I released all the power I'd held. The overhead lights flared, and white arcs of light gushed up from my hands to flash across the stage mirrors that we had so carefully positioned earlier.

I clenched my eyes closed against the blazing brilliance. Loud explosions of pistol shots burst through the hall. Bulbs overhead burst. A man shouted, and I heard someone fall heavily. Then something hit me hard in the shoulder, and I stumbled back a step and opened my eyes.

A few lights continued to flicker through the hall. Deep shadows enfolded the far walls.

Both Hays and Kern lay deathly still on the floor behind Edison. Out of the corner of my eye, to my left, I glimpsed Geula gripping her pistol and aiming for Edison.

"Liz shoots and I will kill you, old man," Guela snapped.

Liz stood in front of me, also holding a pistol and aiming it directly at my head.

"Well, well, well." Edison displayed another ugly grimace of his white teeth. "It would seem you've grown up into quite the conniving little heathen, Miss Naugai. And your pretty friend must be Annie Oakley."

Liz Gorky trembled, but her aim remained steady. The barrel of the gun pointing at my face seemed huge. I couldn't bring myself to look away from it, even to see what her first shot had done to me. My left shoulder ached, and the blood pouring down the inside of my dress sleeve felt scalding hot.

"Now, you, Annie," Edison addressed Geula. "I imagine that a white Christian woman like yourself would be most interested in aiding another white woman. You're the one who wants Miss Liz back with her daughter, aren't you?"

Geula gave him no reply, but I caught her gaze flick to me for an instant. Was she weighing the likelihood that she could shoot Edison before he had Liz blow my brains out?

"What are you suggesting?" Geula asked, and I realized that she had to be stalling—gaining me time to act.

I looked at Liz—at the collar tight around her throat. I didn't even register Edison's response to Geula. Instead, I focused on that seething band of silver.

Sweat soaked the back of my neck. My heart pounded so fast and hard, it seemed to make my vision jump and flicker like the dying overhead lights. I'd spent all of my strength in a brilliant flash, but I still turned my will against the silver collar wrapped around Liz's throat. It seared my senses as I pulled at the heat and power rolling off it in waves. Liz's hand dropped slightly. I took in another gasp of the electric air, swirling up from the collar; it tasted like smoke in my lungs. Liz's arm lowered a little more.

I thought I saw something like pleading in her face.

But both Edison and Geula must have noticed the shift in Liz at the same instant.

"Shoot her!" Edison shouted in a panic. I threw all my strength against the lock of the collar. And in that moment, Geula leapt for me. She wrapped me in a shielding embrace. I felt it as the bullet slammed into her back. She stumbled, and we fell together.

"Shoot her, God damn it!" Edision screamed.

Liz spun around, and I saw her collar laying on the ground at her feet.

She fired the pistol. Edison fell groaning and bleeding to the floor. I thought Liz shot him again at much closer range—he went silent after that. But I wasn't paying attention; all I cared about was Guela, lying so still against me. Tears filled my eyes, and I clutched her.

My hand brushed over the ragged hole torn through her coat and dress. My finger caught on the hard surface of the bullet. It fell from the steel armature under her clothes and dropped into my shaking palm.

"Next time we go with your plan and just run off together, I promise." Geula gave a cough and then grinned at me.

I wrapped my arms around her and kissed her.

❀❀❀

The floor trembled with the steady vibration of wheels rolling over rails. My fingers slipped, but then I caught and unfastened the last button of Geula's dress. The heavy fabric slid to the floor, revealing her lovely bare skin and the lattice of armature that clung to her like an immense silver mehndi. She shifted, and the armature bent with her. It felt almost silken under my fingers as I stroked Geula's back.

She hadn't taken it off since it had stopped Liz Gorky's bullet from killing her, and we'd both grown used to the sight and feel of it.

The sleeping car swayed as our train curved along the track.

Geula kicked her dress up onto the empty bed on the far wall and then settled down beside me on my bed.

"According to the conductor, these mountain passes grow very cold, so we may have to get inventive about keeping ourselves warm all through the night," Geula said.

"Don't worry, I happen to come from a long line a inventors," I replied.

Geula rolled her eyes at the joke but also grinned happily. We'd both had wine while in the dining car and were feeling warm and carefree. Geula kissed my bare shoulder. Then she paused a moment, frowning at the red, dimpled scar.

Miss Starr had been so delighted when we'd brought Liz Gorky back to her that she'd treated my injury. But the skin still felt tender and ached when I extended my arm too far. Given time, the scar would stretch and toughen up. Already it bothered me far less than it had a week ago.

"Does it hurt?" Geula asked.

"Not a bit," I assured her. I picked up the newspaper that the conductor had purchased for me at our last stop in Colorado. Very briefly, I took in Dr. Mudgett's baleful stare gazing up from the frontage. He'd been condemned to hang two days ago—after the Chicago police had discovered the bodies of two more murdered women in the basement of his hotel. It seemed that he'd been making a sideline selling their skeletons to medical students. A maid at his hotel, Elizabeth Gorky, had informed the police.

I felt relieved to know that Mudgett had seen justice, but also happy that it now had nothing to do with Geula or me. I tossed the papers off the bed and drew back the duvet. Geula slid in next to me.

We kept each other quite warm all the rest of the night.

My Road To Romance

SUSAN LEE

I grew up in a very religious home. When I say this, I mean Pentecostal, hands-in-the-air, calling on the "spirit", type church. As I encounter more and more people, I'm finding that this is not in and of itself an original story. But what was a bit different for me was where the church hurt a lot of people by telling them what they could and could not do or be...my experience was being the one pointing the finger. I was the one heading up the exorcism-prayer meeting. I was preaching by the time I was sixteen and a missionary by the time I was twenty. I hated anything "of the world"...and everything that wasn't considered holy was leading you—yes, you! (Whoever my pointing finger could reach)—to hell and damnation. It was *my* duty to save you!

But deep down, I hated myself the most. I lived in constant judgment and self-loathing. Normal, everyday life became my greatest burden. Don't listen to secular music. Don't lay your eyes on any books other than the Bible. Don't you dare lust after that man. Don't you even think about masturbating or having sexual relations before marriage.

My life's journey led me to San Francisco...for a job that I couldn't refuse. I didn't know a single soul. But I was giddy...a new adventure! And because San Francisco was a den of sinners—gay sinners, hippie sinners, artsy sinners—I had *all* this opportunity to save them! And maybe, just maybe, if I saved enough, I could stop hating myself.

And then one night on a prayer walk in the Castro District with my new church, I witnessed two of our church members, one a pastor, physically beating up a gay couple they were trying to preach to. There was violence, there was blood, there were cries for help...and I turned tail and ran.

I got back to my apartment, completely in shock, fell to my knees, and for the first time, had no idea what to say... what to pray. And I had one of those epiphanies. One of those life-altering moments. It was clear as day, and something settled in my heart.

God is not about judgment. God is not about doing right. God is *love*. Period. Love for me. Love for man. I'm not here to preach, but I wanted to share that in that moment, this message changed my life. It saved my life, even.

This pivotal moment redirected me. I started opening myself up to people. Talking to anyone and everyone about stuff not bible-related. I started experimenting with living. I started forgiving myself. And, remarkably, I started reading romance novels. Well, chick-lit at first, then romance, then full-on erotica. And at some point, I stumbled upon a Black Dagger Brotherhood fanfic which opened up my world of reading to M/M romance, and then more.

What has reading done for me? I'm learning every day, with each new book, with each new conversation within this community, with each new interaction with someone I would have completely shunned years ago. I used to think drag, cross-dressing, and being trans were all the same thing. The concept of asexuality I would have declared "a blessing from God" to help one avoid temptation. I cringe at my small-mindedness in the past. But the fervor with which I hated so many years ago, I now use to try and learn, to grow, to experience, to do better, to be better.

Romance opened up my world. LGBTQ romance broadened my horizons. Reading was my portal to exposure and learning. I read with pride because reading is who I am.

Quick story: I recently interviewed for a new job. In every interview, the question is asked: "What are you reading?"

Here I am, interviewing for the VP of Human Resources position. I should say something important. I should say something meaningful. I should say something that would show exactly the kind of HR executive I could be for them. So I did. I replied, "I am a voracious reader of romance books. I particularly read mostly LGBTQ romance." The CEO looked at me, smiled, and said, "Unexpected, but I love the honesty."

I got the job.

Fade to Black

By Josh Lanyon

1.

"It *is* you."

I jumped as though I'd been caught mid-robbery and dropped the trash bag I was carrying. A couple of crumpled coffee cups rolled out, dribbling onto the black cement floor. "I didn't know anyone was still here."

He was standing in the shadows, but even so he was kind of hard to miss. Tall, lean, weathered. Leathered, in fact. Dark hair, dark eyes, skin deeply tanned. Like one of those Victorian teething dolls. Right down to the ugly seam creasing the left side of his rugged face.

"I saw you through the window," he said.

"Oh. Yeah. That." The picture window was Rikki's idea. And actually, it did generate a lot of business—barring those times that the showcase client turned out to be someone who couldn't take pain. Then…not so much.

The man in the shadows didn't move, and the hair on the back of my neck stood up. What was that about? Like he still couldn't believe what he was seeing. Which was…a man about his own age—forty-ish—medium height, slender, black ponytail, sleeves of tattoo tombstones wound with green and blue ivy. Dotted Line being a tattoo shop. The only tattoo shop on the island.

"We're closed now," I said. "You could come back tomorrow."

He shook his head. "No. I don't want another tat."

Good thing. He didn't have room for any more ink on those muscular arms. Not under the revised military regulations—and he was definitely military. Or maybe ex-military, because he was out of uniform. Sort of. Olive drab T-shirts,

faded blue jeans, and huarache sandals are their own uniform.

"Okay. Well…" I picked up the bag of trash again and
nodded for G.I. Joe to head on out the door. It was late. I was
tired. My back hurt. I hoped this wasn't going to turn into
something weird. Off season was usually pretty calm, but
I've been robbed twice off season—and the second time the
dude had wanted to stay for a carving.

This guy? He was still staring at me like he was seeing
a ghost.

Which actually he was. That's my name. Ghost. Okay,
Gordon if you want to get legal about it. Gordon Plymouth,
but no one has called me Gordon in over twenty years.

"You don't remember me, do you?" he asked.

I looked at the ink on his arms again. Nice work, but not
mine. Not from anywhere around here. That looked Asian.
The real thing. *Irezumi.* Not your KYF-00049 or a pick from
2011 Ten Best Japanese Tattoos.

"No."

He reached for the hem of his T-shirt and yanked it up,
revealing a brown and brawny chest. Smooth, hairless, and
adorned with one of the worst pieces of body art a scratcher
had ever carved into a piece of meat.

"What the hell is that?" I stepped closer to get a better
look at what appeared to be a stapler adorned with a skull
and crossbones.

The guy laughed. "You should know."

I gaped at him.

He nodded, grinning, and I got a glimpse of a gold incisor.
"Me?"

I took another step forward, peering at his chest—he
smelled pleasantly, reassuringly of Ivory soap—and dropped
the trash bag again. This time just missing his huaraches. I
gazed at him in horror. "I did that?"

"You sure did." He was grinning like it was the funniest thing ever.

Which...nice he had a sense of humor about it, but... my gaze zeroed back on that evil-looking office product. It was old ink. At least a decade. I felt almost dizzy gazing at those fuzzy lines. I did *vaguely* remember...

"Wait," I said. "It was a cover up, right? I was using the Jolly Roger to cover up...something. Bad."

"Bullet holes. Tats, I mean." He met my eyes. "I do have bullet scars now. I didn't then. This was twenty years ago."

"Twenty years ago," I repeated in wonder. "Dude. You wore this blowout for twenty years?"

"Yeah."

I couldn't read his expression at all. His dark eyes were doing a flickering thing, his gaze roving over my face like he was looking for something from me. If it was remorse, oh hell yeah.

"Come back tomorrow and I'll fix this for you," I said. "In fact, if you want, I'll fix it for you tonight. If you have a couple of hours, I'll fix it for you now."

"No, no. That's not why I..." He stopped.

I couldn't seem to stop gazing into his eyes. Like everywhere I looked, I was somehow staring at him. It was so weird. But he did have pretty eyes. Kind of a black-brown and almond-shaped, fringed with thick eyelashes. Almost like cartoon eyes. They would be fun to draw for a New School stencil.

He gave me a funny, self-conscious smile. "You really don't remember me at all, do you?"

"Twenty years ago." I shook my head. I felt bad about it because it seemed to matter to him, but I'm horrible with faces at the best of times. And that tat...I had probably subconsciously blocked it out. "I had a lot going on back then."

He nodded. "Well, anyway. I'm glad you're good. Glad everything worked out."

And with that, he headed for the door. The evening air wafted in, the scent of the ocean and frying burgers.

"Hey, wait," I said. "You gotta let me fix that for you."

"Nah. It's part of me now."

Bad art was part of him?

"At least tell me your name." I have no idea why I asked because something about him made me uneasy, nervous— and the mention of bullet holes hadn't helped. But that Ivory-soap smell was kind of disarming—as were those big, soft dolly eyes he turned my way.

"Gene Carson."

"Gene, I owe you better. You can't go around looking like the office manager from hell. Seriously. I can see why you have your doubts, but I'm actually a pretty good artist. Plus I don't do nearly as many drugs now."

He laughed, which was good because I was kidding about the drugs. He didn't change his mind though. "It's okay. I saw you through the window and I wondered if it was really you. That's all. I wasn't looking for anything. Well."

An awkward and sudden pause.

What could I say? What did I *want* to say?

"If you change your mind—"

Gene nodded politely. I had a final glimpse of square shoulders, narrow hips, long legs before he vanished into the island-scented evening.

That qualifying "well" had me thinking as I carried out the trash to the dumpster behind the building. Twenty years ago had been a rough chapter in my life, and to be honest, I'd forgotten a lot—and was glad to have forgotten. But Gene… The more I thought about it, about him, the more I wished I could remember. I did sort of recall the bullet-hole tats.

There had been three of them in a row, complete with dripping blood. Gruesome. Especially gruesome for a guy going off to war. Like…not a good omen.

Which…yeah. Something else I could recall. Gene had been leaving for basic training the next day, and he'd wanted those tats covered. And being inexperienced and not at my sharpest, the only idea I had for a cover up was a big black flag. A Jolly Roger. Which I guess would have maybe made sense if Gene had joined the navy.

Anyway.

Even back then I could—and should—have opted for something more creative. Tribal, at the very least. Now days? I could think of a million clever and artful ways to cover up bullet holes. And a half million ways to cover up that black block of a pirate flag. But Gene didn't want to trust his canvas to me, and I couldn't really blame him.

So that was that.

Fade to black.

2.

After Dox split, I'd got in the habit of eating dinner at Luau Louie's. No reason to rush home anymore. Well, even when Dox and I had still been living together, there wasn't much of a reason to rush home. Not after the first couple of months. I like sex as much as the next guy, but I also like having someone to talk to afterwards. Dox was pretty, but no one could accuse him of being overly weighed down in the brains department. I don't like confrontation though, so it was a relief when he decided he couldn't handle island life anymore.

The instant pay raise was kind of cool too. It turned out Dox was supplementing his income with *my* income, fingers applied directly to wallet. That's what you get for falling for a nice piece of ass—especially when that ass is about fifteen years younger than your own ass.

So yeah. Everything works out for the best—I really believe that—but I hated going home to an empty house. Plus I can't cook to save my life.

When I walked into Luau Louie's, the first person I spotted was Gene Carson sitting in a booth reading *A Storm of Swords*.

I haven't read the books, but I love *Game of Thrones*, so I felt a jump of recognition—beyond the other, bigger jump of recognition. I figured Gene had probably left on the ferry because otherwise why the hell wouldn't he let me turn that black block into something beautiful? Something we could both be proud of?

But he hadn't left. He was still here.

"Hey, Ghost," Louie called. "We got fresh oysters on the shell."

"Ha ha ha. You know what I want."

And it was not oysters.

I slid into the booth across from Gene, who looked up. His frown softened instantly into a surprised smile. "Oh! Hi."

"Hey. I thought you'd gone."

"Nope." He put his book down. Picked up his beer.

"You're on vacation?"

"Sort of. I was interviewing for a job at the airport. Flying helicopters. I thought I'd stay a couple of days. Check out the island."

"Did you get the job?" I wasn't sure if I wanted the answer to be yes. I was curious about Gene, intrigued, but experimentation is trickier with indelible ink.

"They said they'd let me know."

I nodded. Then nodded again as Else brought me a Corona and a plate of fish tacos. "You want anything?" I asked Gene.

He drained his mug, held it up, and Else whisked it away.

"You always work with the TV on?" Gene asked.

"Hm?" I asked through a mouthful of cabbage and cod.

"You were watching a movie while you were tattooing that chick."

I swallowed. "*Le Samourai* from the Criterion Film Collection. I do like movies in the background while I'm working, true. It keeps the canvases calm."

"The 'canvases'?"

"Customers. Clients. The wrong music can put somebody on edge. But a movie is like white noise."

He was smiling, and there was that little glimpse of gold. Had somebody punched him in the mouth? Did he chew rocks for snacks? "Plus you like movies."

"Well, I do. A lot."

"I remember."

My smile faded. How could he remember when I had barely any recollection of him? That was kind of weird, no? Maybe a warning sign? The world is full of crazy-ass people. You have to be careful.

I have to be careful. Because I've never picked a winner yet. And I've pulled a lot of cards. "How come you don't want me to fix that jacked-up tattoo I did you?"

He smiled, shook his head.

"Yeah, but I'm serious. That tattoo is an embarrassment to both of us."

He did a one shoulder shrug. Like a little kid. A stubborn little kid.

"I just don't get why you'd come looking for me if you didn't want me to fix it."

"I didn't come looking for you."

"Okay, you didn't come to the island looking for me, but you wanted something when you came inside Dotted Line. Right?" I could hear the accusation in my voice, and I think Gene heard it too.

"I didn't. I don't," he protested. "I was surprised to see you. I thought you were dead."

Dead. The word smacked down on the table between us, hard and flat. I stared at Gene, my heart knocking against my ribs. But then Gene reached across and traced a gentle finger down the tendrils of inked ivy to the Old English R.I.P. on the tombstone. My skin tingled everywhere his fingertips brushed.

Gene said softly, "I don't want anything from you. I'm just really happy you're here."

3.

Else brought us another round. Gene was still talking. About me. My least favorite subject.

"You were scared," Gene said. "Scared to death. You couldn't stop talking about it. But you were brave too. Such a little guy against such a big monster. David and Goliath."

One in a thousand men develop breast cancer. When I was twenty-four, I noticed a BB-sized lump under my left nipple. I didn't think a lot about it. My mom died of breast cancer; I didn't know men could get it too. But the lump kept growing, and I finally went to the doctor. I ended up with a mastectomy and four rounds of chemo.

Brave? No. I don't know about brave. Terror? Oh yeah. And add embarrassment to that because according to my old man, real men don't get breast cancer. But you know, guys make up one percent of breast cancer patients.

I laughed. "But you took it for granted I lost?"

He pulled a face. Kind of sheepish, kind of apologetic. He said, "And you're okay now?"

"So far, so good." I tried to make healthy choices most of the time and keep a positive attitude because attitude is a huge part of it. *It* being life.

"Why do they call you 'ghost'?"

"It's my name. Well, actually my name is, er, Gordon. But I didn't think that was a very cool name when I was younger. So I called myself Ghost, and now I'm stuck with it."

"Oh."

"Yeah."

He said slowly, "I did go back to your old shop. It was about ten years ago. It's a pet store now. Or at least ten years ago it was a pet store."

"So you *did* want a cover up," I said. I was still laughing though, mostly because I was drinking more than I usually do. Or maybe not. It had been a long time since I'd felt... God, sort of smiley, sort of fluttery in my chest. Just from talking to another guy. I couldn't remember the last time. I hadn't felt it with Dox, that was for sure. That had been about sex, pure and simple, and being tired of going home to an empty house every night.

Gene dipped his head. He was half smiling. I studied his sleeves. That beautiful, detailed work. Whoever had done that could have fixed that mess on his chest easy.

"So what have you been doing for the last twenty years?" I asked.

"A little of this. A little of that."

"You were in the army, right?"

"Army Rangers." He said it quietly and with a certain dignity. The dignity that came from knowing you were a certified badass, I guess.

"But you're retired now? From the military?"

"Yeah. Looking for work. Like everyone else."

It was my turn to touch fingertips to his sleeve. Those fierce and gorgeous snakes, dragons, and clouds. He glanced down at my hand, looked into my eyes, and smiled. I felt that smile in my chest.

"Korea."

"Korea?"

He dipped his head in assent. "A little shop in South Korea. That was back in 2014. Training exercises."

"You've probably been all over the world." There was a time I had wanted to travel. My adventures had taken me in other directions. I wore a map of the ancient world on my chest, complete with inked-in monsters, the crooked roads and byways formed by scars.

"A lot of it. Enough of it. How'd you end up on this island?"

"Life's short. I wanted to spend mine in some place beautiful."

He had a funny expression on his face. "You know..." He stopped.

"What?"

He shook his head. "You want to get out of here?"

Did I? Yes. But maybe that was a bad idea. Today had been an ordinary day—and I sincerely appreciated every single ordinary day—but then this had happened. This blast from the past. Even if I didn't remember Gene, I remembered what it felt like when someone looked at you like Gene was looking at me. And it was fun, exciting to feel like there was possibility here, there was a chance for something new and totally unexpected. Potential.

The lesson Dox had taught me was sometimes the potential is the best part.

Safer just to say thank you and goodnight. Safer to go home feeling warmed by imagining what could have been. Disappointment causes cancer.

Well, not really. But sometimes you just want the promise of something nice to hang onto. Sometimes you need that.

I said, "It's an island. There really isn't anywhere to go."

"We could walk on the beach. There's a full moon."

He could have said *Let's go back to my hotel.* He could have said, *Let's go to your place.* Then I could have said, *Thanks, but no thanks.* But where was the harm in a moonlit walk on the beach?

I shrugged. "If you want."

Gene smiled. "I do want."

4.

He paid for my dinner, which was apparently what happened when you hung out with grownups, and somewhere between the door of Luau Louie's and the foamy grasp of the tide, he reached for my hand.

I couldn't ever remember holding hands with another guy, but it felt natural hanging onto Gene. And when he put his arm around my shoulders, that felt natural too.

"Do you think you'll get the airport job?" I asked.

"I think they'll offer it to me. Yeah. Do you think I should take it?"

"Do *I*?"

He was looking at me very seriously.

"If you want it, you should take it," I said.

"Would that make you happy?"

I stopped walking.

"Wait. We've got to…Where does my happiness come into it? You've got to do what's right for you. We don't even know each other." Which was true, although it felt silly saying it somehow when I was already missing the feel of his arm wrapped warmly and securely around my shoulders.

Gene said, "You know how sometimes you meet someone and you feel an instant connection? And you know that at another time and another place, this person would be important to you, would at least be a friend. Would maybe matter more than all the other people in the world? But it isn't that time and it isn't that place and you go on. You never see them again."

"I…yeah. I mean, I guess." I had to be honest because he was truly the bravest guy I had ever met in my life. Or possibly insane. Was that a hatchet in his jeans or was he just glad to see me?

I admitted, "Yes. I do know."

"And sometimes you forget them. And sometimes you don't." All at once, his breath sounded funny, like he was slightly winded, as though we'd been racing down this gentle sandy shore instead of strolling hand-in-hand watching the moonlight pinpoint the shadows. "That's how it is for me."

"How what is?" My voice sounded faint, even to me.

"I used to look at this tattoo and think about you. And yeah, I did figure you...probably died. Because it was clear to me that you thought you would probably die. And you can't think like that and live. Except...you did. Somehow you did."

"I was afraid to hope." I'd never confessed that before. And it was probably too much to concede now. "But I wasn't afraid to fight."

Gene nodded, like that made sense to him. "And then I saw you today. I watched you in that window tattooing a butterfly on that girl's back. I knew you the minute I spotted you. I didn't think it was possible, but there you were. So serious and so...there. It just seemed like fate. And I don't even believe in fate."

I believed in fate. And luck. And omens. And universal healthcare. "What do you believe in?"

"All kinds of things. I believe in the Ranger Creed. I believe in God. I believe in second chances." He said softly, steadily, "I believe in true love."

"Dude..." I mean, I believed in true love too. But who has the balls to say that aloud? It would take a special ops guy. I cleared my throat. "Anyway, if you're asking me, I do think you maybe should probably take that job."

He grinned, and the gold incisor flashed briefly in the uncertain light. "You think so?"

I nodded.

"Okay."

"And I think you should let me fix that mess on your chest. I can turn that into something beautiful."

"It *is* something beautiful."

"It's really not," I said kindly. "It's a black blob. Not that you don't wear it well."

Gene said, "You know what black is? Black is all the colors mixed into one. It's like the…the Omega."

"Gene. You don't have to be afraid. I won't hurt you."

Gene laughed. He bent his head, and our lips met. His mouth was warm, his lips soft, his kiss sweetly off-center. He tasted like something that would soon be familiar to me— and good beer, which was how I knew this was not a dream. He whispered, "I won't hurt you either, Gordon. And I'm not afraid."

I was. A little. But the moonlight seemed to draw a silver line across the ink-black ocean, and I knew I would follow that path.

Wherever it led.

What I've Learned

JORDAN CASTILLO PRICE

Dear Jordan,

I wish I could warn you that school is nothing like you thought it would be. You're standing there with your shiny new diploma, and it seems like you're embarking on a grand adventure where you land a fabulous, secure job, rub elbows with interesting people, and make cool things. Unfortunately, what's ahead of you is more of a long slog.

I'm not sure if it's the recession, or your personality, or simply a matter of wrong place, wrong time. You're not going to find a job you like. Ever. I hope you're not too crushed upon hearing this—I'd actually like to encourage you to relax, because this day-job thing doesn't last forever.

Something called the internet is coming, and that something is really big. Nowadays, it's made of cat pictures and porn. When you first see it, though, it's mostly text. Photographic images will take forever to load, line by line, and trying to stream a video at those speeds would be ludicrous. Even so, having access to any information you care to find is a massive game-changer.

The Internet only evolves from there. Connections improve. Pretty soon most people start communicating via email, which leads to special interest groups on Yahoo and Google, which then give way to MySpace, LiveJournal, Twitter, and Facebook.

So what does this mean for you?

Early on, you'll stumble into a group of women who write fanfiction. Not only will writing with them teach you the mechanics of writing, but it will train you to be able to write sex scenes without flinching away, and in fact you will learn to infuse meaning in every groan and thrust. Sex and sexuality are an important part of the human experience, and being able to handle gender and sexual identity fluidly, without apology, will put you exactly where you need to be when gay romance becomes the hot new genre. And here you were willing to write it for free.

Have faith; it doesn't happen overnight. Initially, you will send out numerous submissions to men's magazines where they either go unacknowledged, are returned unread, or are even occasionally berated. Erotica is probably not the place for you anyway, though I think it's as good a place as any for you to start making sense of the writer's market. Keep practicing and develop your voice. One of these days, the gatekeepers will begin publishing you. And a few years later, once you figure out what's what, you can set up shop for yourself and reach your audience directly, thanks to the internet. Yes, your audience is out there, people who want to read about bent heroes who, up until now, were only allowed a tragic ending.

So don't beat yourself up for not learning more useful things in school to set you up in a rewarding traditional career. You're learning how to interface with other people, to communicate, and to present yourself. Besides, the genre you'll be writing in doesn't actually exist yet. The method for delivery isn't yet accessible to the public, and the devices people will read the stories on won't be around for several years either. Do your best instead to observe your human experience as you navigate the roller coaster ride of your life, friends and enemies, loves and losses. The learning never stops. And every experience has the potential to make your stories that much richer.

DEMONICA

Megan Derr

Shale groaned as Keira set a plate heaped with food in front of him, along with a large pitcher of ale and a platter of biscuits, butter, and cheese. He'd cleared a quarter of his plate before she'd taken her seat.

"Breathe every few bites," Keira said with a sigh. "Are you even tasting any of that?"

"It's delicious," Shale replied before shoving another bite of butter-soaked biscuit in his mouth.

Keira lifted her eyes to the ceiling. "You're disgusting. When your arm doesn't work right tomorrow and you have to spend three hours cleaning out crumbs and dried gravy, don't whine to me."

Shale paused long enough to glance at his left arm, but it was well-covered, from fingertips to just past his elbow, with a special-made, magica-treated leather glove that protected it from far worse than him being a messy eater. He'd also spent the better part of the day getting his arm, eye, and right leg tended, and most of what money had been left had gone to refilling all the medicine he had to take because of them. The Torrien Desert was always hard on his mechanica parts. "Shut up, I'm fine."

Sighing again, Keira tucked into her own food at a much more sedate pace. They'd just started on second helpings when shadows fell across their table. Shale ignored them. Anyone worth taking a job from knew better than to bother them when they were eating.

Keira kicked his good leg under the table, but when Shale only grunted and started massacring another biscuit, she turned to their unwanted visitors—and choked. Shale tamped down on his annoyance and ate the bite of spiced potato on his fork. He chased it with ale as he looked at their guest—and damn near snorted all of it up his nose. He hastily set the mug down and wiped his face with a kerchief he pulled from a front pocket of his jacket.

Six guards stood clustered around the front edge of their table, dressed in the red-and-green garb of the Grand Duke of Soria Bell, who controlled the northeast section of Renmarkane. Peculiar. What would Her Grace want with them? Shale hadn't seen her since, well, a time he was happier not thinking about. It had been made pretty clear to him that she and the rest of the family were done with him. Not a good sign she wanted to see him now, five years after they'd cut ties.

Keira grunted. "We've been gone the past five months and have only been back in Soria Bellmane eight hours. Whoever the fuck said we did whatever Her Grace is pissed off about is lying."

The woman marked as a captain stepped forward, the torchlight gleaming in her dyed crimson hair. "Are you Shale Teor and Keira Mark?"

"No," Shale said petulantly.

Quirking a thin black brow, the captain said, "The Grand Duke seeks to hire you."

Keira sneered. "The Grand Duke can seek—" She broke off with a grunt when Shale kicked her under the table. Smiling stiffly at the captain, Keira said, "With respect, Captain Whoever You Are, of what possible use could a couple of glorified fetchers be to Her Grace? Surely you're capable of doing the job."

"I'm Captain Tula Rumark, and if she wanted me to do it, I would. She wants the pair of you." With a sigh grand enough to make Keira's look a paltry effort, Tula motioned to her soldiers and said, "Take them."

Shale barely had enough time to snatch up his bags and grab a last biscuit before the guards swooped in and hauled them away. As they were dragged along through the streets of Soria Bellmane, he grumbled, "Just once I wish we'd be allowed to finish a meal before another bit of trouble found us."

"I think we both know we'll never be that lucky," Keira said, and they both fell silent the rest of the way through the city and across the great bridge to Soria Bellketh, the castle of Lord Sara Halruul, the Grand Duke of Soria Bell.

It was as beautiful as ever. The sight left him sad and aching. This place had been home once—the only place to feel like home since he'd lost the first one. Mother of All, he didn't want to be here. He twitched as they passed through familiar halls, scents washing over him and churning up further unpleasant memories of the last time he'd been there.

But instead of the north wing, they were dragged into the south wing, where the grand duke's offices were located—and dumped right at her feet, or near enough, with only an enormous table laden with papers, books, and scrolls between them.

Lord Halruul removed her reading glasses and peered at them over the edge of the table. "Thank you, Captain. You're dismissed." When Tula and her soldiers had gone, Halruul regarded them thoughtfully before finally speaking in a voice that, for her, was almost gentle. "Hello, Shale."

"Your Grace."

The formal address seemed to make her droop slightly.

"The captain is new," Keira said.

Halruul sighed. "Yes, Grieger retired last summer. He is missed, but Tula is an excellent replacement. It looks like you're both doing well. I'm glad." Her gaze lingered on Shale. "*Are* you well?"

Shale snorted. "Well enough, not that anyone here actually cares. What do you want?"

Halruul sighed again. "I do care. Stand up. Neither of you need ever kneel, good grief."

Shale cast Keira a warning look as they stood.

Keira was too busy staring down Halruul to notice, not that she would have cared if she had. "How can we be of service, Your Grace?"

Settling back in her chair, the leather creaking with her movements, Halruul asked, "You know of my youngest son, yes?"

"Yes, Your Grace," Keira replied.

Shale nodded. Of course he knew of Annai. Never met him, precious few had, but it would have been difficult to have been engaged to Annai's stepbrother and *not* hear about him.

As always, thoughts of Tellish stirred a sour, curdling sensation in his gut, though it had dulled the way so many other aches and regrets had. With any luck, they'd be gone before he and Tellish crossed paths. Shale might not bear Tellish ill will any longer, but he didn't exactly love him anymore, either.

"Annai currently resides at Korkennet Monastery. Are you familiar with it?"

Keira nodded. "We've worked for them frequently. They make good beer. Good enough to steal, so we often join protection details when they transport it here to sell."

"He's resided there for the past ten years because it was the safest place for him. Unfortunately, I have good reason to fear that is no longer true. For the present, it's best I bring him home. Preparations have been made, and what remains to be done will be finished by the time you return with him. That is your job, my fine mercenaries: retrieve my son and escort him home. I expect there to be trouble. I want to know he is with someone I have known for years and trust implicitly." Halruul's eyes leveled on Shale. "I know you did not part ways with my family on the best of terms, and I will always be sorry for that. I remind my stepson often that he is a fool."

"We were no longer compatible," Shale said with a shrug. "It's over, at any rate."

Halruul picked up a small coin purse resting in front of her on the desk and tossed it deftly to Keira, who caught it just as neatly. "Your down payment. Thrice that to come when my son is safely home."

Keira weighed the bag in her hand, brows rising, green eyes sharp as they stared at Halruul. "He must be your favorite son."

"There will be danger involved. I pay well when I expect people to risk life and limb." Halruul braced her hands on the desk and rose. "The journey is what, four days, roughly?"

"We can do it in three going, and depending on how well your son travels, three again on the way back," Keira replied. "Call it a full trip of ten days to be safe. If you've not heard from us by sunset on the tenth day, be concerned. I'll send you updates as we're able. Do you prefer bird or magica for communication?"

"Magica."

Keira nodded and tucked the money away. "We'll get supplies and leave immediately. Anything else we need to know?"

"There are people after my son, and they'll do a great deal to obtain him." Halruul tossed her something else. "Present that ring to the monks and my son to prove you are there in my name. Without it, the monks will arrest you at best, kill you at worst."

Shale and Keira nodded and didn't bother asking why there was so much fuss to be made about Annai. If Halruul had wanted to elaborate, she would have. Either it didn't matter to the job, or it was something they'd learn soon enough on their own.

Keira turned neatly on her heel and strode out of the room. Shale lingered a moment, something in Halruul's expression holding him. He'd *missed* this place, and being back was as sweet as it was bitter.

"I always liked having you around," Halruul said, a sad smile on her face. "You would have been a good son-in-law. I already considered you one. You would have been welcome here at any time, and still are. I hated most that he drove you away from all of us. I understand why you don't come back, but if you ever change your mind, you'd be welcome. Just know that."

"We'll see," Shale said, more taken aback by the words then he would admit. He'd taken it as understood that the whole family was done with him. Tellish had never given him reason to think otherwise. Had he been wrong all this time? On the other hand, would it have really been a good idea to stay? "Take care, Your Grace. We'll have Lord Annai home soon."

"Thank you. Take care yourself, Shale."

He nodded and left, falling into step alongside Keira as they left the castle, gesturing crudely to the guards in the ward, who laughed and returned the gestures in kind.

"So what is Her Grace not telling us about her son?" Keira asked when they were across the bridge and headed back into the city.

"I don't know much, but what I do know is that Annai is a dedicated Magica."

Keira groaned. "Magica. Anything but that. I hate the jobs that involve magica."

"He went to school when he was young—really young, only five or so—and when he finished with one school, he went on to the next. The last I heard, he was finishing up advanced studies at the Royal University."

"Now he's hiding away in a monastery because it's safest? Why would the son of the Grand Duke of Soria Bell need to hide away in a monastery for *safety*?"

Shale's mouth flattened. "There are certain branches and levels of magica that are difficult to master and highly sought by the more unsavory. It wouldn't surprise me if he's a Wica Angelica or a Wica Demonica."

"Your father was a Wica Demonica, right? He didn't have to be hidden away or fetched home for his own good."

"He was a field Wica, not a scholar Wica, which is what I'm assuming Annai is. They have a tendency to discover, learn, or create things that unsavory types love to misuse."

"So a smart kid is stirring trouble by not leaving well enough alone?" Keira huffed. "Seems like a job that could go to anyone, and not worth the hassle, frankly, even if I like the money. Why didn't you let me tell them to fuck off?"

"Because money is money, and it's stupid to let history or magica keep us from income we could sorely use, especially when we should already be retired and it's—"

"If you say it's your fault, I will break your fucking nose," Keira snapped. "It's not your fault. It was Fishface's fault, and I hope the bastard gets treated in kind thrice over! I should march back in there and tell them to take their fifty gleams and shove 'em up their ass."

"Fifty gleams? That means another one fifty when we get home. We're not turning down two hundred gleams. We'll manage. I'll manage."

Keira's expression soured further. "Fine, but I'm going to bitch about it a lot. To think you were almost married into that." Keira's face soured. "You're better off not, given how pathetic that little rat turned out to be."

Shale stifled a sigh. "We weren't compatible anymore."

"He's a jackass," Keira replied, voice gone flat and cold. "He could have gotten a fuck anywhere. It's not like you cared."

"Can we drop it?" Shale asked sharply. "It's over and done, and that's the way I'd like to leave it."

Keira grumbled to herself a few seconds more, but finally cleared her throat and said, "I'll see to supplies if you wanna go get the horses." She pulled out a few coins and dumped them in his palm. "Anything special I should get?"

"Food enough for six. It'll be a pain, but between me and Annai, we're going to go through a lot of it—especially him, if he's as powerful as I fear, all the more if he winds up using his magica, which wouldn't surprise me."

"What should we be prepared for?" Keira was usually the one in charge; Shale was always happiest when someone else was on point. But she'd grown up in Strea-Accel territory, where magica was one step from reviled and not used outside of limited healing and protection.

Shale, on the other hand, had grown up in the royal capital, the very heart of magica. Both of his parents had been powerful magica, and his sisters well on their way to following in their footsteps. He'd played on university grounds as a boy, used to sit on the wall and watch the students practice until somebody noticed and ran him off.

When it came to magica, Keira deferred to him long enough to learn what was what. Then she was back in charge, and he was happy to retreat to doing as he was told.

That was one of the many reasons he had loved Tellish, who loved to be in charge and taking care of people, matters—all of it. As his stepmother's seneschal, Tellish had plenty to keep him busy. When they'd parted ways, Shale had been training to take the job over from him, and he'd enjoyed it, too, though in a different way. He'd liked knowing he was helping the grand duke and the rest of the family, had liked to see everything run so well, liked working with all the people who helped keep the castle running smoothly. He'd been on the verge of giving up mercenary work for good when everything had gone so wrong.

It would never stop hurting that when Shale had most needed someone to care for and about him, Tellish instead had grown frustrated and impatient.

Not enough that Shale had almost died after being ambushed by a black tail, pretty much the worst possible dragon to encounter. Bad enough he'd lost an eye, an arm, and a leg. Bad enough he'd be on tonics and potions to manage pain and his mechanica parts the rest of his life.

But those medications were taxing, and one of the last casualties of the whole damn mess had been his desire for sex. A fairly common side-effect of the potions that kept his body from hating his artificial parts, he'd been told, but Tellish hadn't wanted to be married to somebody he couldn't be amorous with. He had ideas and plans for his marriage, and they hadn't meshed with Shale's new reality.

So for the second time in his life, Shale had lost a family and home. If not for Keira, he probably would have given up for good.

Now it was just one more old, scarred-over wound that only ached on bad days and when he poked at it. Getting mixed up with them again wasn't helping to keep the ache down, but so it went. He'd deliver Annai and be on his way. A couple more years of work, and they'd finally have sufficient money to take the retirement that had been snatched away when Shale had been unexpectedly abandoned by his fiancé.

"Oi!" Keira shoved him, nearly into the wall of the butcher shop as they passed it.

"What?" At the look on her face, he said, "Sorry."

"Stop wallowing in bad memories, or I'm going to start talking about them again."

Shale made a face. "Good thing this is where we part ways. I'll meet you at the city gates."

Keira nodded, playfully punched his arm, and strode off headed east, whistling as she went, braids swinging wildly back and forth. Shale turned in the opposite direction and threaded through the crowded streets until he reached the Red Street Stables they favored for keeping their horses whenever they were in town.

"Back already?" Jayna asked as she saw him step inside the cool, dark stable, tipping back the flat hat smashed down on her corkscrew curls.

"New job," Shale replied. "Didn't even get to finish my food. *Again.*"

Jayna laughed, not without sympathy. "You do seem cursed. I've got a leftover meat pie—you want it? Bini always brings me more than I can eat."

More than happy to take it off her hands, Shale handed over coin for the scant few hours the horses had been stabled, got them both ready, and led them out into the yard. He climbed into the saddle of his own horse, a handsome roan mare he'd had for five years, a replacement for the one the dragon had killed. He led the horses carefully through the streets, wolfing down the meat pie as he went.

Keira arrived at the gates half an hour after he arrived, bearing supplies in a large leather satchel and a small box. Dismounting, Shale helped her divide everything between their saddlebags. He grimaced slightly when they were done, and dug out his medicines, taking a swallow from each of the four bottles and tucking them all away again.

"You going to be all right, old man?" Keira asked with a smirk.

"I'm sorry, which one of us just turned forty and which of us is still thirty nine?"

She cuffed him lightly and swung into her saddle, laughing. "Daylight's wasting, old man."

Smiling, Shale climbed into his own saddle, settled his mechanica leg more comfortably for a long haul, and followed her through the gates and onto the main road leading away from Soria Bellmane.

❀❀❀

Though braced for trouble the whole way, they made the three-day journey without incident. The only hassle was remembering his medication, which was easy to forget once he fell into the rhythm of work. Everything went so well, he might have forgotten they were on the job if they'd been working for anyone else.

The monastery was the same as ever when they rode through the archways into the courtyard. It was older than the territory—older than the kingdom, carved directly into the mountain it sat on, overlooking the world below. Full of men who spent their days in devotion, managing their magica archives, and making beer. Also imbibing heavily in said beer at certain hours of the night, if one knew where to find them.

Several of the monks in the yard lifted hands in greeting; a few called out. Shale waved back, and Keira called replies, but before they could greet the men further, the abbot came out of the temple, his heavy dark-green robes stirring up dust as he crossed the courtyard to greet them.

Keira dismounted smoothly and bowed to him. Shale dismounted more slowly and followed suit.

Abbott Wistry smiled and bowed his head. "Good to see you again, old friends. I wish the reason was happier for all of us. For formality's sake, I believe there is something you're meant to show me…"

Smiling, Keira pulled out the silver chain around her neck, hidden under her tunic and leathers, and displayed the ring.

Wistry smiled and motioned them toward the temple. "It is comforting to know that our dear Annai will be protected by the only two mercenaries in the world I trust. Come, I will take you to him. You've arrived just in time for dinner, which I'm sure was by design, and there is a new brew to sample."

"That is all the payment I could ask for," Shale replied with a grin.

Keira lifted her eyes to the sky. "Speak for yourself." She shoved the chain back beneath her tunic as they handed off the horses and followed Wistry into the cool dark of the temple.

"All the times we've come here, I never had any idea Annai Halruul lived here," Shale said, his voice echoing softly against the towering stone halls.

"Yes, we are discreet about his presence here, for various reasons. The most obvious being, of course, that he is the youngest son of Her Grace."

And yet Shale was getting the feeling, as they climbed higher and higher into the remotest parts of the temple even he and Keira had never visited before, that Annai's family was the least interesting thing about him.

Wistry pulled a ring of keys from his belt as they came to the end of a hallway and stopped in front of a red-painted door. "This monastery used to house numerous guests, most of them here for the same reason Annai came: to continue his magica studies in depth without having to be concerned about interruption or observation."

"If he was merely a guest, there'd be no reason to lock him in," Shale said. "Is there something someone maybe should have told us?"

"He's not dangerous," Wistry replied as he unlocked the door. "We merely want him safe, and for no one to come upon him accidentally or without our permission, now that we know there are people after him." He pushed the door open and slipped inside. "Lord Annai, your escort has arrived."

"That was sooner than expected," said a soft, easy voice that was reminiscent of Her Grace, but slightly deeper, though not as deep as Tellish's voice.

Shale stepped further into the room, moving past Wistry, and abruptly felt like he'd been knocked over.

Annai had all the best parts of his mother and father. Tellish was nothing to sneer at, not by half, but Annai was the kind of beautiful that existed inside of a storybook. He had his mother's black-brown skin, and his father's tiny, coppery curls and elegantly sculpted face, though his nose was broader like his mother. His eyes were the color of new leaves struck by sunlight, further enhanced by the green-and-gold robe he wore, one of the open styles, pulled on over a short tunic and snug breeches. A scholar's robe, rather than the style worn by the monks.

He was holding books, clearly in the process of carrying them from one of the several bookcases to the trunks in the center of the room. "They have the ring, I assume?"

Keira pulled the chain out, removed the ring, and strode across the room to drop it in his palm. "Your Lordship."

"Good evening," Annai said as he slid the ring onto the first finger of his right hand. "My mother wrote you were coming. You are Master Keira, correct?"

She smiled. "Just Keira will do, my lord." She pointed a thumb over her shoulder. "And that's just Shale."

Annai's eyes shifted to Shale—and widened slightly, mouth gaping the barest bit before he recovered himself. It hurt a bit, to be stared at so hard, so avidly, when the last person to stare at him in similar fashion had been Tellish. But then Annai said, "I've never seen such impressive mechanica parts..." He pushed the books into Keira's arms, oblivious as she scrambled in her surprise not to drop them, and crossed the room to stop barely a pace from Shale. "That is truly remarkable work. Who was the crafter?" He didn't reach out and touch, though Shale had expected it—

and wouldn't have minded. Usually people were afraid of or disgusted by the idea of touching his mechanica parts. "Is that Wica Sylvon's seal?"

"Yes," Shale said, and pulled off the long leather glove covering his arm before tentatively offering it. "You can touch if you want."

Those emerald eyes looked up, bright with happy surprise. "You truly don't mind?"

"Not at all," Shale said gruffly, ignoring the look he could feel Keira giving him. "It was Sylvon. He was an old friend of my mother's. When I wrote to him about needing mechanica, he practically dragged me into his workshop to do it."

He could feel it as Annai's fingers smoothed over the metal, dulled in spots but still gleaming in others, the jewels filled with the fueling magica glittering in the light of flickering lamps. It wasn't the same way he'd feel it if someone ran their hands over his skin—more like the way he'd feel a light touch through several layers of fabric. Sylvon had been extremely pleased with himself for that one; Shale had been his test subject on that new feature. Innovation alongside parts that worked damn near as well as the lost limbs were what gave Sylvon waiting lists that were months long. If he'd been anyone else, Shale would have never been able to afford it, but Sylvon had been a longtime friend of his parents as well as being one of his mother's lovers—and on extremely rare occasions, his father's as well.

"Amazing," Annai said softly, his fingers running along every dip and groove, all the decorative flowers and birds and bees that Sylvon had carved into the arm. His leg had animals: foxes and deer and rabbits, among others. "I've read all his papers. I get all the mechanica journals delivered." He slowly let go and looked up with a smile, stared at

Shale's left eye. "It's beautiful. Could he not recreate the color of your eye, or did you prefer a different shade?"

Shale swallowed, the fingers of his good hand twitching. Even if it was only because of his mechanica bits, it was disconcerting being watched with so much interest and admiration by Tellish's brother—Tellish's beautiful, interesting brother. Annai had a lot of his mother in him, too, which just made it all the worse, because Shale had been looking forward to having her as a mother-in-law and working with her every day. Now he was right back in their lives, and drawn to Annai, and he didn't want to be. He just wanted to do the job and leave. Not tear open old wounds and create new ones.

Finally he managed to say, "I preferred different. It was never going to look real, anyway, so what was the point?" And green was his favorite color, but no way was he saying that.

"Thank you for indulging me. You're most kind," Annai said. "It's an honor to meet you both." He drew back and swept them a bow elegant enough for a king. "Thank you for agreeing to escort me home."

"Why all the fuss?" Keira asked. "Nobody has seen fit to tell us, and normally I deal with that—nobility have always been the cagey sort—but if I'm going to have people trying to murder us, I'd like to know why."

Annai huffed. "Nobody told you?" He rounded on Wistry. "Abbot, not even you? That is shockingly inconsiderate."

"We didn't press for detail either, in all fairness," Shale said.

Keira shot him a look. "Because I trusted that woman enough not to press when she was being purposefully vague. I thought she'd treat *you* better than that, at the very least."

"Mother should have been clear. You shouldn't have needed to press for details," Annai said. "Honestly, Abbot, how could the two of you behave this way?"

"They wouldn't have taken the job, and now they have no choice," Wistry said. "You're too important to me, and your mother, for me to be sorry about that."

Keira's mouth flattened. "Fine words from a man who said he trusted us. I'm not sure I can continue trusting *you*."

Wistry looked sad but resolute. "I did what I felt what was best, though I am sorry it has cost me your regard. I do think highly of you both."

Annai looked even angrier, but before he or Keira could speak, Shale sighed. "You're an Arcana Demonica, aren't you?"

All three of them rounded on him, their faces expressing a range of reactions.

"A what?" Keira asked.

"How did you know?" demanded Wistry.

Annai merely smiled as his eyes turned from emerald green to moonlight silver. "You're astute. Yes, I'm an Arcana Demonica."

Shale swore softly. "That's illegal."

"What is going on?" Keira demanded. "I don't like the word 'demonica' popping up repeatedly. Why did his eyes go spooky?"

"He's an Arcana—possessed," Shale said, unable to tear his own eyes away from that silver gaze. "He was a Magica Demonica who summoned a demon and…screwed up."

Annai laughed as his eyes turned back to green. "Yes, succinctly put. I did something I knew I shouldn't have been doing, and did it wrong, and now I am bound to a demon for the rest of my life. I came here to the monastery for my own safety and that of my family."

Shale swore again, louder this time.

There were three main branches of magic: Elementa, Alchemica, and Angelica. Demonica was a branch of Angelica and the church regulated it with the zeal and ferocity of the royal treasury collecting taxes. Mechanica was a branch of Alchemica, but it was such an enormous industry on its own that it was likely going to be declared its own official branch soon.

Nearly all magic practiced was Elementa, from the most basic spells to the more powerful ones used by city engineers and upper-tier Magica and so forth.

Alchemica had been considered illegal for a long time, an unorthodox—once "unholy"—combination of magica and science. The rise of mechanica had changed that only a century or so ago.

Angelica was the study of holy magic, confined to the church and a select number of special scholars who were responsible for all healing magics, since they were powerful, difficult, and easily abused.

Magica was both the general term and the title for most practitioners. Wica was the title for master practitioners. Arcana was the title bestowed on magica no longer legal to practice, normally only seen in books and other written accounts, never actually used as a form of address.

But centuries ago, back when magica was a very different matter, the summoning of other-worldly beings, was common practice. Those bestowed the 'honor' of being possessed were given the title Arcana.

Bad things happened when non-human beings possessed humans who were not nearly as in control of the possession as they thought. There were scores of books and scrolls and monuments testifying to that fact. The last time someone had been possessed had been two hundred years ago—at least, that was the last possession on record. But Shale was pretty certain the King's Silver, the royal enforcers of all things magica, didn't spend all their time breaking curses and slapping wrists for every minor infraction.

"So you're a demon?" Keira asked. "No wonder your mother paid us so much. I'm starting to think we haven't been paid *enough*."

Annai's mouth quirked. "If it's money you want, that is easily done. To answer your question, no, I am not a demon. I am *possessed* by a demon. We have an accord, however, so you will not have to worry about me doing anything untoward."

Untoward. Shale snorted a laugh. "An accord? Demons don't form accords."

"This one does," Annai said. "Anyway, she is bound quite securely to me, so even if she wanted to run amuck, the bindings laid upon me would not allow her to get very far."

"Just being able to do as humans can do leaves a lot of troublesome options," Shale said.

"Fair enough. Is there anything I can say or do to assure you I am not a threat to you, save insofar as certain people have learned of me and what I am and seek to obtain me?"

Keira shook her head, braids flying about. "No. I'm not getting mixed up—"

Shale drowned her out. "You live peacefully in a monastery, which I take it is still a sound, holy place?"

"Quite," Wistry replied, folding his arms across his broad chest.

Shale glanced at him, then back at Annai. "What is the accord? Why is a demon so willing to live peacefully within you?"

"Rashti is a minor demon, easily overlooked and forgotten in her realm. There is nothing for her there. Within me, alongside me, she enjoys far more than she would have otherwise. She had no desire to be killed or banished. We have many things in common."

"She?" Keira asked. "I don't know much, but I know demons have no such concepts."

"That is how she prefers to be addressed," Annai replied.

"Fair enough. So you managed to accidentally get yourself possessed by a polite, accommodating demon?" Keira asked. "Why can't you send her back?"

"I can't send her back because the terms of the summoning were done wrong, and I accidentally created a blood contract for the span of my life. The contract cannot be broken without killing me."

"Stranger things have happened, so far as accommodating demons," Wistry added with a sigh. "It's not without precedent. There was—"

"Spare me the lesson." Keira rubbed her temples. "I need a drink. Shale, you're the expert here. What's your call?"

Shale tore his eyes away from the fascinating, beautiful Annai and tried to think clearly. After a few minutes, he lifted his gaze to Keira. "I think it won't be any worse than the Waterfall job. I don't think it'll be half that bad, even with the threat of death."

"I don't think attending my own execution would be as bad as the Waterfall job," Keira said. "Fine. But I'm going to insist Her Grace pay us double what she's already promised."

Annai smiled. "If my mother refuses, I'll pay the difference. It is only fair. I did not realize they'd withheld the knowledge. I am truly sorry."

Keira shrugged. "Doesn't matter anymore. Finish packing, my lord. We're going to feast and rest and at first light we're heading out. Your trunks will have to travel separately. They'll make us too slow."

"I understand. I have saddlebags already packed for my trip home. I did not think all of this would be going with me."

"Well, you have some sense to you, then," Keira replied.

She turned on her heel and strode off, saying in parting, "I'm going to let Her Grace know we've arrived and prepare for tomorrow."

Wistry followed after her, but lingered in the doorway. "Master Shale...?"

"Coming," Shale said, but didn't move. Leaving would be the smart thing. The less time he spent around Annai, the less chance he'd say or do or hope something stupid. But his feet didn't want to move.

"He can keep me company, if he's willing," Annai said. "Maybe I can coax him into helping me pack, and we can both join you for dinner." He winked at Shale, then waved Wistry off. "If he wants to linger, I do not mind. Do not let us keep you."

Wistry nodded. "As you wish, my lord." He cast Shale a look, though Shale didn't quite follow what he was conveying, and then was gone.

"You are not troubled by me, by us," Annai said when the door had closed. His eyes glimmered silver for a moment. "You don't feel like magica, certainly not a student of demonica."

"My father was a Wica Demonica. He was killed breaking an illegal curse circle, but something went wrong and it caused a blood reaction that killed the rest of my family."

"Not you?"

"I was adopted."

"I'm very sorry," Annai said softly. "It's never pleasant to lose loved ones, but that seems an especially awful way."

Shale nodded. "Thank you. Did you really want help packing?"

"No, I am particular, best not to get yourself involved." Annai smiled and winked, then nodded toward a chair. "I would not object to being kept company, however. I rarely see anyone outside my family and the monks, and once I am home, that will probably drop to just family. The monks are congenial enough, but most of them are not comfortable around me. It's refreshing to be around someone who is not unsettled." He walked over to the bookcase he'd been in the process of emptying when they arrived. "You and your partner must excel greatly at your job if my mother trusted the two of you instead of hiring an entire army as I half feared she would."

"I have history with Her Grace, and in a job like this, the fewer the better, as the greater the numbers, the greater the chances of a rat infestation." Shale settled in the chair, almost groaning at how good it felt to be off his feet and sitting somewhere more comfortable than a saddle.

"History?" Annai asked. "The only mercenary I know my mother to have..." He trailed off, fingers freezing in the process of reaching for more books, and turned back around. "You're *Tellish's* mercenary. Mother of All, does *my* mother have any concept of decency? I am so very sorry. You must hate doing this."

Shale shook his head. Try as he might, he *didn't* hate it. That would be too easy. He just fervently wished Annai had been someone easy to hate or easy to forget. "I like your family, even if Tellish and I parted ways unhappily. This job is good money, besides. Don't fret upon it, my lord."

"I think you can leave off the formalities." Annai turned back to grab several books and carried them over to his trunk, kneeling to stack them neatly amongst the others. "Tellish was a fool. You've no idea the dressing down we gave him. He still will not speak with me more than he strictly must, and I'm not terribly sorry." He looked up, a sour smile on his face. "I was born with a disinterest in sex, you see. I took his behavior quite personally."

Shale's heart gave a hard lurch in his chest, though he could not say if it was at the mention of Tellish or at realizing that in Annai he'd found a kindred spirit. He was already drawn to Annai—helplessly. Something about him caught, hooked, pulled Shale in. That Annai understood him in a way Tellish had never bothered to try…well, that hook just lodged even deeper.

Foolish, probably, to let himself get dragged back into any part of the world that had already thrown him out twice, but he could not tear his eyes away from Annai right then any more than he could stop breathing. Letting out a shuddering breath, he finally replied gruffly, "As I said, I like your family. It's been a pleasure to finally meet the only one I didn't know."

Annai smiled back, holding eye contact, and the gods must have hated Shale, because that tugging sensation just grew sharper. Shale wanted to hold him close, kiss him soft and sweet, bask in that smile and the warmth of those vivid eyes. Just soak in the pleasure as Annai talked about magica or mechanica or his newest book. Or simply his presence, though Annai struck him as someone who liked to talk.

It hurt, more than anything had in five years. He didn't want to feel this way again—especially not with Tellish's stepbrother, and get himself hurt by people who'd already abandoned him once. Whatever Her Grace said about missing him, no matter how intriguing he found Annai, he couldn't see the matter ending any way but poorly if he was stupid enough to get involved further than retrieve and deliver.

He should have left the room when he'd had the chance.

He finally broke their locked gazes. Annai smiled softly and went back to moving books. The silence lingered, warm and pleasant despite Shale's inner turmoil, interrupted only by the soft shuffle and thump of books as Annai packed.

The bells signaling dinner chimed an hour or so later, startling them both. Annai coughed and cast him a faintly sheepish smile. "I suppose we should go to dinner. I'm sure you would like food after all the traveling you've done. Thank you for keeping me company."

"The honor was my mine." Shale heaved himself out of the seat. "Shall we to dinner? Or do you not eat in the hall? Do they always lock you in your room?"

"No, that's recent, given they fear someone will be attempting to kidnap me. I usually eat in my room, but not always." He led the way out of the room and fell into step alongside Shale as they walked through the wide halls down to the ground floor.

The hall was filled with men in green robes and a small group in yellow acolyte robes, all of them talking boisterously. Some of the talking faded as the monks saw Annai, other conversations turned to poor whispers, and he could feel the weight of their stares as he and Annai walked through the room. Beside him, Annai seemed not to notice, but when he turned his head slightly and caught Shale's glance, his mouth twisted a wry, sad smile. Shale reached out to briefly touch his wrist, which gained him a fleeting but happier smile.

Annai really was irresistible. Seemed to be a family trait. Shale was resigned to not coming out of the job wholly unscathed, but hopefully he could minimize the damage this time around.

They joined Wistry and Keira at the farthest table, at the end closest to one of the small fires scattered about to spread heat throughout the cavernous hall. Though it was only early fall, the mountains were always colder than the rest of the country, and the temple itself colder still.

The tables were heaped with food and pitchers of beer and chilled tea. Shale always ate best when they visited the monastery. Someday, when he was old and gray, it would be a good place to retire. Shale sat and filled his plate, then poured a cup of beer. He grunted as he tasted it. "Delicious. What did you do different? Cardamom?"

"And a touch of cilantro," Wistry said happily. "We're very pleased. I think even Her Grace will be compelled to buy."

Annai laughed. "I'll buy and get her hooked for you, Abbot." He ladled fragrant vegetable soup into a bowl and tore up a hunk of bread to dip in it. "I will miss the food here."

"Sometimes I think we spend more time worshipping the food than the gods," Wistry replied wryly. "No one has struck us down yet, though, so I'm not going to upset the balance until they start replacing the ikons with jugs of beer or hanks of meat."

"Sounds like my kind of temple," Shale said with a grin. He tucked into his food, content to let the conversation carry on without him, occasionally stealing glances of Annai, who smiled and laughed with all the rest.

Around them, Shale occasionally saw a few monks still casting Annai nervous glances. If it was such a well-known secret that he was possessed, that explained how word had spread beyond the temple: nobody gossiped like monks and sailors. He was surprised it had remained a secret as long as it had.

A soft kick to his good ankle stirred him from his thoughts some time later. Shale didn't react, as any motion to prepare would likely be noted by whatever threat Keira had noted. But he readied himself all the same, looking up just long enough to see where Keira swiftly glanced as he shoveled a last bite of food into his mouth.

Voices drew closer to them, three—no, five. Too loud. Too forced. Too casual. They drew closer and closer. Keira shoved a last bite of stew in her mouth.

As the men reached them, she lunged, one of her knives appearing smoothly in her hand. Shale shoved Annai down under the table, and rose just in time to avoid the knife coming at him. Catching hold of his attacker's arm, Shale snapped his wrist and threw him aside. He kicked the bench out of the way, sending it careening into the neighboring table where monks were scrambling to get out of the way.

The man with the broken wrist tried to come at him again, this time with a buddy, but Keira made short work of him, and it took little effort for Shale to disarm and secure the last guy. Keeping him pinned on the ground, Shale looked at the results. All in all, Keira had killed four guys, and he had secured the fifth. They were all wearing acolyte robes.

"Nice work, Kee. You didn't even break any furniture this time."

"Shut up." Keira cleaned her knives and slipped them away again, looked around the empty dining hall and the mess left in the wake of hasty departure. Heaving a sigh, she went to help Wistry and Annai climb out from under the table. "Are you both all right?"

"Fine," Wistry said. "You're the one covered in blood."

Keira looked down at her clothes and heaved another sigh. "I just had them cleaned." She went and started searching through the bodies. "I'm telling you, I'd better get triple pay for this *and* at least a month off before we get dragged into something else."

"Like we wouldn't have been dragged into something else by now, anyway," Shale retorted. "Give me some rope or something, would you? I can't sit here holding him all damned day."

"Quit whining." Keira found some rope on the second body that she tossed him. She found a coin purse next and slipped that to join her own. "It is your fault. If Her Grace wasn't so fond of you, she might have hired someone else for this racket."

"Yeah, yeah." When he got the captive trussed, Shale rose and hauled the man to his feet. "You going to talk?"

"Wouldn't have much to say," the man replied petulantly. He nodded at one of the dead men. "He took the job. Never saw the woman's face, he said. We was to kidnap His Lordship, drop him off at a certain location, collect our money, and call it done. Easy job, or easier than most, anyway. At least until we saw the two of you, but he wouldn't call it off."

Keira preened slightly to be reminded of their reputation as no one to fuck with. "Too bad he didn't have your brains."

"Can I go?" the man asked. "It weren't nothing personal, and I ain't got reason to try anything else."

Keira gave a derisive laugh at that. "That will be for the abbot and Lord Annai to decide."

"Yes, quite," Wistry replied. "I am going to collect my monks. I'll send a few to clean this mess up and take him away, if you'll secure him before taking Lord Annai back to his quarters."

"I'll take care of him. Shale, escort Lord Annai to collect whatever he needs to take with him. Not more than what can fit in saddlebags comfortably. We leave in an hour." She grabbed their captive and hauled him away without waiting for a reply.

Annai stared after her. "Are she and my mother good friends?"

Shale gently took his arm and got him walking. "They never actually met before we took this job, but I'm sure if they stay in touch, they will be before the year is out," Shale replied. "By the end of next year, they'll be running the kingdom."

Annai laughed, then abruptly winced and lifted a hand to his forehead.

It was only then Shale noticed the knot there. "Are you all right? I'm sorry, that must have been from when I shoved you down."

Giving him a look, Annai said, "You saved my life. I can suffer a knock to the head. I've done worse to myself getting out of bed, I promise. Are you all right?"

Shale scoffed. "Whoever hired those three wasn't very smart. They're low-end thugs. You want good work, you pay good money. You don't toss pennies at Sleet Street posers."

Annai smiled. "So never hire mercenaries from Sleet Street. Duly noted. What street should one travel to find you?"

"A smart lord sends his mother's private army to fetch me from Mizzy's Tavern or my rooms on Chestnut Street."

"What if I just wanted to ask you to tea?"

Shale's heart thudded against his ribs and drummed in his ears. Getting involved with Annai wouldn't end any way but poorly. He was better off well clear of the whole family. But he answered the smile with one of his own all the same. "Send a note, Your Lordship."

Annai's smile widened.

Restraining an urge to touch him, Shale increased his pace and hurried Annai back to his room. "Pack quickly. Take only what you absolutely need."

"I'm the spoiled brat youngest child of a Grand Duke," Annai said with another soft laugh. "Anything I need, I can buy. My saddlebags are already packed." He crossed the room and lifted them from where they lay on a chest. "I'm afraid I do not possess clothes like yours, and I prefer to keep the robe for its warmth."

Not surprising. Magica was hard on the body. All magica ate significantly more than non-magica, and the more powerful they were, the more they ate. Even just having mechanica parts left Shale far hungrier than he had been before. There were days he could eat six large meals and still need a bedtime snack.

At Annai's level, that drain also manifested in being always cold or always hot—it varied by the person.

"You can keep it. We're not really trying for stealth, only speed."

"Thank you." Annai swung the saddlebags over one shoulder and pulled a ribbon from a pocket of his robes that he used to bind back his springy hair. "Shall we?"

"Nothing else you need?"

Annai shook his head. "I've always known this would likely happen, and I do like the monastic teaching that the fewer attachments one has, the happier one tends to be. I am very attached to my books and family." He winked. "And a good beer."

Shale forced himself to get moving before he stood there smiling and staring like a moonstruck fool.

Mother of All, Keira was going to mock him until the end of days for mooning over his ex's stepbrother. He cringed just thinking about it, but he'd already conceded he wasn't planning on stopping. Annai was just too compelling. Even the fact he was sharing space with a demon wasn't as off-putting as it should have been. Though it might be once Shale thought about it harder.

But for the present, he was just going to enjoy the unexpected pleasure of being captivated and realizing the feeling was mutual. The details would have to wait until they were safely home.

Back in the courtyard, Keira and Wistry waited with three horses. Annai settled his saddlebags on the black mare, then fed her some lumps of sugar summoned from the depths of his robe.

Keira caught Shale's eye, glanced at Annai, and scowled at Shale. Shale shrugged irritably and ignored her loud huff.

"Let's get moving," she said as she swung into the saddle, her stallion snorting beneath her, annoyed that he hadn't gotten a whole night in the stables.

Shale's mare came over to demand petting, nibbling playfully at him before he moved to mount up.

"Be careful," Wistry said. "Lord Annai, your presence was a pleasure and an honor. Should you ever desire to return, you will be most welcome."

"Thank you, Abbot. I will always be grateful for your kindness and hospitality. I regret my departure is so unpleasant for all of us. I hope the brigands hunting me will trouble you no further."

"Have a care, my lord." Wistry waved a hand in farewell as they rode off into the quickly falling dark.

❀❀❀

They rode for three hours before Keira finally conceded it was too dark to keep going. They made camp in a little field they'd used many a time before, and Shale set to work building a fire while Keira tended the horses. Instead of resting as Shale had expected, Annai stood close to the fire and turned in a slow circle to take in the camp. Then he walked to the outmost edge of the cleared circle and started to walk around it, muttering softly to himself all the while.

Shale completely forgot about the fire as he noticed the glowing silver marks Annai left behind with every step. He'd never seen anyone build a ward so easily. The marks shimmered, curled like smoke and mist, and wove together like fine threads into an elaborate spider web, climbing and climbing until they came together in a dome and slowly faded to invisibility that only twinkled here and there where firelight or moonlight caressed.

"What the fuck was that?" Keira demanded, feed bags forgotten in her hand.

"A protection ward." Annai yawned as he rolled out his bed mat and plopped down. "Anyone who tries to get through it will feel quite the sting, and objects will fail to pass through as well. It won't hold forever if we're attacked, but it will certainly buy time."

Keira stared at him and gave a slow blink. "I can see why people would find you handy. The last time I saw a flasher throw a ward down, it took three hours and a lot of swearing."

Annai wrinkled his nose slightly, but only said, "Yes, Rashti provides many a nifty shortcut."

Keira's eyes narrowed in a way that reminded Shale of Lord Halruul. She'd given him that look a lot when her stepson had announced his relationship with a mangy mercenary. Neither he nor she had expected the relationship to progress so far, though he certainly had hoped…

And thinking about all that might have been hurt too much. It had been stupid of him to believe he could regain some semblance of the life lost with his family. A life that hadn't really existed at all, as he'd found out the hard way when creditors came looking for money or blood, whichever they got their hands on first. Poor money management and a tragic accident was all it had taken to put Shale one step from living on the streets, until he'd crossed paths with a pickpocket who somehow became his best friend.

The mercenary life wasn't a bad one, but they were both getting too old for it and had wanted to settle down years ago. Him to the life he'd first been trained for; Keira to buy a house and work on the family she'd always wanted.

Shale knew it wasn't his fault they were still working the life they'd wanted to leave behind, but it felt like it most days. If he'd seen that dragon. If he'd moved faster. If he hadn't needed the mechanica. If he didn't need the drugs. *If, if, if.* Most days he could ignore the clanging of that damned word. Other days…other days were rough.

"So what does the demon *do* in there? In you? Just… sit there?"

Annai smiled at Keira. "You really are a classic Southern, aren't you? I'm a flasher and you're a dim, is that the term?"

Keira grimaced. "Sorry. I didn't mean anything by that. I'll have more care. But yes, I know next to nothing about magica. Even all our years getting mixed up in one thing or another, we don't cross much more than Magica Elementa and the odd Wica Elementa. There are mercs who specialize in magica matters, so rarely are we called upon to deal with it. I didn't know people could be possessed anymore."

"It happens more often than anyone knows or wants to admit, and only under extreme supervision after the king and half her palace have signed off on it. What I did was very, very illegal." Annai's smile turned sad. "I was young, lonely, and tired of being picked on. Some of my main tormentors dared me to do it, and I knew if I refused or backed down, my life would only grow worse. So I did it, and of course I did it wrong, and now Rashti and I share space. She likes to watch. That's mostly all she does. 'An eternal play that never grows boring' is how she puts it. Sometimes she sleeps. Every now and then she wants a stronger presence, and I'm the one who fades into the background, though never entirely. The bindings prevent that."

"So she's...*always* there?" Keira asked. "In *everything* you do?"

Annai burst out laughing, entire body shaking with it. Shale wanted to kiss him, hold him close, wanted to feel and taste that laughter, that genuine, open amusement. "Yes, everything. I'm certain if I had any interest in sex, that would make things quite awkward. Certainly other, private matters were awkward at first." His eyes seemed to gleam and sparkle. "Though honestly, that is the least embarrassing thing I had to adjust to. I am afraid the whole situation has left me what most would consider quite shameless."

"I guess it would, at that," Keira said with a grunt, and as the horses prodded at her, she seemed to lose interest in the conversation.

Still smiling, Annai pulled his saddlebags close and rifled through them, pulling out a book and a flicker, a magica-made light that would last for hours. If made well enough, which Annai certainly had the money to afford, when it stopped working, an elementa could recharge the glass ball for a small fee.

Shale finished building up the fire and set to work on food. They'd only eaten a few hours ago, but as usual, he was already starving. An hour later, he served up bread, dried pears, and soup made from a few packets. They were expensive, the ready-soups they bought, but worth every penny. Without them, meals would be a lot duller and colder, as Keira couldn't boil water without almost killing them, and they rarely had time for Shale to cook properly.

"Thank you," Annai said as he took the steaming metal cup Shale offered. "You're quite adept."

Shale shrugged. "I like doing it, and the last time Keira tried she nearly burned down the forest."

"It was one sapling, fuck you," Keira said cheerfully as she began gulping down soup. It should have burned her damned mouth, but that was Keira.

Shale drank his own more slowly, interspersing sips with bits of bread dipped in the broth. Keira washed up when they were done, stretched out on her bed roll, and set her sword near to hand. Minutes later was filling the campsite with her soft snores.

"I wish I could fall asleep half so easy," Annai said.

"Yeah, it would be nice." Shale pulled out his bottles and powders and swallowed them in order of bitterest to sweetest, though sweet was a touch overgenerous. He put them away when he was done and pulled out his tin of lemon candies, popping one in his mouth before looking up to offer the tin to Annai, startling to see he was being closely watched. "Um. Candy?"

"Thank you." Annai took one of the sweets and pushed it between his lips. "Would it be rude of me to ask how you and Tellish met?"

Shale shrugged. "I don't mind. He was having trouble with a wine delivery. Turned out the men hired to do the delivering had stolen the wine. Keira and I hunted it down, got back what was left of the wine and the money owed on the rest. He asked me to dinner a few days later." Shale tried to smile, but it faltered, fell.

"I'm sorry. I think I am trying to get to know you and asking all the wrong questions. I still want to punch him in the face, and I am fairly certain I do not even know how to throw a punch."

"It's a useful skill, to be sure, but if you've never had need of it, I'd count that a good thing," Shale said with a small laugh. "Why did you want to know how we met?"

Annai made a face. "It's a trifle awkward to be immediately taken with my brother's former fiancé. I cannot help drawing a comparison, even if I do want to punch him."

Shale flinched despite himself. "The point is that he was formerly my fiancé and he's the one who ended the relationship. There's no point in comparing yourself to him, but I promise you come out the stronger, no matter how much…" He shook his head. "Leave off the comparing. How old are you? "

"Just turned twenty six last month. You're about Tellish's age, right?"

"Yes." A year younger, actually, but thirty nine was still thirteen years older than Annai. "Does it amuse your demon to have an accord with a boy?"

Annai smiled impishly. "She calls me 'babe' most days, 'suckling' if she's irritated with me. She calls *you* boy. *The sad, handsome boy who likes to stare.*"

"I do not—" Shale stopped, then conceded with a grumble, "Fine, I might have stared a bit. You're beautiful. That's no excuse, I know, but you are lovely."

"I've been staring, too. I am the one who so rudely asked how you met my brother. I am also the one who is going to catch it from my mother, sisters, and brothers when they see me flirting. Not that it's going to stop me. Years of being on my own, harassment, and demon possession have made me relentless on top of shameless. I'll only stop if you want me to."

Shale huffed a quiet laugh and looked down at his hands. He might have thirteen years on Annai, but in experience they seemed to draw even, and he'd never minded when someone else was more commanding. "I never minded relentless or shameless. I don't want you to stop." He curled his good hand into a loose fist to still its trembling.

"Good," Annai said softly, and Shale could hear the rustle of his clothes. When he looked up, Annai had lain down and pulled his robes around him. He looked up from the long folds of the hood and gave Shale a sweet smile. "Goodnight. Sleep well. Thank you again for helping me—and saving me."

"Keira did all the hard parts, but you're welcome. Sleep well."

When Annai's breathing evened out into sleep, Shale fussed with the fire and settled down on his own bed roll, wrapped up in his heavy cloak. He settled on his back and stared up at the star-strewn sky until sleep finally carried him away.

✿✿✿

It was chilly, gray, and misty when they woke, and a distant, muffled rumble promised the day was going to get worse long before it got better. Shale made certain the fire was out and helped the others pack up the camp. He downed his morning doses before swinging up into the saddle, munching on hard biscuit and dried apple and pear as they rode.

As threatened, halfway through the day the rain came, pounding down so hard that trying to carry on was pointless and stupid. They took shelter under a heavy copse of trees, and Shale helped Keira tend the horses before wrapping up in his cloak and making them all some tea with one of the firestones he kept around for just such an occasion.

He took a cup of fragrant, steaming tea over to Annai, but had to nudge him twice before he finally took his eyes from the sky. When Annai finally looked at him, the brilliant silver eyes nearly caused Shale to drop the tea. "You're not Annai."

A smile curved the pretty face, but it wasn't any of Annai's smiles. Something more like a parent amused by or indulging a child. "No, I wanted out," Rashti said, and the cadence and accent had changed slightly, like Rashti had learned their language in another time and place, or maybe a different language entirely. But the easiest demons to summon were those that had been summoned before, so she'd probably been summoned decades or centuries ago and learned then. She turned her head back up to the sky. "The weather is not natural. It tastes of manipulation."

"Weather elementa is illegal."

"So am I," Rashti said with a laugh, and Shale half-expected her to pinch his cheek. "Trust me, this weather is fouler than it seems. It dampens my other senses. I cannot read if we are hunted, though the weather is enough to convince me we are. Someone is trying to slow us down, pin us in place."

"Weather elementa isn't cheap. Even Her Grace would flinch at the cost. Is a demon really worth all this money and trouble?" Keira asked. "It's a miracle you—he—whatever—haven't been arrested or executed, for that matter."

Rashti cast one of those parental looks. "Right now I am bound to this body, contracted only for Annai's lifetime, at which point I will return home. The bindings placed on me allow me to do little but observe and come out to play, like this and only like this, for brief periods. After about two hours, I must recede, and cannot do it again until a full day has passed. If these miscreants capture me, they will break the bindings and tear me out, killing Annai in the process, and bind me anew—enslave me, likely, and though I am a minor demon, I am still quite powerful. Weather workings would be a trifling thing for me, and creating that ward was a lark of a moment."

"I see," Keira said quietly. She cast Shale a look. "Your father did this sort of thing for a living? Why?"

Shale shrugged. "Demonica are few. It comes with a prestige of sorts. Money, of course. The challenge." Bitterness slipped into the last word, but he pushed it away like the tired, faded thing it was. "People always want *more more more* when it comes to magica, and demonica is a great way to obtain more, but it's dangerous to summon a demon even if you do everything correctly." He looked at Rashti. "A demon that's already been summoned and safely bound? That's all the best parts and practically none of the hard parts."

"It also sounds extremely lucrative," Keira said. "I doubt we're dealing with people interested in the demon for themselves. More likely we're dealing with people interested in selling." Her eyes skimmed the rain-shrouded landscape before she went to her saddlebags and dug through them before coming out with her spyglass in a weather-proofed leather case. Taking it out, she swept the mountains. "Riders, at least four. They're probably hoping to slow us enough with the weather they can catch up and overtake. Best not to hold still, but we're not going to get very far in all this rain, not when we're traveling down and the terrain is rocky and muddy. I'm definitely not risking the horses."

Shale weighed their options as he gulped down his tea. "We could go on without the horses. The terrain is difficult, but we're not going anywhere we'd be falling off edges, and the road is still fairly visible. It would be the worst day ever, but we wouldn't get pinned, and they can't do such high-level elementa forever. I'm surprised they've lasted this long. They must be bleeding through Magica to maintain it."

"Or they have a demon," Rashti said. "Your plan has merit."

"Damn it," Keira said. "I don't like it, but it's the soundest we've got. Strip the horses of essentials and leave food for them. I don't suppose you can do something to ensure their safety a touch further?"

Rashti dipped her head. "Of course." As Keira and Shale set to work on their own tasks, she circled the clearing under the trees much as she had the night before, trailing a silver ward flecked with green and blue. "That should protect them from the worst of the elements and keep away predators."

"Oh, to have such a thing everywhere we went," Keira muttered. "Though I'm not sure it'd be worth the hassle in the end."

"Probably not," Rashti said with a laugh. "Now, I think I will retreat so that I can be called upon should the need arise. I hope my precautions prove unnecessary. Thank you, truly, for helping us." The silver eyes faded back to green, her posture and demeanor shifting as control was reclaimed by Annai. He blinked several times. Smiled. "Hello."

Keira muttered and shook her head, making the sign of the Mother of All across her breasts before she swung her pack onto her shoulders and double-checked all her weapons were in place. "That will take some getting used to."

Annai laughed. "Sorry. I will try to remember to give warning. I am used to it not mattering since I spend so much time alone in my room, and usually only Wistry comes to see me and is willing to talk to her when she's out. In the dining hall, it's always me."

"I hope life back with your family is better for you both," Shale said. He pulled up the hood of his jacket and double-checked the protective coverings for his mechanica. He was going to be on the table for hours when they got back, but there was no help for it.

Annai stripped off his long, heavy robe and bundled it up tightly. He fastened it to the bottom of the pack he'd pulled from his saddlebags to transfer necessary items to. Then he pulled out a jacket similar to the ones they wore: thigh-length, treated against wind and rain, but it was also decorated with embroidery and shimmered with magica touches that were well out of their price range. He shrugged into the jacket and pulled up the hood, settled his pack, and smiled at them. "Shall we? I will do my best not to slow us down."

"You'll be walking faster than me by the end, no worries there," Shale said with a grunt. "Keira, lead the way. I'll take rear. Annai, do whatever we say without hesitation."

"I will."

"Let's move out," Keira said, and darted out into the pounding rain.

They traveled almost non-stop, Keira pausing only once to see if she could spot the riders chasing them. At her grim expression, they pushed on even harder.

The trip was as miserable as Shale had expected. He skidded and tripped often on the slippery, uneven terrain, swearing every time. Every hour brought increased pain as his artificial parts suffered under the strain of hard travel and brutal weather combined with no rest.

He dug painkillers out of the purse at his waist, the expensive ones that wouldn't make him drowsy, though his stomach wouldn't thank him for taking them without food.

Everything went tits up as they reached the crossroads where the old temple was located—Temple Cross, the area was called, a popular stopping point for travelers, especially large parties.

They'd been so busy watching their back, it hadn't occurred to them to watch their front.

On the positive side, it wasn't a dragon. If it had been a dragon, Shale probably would have lost his damned mind and run all the way back to the city.

On the negative side, it was seven large, well-armed men and five dread wolves.

"Give us the demon," said the man who seemed to be in charge, a scruffy bastard with an eyepatch, a scar that puckered the left side of his mouth, and who was roughly the size of a shipyard warehouse.

As was generally her policy when confronted with scruffy bastards intent on violence, Keira threw a flash-bang. The world exploded in light and ear-ringing noise; Shale lunged at Annai, threw him over his good shoulder, and ran away from the temple, headed over the hill for the cluster of boulders against a sheer wall that might pin them, but meant none of those fucking wolves would be getting them from behind.

Something pinged off his mechanica leg, shooting fire through it and making him stumble. But he'd gotten used to always being one step away from falling on his damned face. It was a near thing, but he kept upright and moving.

He reached the boulders and dropped Annai on the ground, whipped around, and drew his pistols. Please, please, Mother Above, Keira better be all right.

Three men and all the wolves had come after him. That was a good sign. He hoped.

The wolves lunged. Shale fired his pistols, grunting at the recoil because they weren't dainty pieces, but it knocked two of the wolves off course and left them badly injured. Dread wolves were a lot harder to kill than that, but it'd do for a start.

Of course, the other three just kept on coming. Shale dropped the pistols and went for his blades. He heard scuffling and scraping behind him, but ignored it, all his attention on the wolves that were probably about to kill them both while the bastards controlling them just stood there smirking.

The three wolves growled, taking their time, unlike the other two, who'd been young and eager and stupid. One of them crouched, the other two bracing to follow in her wake. The wolf lunged—and yelped in pain as he collided with a shower of silver sparks.

He collapsed in a shuddering, charred, and bleeding heap. The other wolves whined and retreated.

The three men snarled and finally pulled their own weapons: three pistols and a crossbow. Damn it. Shale hissed, "Get down!"

"No," Rashti said. "I can be of use as long as you can keep me protected."

Shale nodded, but before he could say anything, movement caught the corner of his eye. He knocked them both into the mud as bullets and arrows flew. They too hit a shower of silver parks and dropped to the ground, the shaft of the arrow reduced to ash, the bullets sparking madly before dropping like the dead weights they'd become.

The men snarled in irritation and drew their swords.

"I can't hold the barrier much longer," Rashti said. "I'm limited by what this body can take. They'll break through after a couple of tries."

"That's all I need. Stay down. If something goes wrong, you run as fast as you can for as long as you can. Stay under-cover, only move at night, keep going downhill and follow the road." Shale heaved to his feet, using the cliff face for leverage, and stooped to reclaim his dropped sword. He pulled a dagger from his boot, adjusted his grip to throw it, and as the men sparked against the silver barrier, he let it fly.

It caught the left-most man in the throat. One down.

As promised, the barrier broke on their third attempt to slam threw it. Shale charged them, sword in his good hand, triggering the knife in his left. He barreled into the nearest man, sinking the knife deep, through layers of leather and too-thin metal. Cheap armor, tsk. Yanking the knife out, he threw the injured man into his friend.

With them both on the ground, tangled in each other and slowed by mud and rain, finishing them off was quick work.

He dealt with the injured wolves next. Dread wolves were big and nasty, but they were also slow and didn't hold up well against magica. Killing was never pleasant, especially animals, who rarely had a choice in their actions once they were under human control. But they were too dangerous to leave alive.

When that was done, Shale sheathed his weapons and returned to Annai, who was soaked through, covered in mud, water, and bits of clinging rock. He looked as exhausted and bedraggled as Shale felt. "Are you all right?"

"Yes," Annai said. "Thank you."

Shale snorted. "I'd say you and your demon are the ones owed thanks. I couldn't have handled all of that on my own. The wolves alone would have gotten me. I was just hoping to last long enough that Keira could finish the job."

Annai made a soft, indecipherable noise, then suddenly lunged forward and hugged him tightly. "I don't want anyone dead because of me. I'm sorry."

"You saved our lives. There's nothing to be sorry about." Shale held him close, pressed his face to the soaked curls that had come loose at some point. He smelled like sweat and rain and earth, and was warm in Shale's arms despite the fact they were both soaked through. He held fast a moment longer, then reluctantly let go. "We were not equipped for that sort of foe. We were expecting a snatch-and-bolt. We'll do better from here on." Drawing further back, he pushed the hair from Annai's face and rested a hand on his cheek. "No apologies are necessary, all right? This is our job, and we're being well paid to do it. I'm always happy to help your family, anyway."

That just seemed to make Annai more unhappy. "You always look so sad when you look at me, even when you smile, and I can't blame you. I'm sure you'd rather be anywhere else. You of all people should not be risking your life for me. Not after the way Tellish treated you."

"He had his needs and desires and plans, and they no longer meshed with mine. Wrong or right, it's over." Shale squeezed his hand. "If I hadn't wanted to do this, I wouldn't be here. What happened between me and Tellish has nothing to do with you."

Annai didn't look convinced, but he nodded slowly.

"Come on, let's go see if Keira is still alive or if she's become king of the underworld. Stay close, be ready to run again." He drew his sword and headed back the way they'd come, wincing with every step, his damaged mechanica leg getting worse every moment.

As they crested the hill, Shale swept the field anxiously. He nearly sank to his knees in relief to see Keira walking toward them, battered and bleeding but mostly just pissed off. She stopped as she saw them. "Mother's left tit, I was starting to think you were going to make me go back and tell poor mum that her demon and almost son-in-law were dead. I saw those wolves take off after you and thought that was it." She punched Shale's arm as she reached them, then hugged him tightly. "How'd you get them all?"

"I had a demon assistant," Shale replied. "What took you so long?"

Keira gestured crudely. "Suck my left tit. Me against four mountain-sized thugs?"

"I've seen you take twice that in a bar fight for fun."

"Yeah, well, these ones came equipped with some nasty alchemica tricks." She sniffed in offense. "Took a bit longer. Are we done chatting?"

Shale nodded, all of a sudden extremely tired. He'd expected it, but that didn't make it easier to bear. And his damned leg felt like it was on fire and being gnawed on by thorn pixies. "Let's go. Hopefully we don't run into more trouble."

"I do not think we will," Annai said as he pulled his hair back again and restored his hood. "The rain is lessening, the magica in it fading off. If there is to be further trouble, we'll not encounter it anytime soon, I think. I do not know what became of the men chasing us, but I do not think they'll be reaching us."

Keira pulled out her spyglass and swept the mountains again. "You're right. I don't see them. No, I see them. They're unconscious. Maybe dead, but I don't see signs of violence."

"Wore themselves out with the weather elementa," Annai said.

"Probably a combination of weather elementa and pushing hard to reach us in time to pin us between them and the group we just killed," Shale said. "Our plan worked, I'd say, even if it got a little uncertain there at the end."

"Uncertain, my ass." Keira sniffed and tucked the spyglass away. "Even if someone did pay for some high-end mercenaries. I hope they negotiated a lower price, given the shoddy performance. Then again, I think those guys were Nighters, and they're not nearly as good as they think they are."

Annai looked at her blankly. "Nighters?"

"A mercenary group that will do anything and not ask bothersome questions or be terribly troubled about what they're doing, as long as the money is good. Your mother is paying us two hundred gleams to escort you safely home. Those bastards we just killed probably went for at least two thousand, and I wouldn't be surprised if it was closer to three thousand. Whoever was paying them wants you like a sailor wants a whore."

Annai coughed. "I see. I guess we'd best be on our way before the men further up the mountain wake up and make a second attempt."

Keira grunted, turned on her heel, and stomped down the hill. Shale motioned for Annai to go next, and limped behind him.

By the time they made it off the mountain, he was barely walking, and Keira had to help him over to a rock and dig out his tools for him. "Sorry," he muttered.

"Shut up or I'll clobber you with your own leg."

He mustered a faint smile, but it faded as he concentrated on getting the leg off. Laying it across his lap, he inspected the damage. Fortunately, it was to a part he could remove and replace with a spare. It would cost him a painful sum to have it better repaired when they got home, but at least he wouldn't have to repair the whole damned leg.

Swapping the parts out and giving the whole thing a rough cleaning, he fastened it back in place and gingerly tested it out. When he was confident it would hold, he stood to give it a more thorough testing. "I think it's good. Sorr—"

"Don't say sorry!" Keira snarled.

He glared back. "It's not wrong to say I'm a liability these days far more than I'm an asset."

"No, you're not. If you don't stop saying such things, I really will beat you to death with your own limbs. Now let's go. I'm tired and hungry and really fed up with being wet. At least the rain stopped." She stalked off down the road, vanishing over the dip.

❁❁❁

They camped in the hollow of a stack of boulders and rocks, eschewing a fire and simply bundling up in their cloaks. Grumbling about what would happen to anyone who dared to wake her before she wanted to be woken, Keira bundled up in her cloak and went to sleep.

"I hope you will let me pay for your mechanica parts when we return," Annai said softly, sitting so they were pressed shoulder to shoulder, staring up at the sky. "Assuming of course my mother does not do it first. It seems the very least we can do for all the suffering we have caused you. Though if you prefer to simply be on your way, I would understand."

Shale drew a deep breath and let it out slowly. "I did tell you where I lived."

"But you always look sad when you smile."

"Tellish ended our relationship and made it clear I was no longer welcome at the castle. I haven't seen your family for five years. The last thing I expected when we took this job was…" He hesitated, trying to find the words he wanted, but could in the end only managed, "you."

Annai smiled faintly, reaching out to touch his arm. "I'm sorry you no longer felt welcome. I know from my mother's letters that she's missed you fiercely. I had been looking forward to meeting you, and was furious to hear how and why it all ended. I certainly understand why you'd want nothing to do with any of us. I'm sure it's more than a little awkward. But…you're the one who told me not to compare."

"That is what I said. I gave you my address, my lord. If you still want to send a note after you're home and settled in, send a note." He turned and smiled faintly. "We'll see what happens from there."

That got him a smile prettier than all the rest, and Annai leaned in close enough to press his head to the side of Shale's. He turned just enough to bury his nose in Annai's curls, breathe in the scent of rain and earth that clung to him, heart pounding so loudly in his ears he could barely hear anything else.

Annai fell asleep, leaning heavily against him, until Shale finally woke him and Keira and they resumed traveling.

Another day and half, and they finally reached Soria Bellmane. Rather than relax, though, Shale kept ready to draw weapons. Keira, long out of patience and tact, kept her sword drawn. But that meant people cleared a path for them, and Shale could not complain.

They made straight for the castle, where the guards took one look at them and immediately raised the portcullis. Captain Tula met them as they entered the ward and looked them over with concern. "You ran into trouble."

"You could say," Keira grumbled. "Can we skip the pleasantries?"

Tula jerked her head for the guards to fall into line around them and escorted them herself to the doors of Halruul's office. "Your Grace, Lord Annai and his escorts are here."

"Show them in."

Tula bowed them in and faded off, the doors banging shut behind her.

Halruul pushed away from her desk and came around it to hug Annai tightly, heedless of the muck that doing so left on her costly clothes. "It's good to have you home." She drew back and cupped his head in her hands. "You look like you had a rough time of it."

"I'd say Keira and Shale had it rougher—and how could you make him help us? That's impressively rude, even for you, Mother."

"No, it's not," she said with a smile. She kissed his temple before drawing back to regard the others. "I'm glad you're both alive and well. Tell me everything."

Keira did. Shale tried to remain standing throughout, but he was simply too fucking tired and in pain. Limping over to a chair in the corner, he dropped into it and dug out his pain pills. Halruul cast him a concerned look, but did not interrupt Keira's report.

When she was done, Halruul waved Keira to a seat as well. "I'll arrange food and rooms. Hold on." She strode out of the room, and Shale could just hear her bellowing in the hallway. After a few minutes, she returned. "Food will be ready in half an hour, and your usual rooms will be ready even faster. We keep them ready, really. Shale, there's a Mechanica on the way as well, and I'll cover the repair costs."

Shale barely heard the last part, more focused on that 'we keep them ready' bit. He'd been so certain back then that the rest of the family was as ready for him to leave as Tellish, he hadn't questioned the matter when Tellish implied as much. It hurt in ways good and bad to know he'd been wrong, that they'd missed him too. That he hadn't ceased to exist with his relationship.

That maybe becoming entranced with Annai wasn't as stupid and hopeless as he'd feared. "Thank you," he managed, voice rough, and wished he could say more.

Halruul smiled like she heard it all anyway. "I've something to discuss with you, Shale, but it will keep a few days. I want both of you here resting and recovering. It seems the least I can do given all you've endured."

"You can pay them more," Annai said.

She quirked a brow at him, but at his scowl, conceded with a faint huff of laughter. "Yes, I can pay them more. It will be done. Now you come with me, Annai, and you two go devour the meal that has been set out for you. Annai, food is being taken to your room, but first…" Their voices faded off as they vanished down the hallway.

Keira stood with a groan and stretched, her joints cracking and popping. "I cannot wait to fall asleep and not wake up for at least a week."

"I could not agree more." Shale took the hand she offered and heaved to his feet. "Food first, though."

"Race you to the roasted goose."

❀❀❀

Three days later, sore from repairs but otherwise muchly improved, the moment Shale had been dreading finally came. He should have known it would be in the study. He never should have gone into the study. But it had been his place, more than anywhere else in the castle. Everyone had taken to calling it his office. The first time someone had said it, he hadn't been able to speak, his throat was so suddenly clogged. *I put the post in your office, sir.*

Plans to renovate it into a proper office for him had been underway when everything had gone so wrong. He hadn't wanted to see it, but he hadn't been able to resist seeing it either.

Only minutes later, another painful bit of his past finally appeared.

"Hello, Tellish."

He was still handsome, all his mother's sternness tempered by his father's elegance. Lord Miniria was a severe religious figure in the south—severe enough her husband had sought divorce, and the courts had granted him full and sole custody of their son. Shortly thereafter, he'd married

Lord Halruul, and was quite happy managing the finances and what was currently three wineries, and Shale had heard rumors of a fourth joining the collection soon.

"Shale," Tellish greeted quietly. "Mother said you were injured escorting Annai. I hope you are well now?"

"Yes, thank you." Shale sat on the edge of the desk that had once been his.

Tellish hovered in the doorway, hesitation plain on his face. That was odd for Tellish. He wasn't given to hesitation, and he was a closed book if ever there was one, a man shrewd and sharp enough to not only excel as a Lower Councilor but *enjoy* it. He'd just obtained a Lower Seat in the Circle when they broke up.

"Oh, come in and say what you have to say," Shale said, feeling tired.

Tellish stepped inside, but stopped in the middle of the room. "Has Mother spoken to you yet?"

"No, I'm meeting with her after lunch, once she's free of her meeting with the city council. Why?"

"I've won a seat at the High Council."

Shale blinked. "Congratulations. I know you've always wanted that."

"It will require me moving permanently to the capital," Tellish went on. "I've only recently returned from arranging matters, in fact, and am set to move there at the end of the month."

"I'm still not seeing what any of this has to do with me," Shale said.

Tellish made that huff-growl noise he always made when he was irritated someone wasn't keeping up with his thoughts. Shale had always found it equal parts annoying and endearing. Now it was only annoying. "It means mother will be left without a seneschal, and when the subject came up, the entire castle was in favor of convincing you to come back, despite the many other candidates available. You are already trained to it, more or less, and everyone was sorry when you cut ties with them alongside me. Hiring you to fetch Annai was just Mother's way of getting you back here and hopefully willing to listen to the offer."

"You never gave me any reason to think that your family wanted to see me anymore," Shale snapped, holding his hands in his lap so the trembling of his good one wouldn't be visible. "In fact, you implied rather damned heavily that everyone wanted me gone, or wouldn't care one way or another."

Tellish flinched. "I know you won't believe me, but I didn't mean to do that." He stared at the floor for so long Shale wanted to scream to break the silence. Finally, he looked up, his eyes dark and sad. "I made mistakes. By the time I was willing to admit that, it was too late to fix them. I have to live with that. But that doesn't mean the rest of you do."

Shale stared, mouth gaping slightly. Of all the things he had expected Tellish to say, that hadn't even been a remote possibility. He would have laughed if someone had suggested it.

"You were good at the job, better than me, even. I never meant to take that from you. I thought you left because that was what you wanted. I'm sorry, about everything. At least let me fix this much. I'm leaving in seven days. The position of seneschal will be vacant, and Mother says it's yours if you want it. And I have it on good authority a certain spoiled brat recently returned to us would be sad if you left."

Shale jerked at the words, nearly toppling himself off the desk. He swallowed the lump in his throat. "Tellish…"

He shrugged, smiled sadly. "I'm glad you're doing well, Shale. I hope from here on you'll do even better. Take care of them for me, and don't let Mother or the rest of them boss you around too much." He hesitated, then simply nodded, turned, and left.

Shale didn't know whether to laugh or cry. He settled on neither, tamping down the emotions Tellish had turned all to hell and went to get some fresh air.

He really should have known he'd just move from one complicated thing to another.

Annai sat on one of the three benches in the family's private garden, a place Shale technically shouldn't have been visiting, but Halruul had no interest in gardens and could not care less if the cook used it to grab a quick smoke.

Shale hovered, uncertain if he should stay, unable to make himself leave. Annai was bent over a book, occasionally muttering to himself, or possibly to Rashti, as he read. Shale took a step forward, then back, but as he turned to retreat after all, Annai looked up. The way his face lit up when he saw Shale was as gratifying as it was terrifying. He snapped the book shut and stood. "Have you spoken with Mother?" he asked eagerly.

"Not yet," Shale said with a crooked smile, shaking his head in amusement. "However, I did speak with Tellish."

"Tellish?" Annai scowled. "What did that—"

"He said your mother is about to require a new seneschal and I should take the position," Shale cut in. "He said he was sorry."

"Oh." Annai seemed to wilt. "I admit he's not the brat he used to be, now that I have spent real time with him again." He smiled, but it was strained and cracked at the edges.

Shale took another tentative step into the garden, then reminded himself he was a damned adult and crossed the rest of it to stop in front of Annai, though he left plenty of space between them. He clearly had lost his mind somewhere, but whenever Annai smiled at him, he felt less lonely, started to feel like maybe all those things he'd been convinced really were gone might still be there after all. That he really could have a family again. "He also said he had it on good authority that a certain spoiled brat would be sad if I left."

Annai dropped the book he'd clutched to his chest like a shield. "He said what? That *ass*, and after all the glaring and scowling and—" He stopped when Shale started laughing, and as he said tentatively, "So you and Tellish aren't…"

"Trying again? No. What we had is gone."

"So would you accept a new suit? Even if it's from his stepbrother you barely know? Who's spent most of his life amongst students and monks. And is possessed by a demon. And is a little bit shameless and very impatient—" He wrinkled his nose at the metal finger Shale put to his lips, then kissed it playfully.

Shale startled and laughed as he dropped his hand, heart lurching at the gesture how easily and casually Annai had done it.

"I'm also rather bossy. Tellish says it's because somebody had to take after Mother, so of course it would be her favorite and the one with a demon."

"I think you're all bossy brats, but that never bothered me. I *like* bossy."

Annai smiled and moved closer, eyes like green fire, warm and bright and comforting. "Would you like to go for a walk? I haven't been here for so long I scarcely remember it, and if you're going to be our new seneschal, you need to reacquaint yourself with the place."

Shale offered his arm, smiling when Annai took it, the hope and happiness curling through him so familiar and sorely missed that feeling it again almost hurt. "I think that's an excellent idea. We'll have to be sure to stop by the armory. There was a rumor going around the kitchen that the captain of the guard had a mercenary in her bed last night."

"Really?" Annai half-heartedly smothered a snicker with the heavy folds of his robe. "Because I heard there was a mercenary who had the captain of the guard in the storage shed this morning."

"I have every faith both rumors are true, and they'll get worse before the day is over," Shale replied.

Still snickering, Annai wrapped both his arms around Shale's and set off on other topics of conversation as they walked through the castle and over the grounds.

When they finally returned to the keep, it was closer to supper than lunch.

"Oh, good, you're finally back," Halruul said when she saw them, and dismissed the servants gathered around her. She strode across the great hall to them, clapped Shale on the shoulder. "I've been informed you're willing to fall back in with our sorry lot."

"That's one way to put it, Your Grace, but not the way I would put it," Shale replied.

She smiled. "Smart man." She dumped a heavy ring of keys into Shale's hand. "I had those pulled out of storage. Your things are being fetched from the city. The servants are working on fixing up your office to the way you liked it. Dinner is in an hour. I expect to see you both." She gave Annai's robes a reproving look. "Looking presentable. I think you've dragged half the mud in the territory inside with you, Annai."

"Yes, Mother," Annai said dutifully, and shared a look with Shale once she had stormed off bellowing for the servants she'd dismissed a few minutes ago. "Well, I guess it's a good thing you were going to accept the offer."

Shale's mouth twitched. "I am not convinced I had a say in the matter."

"One more thing!" Halruul said, storming back into the room. She jabbed a finger in Annai's chest. "If you drive him off the way Tellish did, I will pitch you into the moat. Am I clear?"

"As glass, Mother."

"Hmph. I can obtain new children more easily than a competent seneschal, remember that." She leaned in to kiss his cheek, then did the same to Shale. "Welcome home, both of you." She stormed off as abruptly as she'd arrived, leaving them alone once more.

Annai shook his head. "I don't know why everyone says I'm her favorite child. It's quite obvious *you're* the favorite."

"That's absurd."

"She's never threatened to throw anyone in the moat for mistreating me," Annai replied.

Shale rolled his eyes. "Uh-huh. I bet she's promised to do extremely violent things to whoever was responsible for those men on the mountain."

"She hasn't settled on what to do with them yet. She's waiting until they've been captured and hauled in, which will be soon to judge by the look in the eyes of the mercs she hired this morning. Rolf, I think, was their leader's name?"

"Good man. Extremely ruthless. He and your mom would get on."

"Mmm, if he gets on with her and my stepfather, I'm sure they'll *get on* very well." He smiled mischievously, eyes sparkling. "I suppose we'd best get ready for dinner. You should escort me to my room. That's not a euphemism for anything."

Shale hugged him tightly, inhaling that scent he was already so fond of, earth and rain and flowers. Annai hugged him back, and Shale started to really believe he was finally home. "I don't need euphemisms. Just your company will do fine."

Annai smiled and halted their steps long enough to lean up and kiss him, quick and sweet. "Thank you again for bringing me home."

"Thank you for the same," Shale said, and escorted him away to prepare for dinner.

About the Authors

About the Authors

Dev Bentham spent some of the best years of her life in the Pacific Northwest but now lives in the marshy wilds of Northern Wisconsin. No tattoos yet, but who knows what the future will bring. She is the author of several gay romances, including the Tarnished Souls series of Jewish holiday romances, *Nobody's Home*, *Painting in the Rain*, *Driving into the Sun* and most recently *Whistleblower*.

www.DevBentham.com

www.facebook.com/dev.bentham

@DevBentham

Jessica Blat sits on the board of Old Growth Northwest and has volunteered at Gay Romance Northwest every year the meetup has run. She has been an avid reader of lesbian romance since she discovered that a genre existed with happily ever afters that were relevant to her interests. She has a particular weakness for romance grounded in speculative fiction and also coming of age stories. Jessica currently works in publishing, which she came to via a circuitous route that wended through a computer science degree and financial systems consulting. She is a Seattle native that never left for more than a few months at a time, and lives with her wife and two cats.

Austin Chant is a bitter millennial, passable chef, and a queer, trans writer of romance and erotica. His fiction centers on trans characters who always, always get the love they deserve. Austin cohosts *The Hopeless Romantic*, a podcast dedicated to exploring LGBTQIA+ love stories and the art of writing romance. He currently resides in Seattle, in a household of wildly creative freelancers who all spend too much time playing video games. He lives on Twitter. His novella *Coffee Boy* will be released by NineStar Press this September.

austinchanted.weebly.com

@austinchanted

Megan Derr is a long time resident of m/m fiction, and keeps herself busy reading, writing, and publishing it. She is often accused of fluff and nonsense. When she's not involved in writing, she likes to cook, harass her cats, or watch movies (especially all things James

About the Authors

Bond). She loves to hear from readers, and can be found all around the internet.

maderr.com
lessthanthreepress.com
@amasour

Growing up a military brat instilled **Samantha Derr** with a love of travel. Time spent on the road, waiting in airports, and crossing countrysides via train gave her an appreciation for a good book. Combined with a love English and a collection of dictionaries & usage guides, editing and publishing only seemed a natural progression in the pursuit of a good read. When not reading or editing, Sam likes to watch professional StarCraft II and League of Legends and stream way too much Netflix.

plus.google.com/+SamanthaDerr
facebook.com/rykaine
@rykaine

Lou Harper is a designer and an author who never has enough time for either, so she keeps an eye on eBay in hopes of a reasonably priced used time machine.

Lou's favorite animal is the hedgehog. She likes nature, books, movies, photography, and good food. She has a temper and mood swings.

Lou has misspent most of her life in parts of Europe and the US, but is now firmly settled in Los Angeles and worships the sun. However, she thinks the ocean smells funny. Lou is a loner, a misfit, and a happy drunk.

LouHarper.com
LouHarper.com/Design.html
@LouHarperWrites

Ginn Hale resides in the Pacific Northwest with her wife and two cats. She spends many of the rainy days tinkering with devices and words and can often be sighted herding other people's dogs, bees and goats. Her novel *Wicked Gentlemen* won the Spectrum Award for Best Novel and was a finalist for the Lambda Literary Award.

www.ginnhale.com
@ginnhale

About the Authors

Marlene Harris is currently a consultant at Reading Reality, contracting with libraries for organizational and process improvements, conducting webinars and workshops on ebook adoption and genre fiction, and writing about genre fiction and other library-related topics. She is also a regular book reviewer at such diverse outlets as Library Journal and Sci-Fi Romance Quarterly, in addition to her own blog at Reading Reality.

Before becoming a consultant, Marlene held positions in public libraries, academic and as a vendor; serving in such diverse places and positions as Technical Services Manager at the Seattle Public Library, the Division Chief for Technical Services at the Chicago Public Library, as the Head of Technical Services at the University of Alaska Anchorage, and as a Project Manager for two Integrated Library Systems vendors.

http://www.readingreality.net
@readingreality

Amanda Jean is an editor, podcast host, and writer. She grew up devouring het romance novels and shifted to LGBT romance as a teen when her thirsty queer nature revealed itself. Amanda has worked with Less Than Three Press, Bella Books, NineStar Press, and serves as Alternating Current's LGBT Director. When she's not wrangling manuscripts, writing about the video game industry, or co-hosting the queer romance podcast *The Hopeless Romantic* with Austin Chant, you can find her watching documentaries, reading too many books on true crime, and caring too much about fictional characters.

amandahjean.weebly.com
@amandahjean

Nicole Kimberling is the chief editor for Blind Eye Books. She lives in Bellingham, Washington with her wife, Dawn Kimberling, two bad cats as well as a wide and diverse variety of invasive and noxious weeds. Her first novel, *Turnskin*, won the Lambda Literary Award for Science Fiction, Fantasy and Horror. She is also the author of the Bellingham Mystery Series.

www.nicolekimberling.com

About the Authors

Josh Lanyon is the author of over sixty titles of classic Male/Male fiction featuring twisty mystery, kickass adventure and unapologetic man-on-man romance. Josh is an Eppie Award winner, a four-time Lambda Literary Award finalist (twice for Gay Mystery), and the first ever recipient of the Goodreads All Time Favorite M/M Author award. Her work has been translated into nine languages. Josh is married and lives in Southern California.

www.joshlanyon.com
VIP newsletter: http://eepurl.com/kZ79D

Susan Lee: avid reader, bourbon drinker, ramen eater, snowboarder...and a true romantic at heart. I believe in fairy tales.

@susannylee

E.E. Ottoman grew up surrounded by the farmlands and forests of upstate New York. They started writing as soon as they learned how and have yet to stop. Ottoman attended Earlham College and graduated with a degree in history, before going on to receive a graduate degree in history as well. These days they divide their time between history, writing and book preservation.

Ottoman is also a disabled, queer, trans dude whose correct pronouns are: they/them/their or he/him/his. Mostly though they are a person who is passionate about history, stories and the spaces between the two.

acosmistmachine.com

Alex Powell is an avid writer and reader of sci-fi and fantasy, but on occasion branches into other genres to keep things interesting. Alex is a genderqueer writer from the wilds of northern Canada who loves exploring other peoples and cultures. Alex is a recent graduate of UNBC with a BA in English, and as a result has an unhealthy obsession with Victorian Gothic literature. Alex has been writing from an early age, but is happy to keep learning to improve on their writing skills. Feedback and comments as well as any questions are appreciated!

www.alexpowellauthor.com

About the Authors

Author and artist **Jordan Castillo Price** writes paranormal sci-fi thrillers colored by her time in the midwest, from inner city Chicago, to rural small town Wisconsin, to liberal Madison. Her influences include Ouija boards, Return of the Living Dead, "light as a feather, stiff as a board," girls with tattoos and boys in eyeliner.

Jordan is best known as the author of the PsyCop series, an unfolding tale of paranormal mystery and suspense starring Victor Bayne, a gay medium who's plagued by ghostly visitations. Also check out her fascinating psychological M/M thriller, *Mnevermind*, where memories are made...one client at a time.

JCPbooks.com

Radclyffe has written over fifty romance and romantic intrigue novels, dozens of short stories, edited over fifteen anthologies, and, writing as L.L. Raand, has authored a paranormal romance series, The Midnight Hunters.

She is an eight-time Lambda Literary Award finalist in romance, mystery, and erotica—winning in both romance and erotica. A member of the Saints and Sinners Literary Hall of Fame, she is also an RWA/FF&P Prism, FTHRW Lories, HODRW Aspen Gold, Bean Pot, and Laurel Wreath award winner.

In 2014 she was awarded the Dr. James Duggins Outstanding Mid-Career Novelist Award by the Lambda Literary Foundation.

She is also the president of Bold Strokes Books, one of the world's largest independent LGBTQ publishing companies.

http://www.boldstrokebooks.com

Rick R. Reed is all about exploring the romantic entanglements of gay men in contemporary, realistic settings. While his stories often contain elements of suspense, mystery and the paranormal, his focus ultimately returns to the power of love. He is the author of dozens of published novels, novellas, and short stories. He is a three-time EPIC eBook Award winner (for *Caregiver, Orientation* and *The Blue Moon Cafe*). He is also a Rainbow Award Winner for both *Caregiver* and *Raining Men*. Lambda Literary Review has called him, "a writer that doesn't disappoint." Rick lives in Seattle with his husband and a very spoiled Boston terrier. He is forever "at work on another novel."

About the Authors

www.rickrreed.com
http://rickrreedreality.blogspot.com/
@rickrreed

E.J. Russell—certified geek, mother of three, recovering actor—lives in rural Oregon with her curmudgeonly husband, where she splits her time between her left-brain day job and her all-the-rest-of-the-time romance writing gig. She enjoys visits from her wonderful adult children, and indulges in good books, red wine, and the occasional hyperbole.

http://ejrussell.com
http://www.facebook.com/E.J.Russell.author
@ej_russell

Karelia Stetz-Waters is an English professor by day and writer by night (and early morning). She lives with her wife, Fay, her puppy, Wila Cather, and her cat Cyrus the Disemboweler. Her interests include corn mazes, lesbians, popular science books on neurology, and any roadside attraction that purports to have the world's largest ball of twine. She is author of *The Admirer*, *The Purveyor*, *Forgive Me If I've Told You This Before*, *Something True*, and *For Good*.

www.kareliastetzwaters.com

Tracy Timmons-Gray serves on the board of the Seattle writing nonprofit Old Growth Northwest, and as a volunteer, leads the organization's Gay Romance Northwest initiative, which includes the Gay Romance Northwest Meet-Up, the first conference that focuses on LGBTQ romance fiction in the Pacific Northwest. Tracy's day job is at FSG, a nonprofit consulting firm focusing on social change issues. In her spare time, she loves reading genre fiction, drawing cartoony monsters, singing karaoke, sending Jeff Bezos irritating letters, talking incessantly about community action and romance fiction, and avoiding her cat when he gets "bite-y".

https://gayromancenorthwest.wordpress.com
@GayRom_NW

Thank You

When you have a volunteer-run program, you have a lot of people to thank. Here are just some of the few people who have helped GRNW grow and thrive.

A big thank you to our long-term sponsors for their continued support over the last three years. Your dedication and steadfast presence have been essential for the program's growth. Thank you to: Blind Eye Books, Bold Strokes Books, Dreamspinner Press, Harmony Ink Press, Less Than Three Press, and Riptide Publishing.

We offer our deep gratitude to these sponsoring publishers who helped support GRNW during our tenure. Thank you for being a part of this journey and celebrating with us. Thank you to: Decadent Publishing, eXtasy Books, Loose Id, MLR Press, Samhain Press, Storm Moon Press, Torquere Press, and Wilde City.

Thank you to the City of Seattle Office of Arts & Culture and Pride Foundation for providing grant funding to support GRNW programming and increasing access to all readers.

Thank you to our partners at Gay City Health Project, the Gay City LGBT Library, and the Seattle Public Library. Thank you for growing with this program and for being a part of GRNW's heart.

Thank you to our family of community partners who have supported GRNW in so many ways. Thank you to: Another Read Through, GeekGirlCon, Hedgebrook, the Inland Empire Chapter of the Romance Writers of America, Lambda Literary, Pride Foundation, Queer Geek, Rainbow Romance Writers, Rose City Romance Writers, the Seattle Lesbian, University Bookstore.

Thank you to all the authors who have joined GRNW, either one year or for multiple years. Your presence and participation is a real gift, and is deeply appreciated by both us and the readers who love your work.

Thank you to author and cover artist LC Chase for creating our amazing designs for the program.

Thank you to the fabulous readers who came to join us at the Seattle Public Library these three past years (and we hope in the future as well!). Your energy and love of these books is the true inspiration that keeps everything else running forward.

Thank you to the GRNW volunteers (which, as a volunteer-run org, is everyone who touches it). Your hard work and dedication power our system and keep us able to serve.

Thank you to the staff and board of our host organization Old Growth Northwest, and especially to its executive director, Erin Fried. You took a chance on an idea and helped turn a spark into a flame that's still burning today. Thank you for your belief that this is a community that needs to have their stories told and their love celebrated.

Thank you to the lovely and wonderful people who are bringing *Magic & Mayhem* to life. Thank you to the authors who have contributed stories, to all the volunteers who have helped through the process, and to the amazing and incredible editors Samantha Derr, Amanda Jean, and Nicole Kimberling who led this project into publication. And thank you to the wonderful and hilarious readers who joined us at GRNW 2014 and 2015 and played "Character Type Love Match" which formed the inspirations for these stories.

And thank YOU for reading.

Tracy Timmons-Gray
Seattle, Washington
June 2016

Contributors AND Supporters

OPEN A WINDOW INTO YOUR STORY

HARPER
BY DESIGN

WEB SITE: LOUHARPER.COM/DESIGN.HTML
PORTFOLIO: LHARPER.DEVIANTART.COM/GALLERY

A place to be you.

Promoting wellness in LGBTQ communities by providing health services, connecting people to resources, fostering the arts and building community.

gaycity.org

Everyone has a heart
Everyone deserves a story

Romance for the whole spectrum

CPSIA information can be obtained
at www.ICGtesting.com
Printed in the USA
LVOW11s0011250817
546309LV00002B/165/P